Whitstead Christmastide

Whitstead Christmastide

A Speculative Anthology

Edited by Abigail Falanga and Sarah Falanga

For our family and friends —
God bless us everyone!

Contents

Introduction

There we were, sitting at the breakfast table, planning for virtual Christmas events to bring some light into a dark year.

"Stories!" one of us said. "Christmas stories, with the same characters or somehow matching!"

"What about all set in one town, in Victorian England?" suggested the other.

"And it could be an anthology! And we could release it at Christmas!"

And so the idea was born.

We suggested it to a few people, and next thing you know the English town of Whitstead was invented, a map made, and characters formed. With an insanely tight deadline but plenty of inspiration, the authors soon began sharing ideas and collaborating on plots and characters.

Before you could say "bah humbug," a community had formed around the creation of the fictional Whitstead. We chatted and shared pictures, debated the history of the Christmas tree and discussed that quite excellent book "A Christmas Carol" released by Mr. Dickens.

The result is a collection of stories that overlap and intertwine and sometimes stand alone. They are truly remarkable, and most beautifully festive!

While we have collated them at short notice and the results are somewhat rushed, we are amazed at the lovely work represented here.

Characters appear in one story who you will know better in another. The twists in one plot are fully explored from another angle in a different one.

We invite you to sit around the fire and explore the town of Whitstead. Visit the Romani camped beyond the graveyard, hear the song of Dermot the blind pedlar, hunt treasures with a professional artifact-seeker, decorate an empty house with a lonely wife, help an injured dog with an eccentric relative, discover dragons, spirits, and doors to the Otherworld.

The genres range through fantasy, science fiction, spiritual warfare, gothic steampunk, mythology, and drama. With themes of hope, discovery, mercy shown and repaid, grief and loss, and those specially chosen to serve those in need, these stories work together on a deep level.

We are sure they will bless you and fill your heart with the wonder and delight of this magical Christmas season!

Abigail Falanga and Sarah Falanga

Map

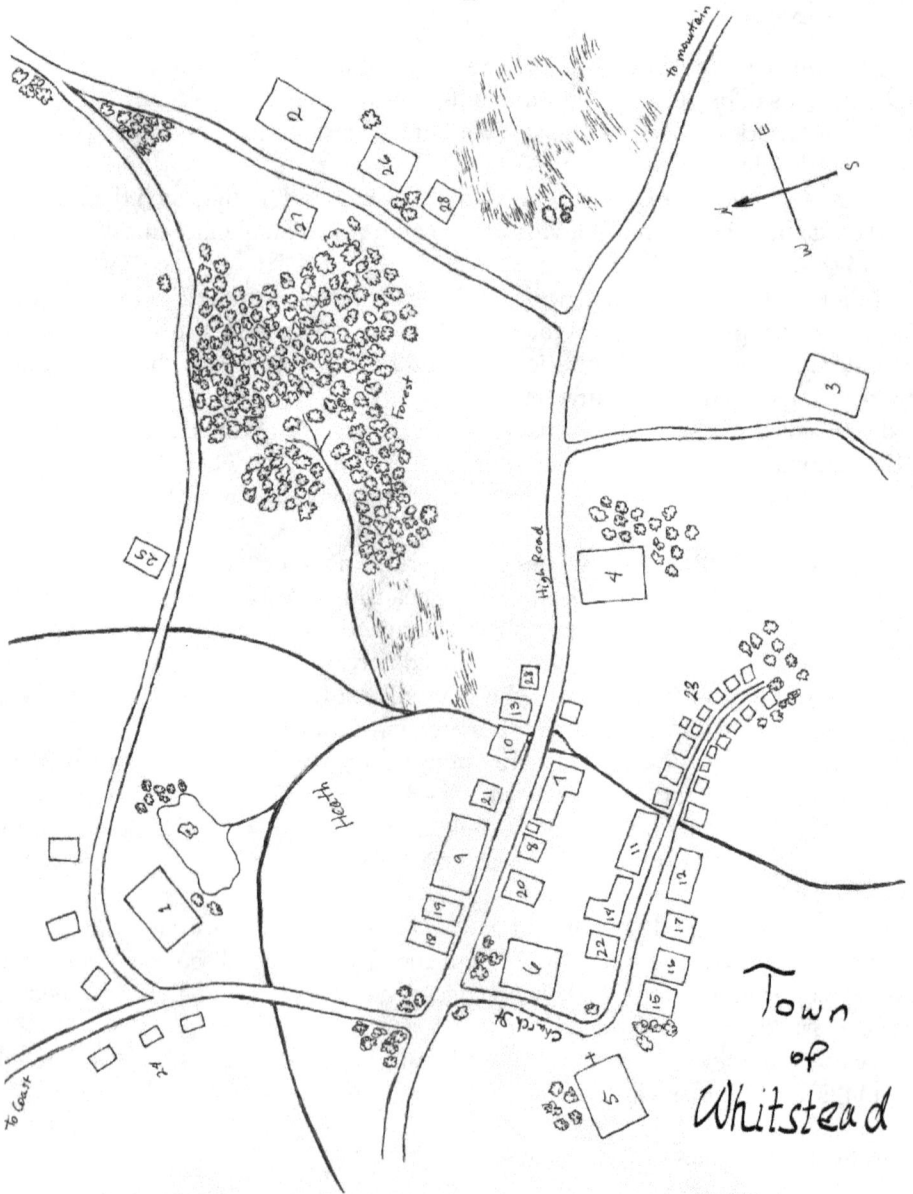

Town
of
Whitstead

Map Legend

A Brief History of the Village of Whitstead

Nestled between low mountains to the east and the coast to the northwest, Whitstead is in an easily farmable area, pleasant though rather damp. The river Whitemead flows through it, making the heath to the north marshy in spring and occasionally flooding, though otherwise the prospect is pleasant and pretty.

In the Middle Ages, it was never an important town, though the Augustinian Wyvern Abbey brought some trade to it. Several large though unfortified houses dotted the neighbourhood.

When the Reformation and the following religious unrest came, Whitstead missed most of the action. Wyvern Abbey, by then fallen into neglect, was emptied and partly destroyed by Oliver Cromwell's roundheads.

Since that time, however, the village prospered.

Wyvern Abbey was repurposed as a residence, some of the building being renovated into a large and comfortable house with associated farms, though part remains in ruins.

Whitmore Park is the most important estate, existing since pre-conquest. It's still large and consequential.

Hedges is a newer house, smaller than either Whitmore Park or Wyvern Abbey, built in the early 1700s to be the height of fashion.

Readfuss Grange is an old and large house, grim and dark, still inhabited by the family which has had it since ancient times.

St. Nicholas Church was repurposed as Anglican. It's old and big and has a venerably tall tower. The vicarage next door is more recent, and rather uncomfortable.

Cobbles is a large, comfortable, rambling old house within the village itself and therefore less than fashionable. Though quite jolly!

The heath and forest nearby were never cleared for farming and are therefore wild and reputed to be haunted by fairies. During the seventeenth and eighteenth centuries, a string of highwaymen and ne'er-do-wells posed more of a threat.

The railway has not yet reached Whitstead. It is a bustling community, populated by ordinary people with lives of love and loss, hope and despair, preparing for a most unusual Christmas season...

The Ghosts of Whitstead, Christmas Past
by David Wayne Landrum (*fantasy*)

everend Hollybrook always went for a walk near Christmastide and always went to the same place. He waited until night and covered the two miles to the ruins of the abbey outside town.

God had given him a gift tonight, he thought as he made his way: snow. It fell straight down in small flakes, silent, still, and beautiful. He smiled. Somehow, he knew she would be there.

Soon he saw the ruins rise up through the snowfall. The abbey had closed three-hundred years ago. The site that once housed a nunnery had gone to ruin. The location had not been a good place to put a convent. The area, sparsely populated and rural, did not generate enough wealth to support the organization. Few girls came as postulants; in 1541, when the decrees of the Reformation closed the site, only four nuns resided there. The land the abbey owned was sold off. Local construction firms took its stones to build houses in the village. The site sat silent and vacant, its empty spaces grown up with weeds and trees, its roofs gone, the ancient windows bereft of the stained glass that once filled the interior with colour and mysterious light.

The Reverend approached the ancient place, enjoying the quiet and dark. On the path that in the past had led to its main entry, he saw Sister Elisabeth standing under the arch. She smiled.

'Greetings, Father Hollybrook.'

Elisabeth had been a nun but returned to the village when the abbey closed. She had married. Her relatives still walked the street of Whitstead. He thought of a relative who bore both her name and a remarkable resemblance to her. Hollybrook bowed.

'Lady Elisabeth.'

'Lovely night,' she said.

'Splendid.' He smiled, 'Of course, it could not be half as splendid as heaven.'

'That depends on how you mean it,' she said. 'Beauty is a gift of heaven. A night like this one partakes of heaven.'

He wondered what his parishioners would think if they knew he occasionally conversed with the ghost of a woman who had died three hundred years ago. He would have doubted his own sanity but that she gave him very tangible proofs that his experiences seeing her were real and not delusional.

'What wisdom do you have for me tonight?' he asked.

'Not wisdom—well, not as you most often use the term.'

She held out to him a cloth bag. He took it from her. It was heavy and made a chinking sound when he grasped it.

'Coins?'

'Gold pieces.'

'For what?'

She smiled. 'You'll understand.'

He touched the bag. 'Where did this come from?'

'From the Abbey's treasury. People donated to the abbey. We were frugal and hid the excess in a site of which only the Abbess and the one of the nuns—I happened to be that nun—knew. There's quite a lot of gold and old, valuable items there. You'll know how to use what I've given you when the moment comes—and it will be soon.'

Then she was gone. That was the way Elisabeth did things. It was not like she faded or suddenly vanished. It was more like she altered reality so that she was no longer a part of it.

He looked down at the bag. Snow had accumulated on it and on his sleeves. He turned back and walked through the splendour and calm of the winter's night.

•◇•◇•◇•◇•◇•◇•◇•◇•

At home, his wife Penelope and the children were huddled together by the Franklin stove. The orange light that came from the isinglass on the front of the stove reflected on their faces. The children's attention was riveted on the words his wife read from a brightly coloured book with gilt-edged pages. He listened:

'Hear me!' cried the Ghost. 'My time is nearly gone.'

'I will,' said Scrooge. 'But don't be hard upon me! Don't be flowery, Jacob! Pray!'

'How it is that I appear before you in a shape that you can see, I may not tell. I have sat invisible beside you many and many a day.'

It was not an agreeable idea. Scrooge shivered and wiped the perspiration from his brow.

'That is no light part of my penance,' pursued the Ghost. 'I am here to-night to warn you, that you have yet a chance and hope of escaping my fate. A chance and hope of my procuring, Ebenezer.'

'You were always a good friend to me,' said Scrooge. 'Thank'ee!'

'You will be haunted,' resumed the Ghost, 'by Three Spirits.'

Scrooge's countenance fell almost as low as the Ghost's had done.

'Is that the chance and hope you mentioned, Jacob?' he demanded, in a faltering voice.

'It is.'

'I—I think I'd rather not,' said Scrooge.

'Without their visits,' said the Ghost, 'you cannot hope to shun the path I tread. Expect the first to-morrow, when the bell tolls One.'

A ghost story, he thought. Penelope had an odd liking for those and often read them to the children as bedtime stories. He had admonished her for this, but she said, 'Such stories will teach the children not to fear ghosts.' And, he admitted, her assessment seemed accurate. The children slept soundly and never seemed bothered with nightmares or fear of creatures under their beds.

'That's all for tonight,' she said, closing the red Moroccan leather covering of the book. The children groaned and protested but their mother was firm.

'We'll continue tomorrow night. Go get ready for bed and we'll have prayers.'

The children changed, their sons into their nightshirts, their daughter into her nightgown, and came to prayers. After they were finished praying, they went through the ritual of bedtime—kisses, short conversations, sudden questions the children always seemed to come up when it was time to retire. After this, they dozed off quickly. Back in the parlour, Hollybrook picked up the ornate book Penelope had been reading.

'What is this?'

'The latest from Mr. Dickens.'

He laughed. 'I hope it's better than *Martin Chuzzlewit*.'

Hollybrook liked Dickens, but his last novel had been tedious and boring.

'Much better,' she said. 'It's titled *A Christmas Carol*. It was released last year and has been quite popular.'

It took books a little while to filter up to Whitstead.

'It's beautifully bound,' he noted.

'I think the author saw it as a gift item—and a book one would cherish and perhaps read year to year at Christmastide.'

A knock came at their door.

It was Elisabeth Stoddard and her husband. She was a direct descendant of the apparition Hollybrook saw periodically at the convent. After seven generations, she looked like the twin of her great-great-great-great-great-great grandmother.

As they received their guests, he remembered that Beth (she went by the diminutive of her name) always delivered the Christmas sweetbread to her friends. He saw the loaf, wrapped in white cloth, beneath her arm.

The two couples had wine and some of the Christmas sweetbread and enjoyed each other's company. Early on, Beth spotted the ornate volume Penelope had been reading to the children.

'*A Christmas Carol*,' she exclaimed. 'It's the most marvellous story ever written.' She went on to describe it, though she was careful not to ruin the ending or spoil the joy of reading the tale by giving out too much of the story.

'I think everyone in town ought to read that story,' she went on. 'If everyone here did, things would be a great deal more charitable in our parish at this time of year—as it should be.'

After the Stoddards left, the Hollybrooks enjoyed their weekly intimacy. Penelope fell asleep. The Reverend lay awake thinking of what had happened with the visit they had received.

Sister Elisabeth often used her living relative as a confirmation of the words she had spoken to Hollybrook. The first time he saw her, of course, he doubted her existence (and his own sanity). He went to Beth's house for a party and saw, in a glass case, an antique painting of a woman—of the woman, the apparition, he had spoken with that very night. It was done in the formal style of early art, but the likeness left no mistake in his mind that this was the figure who had come to him from three-hundred years earlier. Beth had walked up beside him.

'That's my namesake, Sister Elisabeth. She was a nun at the convent but left it when it closed, came back to Whitstead, and married. She's my great-grandmother about six generations removed. And the family legend has it that she appears as a spirit at the abbey from time to time.'

He tried to conceal his astonishment. Beth laughed.

'Don't worry. People who have seen her are unanimous in affirming that she's a nice ghost—a benevolent spirit that only does good.'

'She looks like your twin,' he commented.

'Well, I did not inherit her penchant for asceticism but maybe I did inherit her good looks.'

'So much the better,' Hollybrook said.

Beth and her family were low church. They leant more toward plain worship and were wary of the Oxford Movement; they thought Lydia Sellon's founding of an order of Anglican nuns shocking and scandalous.

As he lay in bed and remembered, he also pondered. Elizabeth had given him money but not instructed him on its use.

Or had she?

He had immediately thought of the poor. In fact, on his journey home from the abbey ruins he had not doubted the purpose of her gift (she had never given him a monetary gift before). He would distribute it to the poor and needy of his parish—of Whitstead and the countryside around it. Now, suddenly, he was not so sure.

The walk through the snow, the wine, and the sweetness of his and Penelope's embrace sent him off to sleep. Otherwise, he might have lain there tossing and turning, trying to sort the matter out. In the morning, after prayers and breakfast, he went to the vicar's office beside the church. In the quiet and warmth of his small library/study, he began to ponder the issue of what to do with the money.

Not even an issue, he told himself, sitting at his desk. *The money will be given to the poor*. The Church had a benevolence fund for helping those in financial need. And such people existed, especially in the rural areas outside the village. The deacons in the church distributed it to those in tightened circumstances. But the stipend was small.

People in the church were generous but the needy were many. Heads of households fell ill. New babies came. Crops failed. Farm animals died. The rural poor suffered such reversals and, living as they did on thin budgets, often could not absorb such setbacks. More than once Hollybrook had given portions of his salary to supplement the benevolence fund. This year he would not have to do so. This year, in fact, he could be extra generous.

But now — it was insane — his heart told him not to give the monies Sister Elisabeth had handed him to the poor; but, rather, to buy a copy of *A Christmas Carol* for everyone in the parish.

If seeing an apparition of a woman who died 300 years ago is not enough to certify me as insane, he told himself, *the idea of spending a bag of gold to buy a ghost story for the people in my town to read would send me packing to Bedlam beyond a doubt.* He had finished the Christmas sermon yesterday, so he had nothing to do that day. He had, in fact, thought of doing some good, wholesome, esoteric theological reading — a thing he hardly ever got to do given the pastoral demands of his job. But he waited and thought.

The idea of buying copies of the Dickens book burned in his mind. He could not dismiss it. Every logical argument he constructed against the notion collapsed — not due to lack of logic but to the burning, unmovable certainty that buying the books was the right thing to do.

It reminded him of when, as a student at Oxford and on the verge of a career as a classics teacher, he had felt the call to take holy orders. He tried for a month to dismiss it. He constructed logical scenarios to defeat its claim on him. But the idea sat in his soul, massive and immobile as a Megalosaurus. No moving it. And it would not go away. He had finally bowed to the thing he recognised as the voice of God.

Could this be the voice of God as well? Would God have him do such a thing — something that would take food and means from the poor in his village?

As if in answer to his question, he heard noise and talking out in front of the church. He stepped to the window of his study and saw a bookseller with a pushcart. A crowd of people had gathered around him and were sampling his wares. Elisabeth Stoddard was among them. The salesman was Elroy Riley.

Riley came to town two or three times a year, his pushcart loaded with books. People eagerly bought them. Hollybrook remembered: this was Riley's Christmas run. People bought and ordered books for holiday gifts or for the onset of cold weather, which meant more time for staying home and reading. Riley always paid a visit to his parish house with theological books he thought would appeal to the Reverend. Sure enough, the knock came to his door an hour after he noticed Riley had arrived.

The salesman's weather-beaten face glowed with cold. He was probably near fifty, a large, robust man with a Dorset accent. Tipping his hat, he laid some tomes on Hollybrook's desk. The Reverend poured whisky. They drank and exchanged pleasantries. Hollybrook saw a text he liked and bought it. Then he knew he had to broach the subject that had its hand on his heart.

'Do you have a copy of Mr. Dickens' *A Christmas Carol*?' he asked.

'Aye,' the man said. 'I had four. They are all sold but one.'

'I have a bigger order in mind,' the Reverend told him. 'Could you get me three-hundred copies?'

Riley seemed to think he had not heard correctly, stuck his finger in his left ear and wriggled it.

'I'm sorry, sir; my ears are a bit waxed up today. What was it you just said to me?'

He repeated his order. 'I really do want that many copies,' he said. 'I will pay cash. And I want this absolutely secret.'

'Of course, Reverend, of course. Could I ask the occasion of this rather extravagant order?'

Hollybrook smiled broadly. 'Of course you can, Mr. Riley. And the reason is very simple: It's Christmas.'

The book cost five shillings—expensive due to the gilt-edge paper and the leather covering. The cost of his large order would be a little over one hundred pounds for what he had calculated as the number of households in the village. He took the money from the emergency fund he kept in a strong box hidden away in his office and gave it to Riley, who said he would need to travel to London to get that many copies. He said the task would take four days.

While he was waiting for the delivery of the book, Hollybrook took the gold to the bank, which sent it out to be assessed. When the assessment came back, the value of the gold was set at just over three hundred pounds. Hollybrook smiled. He could replenish his emergency money and have a bit left over for the benevolent fund.

Doubt about the wisdom of his decision nagged him. He wondered if he had merely squandered the gift Sister Elisabeth had given him. He wondered what he would say to her if his idea did not work; or if he would ever see her again.

Riley returned after four days. The Reverend paid him to quietly deliver the book to each house in the village, to leave four at the local subscription library, and to do so in the small hours of the morning. No one observed him.

Hollybrook prayed he had done the right thing; and, if he had made an error, a bad decision, that God would forgive him.

• ◊ • ◊ • ◊ • ◊ • ◊ • ◊ • ◊ • ◊ •

The buzz the next day was that someone had delivered hundreds of copies of Charles Dickens' *A Christmas Carol* to the people of Whitstead. One had appeared in the postal slot of each house in the village. Four were left at the lending library (and were immediately checked out). When asked what he thought of the matter,

Hollybrook said it was all but miraculous and that maybe Father Christmas was real after all. A copy had been left on his doorstep as well.

Soon the whole town was reading. Ebenezer Scrooge was on the lips of everyone from washer women to bankers and the mayor. People read and re-read the story. In the local eatery, food shops, the two pubs that graced the town, at schools, and on the streets, the tale of Scrooge, Marley, and the three ghosts resounded.

And the reading did not merely generate talk. People were touched. They were moved. Their hearts opened up. Contributions to the church benevolent fund increased vastly. People contacted the less fortunate of the town and asked how they might help them. Committees formed and went to the countryside around Whitstead to look for those in need, those who had suffered financial setbacks, required assistance with medical debt, were short of food or goods and equipment. The overflow of generosity, too, did not seem impulsive. Hollybrook could see, from his years of dealing with charitable events and organizations, that this would continue; that it would remain a sustained movement of grace, that it would provide lasting results of charity in the years to come.

He wanted to thank Sister Elisabeth. But one did not seek her. When she wanted to speak to him again, she would summon him. One did not summon her.

On Christmas Eve the church was full. His homily centred on the shepherds and how they met Mary, Joseph, and, above all the Christ child. His text was Saint Luke 2:17-18: *And when they had seen it, they made known abroad that saying which was told them concerning the child. And all that had heard it wondered at those things told them by the shepherds.*

He focused on their obscurity, their lowly place in the social order, their simplicity and honesty. The most profound sentence in the entire Christmas story, he said, might be what the shepherds said after hearing the angel and the angel choir: *Let us go even unto Bethlehem, and see this thing which is come to pass, which the LORD has made known to us.* 'What the Lord had made known to them,' he said, 'he has also made known to those of us here in this sanctuary. Their wonderment is ours as well; and their discovery and the words they spoke, which caused wonder for all who heard them, are ours as well.'

People thanked him when he shook hands with those leaving the church. Elisabeth Stoddard, dressed in white that day, looked even more like her ancestor of seven generations past, whose blood ran in her veins. He saw Sister Elisabeth's smile on the face of her descendant and knew she had to be pleased with what he had done.

The words of the Gospel narrative of the Bible ran through his head; but so did the last line of the secular book that had also done so much this Christmastide, *God bless us, every one.*

A Hundred and One Uses
by Hillari DeSchane *(fantasy)*

'Isaac, I have a note here from your Aunt May.' My father slid an oblong card across the table. It looked like one of those new-fangled Christmas cards that people had just begun sending through the penny post.

'Who's coming?' I examined the image, an ornate sleigh drawn by a large deer, the driver swathed in a hood and cloak of bright red. It was a beautiful thing. There were even bits of metallic embossing. The light from the big lamp suspended over the kitchen table winked on gold-mounted harness, and flashes of silver about the driver's face.

'May Nichols. She's your mother's aunt, really. Makes her your great-aunt. But still your aunt, and mine by marriage.'

'Why is she coming here?'

'Because I invited her. She went off traveling the world with her husband before your mother and I married, so I've never met her. We're the last of her relatives here, now that—' He shied away from finishing the sentence, his grief hauling his words off track like a wilful carthorse.

Now that your mother is dead, I filled in silently.

He cleared his throat. 'You'll need to take the pony and trap into the village to fetch her. Read what it says so you know when she's arriving.'

He looked down at his dish as if spooning up his breakfast porridge required his full attention. He was one of the most successful farmers around Whitstead, but the years of grinding labour that had enabled him and my mother to finally buy our farm had left him no time for school. He was a proud man, and he considered being unable to read a weakness. It rankled him.

My spoon slipped from my numb fingers. A drop of cream spattered the card. 'What if I bring the wrong old lady home with me?'

He pointed with his chin. 'Hold that up to the passengers as they get off the coach. I imagine that's why she wrote on one of these new illustrated cards.'

I squinted at the spidery writing. As if God had played a cruel joke on my father, reading had always been a problem for me, his son, the focus of all his hopes and pride. He meant for me to achieve in my life the only thing he been unable to accomplish in his—become a man of learning, not a man of labour. But none of the tutors he hired for me, the hours he spent standing over me as I pored over my schoolbooks, had helped. The harder I concentrated, the more the letters wandered across the page like mouse tracks. Sometimes they disguised themselves one for the other, like 'b' for 'd,' or they changed order or hid, 'saw' becoming 'was,' or 'started' becoming 'stared.'

Things had only gotten worse after my mother died in the spring. Her idea of helping me was to just have me read to her — anything I wanted, which for me was any book touching on animals, or farming, or agriculture in general.

It wasn't my brains. I knew I was smart. But I wanted to farm, and not just anywhere, but right here at Abbey Farm where I'd been born. My father was horrified by my ambition. We'd just had our worst argument about it a few minutes ago, when he came down to the breakfast table to find me reading a pamphlet on doctoring animals. *A Brief Treatise on Advancements in Chirurgy and Physic of Livestock and Farm Animals, With Some Practical Techniques and Materia Medica,* the seal of the London Veterinary College stamped on the tan cover. I'd camouflaged it between the pages of my Latin textbook.

He'd shaken the pamphlet at me. 'Why do you think your mother and I drove ourselves all those years? So our son could have better than we had. You're going to be a man who works with his mind, not his hands. So bear down on that—' He stabbed with one thick finger at the textbook. '—and forget about this.' Then he'd tossed the pamphlet into the hearth.

I knew he loved me, but I also knew I was a disappointment to him. I prayed every night for months that words would line up straight and obedient for me as they did for most everyone else. But God didn't seem interested in giving me what I wanted, so I gave up praying.

My father used to pray too. I'd see him standing at twilight, arms draped over the farmyard gate staring off toward the woods that bordered our farm, lips moving. I hadn't seen him do that lately, at least since my mother died. I didn't know if he still prayed, but he'd stopped going to church.

With those memories and our argument still knotting my stomach, I gave up and read out my best guess. '"I will stare early because I want to breathe the snow. It is good for families to be untied on Christmas Eve."'

My father sighed. 'I'll warrant it's "*start* early," because she wants to "*beat*" the snow. And families should be "*united...*"' He looked at me from under his brows. 'Ah, well, no matter.'

'Don't you want to meet her yourself?' I hated the quaver in my voice.

'Of course, but I can't spare the time.' He had already pulled on his heavy hobnailed boots. 'That tree that came down in the east field last night has to be cut up and cleared before the men can get on to mending the fence it took with it. With snow coming tonight, I can't take the risk the in-lamb ewes will wander off'.

Despite the distance between us, sometimes my father could still read me. He paused in pulling on his heavy coat. 'Your mother used to say her Aunt May was like a sparrow. Bright and chirpy, with a hundred and one tales to tell. That's why she was your mother's favourite.' His calloused hand scraped the back of my neck in a rough caress. 'Her visit might be just the thing we need.'

•◇•◇•◇•◇•◇•◇•◇•◇•◇•

The signboard said something about the Baby, a well, and a cross. It was Christmas Eve, true, but why would that change the coach's regular stop? I pressed my balled fists into my eyes. Now I saw it wasn't 'Baby,' but 'Abbey.' I filled in the rest quickly. The coach had broken a wheel, not a well, and let out its passengers at the Abbey crossroads.

I'd missed her. Aunt May was somewhere out there—I cast an uneasy glance at the mackerel sky, grey clouds pregnant with snow, strung across a darker grey background—a sparrow-like old lady alone, dragging her luggage toward a house she'd never seen.

I pushed the pony into a spanking trot and set out east on the High Road toward the crossroads. On the north side of the road, the forest pressed close. There were numerous footpaths that struck off into the trees. Surely, she wouldn't have taken one of these. The trees were thick, and a person could easily become lost.

Something fluttered at the stony edge of the road. A bit of bright red cloth, torn from a woman's skirts or cloak, perhaps, and a set of footprints. I hauled the pony to a halt and tumbled down off the seat. Before I could do more than snatch up the scrap of wool, I heard a high-pitched cry. I tore off toward the sound.

A few yards into the cover of the heavy trees, the footprints ended. The cry ended too. Then a flash of light caught my eye. It blinked once, then again, ahead and not too far. Within a few steps I saw something bright red moving within a thick stand of holly. I pushed through the thorny mass and into a little clearing.

The woman bundled in a red cloak and hood didn't seem surprised to see me. 'Oh good, Isaac, you're right on time.' Light flashed from the little pair of spectacles that had slipped down to the end of her nose. 'I'll need help carrying this fellow to your trap.'

Like a dreamer I passed forward wordlessly. Aunt May—for who else could it be— was kneeling beside a large black dog, holding a rough bandage around one of his front paws. She shifted a little and I saw she was only wearing one boot. It was her stocking she had wrapped around his paw. 'There's a hundred and one uses for stockings, didn't you know?' she said, wiggling her bare toes.

The dog thumped his thick otter-like tail against the ground in greeting. But when he tried to shift himself onto his chest, the cry rang out again.

'He'll freeze to death if we don't get him up off this cold ground,' Aunt May said. 'He can't shift himself.'

I was eying the big dog. Every bit of five stone, or more. Too heavy for me to carry without hurting him. There was a carpetbag nearby. 'Do you have another cloak, or something of strong cloth we could use as a sling to carry him between us?' I asked Aunt May.

'Strong cloth, you say?' She cocked her head. 'I believe I have just the thing.' May began pulling things out of her bag. A shiny crimson gown, two, no, three more pairs of stockings, a sack of sweets and what looked like one of coal—I soon lost track, struck dumb by the number and variety of things she'd managed to pack into one smallish bag.

She crowed in triumph, brandishing some sort of vast, ribbed garment festooned with lacing and straps. She pulled at each end like a concertina, as if testing its strength. 'Not that I have any doubts,' she explained. 'Any corset stout enough for me could be used as a mainsail. There's a hundred and one uses for a corset, don't you know.'

Faster than I could have imagined, we had the garment passed beneath the dog and all Aunt May's items were tucked back into her bag, seemingly with room to spare. Then we hoisted the dog and carried him between us out of the trees. I was panting by the time we reached the road, but Aunt May, silver haired, face as wrinkled as a dried apple, scarcely drew a deep breath.

My father was standing at the farm gate, face set, lantern held high, as if he was just about to set out to track us down. 'May? Are you Sarah Wharton's Aunt May?' He peered doubtfully at her face, at least what he could see of it beneath the swathes of red wool that hid her face.

'Are you my own dear Sarah's own dear Hugh?' She wrapped her arms around him and pulled him close in a hug that rocked him on his feet. 'I've brought you and young Isaac all sorts of gifts,' she said, stepping back, 'but first, see what I found for you along the way! Isn't that the way of it, when you seek one thing, you find another, and it's often the one thing you really needed, though often not the one you wanted.'

She steered him to the back of the trap then whipped the tarp away with a flourish. 'It's a dog!'

'Aye, I can see that', my father said. 'A sick one.'

'Just a bit of an injury to one paw is all. Isaac here can set him to rights. Be a good trial for that animal doctoring he's been reading up on.'

'Told you about that, did he?' My father's lips thinned.

May nattered on as if she hadn't heard him. 'You two farmers will find a hundred and one uses around the place for a dog like him. Now—' She clapped her gloved hands together. '—shall we get started? There's much to do, and little time left.'

My father sledged in Aunt May's carpetbag, muttering under his breath and shooting an odd glance toward May when she took it from his hand as if it weighed no more than a loaf of bread. 'Sparrow?' he mouthed to me. I just rolled my eyes and shrugged.

Finally, it was the dog's turn. We eased the improvised sling from beneath him, my father's eyes climbing nearly to his brows at what he found himself holding.

The corner of May's mouth twitched at his reaction. 'Any bigger of a beast and I'd have arrived in my shift.'

When I eased the makeshift bandage free, we all sucked in our breath. The dog's left front paw was badly broken.

My father speared his hand through his hair. 'Too bad. Might have been nice to have a dog like him around the place. Saint John's Dogs, they call them. First ones came from the Labrador coast of Canada, then the big landowners in the Scottish Borders started breeding them for retrieving game. Smart, work all day without a complaint, kind.'

As if he knew we were talking about him, the dog thumped his tail, his dark brown eyes pools of trust.

'Why can't he stay? I'll take care of him,' I said.

'It's not a matter of staying, son, but of suffering,' my father said. 'He needs that paw fixed now, not days from now when it will heal all awry and lame him for life. It's Christmas Eve and coming on to snow. Who's to be found with the knowledge to do it? No, Isaac, kinder to end it now. He'd be weak and useless to me.'

Weak and useless. Like you. He didn't have to say it. My heart heard. I scrambled to my feet, aching to be anywhere but here.

May's hand shot out and caught hold of my wrist, casually, but holding me in place like a fetter. 'Momentous times we live in now, Hugh,' she said to my father. 'All the discoveries being made every day. Why, even the doctoring of animals has become a modern, scientific pursuit. I understand there are some very learned men who devote their energies to this branch of study. What we could do with their advice just at this moment,' she mused. 'Even just one of their pamphlets.' She cocked her head as if listening, then plucked a booklet from the heart of the glowing firebox. 'Like this one.'

She handed it to me. A light, almost pleasant scent of woodsmoke drifted up when I fanned the pages. The seal had collected a smudge of ash, and one corner of the cover was lightly toasted, but it was my pamphlet, intact. It fell open to a later chapter, one I hadn't read yet. I saw drawings of a dog's paw, the bones and muscles revealed.

'Of course, we'll need someone with an open mind and fresh eyes to put it in practice. Not old and set in their ways like me or you, Hugh.'

My father kicked a coal back into the fire. 'Aye, Isaac has the open mind. The eyes, rather his reading, now — best not to rely…'

Still on her knees beside the dog, May reached up and snagged my father's hand. 'Help a frail old lady to her feet, Hugh, if you please.' She smiled sweetly then yanked, nearly pulling him over.

The dog shifted his head until it rested on my knee. He looked up at me, patient, uncritical. I put my finger to the text below the drawing. '"The metacarpals and distal phalanges…"' I began.

Behind me, May's voice was a soothing background that reassured me no one was staring at me while I read. 'I seem to recall a certain man who had an affliction', I heard her tell my father. 'The man prayed mightily that God would remove it. Though God did not answer his prayers to remove what Paul called a thorn in his flesh, Paul—that's right, isn't it, Hugh?'

My father grunted in confirmation.

'I've never heard the exact nature of Paul's affliction, let's call it a weakness, but some scholars believe it was something to do with his eyes. Nevertheless, this man Paul went on to lead a very useful life, indeed, though a life no doubt far different than what his family, or his father, had envisioned for him.'

I heard the scraping of chair legs across the floor then a creak as my father sat down heavily.

'I also know of a woman who prayed mightily too,' May went on. 'Not for herself, but for her beloved husband and son. She prayed for her son to be healed of his affliction—I believe it was also something to do with the eyes, perhaps reading.' May waved her hand as if the detail scarcely mattered.

Against my will I was listening, staring sightlessly at the pages in my lap.

'But even more, this woman prayed that her husband would be healed of his own affliction. His weakness was something to do with pride, I believe, and perhaps a touch of embarrassment. Most of all, the woman prayed that her husband and her son would not lose the great love they had for each other. She prayed for them because she loved them so much, and because she knew she would be leaving them soon.'

My father gave a harsh sob, then he buried his face in his arms. My heart pounded. Even when my mother died, I had not heard my father weep.

May laid a hand on his shoulder. 'Sometimes God in His wisdom answers our prayers by saying "no," so we can learn to rely on His strength, not our own.'

We were gathered around the dog, May holding him still, my father with freshly washed hands in readiness, a tray of bandages and other supplies at his elbow. He nodded at me. He would follow my instructions as I read. I raised the pamphlet, took a breath—

'Wait!' May interrupted. 'We've forgotten something.' She took off her spectacles and settled the frames on my nose, looping the silver wire armpieces behind my ears. 'Every learned man I've ever known has worn spectacles. Must be all those academic tomes, that tiny type that looks more like mouse tracks meandering across the page.'

I blinked owlishly through lenses that were so strong, they were almost opaque.

May made a *tsk* sound. "They need just a bit of an adjustment… Clearer this way?' She did something to the loop behind my ear and a window of clarity appeared in the very centre of each lens. 'What about now?' With each tweak and adjustment, what I saw through the centre of the lenses cleared until the print was sharp-edged and crisp, while everything else was blurry and indistinct. I had to turn my head to see Aunt May or my father, like a horse wearing blinders.

Just then the dog whimpered. 'Son', my father said, 'we need to do something for this dog now.'

It wasn't a miracle. Aunt May's glasses just helped me focus on my reading, not on the others' reactions to it. The medical words were long, the sentences complex. Sometimes we had to stop and figure out how to carry out what the pamphlet called for. Aunt May even had to change places with my father when more nimble fingers were needed. But eventually we were rewarded by the sight of a normal paw, all the bones neatly aligned.

Later, the three of us drowsed before the fire, the dog resting comfortably on his blankets. We talked, at least my father and I talked. May murmured the occasional question. I don't recall she told any stories of my mother's childhood, as my father had said he wanted to hear.

But even now, decades later, I recall the tears on his cheeks through his laughter, and the answering moisture on mine, when we told our own stories of the woman we loved and missed. And woven around and through our talk was the shared refrain of how much my father and I had missed each other and needed each other in these long months that our grief had separated us.

Much later, a cool draught roused me from a sweet dream. It was as if Aunt May's spectacles had been lifted from the bridge of my nose, then a hand fleeted across my brows and down over my eyes, the way my mother used to do before she said 'good night.'

I trailed across the kitchen, half asleep. Through the partially open door floated the midnight peal of the bells from the church across the fields. Christmas had arrived. I closed and latched the door then curled up again in my chair. The flames chuckled quietly as if they'd been freshly stoked, and my father slept on, smiling softly in a dream of his own.

The dog woke us at first light that Christmas morning. He was balanced on three legs, just dotting that front paw to the floor, but he was bright eyed and clearly doing well. My father said nothing, just nodded once at me in congratulations, but he retrieved the pamphlet from the table, smoothed its covers carefully, then tucked it among my schoolbooks in the bookshelf.

May's chair was empty, blankets folded neatly over the back. I looked out the window and beheld a world decorated with drifts and icicles, silver-blue where the sun hadn't yet reached. 'I don't see any footprints,' I told my father.

'Her carpetbag is gone.' My father replaced me at the window and craned his neck, checking the sky. 'Get your boots. We have to find her before the snow starts again'.

My father opened the door onto a farmyard hidden beneath a cloak of snow. The rising sun picked out a trail of footprints. They began at the stone steps where we stood, then led across the farmyard toward the big gate.

'She headed to the woods!' I plunged forward.

My father caught my elbow and hauled me back. 'Wait a moment, Isaac. To the woods, then where?'

'Where—oh.' The footprints led to the gate and continued unbroken on the far side, though the undisturbed snow on either side showed the gate had not been opened. A few steps farther along, the trail of footprints just... ended.

My father rocked back and forth on his feet for a moment or two, humming thoughtfully to himself, then he led me back inside.

I squinted as a sharp reflection struck my eyes. Aunt May's spectacles! I'd never given them back to her. What would she do without them?

My father was hunkered at the hearth, one hand stroking the dog, the other holding something small, turning it over curiously. 'Isaac, have a look at this.' Balanced on his palm was a stocking, the Christmas card and a pair of spectacles tucked inside. 'Read the card for me.'

I didn't want to mar our precious newfound closeness. 'Don't you remember? She just wrote the time she was arriving...'

'...and how she wanted to "breathe" the snow. Yes, I remember what it said. Yesterday.' He paused briefly. 'Read it this morning.'

'Well, maybe with the spectacles...'

My father made that thoughtful humming sound again while he polished the lenses on his sleeve, then he held them up for my inspection. From edge to edge, I saw the flames, straight and undistorted. The lenses were made of clear glass.

I angled the back of the card toward the light and began to read. *'For this thing I besought the Lord thrice, that it might depart from me. And he said unto me, My grace is sufficient for thee: for my strength is made perfect in weakness.'*

I stopped. Those verses from the second book of Corinthians had been my mother's favourites, particularly toward the end.

Father's hand settled on my shoulder. 'I never told you, son, but in those last days, when your mother had gotten too weak to read her Bible for herself, I used to stand outside the door and listen to you read those verses to her.'

Below the verse, May wrote, 'On this night our Lord came to us in the form of a babe, seemingly weak but with the strength to save us all. There is none of us so strong we do not need His mercy, and none so weak we cannot serve Him, by His grace. Have a blessed Christmas, my dears, all three of you.'

There was a postscript, added in writing that snaked along the edge of the card.

15

'P.S. I didn't want to disturb you all, so I didn't retrieve my corset from under the dog. I'm sure you modern, scientific farmers will find a hundred and one uses for something like that.'

I turned the card over. Surely, she had bought two of the rare things? I held it so close to the fire the skin of my knuckles began to sting. No, it was the same card, down to the cream stain in the corner. I had assumed the sleigh driver was a man, but now I wasn't so certain. Just above the hooded head with its silver spectacles was the cancellation mark. The ink was too thick and smudged to read.

Father peered over my shoulder. 'I'll tell you one thing—' My father gave the dog a last pat before he pulled himself to his feet. '—if we could see where she mailed it from, that would be a starting place to wonder at. Now get along upstairs with you. We need to wash and dress in a hurry if we're to make it to church on time.'

I threw open the window of my little room high up under the eaves. It felt too small to contain all the gratitude my heart was holding. From far across the fields, from every tower of every church in the village, the bells were tolling. I leaned out in my shirtsleeves, despite the cold, letting the glad tidings wash over me.

A flash of light drew my eyes to the forest just beyond our farmyard. I caught a sweep of bright red, as of a hooded cloak. I watched as it receded rapidly into the distance until finally it disappeared in the rising sun. 'Thank you,' I whispered, then I bowed my head and began to pray.

The Occupied Mirror
by John K. Patterson (*fantasy*)

Velith maintained her camouflage, watching the inhabitants of Whitstead draw indoors from the storm and crowd around their fires. Her skin and clothing alike mimicked the piling-up snow drifts and the dark masonry of the houses behind her. If anyone had been close enough, they would have seen a distortion in the air, like a shimmer of heat.

Humans grew more wary by the day, even in such a subdued village as this. So far from the grove, a Dryad needed to keep her wits close at hand.

Doubly so when her mission required breaking into a haunted house.

Haunted by what, that is the question, she thought. Days of observation had provided no answer. The abode in question was a small two-story affair, well-maintained but with windows dark as hollow eyes. Johann Schneider, reclusive tinkerer and sole human occupant, was attending to a chair at Wyvern Abbey. A chair she had broken, counting on Schneider's good standing at the Abbey to lure him away from home for some hours. Maybe the storm would force him to spend the night there.

Candles and lamps shone with amber light in the windows of the adjacent houses, and families gathered around their tables for supper. She would have to be careful to not catch their attention.

Resident spirits were nothing uncommon, and normally her senses could work at a distance, distinguishing Fae from ghosts, or demons from sprites. But Velith's perception felt blunted, only allowing her to notice the presence of *something* inside. She hadn't been that ill-informed in centuries. It worried her.

The presence sent out a simple message, inaudible but picked up in the background of her thoughts. A cry for help, like a bottled letter thrown into the ocean. *I'm trapped. Come destroy the mirror. The Fae lives inside the mirror. It's not letting me leave.*

Fae. The very word tightened the muscles in her shoulders, and scars from a Fae knife felt as if they burned all over again.

Liberate a Fae's captive and dispatch the monster itself? Christmas was for most a time of celebration and rest. For Velith, it was a fight against evil.

The wind picked up, and wraiths of snow snapped and twisted across the wide road. She could no longer wait to see if the fog would lift from her mind. Velith stepped across the street, all too aware of the footprints she left even as the snow filled them in.

Her uneasy hand kept drifting to the small pockets and compartments sewn into her cloak, full of various useful seeds, and checking to see if they were still there. Not that her tools had ever gone missing in her travels. But experience had punished her lapses in vigilance. Some of her scars still ached in the cold, though the rest of her stood up well to the icy tempest.

The closer Velith came to the house, the more she felt as if she walked a tightrope. Even an arm's length from the door, she felt vertigo clutch her chest.

Since Schneider had installed many locks on the back door, it would be faster — and riskier — to enter here. Taking one more chance to glance left and right, she withdrew the seed of a picking vine from her coat.

Even camouflaged, Velith slowed her movements as she bent down to take a pinch of snow off the ground. She let the clump of frigid flakes rest in her palm and set the fingernail-sized black seed on top, then wrapped her fingers around it. She let her body heat melt the snow, to both nourish the seed and activate its magic.

Velith leaned forward as she felt the seed split, and the picking vine grew out. A tight-fingered grip was needed to direct the growth in one direction: toward the keyhole on the front door.

A dark green vine emerged between Velith's thumb and index finger, thin as a knitting needle. Its tapered end grew into the keyhole, and she could feel it searching out the gaps. The wind kept her from hearing the lock opening, but she knew it was ready when the vine stopped growing.

Velith twisted the freezing iron knob, and the door opened. When Schneider returned, he'd find a curious wooden vine that had somehow grown, in the dead of winter, into his lock. She slipped inside and shut the door, idly wondering if a human tinkerer would bother trying to extract the plant, instead of replacing the mechanism.

Indoors, she let her camouflage relax, drawing back her hood. She removed her cloak — now a rich and dark green — and draped it over one arm, inside-out so she would have easy access to the pockets of seeds. The entrance hall was crowded with tools and devices, leather satchels with holes worn into the bottoms and patched-up shoes and waistcoats that should have been discarded ages ago.

He'll definitely try to keep the lock, she decided. Men like him would find uses for any old refuse until the trumpets blared for Judgment Day.

The house's cold was deeper than the mere chill of winter. Even Velith shivered, though she could have strolled the Arctic Circle in a gossamer dress and would call the weather 'brisk'. This was a deeper cold, pouring out of the spirit realm. The house had been soaking in it for a long time. The owner probably could not feel it as cold, but perhaps as a melancholy atmosphere that robbed his surroundings of colour or humour.

She decided to think of this little mission as spreading Christmas cheer rather than assassination, but the scars on her fingers smouldered.

Velith turned around as the presence she felt from afar came to meet her. It coalesced soundlessly, mist slipping together into a human-like shape, half Velith's height. A little girl took form. She wore a tattered brown dress, tiny hands folded in front of her. She only appeared solid, but it was the most convincing apparition Velith had seen by far.

The ghost looked up at Velith, all red curls and blue-eyed pity, with a lip trembling at just the right rhythm to tie a knot in Velith's throat.

What had happened to such a pure and tiny girl to cut her life short?

The shaking lips opened, and the spirit pleaded, 'Have you come for the mirror?'

Velith nodded. Human ghosts rarely spoke with their living counterparts. But Dryads and many other spirits could converse with them readily.

'I have. What is your name?'

'Deborah,' the girl said.

'How many years have you been here, Deborah?'

'I don't know.' Tears broke free and slipped down her cheeks.

'It's all right,' Velith said. She knelt down instinctively to wipe the tears away. The little girl drew back, floorboards creaking faintly beneath her.

Velith felt a fool. She could not wipe a ghost's tears away any more than she could grasp a rainbow. Her hand would just go right through.

'Does the owner know you're here?' Velith said, trying to redirect the girl's thoughts.

Deborah's tears multiplied, and Velith felt a pain in her chest. 'Maybe. I try so hard to be quiet for Mister Schneider. But sometimes the Fae scares me, and I break things or move them. I don't mean to!'

Velith clenched her fists. The beast would pay with its life.

'I need to move on, but it won't let me. Please help me. It's upstairs.' She evaporated into mist, and the house would have been silent but for the faintest echo of weeping.

Velith felt her hand steady, and a heaviness seemed to lift from her mind. Light and clarity poured back in. If there was a chance she could free a chained spirit, especially of one so young, she would see it through to the end. Especially if it meant one less Fae in the world. She had done right in deciding to help.

She ascended the narrow stairs to the second floor, the boards squealing under her feet. She paused, looking down at the dusty steps.

Deborah had creaked the floorboards when she flinched away and stepped on them. How was that possible for a ghost?

Velith shook her head, dismissing it. Maybe Deborah was simply one of the stronger poltergeists. But even the most raucous ghost did not have mass or shape in the world.

19

More of a loft than a full floor, the upstairs carried the same burden of clutter as downstairs, with a writing desk and a workshop table on either end as the only clear spaces. A thin film of dust settled here, as if no one had been up here for weeks.

Velith found the mirror, propped up like a portrait on the writing desk. It was framed in wrought iron, shaped like black vines and leaves that twisted around the glass. A most peculiar mirror for a human to possess. The iron frame was a good cage for containing creatures from Faerie.

Her scarred finger idly traced the small knife made of polished iron, tucked away in a little sheath next to the seeds. She could kill the creature while it was trapped inside.

Velith clutched her cloak against her stomach, leaning in closer. Out of the corner of her vision she saw Deborah fade into existence once more.

Velith glanced at her. 'How did the owner come by this mirror?'

'The Gypsies camped by the town. He accepted it as payment for fixing a cartwheel. He's used it as a shaving mirror, but he saw things in it. Just little flashes. He looked bothered by it. So he left it up here.'

'Why didn't he pack it away, or break it or give it to someone else?'

Deborah hesitated. 'He tried. But it... it comes back. He's afraid to break it. Maybe he's worried about what might come out. But I think it likes staying here.'

That made sense to Velith. Trapped Fae wanted to stay in one place and wait for their cohorts to rescue them. Something else about this did not add up, but what was it?

'Look in the shadows,' Deborah whimpered. 'It's there.'

Velith carefully picked up the frame with her free hand. Warmth radiated from the iron, as if it had been left too close to a fire. Her eyes searched the shadows in the mirror, behind closed doors and within bookshelves. There. In a gap between stacks of books piled atop the bookshelf, she saw two faint red spheres. Eyes. The red flared brighter, as if their owner had noticed her.

Velith glanced back at the bookshelf. No eyes there. She glared back at the mirror, staring into the monster's gaze. She had found her quarry.

'You have to kill it!' the girl said in a panic. 'Smash it! You must do something!' The shout echoed, and some of the looser tools on the worktable clattered to the floor. She was a stronger spirit than Velith remembered seeing.

Something in the girl's voice and presence felt just slightly out of place. Velith couldn't quite find the words for it. Too pitiable, maybe. Too wounded. Something that gripped Velith's heartstrings tight and yanked her like a marionette.

It was as if the girl was the perfect image of someone Velith would help. A cause she would fight for.

She bent down to look closer at the girl, at the diamond glimmer of her tears.

'What are you doing?' the girl said.

'Just a moment,' Velith said, holding up a finger.

The closer Velith stared, the more the image of the little girl spoke of fakery. It was more than the illusion a spirit could cast, almost like something trying to *mimic* a helpless child. It made a convincing mask, and Velith had quite nearly missed it.

A chill shuddered down Velith's backbone and dripped over her ribs. Whatever this was, it was no human ghost.

'Is something wrong?' the girl asked. The mask righted itself anew, all but convincing. But Velith could not deny what she had perceived, no matter how her pity demanded her to help this poor trapped spirit.

The conviction and impulse to help stepped back, suspicion taking their place as Velith narrowed her eyes. A deep-set fear flowed to the front of her thoughts, fear of a snare tightening around her.

'How did you die?' she said.

Deborah tilted her head and pushed aside tumbling curls of red hair. Bruises showed black and purple along her neck, almost too strong, like ink stains. 'Mother strangled me.'

Sympathy hit Velith like a crossbow bolt, even though she was certain the girl was not what she seemed. More likely a disease or an injury should have taken her life this early. Everything about Deborah seemed tailored to encourage Velith to protect her. And the bruises hadn't been there before. Velith was certain of it.

'I'll need to take it to the woods,' she said. 'I can destroy it there.' She needed to get out of this house. She reached into one of the pockets on her cloak, where spear-seeds awaited use, and drew one of them out.

Looking remarkably like hazelnuts, they were imbued with magic stronger than the picking vine. Velith cracked the shell between her fingers, and the insides rapidly grew, twisting and sprouting miniscule twigs and leaves, until there formed a javelin nearly matching her height. The grain of the wood circled the shaft in an elegant spiral pattern. As Velith let the shell fragments clatter to the floor, she watched Deborah's expression. Closely.

Concern. Maybe a little surprise. But not nearly enough for a human girl, even one who had been dead for some time.

'I'll need this to kill the creature,' Velith said.

A flash of suspicion in the ghost's eyes, if it was a ghost, as if it nearly shook its head in disagreement and caught itself.

It knew this was the wrong method.

'Oh, so you know a better way to kill it, then? How does the spirit of a little girl come by that knowledge?'

Deborah's mouth opened and closed, her little fists coiling tight enough to turn white. 'I've seen your kind from time to time in the woods.'

Velith nodded. 'Maybe you've even talked to one or two of us. And we certainly have no love for the Fae, but I cannot imagine that the proper method for dispatching a Fae trapped in a mirror was ever a topic of conversation.'

The inner pleas for pity surged again, but Velith beat them back... and lifted the spear's sharp end toward Deborah.

The little girl flinched. As if she were something the spear could hurt. Even now, the mask was starting to crack. Anger, even fury showed in the eyes, her blue irises darkening almost to midnight.

A tremble arose from the mirror itself, a silent vibration as the metal frame grew hotter.

'You can't destroy it yourself, can you?' Velith said, adjusting her grip on the spear so she held it like she prepared to throw it. 'A curse, a spell, something binding you to it. You want the Fae dead, but you needed someone else to do your dirty work.'

Deborah's lips cracked open, showing a smile so white it glowed, a parody of a human. By now the eyes had gone all dark blue, with an oily sheen over their surfaces. Velith felt a deep-set revulsion at the image, like a doll had come to life and was deciding whether to eat her.

Deborah's voice started out almost the same as before. 'Velith Nightlock. Mighty warrior of the Yorkshire Unseen, slayer of the last minotaur, defiant to the Fae queen of the Lochs.' Now the voice turned more mocking, broken like a violin's strings frayed almost to snapping. 'That knife must have hurt. They say the scars never go away, even for a Dryad.'

Deborah grew taller. Her appearance did not age, but was stretched out into a gangled form, matching Velith's height and then rising above it, nearly hitting the ceiling. Velith fought back a scream and kept a lid on the primeval terror clawing for release. In some realm at the edge of Velith's perception, there was a sense similar to that of a snake flexing its jaws before devouring prey, or of a dragon unfurling giant wings. The predator was about to spring the trap.

Velith clenched her grip around the spear, with fingers that would never stop straining against the marks left from that encounter with the Fae queen. The nearest way out was a window in the kitchen, the glass marred by dirt and lack of care.

Though the iron frame of the mirror grew hotter, she held it fast between her cloak and her side. Whatever the red eyes belonged to, she dared not kill it now, and give Deborah what she wanted.

She channelled all the tension in her arm and grip into throwing the javelin. Before the thing that had been Deborah could evaporate out of being, the spear hit her in the shoulder. She screamed, only then disappearing in mist, and a hideous cry tore through the air like a knife on slate.

I hope that *will leave a scar.*

The spear clattered to the ground; but instead of gathering it, Velith hugged the mirror close, raced to the window, leapt, and smashed right through it.

A human would have been cut to ribbons by the glass. She would have only a few scrapes and cuts on her clothing to deal with. She hit the ground running, pounding the snow as she raced into the storm.

She ran as quick as the snow and wind allowed, cutting to the right. Somewhere ahead lay a stream, and then High Road and Wyvern Abbey. Past them, there were the woods. Any hope of leaving Deborah behind was gone as she sensed the presence take form once again, racing toward her, the sound of footfalls numerous and rapid. Whatever she was, she must have taken a form with more than two legs, and some inner warning kept Velith from looking over her shoulder. She could only run, all but blind. Where was the stream?

The creature caught up to Velith, sweeping a hard limb to knock her off-balance. The cloak and mirror flew out of her hands, and she went sliding in the snow and came to a stop. Velith caught herself, struggled to her feet, and found a dark, slowly churning current of water just ahead.

The stream. It hadn't frozen over yet.

The mirror was just an arm's length away, next to the cloak. Her precious seeds had spilled from their pockets, scattered, and were already being lost to the snow.

The mirror's iron frame had grown so hot it was actually melting the snow and steaming in the cold air. She picked it up, surprised at the pain. It was hot enough to hurt *her*. A human's hand would have fared much worse.

Whatever was trapped inside, it wanted out. Would it kill her for her offense of the queen? Would it aid her, and then merely imprison her for the royal court's amusement? Would it simply make its escape and abandon Velith to her fate?

Deborah's unholy scream rose above the wind. Somewhere behind the flurries and icy fog, an angular shape stalked, gloated with a sound like rasping laughter. Velith made her decision and threw the mirror into the water. The glass had picked up the heat of the iron frame, and even as it sank into the frigid current, she heard a distinct *crack*.

Next to her foot, she found one of her spear-seeds. She snatched it up, breaking the shell and letting a new lance grow in hand.

She held it out defensively, waiting for her attacker to come forward. The jointed legs of a spider or mantis rose over the shape of its body, crawling closer.

Velith sensed the Fae emerging from the mirror's broken pieces. It burst out of the river in a torrent of icy water, spreading dark wings, and emitted a high-pitched cry so strong and commanding, it brought Velith to her knees.

The silhouette was familiar to Velith. A Fae Sentinel. The creatures guarded the royal court and scouted ahead when they travelled. Through the ice and fog, its immense red eyes shone like glowing coals, blazing with flashes of gold and white. Its shape resembled a torso and two legs, without any head or arms to speak of; the eyes bulged from where shoulders would have been. The creature's wings were immense expanses of skin, triangular and with mottled patterns in the fine brown fur that covered its entire body.

It seemed indifferent to the wet and cold as it landed next to her. The Sentinel's clawed feet drove into the earth like a hawk's talons. Its cry burst forth again, but Velith could brace against its main thrust and get back to her feet.

Ahead, the air cleared of fog, until all but a thin film of the blizzard lay between her and the corrupt creature that had deceived her, had so effectively played on her sympathy and her hatred. She knew its form and could finally name it. *Demon.*

Demons were enemies of the Fae and vulnerable to the Sentinel's screams. Even now the shapes of its jointed legs kicked and writhed. In this state, the creature was unable to vanish into thin air.

She drew her arm back, adjusted for the wind, and hurled the spear. It hit the fallen angel's centre of mass, and it gave a final, brief cry of pain.

The Sentinel's cry lessened, faded, and stopped. Velith had just enough time to watch the demon's body and her spear, both blackening and turning to ashes, then disintegrating and scattering, blown away as the ice and fog drew back together.

Velith turned and faced the Sentinel as it folded its wet wings around its body. Sentinels did not communicate in thoughts or words, but they could bring images to your mind. Sometimes even emotions.

She was struck by the force of just such an emotion: gratitude.

Gratitude? From a Fae? For her?

The images came to her from the being's strange mind, totally unlike her own and yet so efficient in showing meaning to her:

The demon imitating another hurt child to exploit its sense of compassion.

The Sentinel being lured into its iron trap and kept there for years, suffering in isolation from its brothers and the royal court, dying slowly as it languished inside the mirror.

Johann Schneider replacing the spokes on a cartwheel and receiving the mirror in exchange.

The Sentinel appearing in the glass, appearing sinister, trying to scare Schneider into breaking it or giving it to someone who would.

Schneider almost breaking the mirror with one of his many hammers but putting it away for suspicion of releasing bad luck.

Deborah feeding those fears by bringing the mirror back every time he tried to give it away, and Johann deciding to live with the supposedly cursed object, as long as it didn't hurt him.

Velith had come so close to falling victim as well.

The creature drew back from her, unfurled its giant wings, and sent one last image to Velith. It promised a new cloak and new seeds, provided by the Fae, as repayment. No strings attached, nor curses, nor conditions. And Fae did not break their word.

Since when had any of them made such an offer? Velith found her own inner Armor and resentment breaking, as tears gathered in her eyes.

And with that, the Sentinel lifted its wings high, swept them down, and took off into the storm. In a brief moment, she could glimpse its silhouette through the fog, like the shade of a dark guardian angel, until it was lost from sight.

Even for Velith, the storm was starting to grow cold. She gathered the remains of her cloak and wondered if the humans of Whitstead would attribute the unearthly cries to the fierce wind. Schneider might be relieved to see the mirror gone, and Velith would leave behind some gold to pay for the window. For now, she listened to the storm and to the faint sound of Christmas carols being sung at Wyvern Abbey, somewhere unseen in the tempest.

A Christmas gift. As Velith donned her camouflage once more, she laughed at the surprise. Here she was, apart from human concerns, and the Fae, of all people, were sending her a Christmas gift.

The Legend of Wild Wilda
by E. S. Marsh (fantasy/mythology)

ush now, child. Shall Saint Nicholas leave you a switch for Christmas? No? Then settle into bed. Up you go. Oh, my bones. A storm must be brewing. Mark my words, the windows will be half buried in snow when you wake. Peace, child, or I'll ask Wild Wilda to blow her horn and judge your soul. Who is Wild Wilda? Mercy, what are you learning in that fancy school? I'll tell you once you're tightly tucked. There you are.

Do you truly know nothing of Wild Wilda and the Huntsmen? Not a bit? It'll have to be the whole story then. Listen close. It is said that when a fog rolls in or the snow falls heavy and quiet, Wild Wilda roams Whitstead, a hunting horn in her hand. What's that? I don't know exactly how she got the horn. No one does, really. Some think Erlkönig, the elf king, stole her as a babe and gave the horn to her as a gift. I've also heard whispers that Wild Wilda is really a changeling, found as a child by a widowed woodsman. Upon his deathbed the woodsman gave her his horn which he told her would call the hounds of hell to bring wicked men to the destiny of their own making.

Don't interrupt. Of course, Wilda is a real person. Or at least was. My grandmother's grandmother met her. It's true. Every Christmas the tale is told. Now I will tell it to you.

My grandmother's grandmother knew the art of listening, she did. She traded her family's pelts at the Abbey for tea leaves and spice, but she also traded gossip. Word from town for word from the Abbey. One day the Sisters told her they feared a certain Bishop whenever he came to visit. No, I'll not tell you why. You are too young to know such things. Just know he wore Christ's cloth, but practiced none of Christ's principles.

My grandmother's grandmother told the Sisters of a strange woman in the woods that the townsfolk sometimes went to for advice or a tincture. The next month the Sisters had news. The Bishop had gone missing. If you do not calm yourself, child, I will not tell you how he met his end. That's better.

Now the Bishop adored the hunt. He led a hunting party into the woods where Wilda was known to live. The hounds took after a great elk, but when the Bishop caught up to them, he found the dogs with Wilda. They lay belly up at her feet and ate from her hands as if they knew her better than their own masters. The Bishop, enraged at the loss of his quarry, made threats. Never you mind what kind of threats. Wilda cautioned the Bishop that her friends, the spirits of the forest, would come for him should any harm come to her. To that, the Bishop laughed and drove his horse deeper into the wood.

At dusk, the hunting party returned to the Abbey, but without the Bishop. They said his horse spooked, the Bishop fell, and his foot caught in his stirrup. His horse dragged him away faster than the hounds could run. The hunting party searched until the sun waned, but neither they nor the dogs could find the Bishop or his mount. For a fortnight, half of Whitstead combed those woods, my grandmother's father among them. They never saw so much as a hoof print. What they did find was Wilda's hut, but neither she nor her horn there.

No, that is not when my grandmother's grandmother met Wilda. Don't get smart with me, I'm the one telling the story. Now after the Bishop disappeared the Abbey looked more and more unkempt by the year. The Sisters had to seek work in Whitstead to keep the Abbey in good repair. My grandmother's grandmother hired one of the Sisters to help tend the animals and make the butter and cheese. The two of them were milking one morning when they witnessed what happens when Wild Wilda blows her horn.

My, is it late. Perhaps I'll finish the tale tomorrow night. No? You promise not to be frightened when I snuff out the candle? Very well. I will tell you the rest.

As I said, my grandmother's grandmother and the Sister she hired were milking one morning when they heard a ruckus outside. The son of the smith was chasing Wild Wilda through the potato patch. Now, the son of the smith was as pompous as his father was humble, so my grandmother's grandmother grabbed the pitchfork and started after him, but the Sister held her firm. 'Wild Wilda can hold her own', the Sister said. And she spoke true. Wilda was stronger than she seemed, and that man's backside met the dirt more than a few times. Even so, the son of the smith kept on. Wilda brought the horn to her lips and gave a great blow.

The sound, I'm told, was so awful the chickens wouldn't lay for two months. A great many hounds could be heard a-howling, yet Wilda and the son of the smith were the only creatures in that field. If the smith's son had a lick of sense, he would have run then, but, be it bravery or foolishness, he stood his ground. When the horrible echo of the horn faded, snow began to fall. Clumps of flakes as big as your fist, they say. Out of the white haze came the Huntsmen. Already a layer of snow covered the field, but these men and their mounts left no tracks.

My grandmother's grandmother got a good look as they rode up and she said she almost died of fright. The tallest of the men was on the tallest of horses. He wore a helm adorned with antlers whiter than the snow around him. His hands holding the reigns were hardly more than bones. Some of the mounted Huntsmen held chains that bound poor souls whose judgment had already been cast. The Sister pointed to one of them. A thin man in a frayed white robe and a pointed hat. Yes, the bishop. How smart you are.

The horned Huntsman pointed a rotten finger at the son of the smith. Up from the very ground came a large black dog. Big enough for you to ride like a pony, I'd wager. It circled the son of the smith, sniffing about his feet. The dog gave a growl so sudden and fierce it put the son on his backside again. The horned Huntsman flicked his wrist and a chain wrapped itself around the son's neck. Then the whole lot of them thundered into the woods with the smith's son dragged along behind them.

And do you know what Wilda did? Wild Wilda walked right up to the barn as if she knew all along the women had been watching. To my grandmother's grandmother, Wild Wilda said, 'His soul was stained. Be sure to wash yours.' She left then, in the same direction of the Huntsmen. Whenever her horn, is heard another citizen of Whitstead goes missing, though not anyone that anybody cares to see again.

Hm? Don't believe me? Ask your parents. The disappearance of the smith's son was the talk of Whitstead for decades. Rumours spread like the black death. Some thought the son of the smith had too many debts to pay to too many people and left the village to spare his life. Others said he was murdered by the father of an unwed woman that carried his child. I've also heard that he made the mistake of entering the forest during a blizzard, got himself lost, and perished from the cold. Nonsense, I say. The truth has been passed down from generation to generation in my family. Now you can pass it to yours if you wish.

Look! The window. Didn't I tell you? It's snowing. Sleep well. Say your prayers and mind your manners tomorrow or I'll ask Wild Wilda to blow her horn once more.

A Flickering Candle
by Marla Schultz *(drama)*

Emma awoke, her body tense. Out of habit, she stretched her hand towards the space beside her only to feel the chill of empty sheets. Realization seeped in. Jasper was away, but there was something else. Was that a cry? She tugged back the covers — *Sophia*. But then the familiar wave of despair slammed into her.

Blackness. The weight of it unbearable. She couldn't breathe. Fumbling in the darkness, heart pounding, her hand searched the small table near her bedstead. Panic shot through her when her hand didn't make contact with the item she sought. Then suddenly — like a tiny miracle — her hand wrapped around it.

Scritch. Scritch. A grating noise filled the room. A tiny flash from the match. Whoosh. A flicker of light — soft and golden — met the darkness head on, defying its power. It crackled and sizzled as she held it against the blackened wick of the candle. It sputtered for a moment, causing her heart to flutter in fear, but then it leapt high, confidently swaying in the darkness. Tiny in contrast to the size of the room, but its brightness seemed mighty. She stretched out a hand to the flame gathering strength from its boldness. Its warmth. Its ability to push back the darkness even for a little while.

•◇•◇•◇•◇•◇•◇•◇•◇•

Emma pulled her cloak over her black bombazine gown. Years before she scoffed at the tradition of donning mourning clothing when a loved one died. Even when her beloved grandmother passed away, she had worn the sombre clothing for the required time but longed to dress in the grey and lilac colours of half-mourning, and then transition quickly to the lighter colours Grandmother had loved so much. At the time, wearing the dark clothing seemed so attention-seeking — so demanding of sympathy. Now, she couldn't imagine wearing anything else. Colour had seeped from her world leaving it monochromatic. Black dominated it — its intensity a harsh reminder that she still existed.

She stood for a moment, eyes closed, one hand on the doorpost. The grief. It still left her paralyzed at times.

'Ma'am?' A young voice filled the space near her.

Her eyes flew open. Polly, her housemaid stood near her, her eyes filled with concern. Emma attempted to smile. 'Oh, Polly! I'm... I'm preparing to go into town.'

'Yes, of course, ma'am.' Polly's eyes searched Emma's. 'Should I order the carriage for you now?'

Emma studied the cloud-darkened sky through the window. The weather matched her emotions. 'No, but thank you. I think I will walk.' She nodded her head in dismissal.

'Yes, ma'am.' Polly curtsied and left.

Emma watched as she retreated from the room. She felt weary of all the niceties of polite society. The pretence. The 'I am doing wells' when it was the furthest thing from the truth. 'I am NOT fine!' she wanted to scream through the doorway at poor Polly's retreating back. 'I feel like I am dying!' But whom could she tell? Jasper, her merchant shipman husband, was far away on a ship destined for China. Away from the reality of the loss of Sophia. This grief was hers alone. No letter had been delivered from him yet acknowledging Sophia's passing.

No! She hadn't 'passed.' Death with its ugly, long claws had snatched their infant daughter from her arms. And it had stolen Emma as well, leaving behind a fragile shell. Humans had a plethora of feelings and emotions. She only had two. Grief and pain.

She couldn't share her sorrow with her servants. It wasn't done. At least that is what Jasper insisted. She had no one.

Outside, a chilly wind blew over the colourless landscape—grimy snow, a few skeletal, deciduous trees, and a dark, wooded area in the distance. Nearby, the half ruins of Wyvern Abbey loomed against the grey sky. The medieval architecture, with its carved, stone columns and peaked arches exposed to the emptiness surrounding it, gave the impression of a behemoth skeleton picked clean. The carcass of what had once thrived hundreds of years ago. She shivered, averted her eyes, and hurried towards the village.

•◇•◇•◇•◇•◇•◇•◇•◇•

Twilight had fallen, though it was scarcely five o'clock. A crescent moon, partially obstructed by cloud-covering, cast a faint light on the few bare trees and the carved gravestones poking up out of the frozen earth. Emma shivered as she became aware of her isolation. She glanced towards the path leading out of the cemetery. She had lingered too long at Sophia's tombstone tracing the letters of her name, the numbers of her birthdate and date of her death. The dates were too close together. *21 January 1844* to *30 July 1844*. No years to separate the two.

Angrily, she swiped at the snow that covered the top of the tombstone, knowing that the wind would sweep it up and redeposit it, covering her baby's resting place again with a frigid blanket. Hot tears formed. Sophia couldn't feel the chill of the snow, but it hurt her to think of her infant lying there under the frozen ground.

'It isn't fair!' she choked out, her words a faint whisper. She touched the silver locket hiding under her cloak and pulled it out. The metal caught the moonlight and glimmered. She left it closed, knowing she wouldn't be able to see the miniature of Sophia inside, but it was enough to hold it in her palm. Emma's throat swelled with unshed tears. She needed to go. The walk home would be long and cold in the dark.

A muffled sound on her right caught her attention. She turned towards the noise only to be rewarded with a heavy weight slamming into her, followed by a sharp slicing pain around her neck. She sprawled on the ground, breathless. A tingling surged through her body. Searching the area, she saw a copper-haired figure dash past the church, a shimmer of silver dangling from his hand.

With a gasp, she reached for the locket, but found nothing. The unshed tears from earlier began to flow, but to her horror, something began to form in the pit of her insides. She couldn't stop it. A deep, keening wail poured out of her. She wanted to stifle it—someone would hear. But she couldn't. It filled the air around her. She allowed her grief to consume her. The frigid snow beneath her, the icy air around—it no longer mattered.

Her weeping subsided, and she became aware of a presence. She stiffened.

'Ach, child.' A rich, female voice said. 'Why are you grieving so?'

Oh, Father in Heaven. Someone had witnessed her anguish.

She clucked. 'You're shivering.' The voice had a slightly foreign hint to its timbre. Emma lifted her head. Tears blurred her vision, but she was able to make out the figure of an older woman. Golden hoops hanging from her ears glinted in the faint light. The woman was swathed in layers of clothing, a shawl wrapped around her shoulders. A slightly exotic scent permeated the chilly air. The woman reached down and picked something off the ground, then with warm, ungloved hands lifted her up. 'Come.' She patted Emma's arm. 'My name is Elena, and you need warmth, child.'

Emma found herself being led through the graveyard away from the lamplit street. Glancing anxiously around her, she confirmed her suspicion that they were alone. Could this stranger be trusted? She knew a group of gypsies—Romani—were camped near the church. People shunned for their supposed pickpocket skills and fortune telling abilities. This woman with her unusual clothing appeared to be one of them. Was the thief a gypsy too? Emma slowed her pace. She was being foolish.

In the thicket of trees in front of them, light flickered, and sweet strains of music spilled out into the night. The tune sounded familiar, yet she couldn't quite place it. The song urged her forward. A rich tenor voice sang the melody while a deep baritone and a beautiful alto harmonized with him. The words greeted her ears. 'Silent night, holy night…' Her heart leapt. *The music of Christmas*. The notes danced from the strings of a fiddle accompanied by a squeeze box, and the silvery tinkle of another instrument. Wagons of emerald, scarlet, canary yellow, and cobalt blue—all of them gilded—were lit by a blazing fire crackling in the middle of the encampment. Several men, women, and children warmed themselves near its flames.

As the two women drew closer, some of the people turned towards them—the smoky, woody smell of the campfire filling the air. The music trickled to a stop. More than a dozen faces stared at her. Some were shadowed. Others, coloured by the flickering light of the fire, were either inscrutable or wary. Emma held back, but Elena pulled her gently forward.

'Forgive them. We tend to be a little distrusting of strangers,' she said. 'Sharra, would you share a little of your supper with my guest?'

A thin, dark woman dressed in a crimson and black fringed shawl stood up from her place near the campfire, a guarded look in her eyes. Emma flushed in embarrassment. She couldn't take food from these people who owned far less than she.

'Oh, no! I don't need—' As Emma began her refusal, her stomach growled.

One of the men began to chuckle. 'I think your belly disagrees.'

Emma felt something lighten inside of her. 'Maybe you're right,' she said. A small boy sidled up to Sharra's side and leaned against her. He studied Emma from under the flop of brown hair covering his eyes.

'Kit,' Sharra said, glancing down at the boy. 'Get our guest a bowl of stew. And be quick.'

Kit hurried away to a cobalt blue wagon on the other side of the encampment. A few minutes later he came out holding a steaming bowl.

'Here, Miss,' he said as he approached, holding out the delicious smelling fare.

Emma's stomach growled again. 'Thank you, both,' she said. She smiled hesitantly. 'I appreciate your generosity.'

Sharra gave a quick nod and returned to her place by the fire. One of the men raised a fiddle to his shoulder and, a moment later, strains of music filled the air around them again. Sharra joined in. Surprised, Emma realised that the beautiful alto voice from earlier belonged to this quiet woman.

'Come, my friend,' Elena said. She gestured to the crimson and gold wagon closest to them. Accents of amethyst purple, vibrant green, and cobalt blue, shimmering like jewels in the flickering light, decorated the ornately carved grapevines and flowers on either side of the door. 'This is my vardo—my wagon.' Her friend. 'Inside you can eat your supper.'

Emma glanced up. A small pipe chimney stuck out of the top, puffs of smoke making trails in the chilly air. As she followed her hostess through the doorway, she gasped. Glorious colours, textures, and fabrics filled the tiny space. Her colour-starved eyes surveyed the visual feast.

'Elena,' she breathed. 'It's beautiful!' Fascinated, she stared at the red and gold mantle on the left side that housed a tiny, black stove. Green tiles enclosed the space around it. A copper kettle perched on the range, steam huffing out of its spout. A richly textured, cosy bed at the back; sparkling glass and porcelain dishes; and a built-in velvet-covered sofa all added to the interior's charm.

'It's humble, but it's my home,' Elena said, pleased by Emma's praise. 'Here,' she patted the sofa. 'Sit and eat your supper before it grows cold.'

Emma removed her cloak and sat down on the comfortable seat. She spooned a bite of stew into her mouth, unsure of what the unfamiliar cuisine would taste like, but her first mouthful delivered a medley of flavours. The spices and herbs were unfamiliar, but delicious. As Emma ate, Elena bustled around, opening cabinets and clinking dishes. A few minutes later, a cup of spicy-smelling tea and a slice of bread on a delicate rose-coloured plate sat on a carved table to Emma's right.

'Now', Elena said, as she sat down next to Emma. She stretched out her hands. 'Tell me your troubles, child.'

Emma's eyebrows furrowed. Did Elena plan to tell her fortune?

The older woman gave her a gentle smile and shook her head. 'I am neither a fortune teller nor a prophetess. Just another traveller in life who has experienced much grief, but also much joy.' She took Emma's hands in her own and squeezed. 'I feel you need to share your sorrow. You have been carrying your burden alone for too long, I think.'

The look of compassion in Elena's dark eyes and the tender expression on her face were too much. Emma's throat swelled and she felt the grief begin to well up to the surface again. As Elena held her hands, Emma realised she wanted to share her pain. Through tears, she told her about Jasper's absence. His current voyage to China as a captain and that, most likely, she wouldn't see him for another two or more years. Her isolation. But, mostly, about the loss of her precious baby, Sophia. Sophia, who had only been six months old when she died. The stolen locket with her baby's miniature. Emma wept and this stranger, yet new friend, listened like her beloved grandmother had years ago.

'Where are your parents, child? Your mother?' Elena asked as Emma righted herself and blew her nose on her handkerchief.

'My parents died when I was young. My grandmother raised me, but she passed away several years ago.'

Elena clucked. 'Not only have you lost a child, you are also an orphan.' She patted Emma's hand. She studied the glass shelves across from them, emotions playing over her face.

'Did you lose someone, Elena?' Emma asked softly.

The older woman wiped her eyes. 'I am a widow — my Sampson passed from this earth in the spring.' She gave her a sad smile. 'You and I. We are the widow and the orphan.' She gazed at Emma intently. 'But joy *will* come again. This I believe.'

Elena insisted on walking Emma home. The boy, Kit, and Elena's son-in-law, the fiddler, accompanied them. As they passed through the village, she heard the blind pedlar, newly arrived in the village, singing a Christmas carol. 'O come all ye faithful…' He strummed a lute and sang in a rich baritone voice.

The walk to the village, which had felt so lonely that afternoon, contrasted sharply with the journey home. The man, Victor, was silent, but it didn't make her uneasy. Kit was also quiet, but content, it seemed. Before they departed, Elena handed her an unfamiliar, grey, knit glove.

'Perhaps it belongs to the thief,' Elena said. 'I found it in the cemetery.'

•◇•◇•◇•◇•◇•◇•◇•◇•◇•

In the middle of the night, Emma awoke to silence. Pressing blackness. Her heart raced as she fumbled for the matches by her bed. She scraped the match and with a whoosh, the flame leapt up high, its golden light lessening the darkness — removing its weight. Emma breathed in deeply as she lit the candle on the table beside her. She reached for her locket only to discover empty space. The memory of her assault swelled to the surface. In the Romani camp, the loss of her locket had receded, but now she felt its absence sharply. As she touched the raw place on her neck, tears formed and anger at the thief surged through her. She would go see the constable the next day. She needed justice.

Again, the next night she repeated the familiar pattern. Panic. Groping for the matches. The sizzle of the flame making contact with the candle's wick. She watched the flicker of the tiny blaze and remembered the Romani campfire. The rich and vibrant colours of the vardos. The taste of the delicious stew. Elena's acts of kindness and her newfound friendship. Emma peacefully slipped back to sleep.

•◇•◇•◇•◇•◇•◇•◇•◇•◇•

In that thin place between slumber and wakefulness, the next morning, Emma became aware of an unsettledness. A need to share. To look outside of herself. Like Elena had. But to whom?

The blind pedlar in the village green.

She ordered the carriage to be prepared for her trip, added a couple of lumpy bundles to it and, by ten o'clock, was on her way into town. Flashes of colour caught her attention. Redwings and red breasted robins perched in the bare trees near the road. A red fox outlined against the grey winter sky surveyed the carriage as it rolled by. Holly leaves adorned with bright berries decorated cottages.

'Henry, please take me to the pedlar's wagon.'

Henry started to turn in his seat towards her, but then gave a quick nod.

The carriage turned left onto Church Street towards St. Nicholas Church and the village green. Henry brought the team of horses and the carriage to a halt with a 'Whoa!' and a slight tug on the reins.

Across the way from the church sat the pedlar's emerald green, barrel-shaped wagon. Green? She could have sworn it was grey. She had purchased something from him a couple of days ago but, somehow, had missed its beautiful colour.

Henry helped her out of her carriage and picked up the bundles.

Her insides tumbling a little, she wondered what the pedlar would think. She crossed the snow-covered ground, uncertain of her decision.

The blind tinker tilted his head as they walked towards him. 'A very good mornin' to ye!' he called out. He had his hat pulled low over one side of his head.

'Good morning,' Emma replied as she approached him. She faltered. 'I... I need to purchase a couple of items.' But what? Her mind scrambled. Ribbons? What an odd thought.

As she watched him bring out a selection to choose from, she noticed for the first time his scarred and crippled arm. Tears formed and she felt the familiar knot in her throat. Another one of life's travellers who had experienced much sorrow. Emma tried to swallow the lump of emotion.

She reached for a black ribbon, but one the colour of holly berries and another, a rosemary green, captured her attention.

'These two, please.' She said, placing them in his hand.

The pedlar smiled; his sightless eyes turned in her direction. 'Will ye be needing anythin' else?

She remembered her dwindling match supply. 'Maybe...' Her voice caught. 'Maybe a packet of matches?'

Dermot's expression softened. 'I am sorry, but that's not somethin' I have.' He tilted his head again and paused for a moment. 'It seems ta me, ya won't be needin' those matches so much afore long.' His tone seemed to give extra meaning to the simple words. He handed the ribbons back to her. 'No charge, Miss. A happy Christmas to you.'

She felt her face flush. 'I have something for you too.' Emma took the first bundle from Henry, unwrapped it, and lifted out a small crockery pot. As she raised the lid, the tantalizing smell of roast beef and potatoes flavoured with herbs filled the air.

'Och, but don't that smell morish? My belly and I thank ye.'

'I also have some hot cider if you like.' Feeling awkward, she held out a jug filled with the beverage. 'My name is Emma Williams, by the way.'

'A pleasure to meet you, Emma Williams.' The pedlar gave a slight bow. 'Dermot Sheridan is what I'm called.'

●◇●◇●◇●◇●◇●◇●◇●◇●

Colour continued to seep back into her world. On Sunday, a breath-taking sunrise streaked the sky. The snow glistened in the new light of daybreak. It seemed a painter had traded his charcoal sketch for a palette of pigments and a fresh canvas and began brushing daubs of colour onto the white expanse. Emma blinked away the moisture that sprang to her eyes, surprised that these tears were a response to beauty and not grief.

She attended the church service that morning.

•◊•◊•◊•◊•◊•◊•◊•◊•

More colour appeared. This time on the flushed face of Mary, the cook, who stood coughing in the kitchen, and upstairs in the red-rimmed eyes of Polly. She gave both of them the day off. They stared at her, eyes wide, twisting their aprons.

'With pay, of course,' Emma said. She assigned other servants to tend the fires that day.

In the village, Emma stopped by to see the constable, but there was no news regarding her locket or the thief. Next, she visited Elena in her beautiful vardo, drank more of the spicy tea, and shared some sweet buns she had brought. As she and Elena left the cemetery together, a few villagers scrutinized them. Emma glanced around at the villagers, then grasped Elena's hand and thanked her for the visit. Elena then slipped back towards the security of her camp.

•◊•◊•◊•◊•◊•◊•◊•◊•

On Wednesday night, a snowstorm hit Whitstead with a ferocity the village hadn't seen in years. In the middle of the night, Emma awoke. The night sky looked odd through the partially opened drapes, and a quick inspection revealed thick snow swirling outside her window. *Elena and the other Romani. The pedlar.* A prayer spilled from her, an appeal for protection for them and any others caught in the storm. As she stood by the window with the scant moonlight her only illumination, she realised — she hadn't lit a single match.

The amount of snow the next day required a trip into town by sleigh. They delivered a meal to Dermot, who declared he was none the worse despite the storm. Elena and the Romani seemed fine as well. As she and Henry were leaving the village, a commotion near the river running through town caught her attention.

'They found a body on the riverbank!' a dark-haired boy hollered as he ran past the sleigh.

Emma clasped a hand to her mouth.

'Terrible news, that,' Henry said, turning around in his seat. 'Especially during Christmastide.' He shook his head and clicked at the horses.

The fourth Sunday of Advent dawned as bright as the Sunday previous and again she attended the service. As she exited the church, the portly constable hurried over to her.

'Mrs. Williams. I was hoping to see you today. I have some news.' He had a sombre look on his face. 'We found your thief.'

Emma's heart leapt and she put a hand to her chest. 'And my locket? Was that recovered?'

'It was.' He produced the necklace from a pocket.

Emma held out her hand and the cold metal slinked into her palm. Her hands trembled as she opened the oval locket eager to see Sophia's likeness. Instead, Sophia's tiny face was barely identifiable. The watercolours smeared.

'I am sorry. Truly.' The Constable looked at her with compassion. 'I expect the water's what damaged your painting.'

She tried to keep her voice steady. 'And the thief? Is he locked up?' she asked.

'Actually,' the constable said. 'He drowned.'

Emma's eyes widened in shock. This wasn't the justice she sought.

The constable continued. 'Someone found him the day after the snowstorm.' He shook his head. 'It looks like he may have slipped and hit his head.' He pursed his lips. 'Poor fella. He left a child behind too. A little girl.'

'Oh no!'

'And Mrs. Williams?' He glanced down and cleared his throat. 'I am sorry for your loss. My missus and I, we lost a wee one as well a while back.' Awkwardly, he turned and left.

Her heart wrenched for them. More of life's wounded travellers. And the thief, now lying cold and lifeless, had left behind another. Was she at the Charitable School? Emma shuddered. She had encountered Miss Rossiter, the matron of the establishment, once. A cold, stony-faced woman lacking any maternal sensibilities, it seemed.

●◇●◇●◇●◇●◇●◇●◇●◇●

On Christmas Eve, Emma attended the evening service. As she walked out into the chilly night, her heart felt lighter. Although it had been just two weeks since meeting Elena, her world felt different.

Across the street, Dermot the pedlar emerged from his wagon, his beautiful lute in his hands. She thought of her remaining matches, unused for the last few nights. Somehow, he had known.

'Happy Christmas, pedlar,' she called out. She could feel her joy spilling out.

'Happy Christmas, Emma!' he responded. He raised the lute and touched the neck of it, his damaged fingers surprisingly limber.

A few moments later, he began to play. In wonder, Emma listened as the music of angels poured from his instrument. The pedlar's fingers flew over the strings; his rich baritone voice singing the unfamiliar song.

'Babe in the manger, sweet holy child…'

A babe in the manger. She still longed to hold Sophia, she couldn't deny it, but grief had lost its sharp edge.

Her chest constricted as Dermot sang the next verse.

'Born for the shunned, the orphan, the poor,

Born for the broken, the lost, and the lame…'

Orphan. Broken. Lost. All words that had recently described her. An exotic scent greeted her nose as someone slipped up next to her and gently squeezed her arm. She turned to see Elena's warm, dark eyes looking at her, understanding and compassion filling them.

'Here we are again,' Elena whispered, squeezing her hand. 'The widow and the orphan.'

Dermot sang the next line.

'For this dying world, the Christ Child came.'

'I will not leave you comfortless; I will come to you.' The words of a scripture her grandmother had taught her years before came unbidden. Tears filled Emma's eyes. *He hadn't left her comfortless. He had come to her.*

'A-la-la-la-la-la Alleluia, A-la-la-la-la-la-la Alleluia.'

As Dermot sang the chorus, repeating it over and over, the villagers and Elena joined in, their voices joyous. Emma sang as well, her throat tight, and her voice breaking a little, but her heart full.

A small boy, no more than five or six, sang as well, his voice angelic. A tiny girl stood next to him clapping her hands. From the Romani camp, Emma heard their instruments adding their own joyous strains to the music under the stars.

•◊•◊•◊•◊•◊•◊•◊•◊•◊•

As the cobwebs of sleep fell away the next morning, and Emma began to stir, the words fluttered through her mind again. *I will not leave you comfortless; I will come to you.*

A couple of days after Christmas, Emma swallowed her anxiety and made the trip to the Charitable School. She trembled as she walked towards the front doors. Frowning, she surveyed her surroundings. Dark, muddy patches with tufts of dead grass spotted the yard like a disease. The building seemed as cold and stonehearted as its matron. She looked back towards her carriage. She could leave now; no one would know of her indecision. It was so tempting.

As she hesitated, a tumble of children burst out of the side of the house bundled in a shabby array of winter wear. A group of brunette and blond children with an occasional black-haired child mixed in. Another child, a little boy, raced out after the others, a nut-brown cap covering white-blond hair. Hair the colour of Sophia's. The familiar pain surged through her. She breathed in deeply, steeling herself against it. She could do this.

A tall young man, a bright red scarf wrapped around his neck, trailed after them laughing and calling. 'Let's play Hide-and-Seek. John! It's your turn to count.'

The child raced to a tree, a spray of snow shooting out behind his flying feet. He leaned his arms and head against the rough bark and began to count. 'One, two, three…'

Emma watched the scene in puzzlement. Hide-and-seek? In the snow?

'Uncle Mattie!' a small voice called. 'Help me hide!' The voice came from behind a boulder. A moment later, a little boy appeared, dark hair half-hidden under a limp hat, trailing after the young man.

'Sorry, Charles!' the young man's warm, friendly voice replied. 'You have to find your own hiding spot.' He turned and slipped down a small hill, disappearing behind a dip in the landscape.

The boy tumbled after him.

But which one was the thief's child?

A moment later she knew. A young girl, her bright, red curls a tangled mess, stood alone by the building her head bent down. In the girl's hand she held one large, grey glove. The twin, Emma assumed, of the one Elena found. Emma's heart wrenched. She saw herself standing there. Alone. An orphan. Undesirable.

Her adoptive parents found her at an orphanage years before and had chosen her, not as a servant, but a daughter. Later, when they were tragically killed in an accident, her adoptive grandmother warmly welcomed Emma into her home and raised her as her own.

Emma walked over to the girl. 'Hello,' she said. 'What's your name?'

The girl didn't answer at first, but then whispered, 'Lucy.'

'Lucy. That's a beautiful name,' Emma replied.

•◇•◇•◇•◇•◇•◇•◇•◇•

A few days later, Emma brought the little girl home. That night Emma tucked Lucy into a cosy bed in a rosemary green bedroom, with accents the colour of holly berries, that she had prepared for Lucy herself. The ribbons purchased from the pedlar lay on the bureau.

After bidding Lucy good night, Emma walked out of the bedroom into the lamp-illuminated hallway.

A small whimper came from the dark room. 'Miss Emma?'

'Yes, Lucy?

'I'm afraid of the darkness.'

Emma could hear a tremble in her voice.

Scritch. Scritch.

The grating noise filled the room. A tiny flash. *Whoosh.* A flicker of light met the darkness defying its power. It crackled and sizzled when laid against the wick of the beeswax candle. It sputtered, but then danced a victory dance. Tiny in contrast to the size of the room, but its brightness mighty.

Lucy stretched out her fingers toward the glow, gathering strength from its boldness. Its warmth. Its ability to push back the darkness.

'I'm here,' Emma whispered, gently touching Lucy's tousled, red curls. 'I won't leave you.

Dermot's Alleluia
by Melinda K. Busch (*drama/fantasy/poetry*)

ou're not good enough.

The hissing whisper woke Dermot Sheridan from a sound sleep. He sat up, heart pounding, breathing heavy.

They'll never want you.

A bitter wind cut through Dermot's ragged tunic, chilling him to the bone. Flynn, still curled on the ground, whined softly. Dermot lay down again and wrapped his good arm around the hound. 'Good lad.' The dog's tongue swiped his cheek, the right one, where he had no scars to rob him of sensation.

He was accustomed to the taunting words. All his life he had heard them, long before the burns had scarred his face and rendered his left arm near useless. His people encountered hatred and derision almost everywhere they went. Mam had taught him when he was young not to listen to the hoots and jeers of the settled folk. 'Hold your head up, boyo,' she'd say when their caravan was forced out of one town after another. 'We're as much children of God as any of 'em.'

How he wished she were here now to still the whispers on the wind. He pressed his face against Flynn's back, remembering the days when he would run to Mam for comfort and she would hold him close to her chest so he could hear her heartbeat.

The fire had stolen more than his handsome features and his sight. Mam was gone, passed through Heaven's gates. Dermot travelled alone now. Well, except for Flynn. As soon as he could put one foot in front of the other without tripping over it, he walked away, leaving his people behind. Flynn was all the friend and guide and protector he needed. Together, they avoided all but the most fleeting of interactions with other humans. In spring and summer, they lived by foraging. In the colder months, they would venture into towns and villages, never staying long enough to develop attachments. When he could sing for his supper or a few coins, he ate. When he could not, he went without. So far, he had managed to keep body and soul together. Well, after a manner of speaking. Sometimes he wasn't so sure about the soul.

You're not good enough. The whisper was louder now. His ears fairly rang with it. He twisted his good hand in Flynn's fur and wept until he drifted into sleep.

•◇•◇•◇•◇•◇•◇•◇•◇•

'Dermot Sheridan, rise up. We would have you come and sit with us.' A woman's soft voice reached into his dreams and tugged him to wakefulness. At least, he thought it had awakened him until he blinked open his eyes and found that he could see. That only happened in dreams, a nightly respite from the suffocating darkness. A black-haired beauty stood over him, a gentle smile tugging at her lips, hand stretched down to help him up. She wore a white gown under a green cloak. His eyes fastened hungrily on that green... the colour of life. He took her hand and let her pull him to his feet. Once standing, he turned in a slow circle, eagerly drinking in everything he saw. His own breath puffing out in a cloud... a silvery sliver of moon hanging in a black velvet sky... a myriad of glittering stars strewn across the inky expanse. In one direction a line of birch trees marked the edge of a wood, their bare branches stretching upward; in another, a few flickering lights illuminated the windows of some farmhouse in the distance. Dermot stopped his turning with the wood to his back as his gaze landed on a campfire blazing not twenty paces away. A pleasant heat soaked into him, chasing away the chill. In waking life, fire terrified him. It dredged up memories of pain and the anguish of loss. But in his dream, the sight of the dancing flames sparked joy within him. He glanced behind him and saw his own form still asleep on the hard ground, Flynn curled close against him. *Naught but a dream. But if that is so, why is my arm still crippled?* He shrugged the question away and followed the woman who had awakened him.

Around the fire a small group had gathered. Travelling People like himself, if the green barrel-shaped wagon parked a few yards away was any indication. Sitting on a log facing away from Dermot, a white-haired fiddler played a merry tune. A second man stood nearby, playing along on a penny whistle. And the singing, och, there was a heavenly blend. The soprano was a lithe woman, clad all in white, with flowing red curls and green eyes that flashed in the firelight. Her skin was like porcelain and her clear sweet voice soared its way to God's ears. As she sang, she played a bodhran, her hand a blur as she skilfully wielded the beater. The fiddler sang tenor. He was a slender man, but wiry, nothing weak about him. His voice rang through the cold air, making Dermot's feet itch to dance. The alto was the very lass who had pulled him to his feet. The bass, a hulking man who looked like some ancient warrior stepped out of the old tales, served as an anchor for the higher voices. They sang a joyful *Alleluia* to a tune he'd never heard but hoped he would remember when he awoke. Dermot found his heartbeat quickening as the song chased out the darkness from his heart. Intrigued, he settled himself beside the fiddler and listened, his heel tapping out the rhythm.

As the music faded, the fiddler lowered his instrument and called to the soprano. 'Trócaire, food for our young friend here. Looks like a crow's age since he tucked into a proper meal.'

Before he had a chance to ponder the woman's odd name... *Trócaire*... Mercy... she was thrusting a bowl into his good hand and the heady aroma of rabbit stew wafted up to tickle his nose. 'God grant ya health and long life, lad,' she said as she stood back and smiled down at him.

Dermot balanced the bowl on one knee and gave her a nod. 'I thank ye, mum.'

The tenor clapped him on the back. 'Eat hearty, lad. Put some meat on them bones of yours.'

Dermot nodded, then set to eating. Living wild for so long, he had little use for table manners. He plucked a chunk of meat from the bowl with his fingers and put it in his mouth, then went for some potato. His hosts gave no show of offense.

While Dermot shovelled in his meal, the fiddler talked. 'My name's Rafe.' He pointed to each of the others in turn, starting with the burly warrior. 'That there's Mick. Him with the whistle is Gabe. And the alto is Dóchas.' Then he pointed beyond Gabe to a horse Dermot hadn't noticed before, an old grey nag with a ragged coat and a crooked back. 'And that's Beauty. She's to be yours, along with the wagon and all within it.'

'Beauty?' Dermot let loose with a derisive snort as he set his empty bowl on the ground. 'What sort o' name is that for such a bag o' bones?'

'Whisht!' Rafe gave him a light swat on the back of his head. 'Courtesy, lad!' Suddenly, they were standing beside the horse. Rafe reached for Dermot's good hand and placed it on the animal's side. 'Appearances are a cheat, lad. Have you forgotten what your mother taught you? "Look with your heart instead of your eyes. What seems ugly outside may be beautiful within."'

Dermot closed his eyes and tried to look with his heart. He stroked Beauty's nose. She nuzzled him and nickered softly in his ear. When he opened his eyes again, she was still ragged and skinny. Her back was still crooked. But he saw beauty shining in her eyes. 'What makes the difference?' he asked in an awed whisper.

Rafe's eyes twinkled. ''Tis simple, lad — ye chose to look on her with love.'

Back by the fire, Dermot determined to remember every detail of this strange dream. He studied each of the singers carefully, letting his eyes linger on the alto. There was something timeless about her face... when her eyes sparkled in the firelight, he thought she looked like a young slip of a lass. And yet, a deep wisdom in her gaze bespoke long years of not just surviving but finding joy amidst sorrow and struggle. In that, she reminded him of his mother. *Dóchas... Hope. Aye, I've been sorely needing some of that for years now.*

When he turned back to Rafe, the fiddler passed him a simple lute. It looked just like the one Dermot had carried when he had two good hands, crafted of cherrywood, with strings of sheep gut. 'Will you join us?' Rafe asked, though the words came across more as a command than a request.

Dermot frowned, thrusting his chin toward his injured arm. 'And just how do you think I'll play with this useless wing?' he retorted.

If Rafe took offense, he didn't show it. He just pressed the lute into Dermot's hand. 'It's made special for you, lad. Hold it just so and it'll give ye no trouble.'

'Please, Dermot.' Trócaire sat herself down beside him and lay a slender hand on his shoulder. 'It's been far too long since you played.' Something in her voice compelled him to do as she asked. It was all just a dream, anyway. He accepted the instrument and let Rafe show him how to hold it.

He strummed the lute strings, listening carefully to be sure they were properly tuned. Rafe had been right—he was able to play. His damaged fingers had just enough strength to work the frets. Once he was satisfied with the tuning, he launched into *The Wexford Carol*. It had been his mother's favourite. A poor choice, he soon realised. Before he was halfway through, he felt tears forming in his eyes, then running down his cheeks and soaking his collar. As he reached the final verse, his voice wavered with emotion. Still, he forced himself to keep singing.

As the song faded to silence, Rafe's hand settled on his shoulder. 'Well done, boyo. From the heart. Now set the lute aside. Sit awhile and talk with me.'

'Aye.' As Dermot lay down the lute, he thought that he'd never had a dream so vivid, so detailed. It was just a wisp of a thought, gone as quickly as it had come.

'Are you so certain 'tis a dream, lad?' Rafe asked.

Dermot's heart clenched. He did not like the feeling that Rafe knew even his private thoughts. 'What else could it be?' He spit out the words as if they were spoiled food, then pointed his chin to the spot where he could still see himself lying in the dirt beside Flynn. 'With me sleepin' yonder and you pluckin' the thoughts from me head,' he sputtered, 'and all of the sudden me seein' like a hawk. Aye, 'tis a dream and nay more.'

Rafe didn't argue. He just lit a pipe and stuck it between his lips, then leaned his head back to gaze at the stars. Fragrant smoke drifted up to Heaven like a prayer. 'I bring a message for you, lad. You're as much a child of God as any of 'em.'

Stunned into silence, Dermot blinked. *Mam's words.* He hadn't believed them for years. He wasn't sure he ever could. 'Bloody cruel Father He is, to leave me thus,' he muttered.

'Och, boyo…' Rafe's eyes seemed to bore into his soul. 'There's beauty in them scars you bear. The Father knows the ache that's in your heart. He wants to heal it. He wants to bring you home.'

Home. And where was that supposed to be? Ire bubbled up inside Dermot once more, burning from within. A fleeting thought shot through his mind that he wasn't sure which of his scars were worse—the ones that could be seen, or the ones he carried in his heart. 'I've got no home,' he growled.

'Ah, but ya do, lad,' Dóchas said quietly. 'And folk who have never stopped longing for you to return. But the Father is patient. You have time yet.'

'Aye,' Rafe agreed. 'You have time. Go back to your sleep. When you wake in the morning, you can judge for yourself whether this was only a dream.'

And suddenly he was lying down again, his good arm wrapped around Flynn, drifting back to sleep while Dóchas sang a lullaby.

•◇•◇•◇•◇•◇•◇•◇•◇•◇•

Lilacs and honeysuckle. The fragrance drew Dermot from a sound sleep—the best sleep he'd had in years. 'High time you woke, lad.' A woman's voice, but not one of the voices from his dream. A warbling voice, soft and deep, with laughter somewhere in the back of it. Tears too.

He could feel the weight of Flynn asleep on his feet. When he blinked open his eyes, a blur of light told him it was day. Other than that, he couldn't see more than the occasional hazy shadow. 'Who are you?'

''Tis Maisie Bloom I am and pleased to meet ya.' She pushed something into his hands. 'I found this on the ground outside. Wouldn't want it damaged.'

When he realised what she had given him, he sat stunned for a moment. It was a lute. The very lute Rafe had given him. But that was all a dream! 'Where did you get this?' he demanded once he had found his voice.

'Outside your wagon, lad. Lyin' on the ground near the fire ring.' She answered matter-of-factly, as if the blending of dreams and reality was a matter of common occurrence for her.

It took a moment for him to realise what she had said. 'Wait... wagon? Fire ring?' Only then did he realise that he was not outside, lying on the cold hard ground, but inside on a cushioned bench, and it was warm. Too warm. The odour of burning wood caused him to stiffen.

A hand on his back calmed him. 'Peace, lad,' Maisie Bloom crooned. 'This stove'll give ye no trouble.'

'But... how...' Words failed him. 'I mean... I... I must be dream—Ow! What was that for?' He rubbed at his cheek, which she had given a hard pinch.

She chuckled. 'Now ya know you're wide awake. Time to break your fast while I hitch up the horse for ya. A real beauty she is. She and I had a nice little chat this morning while you was sleepin'. She said ya wasn't so sure about her finer attributes, but she's willin' to work hard to prove herself to ya.'

Dermot sat stunned, murmuring to himself as his mind attempted to catalogue every impossible thing that had happened to him. 'Beauty... the wagon... Rafe said... but it was all a dream... it's can't be—'

'Och, boyo.' He heard Maisie rummaging about as she talked. 'Don't ye know, most anything is possible in one of the thin places.'

Thin places? Mam had spoken of them, those places where Heaven and earth seemed to touch, where the veil between them is lifted. Could this cold bit of English heathland really be such a place?

'God can make a thin place wherever 'tis needed, lad,' Maisie said.

Dermot had found it irksome enough when Rafe heard his thoughts. For Maisie Bloom to do it too was even more disconcerting, but he kept his silence. Doubtless, she already knew.

'Aye, I know.' Her laugh sounded like bells ringing for just a moment before she let out a satisfied crow. 'Seek and ye shall find! Have ya been missin' this, Dermot?' He felt something new pushed into his good hand.

Even without sight, he knew immediately what he held. He would never forget the heft and texture of Mam's old Bible. Mam couldn't read, but she knew the stories this old book held inside and out, and she loved to tell 'em. She always said she hoped one day Dermot would learn to read it for himself, to nourish himself after she passed. But the Bible had been lost to the flames along with Mam, the yellowed pages burned all to ash, and even if it hadn't been, Dermot would never be learning his letters now. He opened his mouth to question Maisie, but then closed it again. There was no possible explanation other than what he had already been given. 'Thin places,' he murmured.

'Aye.' She bustled about, seemingly never at rest. 'Thin places.'

His fingers stroked the leather cover of the Bible, tracing the embossed letters. He lifted it to his nose and inhaled the familiar earthy aroma of the cracked leather. No hint of smoke clung to it.

'Here ya go,' Maisie said. She gently slid the Bible from his grasp, exchanging it for a bowl. 'I'll set it away safe. Eat. Spoon's in the bowl... use it an' not your fingers. I'm goin' to hitch up Beauty and drive ya into Whitstead. There's wares to sell and the day is wastin'!'

Wares to sell... how long's it been since I done that? Dermot frowned, thinking back on the old days roaming the country with his people, occasionally finding acceptance but more often rejection. 'But will they have me? I mean... settled folk don't want my kind hangin' about.'

Maisie gave his shoulder a comforting pat. 'No doubt,' she said, 'there's some in Whitstead what think that way, but most are decent folk who'll be glad to have an honest tinker settin' up with his wares. And if any of 'em doubt, you just take that lute and play 'em a tune that'll set their hearts singin'. No one'll think of sendin' you packin' then.'

The next thing Dermot heard was the swish of Maisie's skirt, the creak of hinges, and a quiet click as the door closed. Before Dermot had finished eating the steaming bowl of porridge, the wagon creaked into motion.

•◇•◇•◇•◇•◇•◇•◇•

Throughout the next two weeks, Dermot's rich baritone echoed through the streets of Whitstead as he hawked his wares. Mam had always said his voice carried well, and it had brought him a great deal of business. Maisie Bloom had helped him to set up shop when he arrived and then she flitted off without a word. On occasion, he doubted that she was real, but if she weren't, how could the wagon and wares be?

Business had been brisk, allowing him little time to think about what exactly had worked this radical change in his life, but he was convinced he'd encountered angels that night on the heath. He had considered that maybe Maisie was an angel too but had decided there was something too earthy about her. Still, it seemed to him she lived her entire life in the thin places.

The first few days in Whitstead, he'd worried every moment that some authority would come to tell him he had to move along. He had expected taunts and jeers and possibly even to be pelted with rotting tomatoes or, worse, a hail of stones. Sure, and he'd heard a snide remark or two, but beyond that, he'd not been bothered. On the contrary, he had experienced such kindness as he'd never before received from settled folk. Hearty meals and hot cider were a healing balm for his soul, but even more so the kind words and honest praise that were offered him. He had returned their generosity in kind — truth be told, he'd given so many things away that he'd added little coin to his coffers. The wares had been given to him freely, after all — why not give them freely where they might bless others? Strangely, no matter how many items he might sell or give away, his stores were never depleted. Whatever a customer might need, Dermot the Pedlar had plenty to offer.

Each evening, once his wares were stowed away, Dermot would take out his lute and sit by the wagon to play and sing. Sometimes the Romani who were camped nearby came to join him, and he took great pleasure in jawing and singing with fellow travelling people. Best of all, though, was when the villagers joined in the merry tunes. On his second evening in town, long after the crowd had returned to their homes and settled in for the night, Dermot was still sitting outside his wagon strumming the lute and singing softly. When he heard a high pure voice take up the descant on *Hark the Herald Angels Sing,* he kept strumming, but stopped singing. After the song was done, he breathed out, 'Sure, and it's an angel giftin' us with song.'

A childish giggle answered him. 'I'm afraid I'm not an angel! I'm only a Robby!'

Dermot ducked his head in greeting. 'Well, Robby, 'tis right pleased I am to meet ya. I'm Dermot. You come again tomorrow when my wares are out, and you can choose anything you like as a gift of thanks.'

'Could I choose something for my sister, sir?' Robby asked shyly.

The child's thoughtfulness touched Dermot's heart. 'Aye, something for your sister and something for yourself,' he said with a nod.

Robby went on to confide that he and his sister were orphans and that wee Margie had not spoken since their mother's death. Dermot understood the child's grief and

47

hoped that in some small way he might help restore joy to the children's hearts, as the angels had done for him. When he learned that the boy and his sister had run away from a dismal orphanage, he had willingly offered his wagon as a place of refuge. No one would think to look for them there, and with all the food Whitstead's citizens had brought him, he had plenty to share. He was certain that the children were a greater blessing to him than he could ever be to them. Each time little Margie wrapped her arms around his neck and kissed his cheeks, his heart nearly shattered with the healing power of her love. He longed to offer them a permanent home, but what kind of father could he be, blind and crippled as he was, never settling anywhere for longer than a few weeks?

You'll be a good father, but not for these children. They are meant to remain here in Whitstead, and you are not. Dóchas' voice had whispered in Dermot's ear more than once since that night on the heath. He was growing accustomed to it. He had come to think of her as his guardian angel. Whether it was with a word of encouragement, prompting to give a particular item to a customer, or a warning when someone tried to take advantage, she made it known that she was watching over him.

Thanks to her whispered assurances, when the children found a home, he was able to say goodbye. Still, he felt the loss acutely. For so long, he had avoided human relationships. Now he craved them. But at least Robby and Margie stopped by daily to greet him. And little Margie always tugged at his tunic so that he would kneel down and let her pat and kiss his grizzled face. Just this morning, he had imagined that even his damaged cheek could feel the touch of her tiny fingers running themselves across his scars. Though she did not have the words to say it, he knew she thought him beautiful... that her innocent eyes chose to look upon him with love rather than fear or disdain. The knowledge humbled him.

He sighed, then bent to throw another log into the small wood stove that heated the wagon. For the sake of the children, he had forced himself to overcome his fear of fire and now he enjoyed the warmth the stove provided. He straightened up, then picked up his lute and began to strum.

For the last two weeks, the joyous *Alleluia* sung by the angels had danced through his thoughts, drowning out the whispering voices that once plagued his nights. Now it was Christmas Eve and the chorus played itself over and over within him, eager to burst forth and rise up like the smoke from Rafe's pipe, a grateful prayer to the Father who had reached down to him in the thin place and raised him out of his self-pitying resentment. But was he worthy of singing such a song? His memory of the verses was hazy at best, the words he put to it only a rough approximation. And yet it was a gift he longed to give his Maker.

Wanting nothing to stand between him and God's Heaven, he took his lute and stepped outside into the brisk air. The early evening mass had ended, and he could hear cheerful greetings from people as they walked past. 'Happy Christmas, pedlar!'

a young woman called. He recognised her voice, though now it seemed to possess a joy that had been absent on their last encounter.

'Happy Christmas, Emma!' he returned. He raised his lute and positioned the neck so that his scarred fingers could manage the frets. Was he imagining it, or had his fingers really grown more agile?

He checked the tuning, then began to play, his fingers flying over the strings. As he sang, he forgot his scars. He forgot all but the music that seemed to bear his heart Heavenward. And though the longing for his mother never faded, he felt the anger he'd harboured over her loss slipping away.

> Babe in the manger, sweet holy child,
> Mary doth tend thee, gentle and mild,
> Joseph stands guard, so stalwart and strong,
> While angels sing their heavenly song.

> A-la-la-la-la-la Alleluia, A-la-la-la-la-la Alleluia

> Ye came for the king upon his gold throne,
> Ye came for the outcast who wanders alone;
> For strong and for weak, for foolish and wise,
> Ye came, dear God, in a fragile disguise.

> A-la-la-la-la-la Alleluia, A-la-la-la-la-la Alleluia

I was the outcast, Father. I cast myself out, fleeing from my friends, my family, You. And yet ye never stopped chasing after me. I understand that now.

> Born for the shunned, the orphan, the poor,
> For all those who languish, longing for more,
> Born for the broken, the lost, and the lame,
> For this dying world, the Christ-child came.

> A-la-la-la-la-la Alleluia, A-la-la-la-la-la Alleluia

Och, Father of the fatherless… Ye saw the hearts of wee Robby and Margie. May they grow up knowin' well the joy I took so long to find.

> Praise to the Father who reigns o'er the earth,
> Praise to the Son this night at His birth,
> Praise to the Spirit who comes here to dwell,
> Welcome the Christ-Child, Emmanuel.

> A-la-la-la-la-la Alleluia, A-la-la-la-la-la Alleluia

He sang the chorus over and over, gradually becoming aware that he no longer sang alone. He could hear the squeeze box and several fiddles from the Romani camp... he could hear the villagers adding their voices. Wee Robby sang, and Dermot fancied the clapped rhythm he heard came from little Margie. The whole town, joining him in this thin place, seeing if only for a moment, beyond the veil. And then he heard voices close, echoing around him. Maisie. Rafe and Mick. Gabe's exuberant piping. Dóchas and Trócaire. He closed his eyes and sank to the ground, suddenly exhausted with the joy of it all. Christmas had come with healing and hope and the blessing of love. And Dermot's heart would never be the same.

The Alton Chronicles: Home by Christmas
by Sarah Earlene Shere *(fantasy/steampunk)*

Two children huddled behind the largest monument in the graveyard of St. Nicholas' Church, avoiding visibility from the main road. Songs were filling the air. It was Christmastide, again! Lyrics danced upon the wind, spreading peace on earth, goodwill toward men. 'Hope'. Could it be? There seemed to be none for these.

Five-year-old Robby Alton could remember so clearly his mother and Christmases past. Although they lived in one of the poorer houses in Whitstead, their mother had seen to it that all their celebrations had been merry. Robby looked down at his three-year-old sister, Margie, curled up, asleep in his arms, clutching her beloved cloth doll close to her scantily clad bosom. He wondered if she would compare the contrast of his small, bony frame to that of the comfort they had often found lying against their mother. Leaning on his mother's chest, Robby had found love and rest. But now his mother's soft form was gone, laid deep within the earth, a stone's throw from where they now sat. Who would he have now to lean upon?

Songs of hope continued to surround them. Where could hope be found? The icy earth seeped into Robby's thin layer of clothes till the skin around his slender body became numb. The candlelight in the window of the church began to dim. Through the carols, the last sound to fall upon his small ears was his mother's whisper, 'Child, I am here.'

•◇•◇•◇•◇•◇•◇•◇•◇•

Mrs. Winterhaven descended the stairs into the basement to check on her husband. She had allowed dinner to wait as long as she dared. Now she tentatively entered her husband's workshop to see if he wouldn't come join her. There she found him, hard at work, bent over the project he had been working on for the last two years. She saw a jerk of his hand as a spring flew loose. His shoulders drooped. He sighed. Mrs. Winterhaven's heart ached for him. She hurried up behind him and embraced those strong, broad shoulders that had been so dear to her since their youth, before her dark brown hair had been streaked with silver threads. She leaned over him and whispered in his ear, 'Come away from it for a little while, Ebby. Come have some dinner while it's still warm.'

Mr. Winterhaven removed his magnifying goggles and rubbed his eyes with another sigh. 'Perhaps you're right. I don't know why I even keep trying. Only that' — he reached back and took one of his wife's hands as he turned to look into her soft, blue eyes—'I keep having that dream!' His aged, brown eyes filled with tears. 'If only I had known! If only Penelope had written to me! I would have taken the boy in! We could've had the son we always wanted, the child we could never have!'

Mrs. Winterhaven caressed her beloved's greying hair as she pulled his head against her and fervently kissed his face. 'Hush, Love. It was not your fault. Your sister lived as she thought best when your father sent her away.'

Mr. Winterhaven sobbed against his wife, 'But to live in such poverty! To have your small boy taken and used as a brush for chimney sweeps! For him to die that way! Trapped! So small! So young!'

Mrs. Winterhaven's own tears rushed to her eyes. 'Hush, my Love! He is safe in the arms of our Lord! Clean, wealthy, healthy and free!'

Mr. Winterhaven suddenly pulled away. He looked up at her with a frenzied expression. 'But, Katy, he's not the only one! Children all over our world are being bought and sold like livestock and used as slaves for the ease and comfort of man.'

Mrs. Winterhaven took her husband's face in her hands and brought hers down closer to him. 'You aren't meant to change the whole world. But you can make a significant difference in your little corner of it! Come now, my darling. Say a prayer over your dinner for the children of our world, then nourish yourself, so that you may be of better use to their cause.'

$$\bullet \Diamond \bullet \Diamond \bullet \Diamond \bullet \Diamond \bullet \Diamond \bullet \Diamond \bullet \Diamond \bullet \Diamond \bullet$$

Robby felt a softness under his head and warmth encircling him. Slowly he was brought to full consciousness by the sound of a soft alto voice humming near his ear. He immediately recognised the song as 'O Come Every Christian', the Welsh carol his mother used to sing to them every Christmas Eve as they fell asleep in her arms. Looking up, he saw a dark-haired woman gazing into a small fire that burned quite near their hiding place behind the graveyard monument. She had him and his sister wrapped in her warm, green cloak on either side of her, close to her silken, white gown. Robby noted how much she reminded him of their mother.

He whispered, 'Have we died?'

The young woman gently smiled down upon him, then shook her head. Feeling strengthened by the fire, Robby slid away to get closer to its warmth.

The woman finished her song and rested her eyes upon Robby, as if waiting for him to speak. He was not accustomed to an adult being interested in what he had to say. Ever since he and Margie had been admitted to Miss Rossiter's 'Charitable School,' he had been trained to not speak unless he had been spoken to. But this angelic woman looked at him so attentively that he was compelled to pour out the words that had been troubling his little mind.

'I had felt so sure of myself when I began this journey. But now I'm not certain.' Robby continued to tell of how he had run away with his sister earlier that evening after overhearing Miss Rossiter arranging with Mr. Penterwidth for Robby to become his apprentice as a chimney sweep. He explained that this had filled himself and his sister with fear, since they both had heard the horrible story that had spread from another village about a chimney sweep's apprentice, around his age, who had gotten stuck in a chimney and could not be retrieved in time to save him. Besides a fear for himself, Robby did not want to be separated from his little sister, Margie. She was quite dependent upon him. And yet, she hadn't even spoken a word to him, much less anyone else, since their mother had died last winter.

Robby wondered why the woman with the kind eyes did not respond to him. She only looked at him patiently, as if waiting for him to continue. But he could think of no more words. He brought his knees to his chest and wrapped his arms around his legs as he stared into the fire. He then looked over at Margie, curled up beside the lady, asleep with her head in the young woman's lap. He mused aloud, 'I only want to find a good home for my sister, like Mama gave us.'

The woman's smile broadened a bit as she stroked Margie's wispy, blond curls. Then she stretched out her other arm to Robby. He accepted the invitation, making his way to her side, under her arm, inside the shelter of her cloak.

Margie stirred and raised her large, blue eyes to her brother. He smiled down at her. 'Don't worry, Margie. We'll be all right. Hope will lead us.'

•◇•◇•◇•◇•◇•◇•◇•◇•◇•

Mrs. Winterhaven dabbed the tears that had escaped down her soft, rosy cheeks. Taking a deep breath, she inhaled the lavender scent on her handkerchief and composed herself before going back to straightening the garland on the banister. While Mr. Winterhaven's grief kept him blind and indifferent to all festive decor of the season, his wife found a kind of therapy to the pain by recreating the holy warmth of the Christmastide that she had experienced in years gone by. In those days, their comfortable, spacious home held one of the most anticipated parties of the year in Whitstead. But since the accident and loss of her husband's nephew, his mourning had become her mourning. After nearly forty years of marriage (not to mention the years of friendship that turned to courtship in the years previous) Mrs. Winterhaven had learned well how to adapt herself to her husband. Additionally, her undying love for him made it no trouble for her to do so. Still, she was grateful that decorating their home was one pleasure she had not needed to sacrifice.

Finally, Mrs. Winterhaven stepped back with a sigh to examine her work. 'Yes,' she quietly thought aloud, 'A lovely display, I must say.' These moments in the late hours of the evening, when her husband and the servants had turned in for the night, were precious to her. So tranquil and peaceful. 'Just me and the Lord', as she would put it. Suddenly, the sound of a sweet soprano voice outside her front door fell upon her ears. Surprised, she glanced at the floor clock nearby. *Who would be out at this hour?*

Hastening to the door, she opened it to find a small boy standing there, softly singing, 'Silent Night'. A petite girl stood by his side, holding on to his arm and a little raggedy doll. Mrs. Winterhaven's heart went out to the waifs. At the close of his song, the boy smiled and tentatively held out a hand. 'Ha'penny for the song, Madam?'

Mrs. Winterhaven bent down and, like a mother hen, with outstretched arms ushered the two ragamuffins inside.

•◇•◇•◇•◇•◇•◇•◇•◇•

Robby sat curled up in the chair by the fire, wrapped in a warm blanket, sipping his tea. His eyes were fixed on Margie across from him. She stood close to the towering Christmas tree, mesmerized by its jewelled baubles, beads, tinsel and paper ornaments. Slowly she reached out a finger to touch one of the shining trinkets, but stopped suddenly at Robby's whispered command. Mrs. Winterhaven smiled as she re-entered the room, carrying a tray of delectable things to eat.

'It's quite all right. She can't hurt anything.' Setting down the tray, she knelt at Margie's side. 'I don't suppose you have seen many Christmas trees. This is the kind of tree my father put up for my sisters and I every Christmas, when I was a child.' Beckoning Robby to her side, she began to show the children all the different ornaments on the tree. Each one carried a story and a special memory; some of them she had made with her sisters when they were children.

Finally, Mrs. Winterhaven sat back on the floor, watching the two strays gently play with the hand carved Nativity scene under the tree. Robby having told her that they had no home, at the present, she was determined that these babes would not go back out into the cold tonight. They would stay here. The guest room was always kept clean and made ready. They would have a good night's sleep and a hearty breakfast in the morning. She would talk to her husband as soon as he awoke. She would try to ease him into the idea of their new visitors before he would come across them at the table. She feared their presence would only add to the pain of his loss of his nephew, and the lack of children in their own lives, as had seemed to be the case whenever children were near him. However, she clung to a small strand of hope that these two could be just the balm he had been needing to heal his heart. Perhaps she could talk him into letting them stay through Christmas, before they decided on the next course of action.

•◇•◇•◇•◇•◇•◇•◇•◇•

Robby snuggled down against the fluffy pillow under the warm covers, close to his sister. How different it was here in the Winterhaven's guest bedroom from the near freezing nights at the school! Even the wagon of the kind, blind tinker they had met the night before could not compare to the luxury these two vagabonds were now experiencing in this soft, canopy bed. Robby started at the feeling of something hard clutched in his sister's hand. He smiled when he realised it must be the small, mechanical trinket the tinker had given her. Shaped like a heart, the metal had shown brightly in the candlelight. The exposed wheels, gears and cogs looked like they were just waiting for someone to bring them to life. Margie had been drawn to it the moment she saw it. Dermot, the tinker, had smiled at the choice that was made. He had offered for each of them to take something in gratitude for the lovely song Robby had given in accompaniment to his lute playing and his own soft baritone. Robby had politely declined, feeling he needed no thanks, but he was happy that Margie had found something that made her eyes light up and shine.

As Robby lay there, he began to slip between sleep and wakefulness. He could almost see his mother's pale face framed by her black curls atop the white pillow on the other side of Margie as he remembered her words to him. 'Robby, you and your sister are very special children. Beyond having guardian angels, as every child does, each of you has a gift that is unique to you. No one can tell you what it is (in fact, some may never see it), and no one can take it away from you (although many may try). It is your duty to discover what your gift is, dedicate it to God, and use it wisely.'

Robby wasn't sure he would ever discover his gift. What could he offer, as poor as he was? Still, he chose to believe her words. After all, he felt sure the woman he had seen last night in the graveyard was an angel. Perhaps she was one of their guardian angels Mama had told him about. She was certainly beautiful and mysterious. He recalled the way she had suddenly gone from between him and his sister. When he and Margie looked for her, they found her standing on the road, staring at them, with a robin redbreast perched on her shoulder. In a flurry of snow, she was gone, and the robin was in flight. Down the road, they could just make out a green, round wagon. Margie had suddenly bolted toward the little bird, as if someone had called her name. Chasing after Margie, Robby and his sister followed the bird to the wagon, where it happily perched on the top. That's where they had met Dermot, and Robby had joined him on the descant of 'Hark, the Herald Angels Sing'.

As Robby's eyes grew heavy now, he wrapped his slender fingers around the small key on the chain around his neck, the last thing his mother gave him before she 'passed on to sing with the angels', as she had described it to him. She had slipped it over his head with an admonishment, 'Keep this around your neck always! You will come across many keys in your life, but there is only one that will unlock the answers to all your questions.' Robby had worn it as often as he could, when it didn't need hidden from Miss Rossiter's scrutinizing glares. Would he ever understand all the mysteries his mother had imparted to him? Were they all pieces that fit together to make one picture? He wondered as he slipped into dreams of happier Christmastides.

•◇•◇•◇•◇•◇•◇•◇•◇•

Mr. Winterhaven stared into the shiny, metal face of the automaton that sat before him on the workbench. He was often found in this position, usually trying to figure out what he was missing, why he couldn't get his creation to work. But today he was not merely looking at a mechanical form of a minute human, he was gazing into the face of a small child.

Mrs. Winterhaven had broken the news to him that morning that they had two unexpected guests of the juvenile variety. One would suppose that the fact that he and his wife had always wanted children, combined with the loss of his nephew, would have made him delighted to be around little ones. But, in fact, the opposite was true. Now, sitting alone in his workshop, he had to face the demons that haunted him: the thoughts that plagued his mind, that all of this was his fault. He was the reason his wife could not have the babies she had always longed for. *She should have married a healthier man.* It was his fault that his nephew lost his life. *I should have kept in touch with my sister when Father sent her away. More than that, I should have taken her into my own home.*

The cold, dark eyes of the automaton seemed to rebuke him, as well. His only invention that might give him an ounce of redemption refused to come together and work. Mr. Winterhaven had created dozens of other marvellous things that had given ease to many jobs and daily tasks. These inventions had allowed him and his wife to live comfortably and to give to others generously for years. Perhaps that was part of the problem: he had little to no obligations; he had nothing to occupy him but this newest, driving passion. His goal was to create a machine that could assist chimney sweeps. In this way he hoped to save hundreds of children, like his nephew.

Mr. Winterhaven slowly traced the face of his creation with his finger. He whispered, 'I'm sorry, little Thomas. I have failed you twice. Like I have failed everyone.'

•◇•◇•◇•◇•◇•◇•◇•◇•

Robby and Margie knelt on the landing and pressed their faces between the rails. They could just see Mrs. Winterhaven offering Miss Rossiter a seat by the fireplace. The unexpected guest declined coldly. 'I do not require much of your time. I only ask that you produce the children, and we shall be on our way.'

Robby answered Margie's fearful expression with a whisper, 'Uncle Mattie kept our secret as long as he could, I'm sure. We knew she'd find us eventually. But don't worry. We know how to escape, again.' Uncle Mattie (as they lovingly referred to him) was Miss Rossiter's benevolent brother who had come for a visit during the holiday season. A friend to all the children in the school, he had discovered where the runaways were staying, but had promised to not divulge the knowledge, especially to his hard-hearted sister. Margie seemed little consoled by her brother's words as they turned their attention back to the conversation downstairs.

Mrs. Winterhaven spoke calmly, although the children could see her gently twisting the handkerchief in her hands. 'My dear Miss Rossiter, you must be overwhelmed at this time of year with so many children under your dutiful care. Please, let me help ease the burden and watch these two for you, at least for the next couple of weeks. Allow me, in this way, to help you stretch your hard-earned funds.'

The children watched and listened breathlessly as they awaited a reply. Miss Rossiter's greed suddenly altered her demeanour. Her shoulders relaxed as she thoughtfully ran her fingers through the tassel on her purse, as if considering exactly how those 'funds' might be better used. As always, Miss Rossiter found the perfect words to give herself an air of compassion and potential benefactors a desire to open up their hearts, and consequently their pocketbooks. 'Well, I suppose there would be no harm in that. Of course it would be wonderful if all our children could benefit from such generosity and hospitality as yours and Mr. Winterhaven's. Very well, then. We shall reconvene at the beginning of the new year. Good day, Mrs. Winterhaven. And thank you for your time.'

Mrs. Winterhaven closed the door behind the unwanted visitor and breathed a sigh of relief. Turning, she looked up and returned a smile to the two faces beaming down from the landing.

•◇•◇•◇•◇•◇•◇•◇•◇•

The Heavenly music from the Christmas Eve service at the church down the street drifted into Mr. Winterhaven's workshop and began to soften his heart. He inspected the heart shaped gadget that little Margie had inserted into the chest of his automaton. Her large blue eyes suddenly looking up at him, filled with fear, stuck in his mind. He shouldn't have been so gruff with little Robby and Margie. They were only children, after all. Who could blame them for wanting to explore such a large house? They would, of course come across the basement, eventually. And who could resist touching the shiny inventions and tools he had left lying about?

Mr. Winterhaven ran his finger over the piece Margie had inserted and noted how well it seemed to fit. The only space where it was not flush almost seemed to belong there. In fact, it looked like a keyhole. Just then, something on the workbench caught his eye. He remembered seeing it fly out of Robby's hand when he had startled them with his harsh reprimand. Picking it up now, he turned it between his fingers. It was a small key. He looked back at the automaton and mused aloud, 'I wonder...' Carefully, he inserted the key into the hole and turned it clockwise. Suddenly, there was a click and a gentle hum as the exposed wheels, gears and cogs inside Margie's trinket began to stir gracefully into motion, almost hypnotically. Mr. Winterhaven was awestruck as he watched his creation slowly come to life. First, the dark eyes lit up like two green jewels. Then the head slightly turned. The slender fingers each began to move, then the arms. It stopped, holding out its hands, as if waiting to be given a task.

Mr. Winterhaven's eyes filled with tears. Two years of hard work and trying everything he knew had all come to culmination! And to think, this moment would have never been possible had it not been for those two children who had come into his life so unexpectedly. Robby and Margie! They were at the church with Mrs. Winterhaven now. It was Christmas eve. Christmas day, technically, given the fact that it was past midnight. How selfish he had been, shutting out the living world in exchange for walking in a daze amongst the ghosts of the past, and the phantoms of what could have been. And here he had pushed away the only people that could actually make his dreams come true!

•◇•◇•◇•◇•◇•◇•◇•◇•

Mr. Winterhaven slipped into the back pew of the church next to his wife who greeted his tardy appearance with a surprised expression. Without a word, he smiled down at her and slid one hand around her waist while reaching with the other to light his brand new candle on her already melting one. Her face relaxed into a smile as she studied the soft, peaceful look upon her beloved's face. Together they turned their attention to Robby who was just beginning his solo for the evening's program.

As the angelic soprano filled the sanctuary, Mr. Winterhaven looked down at his bride of forty years and whispered, 'He and Margie might have been ours.' Mrs. Winterhaven slowly nodded as tears welled up in her eyes. Mr. Haven leaned close to her ear and whispered, again, 'And is there any reason they may not yet be?'

Mrs. Winterhaven turned sharply toward him, her eyes wide and questioning. After taking a moment to study his countenance, she determined that he was in earnest. With a smile, she shook her head and whispered her reply, 'No reason I can think of, I'm sure!'

The elderly couple beamed at each other like children on Christmas morning as they turned their attention back to the ceremony. Margie now was at the centre of the group of children. Taking her role as Mary very seriously, she was kneeling down, cradling her treasured cloth doll as if it were the new-born Holy Babe.

•◇•◇•◇•◇•◇•◇•◇•◇•

Every year, there's a kind of magic in the air on the night of December the twenty-fifth, a magic that can only be felt by a child, and the child at heart.

Clutching her raggedy doll close to her face with one hand, Margie grabbed at the bright red ribbon on the ground with the other and gave it a sudden tug, pulling Mr. Winterhaven toward her. His over-exaggeration as he fell toward her with a cry as if he were falling from a tree caused Robby and Mrs. Winterhaven to erupt with laughter. Margie's face was all smiles as he suddenly grabbed her and pulled her into his arms.

Robby playfully pounced on him in a mock effort to 'save' his sister. Mr. Winterhaven reached for his wife and called out in a helpless plea, 'Mother! Come save me! The children are attacking me!'

Mrs. Winterhaven laughed as she joined the pile of bodies. 'Oh, that's not how I saw it happen, Papa!'

When the dust had settled, and the giggles had died down to contented sighs, a small family sat wrapped around each other in front of the Christmas tree watching the candles flicker on the branches, listening to the fire crackle in the fireplace, accompanied by a three-year-old little girl softly humming 'Silent Night'.

The Miracle of Whitstead
by E. J. Sobetski *(fantasy)*

My name is Thomas Winterhurst. The oldest of three children, I am fifteen and a blacksmith, living in the small town of Whitstead, England. Every house is close to every other house. There are shops, the church, a forest to the north, and the townsfolk are always fun to be around. At Christmastide, each building has a candle placed in the largest window for the holiday.

My sister Emily, two years younger than I, helps at the bakery next door every year during the holiday, bringing fresh buns to everyone in town each day. Our little sister Ava, eight in the year of my story, has a wild imagination, some would say. But to Emily and me, that day, we saw something incredible.

You see, I had just come downstairs that morning to begin my daily routine of getting the forge ready for the day. My father had taught me much about every metal, and after he passed, I continued in his work. I could make just about anything you asked, from a hammer to a sword.

My mother, Amelia Winterhurst, had prepared breakfast for my siblings before taking Emily to the bakery. I was left to watch Ava for the morning. My sister usually kept to herself, talking to her imaginary dragon she called Silven. After lighting the fire under the forge, I gathered a few old hammer heads and laid them in the flames. The heat kept the smithy warm as Ava sat in a chair near the house. A knock on the door brought in a neighbour from across the street wanting a new shovel handle. As the metal turned red, Ava asked if she could look closer. She climbed up on a stool, and her brown eyes glowed from the fire.

'Could Silven help with the fire next round?' she asked.

I grinned. 'As long as he does not burn the house down.'

'Thomas, do you think dragons were ever real?'

'You have always believed they were,' I replied. 'Father used to say, "if you believe in something hard enough, it will become." Or something like that. People always thought they were real in medieval times.'

'I should like to have been there, living in a castle, as a princess. Maybe I could ride a dragon!'

I took my steel grip and carefully turned the metal in the forge. 'And who would I be in your castle?' I inquired.

Ava smiled. 'Captain of all the knights.'

'Now that I would love. I'm glad you did not say a servant.'

Ava reached out with her right hand as if petting something while humming. 'Silven purrs like a cat. I wish others in town could believe in him.'

Ava felt like an outcast among the townsfolk. People around here found it hard to understand imaginations like hers and most just laughed. But in the light of the forge fire, I caught a glimpse of something. Shaking my head, I continued to work. As I turned the metal in the flames, a sudden chill crept up my arms. The wind chimes above the building's entrance moved with greater speed each passing second.

'Thomas?' Ava asked shivering. 'What's going on?'

'Stay here,' I answered.

As I looked out to the sky, all became dark and the wind picked up. Suddenly, church bells sounded at St. Nicholas Church as Reverend Hollybrook ran from building to building.

'Thomas Winterhurst!' he cried out. 'A storm is coming! It's closing in! Get your sisters and mother inside.'

I called for Ava and we ran to the bakery. When we threw open the door, our mother spun around to look outside and see the trees sway.

Jeremiah Ellicott, the baker, stopped cold when we entered. 'You two seem to have a ghost on your trail.'

I tried to catch my breath. 'Reverend Hollybrook has ordered the warning sounded on the bells. We need to get home and inside. A snowstorm is coming!'

'You must be kidding, dear boy,' said Jeremiah. 'These biscuits have only a little time before they are done.'

'Biscuits will have to wait,' Mother said as she hurried to the back room to fetch Emily.

We returned home and none too soon; the wind picked up as snow blew in, creating clouds of white. Mother hurried to light some candles while Emily and I closed what windows we could. Ava huddled in the parlour corner with a blanket around her. I could hear the wind howling like a hundred wolves.

'I'm scared,' said Emily as she tried to light a fire under the stone mantle in the kitchen.

'We will be fine.' I tried to comfort her. 'God will protect us.'

Crashing sounds came from the shop, and I knew my tools were being blown around. Suddenly, the parlour windows blew open, causing snow to blow inside. Ava screamed at the sudden burst. Mother rushed into the room and, taking a chair, propped it against the wooden planks.

'That may not hold long,' she said, frowning. 'And the candles won't stay lit.'

'What if the storm ruins Christmas?' cried Emily.

'We should gather what blankets we have and stay together for warmth,' I stated, glancing to Mother.

'Yes, good,' she replied, seeming panicked. 'Oh, if only your father were alive, he would know what to do in these times.'

Emily and I grabbed what we could from our rooms and, bringing everything to the only room with no windows, we huddled together with one candle nearby. Ava sneezed as I wrapped an extra blanket around her.

'There must be something we can do,' she said looking up at me. 'What about Silven?'

Emily shivered. 'He's… not… real.'

'Yes, he is… if you believe in something hard enough… it will become.'

Emily looked away, sniffing as she brushed her black hair from her face, and I knew why – she missed Father. It was then I heard Ava whispering words I could not make out. Suddenly, I heard something crackling.

'Oh no,' I thought, 'trees are breaking outside.'

But what I saw was a glowing light coming from the kitchen. Mother sent me to make sure nothing was on fire. As I came around the corner, it was hard to grasp what I saw.

I whirled around to see Emily following me. 'What are you doing? You all must stay back! Whatever is causing this storm could crush everything and…'

But I stopped as Emily pointed and her eyes grew. Slowly, I saw shadows appear on the ground as a great light rose from behind me. I turned and saw a sight that made my heart leap. Was it the blazing fire that now burned in the fireplace? No. It was more the silhouette of something around the flames. I was not sure whether to run, scream, faint, or all three at once. In front of the fire was an almost see-through creature with what appeared to be wings, like a ghost. Within the flames, logs had been gathered, but from where?

'What in the world is this?' I asked.

'It's Silven. Do you see him?'

Emily and I looked behind us to see Ava with Mother behind her.

'What do you mean?' asked Emily. 'That's impossible!'

No one said a word, except for Ava. 'My dragon.'

Mother knelt to her, 'My dear, I want to believe what you say, Lord knows I do. You have an incredible gift for imagining.'

Ava turned slightly red. 'He is real, and he started this fire so that we would have warmth in the storm. How could I have started this blaze? He is only seen near fire as I have always imagined him – that's why no one else could see him.'

I had not taken my eyes off the winged creature still near the flames as I remembered that morning at the forge. The dragon was half the size of the room and stood on all four legs. Could this be real? Emily, too, investigated the fire and smiled.

'It was Silven!' I called out. 'I don't know about the rest of Whitstead, but this is a miracle. A storm covered us in darkness and now this fire has given us more light than we could have gotten ourselves. We should give thanks to God for this miracle, and to Ava, for bringing her dragon to this world.'

A tear formed in Mother's eye as she stood. 'If you believe in something hard enough…'

'It will become,' Emily finished.

Mother walked to the window, listening as harsh winds howled behind the panelled doors. When she turned back to us, a smile spread across her face. 'We could share this.'

'What do you mean?' asked Emily.

Mother held up a hand. 'What if we went to our neighbours, for surely they are in need of warmth too?'

I stood still, thinking hard. Catching my mother's idea, my eyes widened. 'Ava, could you take Silven to each building in town?'

Ava grinned. 'Of course! I always do. Anywhere we go, he comes too.'

'Then let us go to the bakery first.'

'Why is that?' I asked Emily.

'I think Jeremiah wants his biscuits to finish baking.'

•◇•◇•◇•◇•◇•◇•◇•◇•◇•

A week later was the Christmas Eve party with dinner in the evening. Jeremiah and Emily brought out dozens of cakes and pies to serve, and everyone said there had never been any sweeter. After some games were played, I sat near Ava and several friends. Emily and her best friend Evelyn sat next to us as we laughed and told stories. Most of the children gathered with Reverend Hollybrook to hear tales of Christmas ghosts.

Before dinner, Ava nudged me. 'Do you think something will happen tonight? It is Christmas after all.'

I glanced at her brown eyes, 'Why do you ask?'

Ava giggled. 'No reason. Just in case Silven is needed for another miracle.'

The Clockwork Study
by Sara Francis *(gothic steampunk)*

o one liked Theodore Readfuss. If even one man in Whitstead found him the slightest bit amicable, he would be passed off for a drunk or a liar. Was it because Theodore Readfuss was a horrid wretch? Absolutely not. Did he go out of his way to offend others? Never.

He was simply peculiar.

Theodore Readfuss never left his land. He'd talk to himself in his hall of clocks or wander the fields while staring at the ground. The Readfuss Grange was a beautiful estate, but a grim, dark, eerie feeling floated through the rooms of the house and hung above the farm. No one dared to get too close, fearing they may never come home.

Alas, those were only rumours. Because of them, no one tried to extend a warm hand to find the truth. The Readfuss family grew ostracized from the rest of Whitstead.

This misconception made life difficult for Theodore's twin sons: Terrence and Thaddeus. A mischievous pair. With their mother disappearing (presumed dead) when they were toddlers and their father's oddities, the boys were left to their own devices — until their maid decided to raise them right.

Miss Willow was a beautiful woman despite the wrinkles beneath her eyes and the scars covering her flesh. She tended to Theodore Readfuss since he was a child and chose to do the same for his sons. She vowed not to let the same mistakes fall upon the Readfuss twins as it did to Theodore. Theodore Readfuss was a lost cause, but not his boys.

However, Theodore Readfuss did something that perplexed his family and all of Whitstead.

It was a brisk Christmas Eve morning in 1844, and the Readfuss family gathered around their long walnut table enjoying a bountiful breakfast. The twins sat across from each other, slurping up porridge and scarfing down eggs. Theodore poked at his meal with his knife, staring at the oil paintings hanging on the wall. His dark eyes were fixated as they scrutinized every little detail.

And he never blinked.

That quirk was the final straw that caused the villagers of Whitstead to avoid him like the plague. While the Readfuss twins agree that their father's condition was unsettling, they never understood why it would cause such division between their family and the village. They thought nothing of it until their father travelled into the village to speak with Reverend Hollybrook about his wife's memorial service many Christmases ago. It only took one passer-by to notice his oddities and the rumours grew like a weed.

The mindset of the village made Theodore bitter and angry. He holed himself up in the grim Readfuss Grange and ordered his sons to do the same. Only six times out of the year did the Readfusses leave their home and Christmastide was never one of them.

Theodore let out a deep breath, causing his sons to stop and look at their father. 'Terrence, Thaddeus, I have been pondering something,' Theodore began. His voice was deep and throaty. 'It's around this time your mother left many years ago. I know I have not been the best father during Christmastide, nor a joyful one at that, and I hope to make it up to you.' Laying his knife down, he coughed once then continued, 'While I don't prefer you boys leaving the house, I've decided to make a change this season.'

The boys' eyes sparkled. 'What change, father?' Terrence, the stockier of the twins, asked.

'I know the past years have been difficult for you,' their father sighed. 'I've been debating this for some time and my mind is made up.' His unblinking eyes met his sons'. 'This year, I shall allow you to attend the Whitmore Park Christmas gathering and' — he paused and clasped his hands together — 'we shall host our own event here at Readfuss Grange to celebrate the New Year.'

Stunned, the boys sat in silence. Even Willow the maid stood quietly in the doorway.

'Father, are you sick?' Thaddeus asked slowly. 'Did something happen to make you decide?'

A grin spread across Theodore's face. 'Of course not, son. This didn't happen overnight.' He slowly rose to his feet. 'You boys must enjoy your Christmas out of this house. While I won't go, I want you to have a pleasant time.' He walked around the table and clasped a hand on each son's shoulder. 'While you're out,' he whispered, 'you must select the perfect guests for our Readfuss Party, you hear?'

The boys nodded quickly. Theodore patted them on the backs and left the room, not even touching his breakfast.

The twins turned and looked at each other. 'Terrence, do you think Father really had a change of heart?' Thaddeus asked. While the two boys were twins, Thaddeus was slimmer, timid, and always desired Terrence to take the lead.

The other boy shook his head. 'I'm not sure,' Terrence confessed. 'We know he's been acting stranger than usual, spending time in the Clockwork Study again. Maybe he's been doin' some thinking.'

The Clockwork Study was a vast room hidden in the centre of Readfuss Grange that housed their mother's clock collection. Longcase clocks, pocket watches, wall clocks, cuckoos, and every type in between. Theodore would often sit and stare unblinking as he pondered life. The boys assumed it was a way he mourned their mother.

Thaddeus shrugged. 'I hope so. This seems too good to be true.'

Willow stalked across the room with an empty platter in her wrinkled hands. 'Too good or not, take advantage of this day!' she put in cheerily. 'I haven't gotten to adorn the Grange for a party in a long while.' She bent over and whispered into their ears. 'Besides, I'll keep an eye on your father.'

The boys grinned from ear to ear. 'Thank you, Willow,' Terrence said sincerely then turned to his brother. 'Shall we enjoy the festivities early?'

Thaddeus nodded vigorously. 'Yes! Let's go!'

The two took a few last bites of their meals and ran for their coats and boots.

As Thaddeus threw on his red scarf, he heard a strange thump and a yelp from the Clockwork Study. He jumped up and ran to see what it was. He almost reached the door when his father stepped through and stopped him.

Theodore's stare was cold. 'No need to worry, Son. I have it under control,' he whispered in a drone.

A shiver ran down Thaddeus' spine. 'S-sorry, Father,' he stammered.

Without closing his eyes or blinking, Theodore shook his head and spoke again. This time his voice was lively. 'Make sure some villagers join us for our event! It is going to be a grand one.' Saying nothing else, he slipped through the door of the Clockwork Study and shut it tight.

Thaddeus shook off his uncomfortable feeling and scurried back to meet Terrence. 'Everythin' all right?' Terrence asked as he tightened his own black scarf.

Thaddeus shrugged. 'Father is acting strange again.'

Terrence scoffed. 'I've heard that one before. Forget him for now, let's go into the village!' With a skip in their step, the boys ran out the door and headed towards the village of Whitstead.

•◇•◇•◇•◇•◇•◇•◇•◇•◇•

Theodore heard the slam of the front door and let out a long breath. He strode across the room and picked up the cuckoo clock that landed on his foot moments before. 'A few more nights of this,' he mumbled as he changed the time. 'A few more, then I will fulfil my promise.' He hung the clock back upon its nail. The wall was completely covered by clocks once again. 'Soon, I will be free,' he whispered with hope.

•◇•◇•◇•◇•◇•◇•◇•◇•◇•

The Readfuss twins marched through the snowy streets of Whitstead, looking around with wide (blinking) eyes. The villagers of Whitstead cheerily went to and fro, preparing for the glorious night.

'We have several hours before the celebration at Whitmore Park begins,' Terrence said as he crunched the snow beneath his boots. 'Should we seek out Father's guests?'

Thaddeus shuddered, although he didn't know why. 'I suppose so,' he said slowly.

Terrence ignored his brother's discomfort and led him through the streets. The two fair-haired boys approached several villagers who seemed friendly.

However, once they heard the name 'Readfuss' they shook their heads, scoffed, or simply turned away.

The boys' hopeful hearts started to sink with the setting sun. No one seemed interested in their father's New Year's celebration. No one cared that Theodore Readfuss seemingly desired to extend a warm hand. They still didn't trust him.

For what reason? The boys didn't know.

'Don't worry, Thaddeus,' Terrence comforted. 'There are several days left until the New Year.'

'I suppose.' Thaddeus pulled his jacket tighter. 'Maybe their hearts will change tonight.'

Terrence nodded. 'Now, let's stop bothering folks. Time to have some fun!'

Whitmore Park was overrun with giddy villagers overflowing with Christmas spirit. There were the Roebucks, the Westons, the Cobbetts, and almost the rest of Whitstead. The Readfuss twins were in awe at the joyful singing, the delicious delicacies, and the happiness and love that floated through the air. Thaddeus and Terrence wanted to bottle up that feeling and unleash it in their grim home. They spent the evening laughing, playing, and intermingling with the other children.

They hid the name of Readfuss just for one night.

It was almost midnight and Thaddeus wrapped his cold fingers around his third cup of warm punch. The delicious aroma filled his nostrils. Its warmth and sweetness unlocked a memory of his mother that was tucked away for years:

'Mama!' Little Thaddeus called as he waddled across the polished floors of Readfuss Grange. 'Where go, Mama?'

Mother slipped through the door to the Clockwork Study.

Tears filled Little Thaddeus' eyes. 'Mama,' he whined. As he reached for the door, he fell on his knees. He didn't cry. Not yet. He scooted along the ground and peered into the study.

Mother stood in the centre of the hall, staring at the wall of clocks. She didn't move.

Little Thaddeus sniffled. 'Mama?'

Mechanically, Mother took a small pocket watch off the wall, stuffed it in her overcoat, and turned to leave out the side door. Before going, she looked at Thaddeus who sat in the hallway.

Tears dripped down Mother's unblinking eyes.

'Thaddeus!' Terrence called.

Thaddeus gasped as if he'd forgotten to breathe. The warm punch sloshed in the cup, dampening his mittens. He shook out his hands and apologized, 'Sorry, brother. I remembered something.'

Terrence cocked his head to the side. 'About what?'

Thaddeus swallowed the lump in his throat. 'Mother,' he whispered. 'The day she disappeared.'

Terrence was silent. After a moment, he said, 'Maybe God let you remember for a reason. Maybe we're supposed to pray for her during the service tonight.'

Nodding, Thaddeus took a final sip of whatever was left of his hot chocolate. His mind didn't think about the rich sweetness, but only about the cold sorrow of his mother leaving.

Terrence patted his twin on the back, and they departed for the midnight Christmas service.

•◇•◇•◇•◇•◇•◇•◇•◇•◇•

Tick. Tick. Tick.

Theodore Readfuss sat in the middle of the row of chairs he aligned, facing his wall of clocks. His unblinking gaze watched the largest one in the centre. He felt time was going too slowly. It reminded him of that Christmas Eve years ago.

The night his wife disappeared.

Theodore's heart ached. He knew it had to happen. That was the nature of the Readfuss family, but that was the issue.

It was supposed to be Theodore.

Cupping his forehead, Theodore let out a long shaky breath. His eyes burned, but he could do nothing to fix the discomfort. His mind was warped like a reflection in the lake. He knew why people didn't like him. Certain villagers of Whitstead *knew* what the Readfuss family was capable of. Theodore wanted nothing more than to dispute the lies. To dispute the rumours.

He was ready to end it.

Tick. Tick. Tick.

Theodore sat up straight, watching the clock earnestly. Without averting his gaze, he raised the glass of wine in his right hand.

The clocks struck midnight.

As the different chimes, cuckoos, and tings filled the room, Theodore gulped down his red wine then proceeded to drink straight from the bottle.

One more week, his groggy mind thought. *One more week, darling. Then, our family will be free.*

~

Thaddeus and Terrence pulled their jackets tighter as they marched down the dark streets to return home. They were cold and sleepy, but there was still a long way to go. The brisk air nipped their skin and the full moon shone down upon them.

Through chattering teeth, Thaddeus asked, 'T-T-Terrence, may we stop somewhere f-f-for the n-n-night?'

Rubbing his shoulders, Terrence replied, 'Where would we stay? No one will take in a Readfuss on Christmas Eve. We must keep going.'

Thaddeus shivered and tried to regain feeling in his hands. His mittens that were wet from his spillage started to frost over. He felt his fingers going numb. 'Brother, p-p-please,' he begged. 'At least let us stop to w-w-warm up.'

Terrence let out a long sigh. They stopped in the middle of the High Road and looked around. To the right, he spotted a flame in the centre of the snowy field. It was halfway to Readfuss Grange.

'We can cut through and stop there,' he suggested.

Thaddeus nodded and the boys ran through the snow. Their tired legs wanted to give up, but they refused. They wanted to get home.

The twins approached the homes of the less fortunate of Whitstead. Outside these modest structures were a few villagers gathered around a fire. Despite their poverty and the frigid weather, they seemed content.

An elderly man in rags saw the boys approaching and stood up. His grey bushy eyebrows furrowed, and he called, 'Ay! What brings you boys out this way?'

'We don't mean to bother you,' Terrence replied.

'May we warm ourselves by your fire?' Thaddeus pleaded as he rubbed his frozen fingers together.

The elderly man looked at the others who nodded. 'Of course, lads. It's Christmas Eve.'

Thanking him, the twins ran to the warmth. They held their hands so close the flames tickled their palms. The Readfuss boys were so cold, the fire didn't hurt.

'Where is your home?' the elderly man asked. 'It's quite late.'

The two looked at each other, waiting for one to speak.

Terrence took the lead. 'We live at Readfuss Grange.'

An uncomfortable silence fell upon the poor villagers. All eyes went to the boys.

'Awfully brave of ya,' the elderly man said. 'The trek from the church to the Grange is quite far.'

The twins were surprised at his reply. He didn't bash their father or apologize for their ancestry.

'We didn't mind,' Thaddeus told him. 'Our father wanted us to enjoy the Christmas festivities.'

'He wants to bring joy back to the Grange,' Terrence put in. 'He even is hosting a celebration for the New Year for some villagers of Whitstead, but...' he trailed off.

Thaddeus sighed and whispered, 'No one wants to join us.'

The villagers around the fire mumbled to each other. Some were amazed that a party was even a thought that crossed Theodore Readfuss' mind. Others did not blame those who turned down the boys' invitation.

Leaning forward, the elderly man met the gaze of the twins who blinked several times. He chuckled. 'No need to prove anythin' to me. So, your pa is a bit peculiar. Is that why no one will come?'

They nodded simultaneously. 'Our father is not a bad man,' Terrence explained. 'No one realises how he suffers from losing our mother.'

'Not to mention how the villagers treat us,' Thaddeus grumbled.

The elderly man sniffled and rose to his feet with a grunt. 'Well, boys, I'll tell you somethin'.' He limped over to them. His wrinkled face glowed in the firelight. 'Not everyone will understand your pain. Just like no one will understand ours,' he gestured to the others around him. 'But it's how you *endure* pain that will make people think differently.' He patted the boys on the back. 'Those who turned you away have hardened hearts. But keep searching. There are folks whose hearts are willing to give others a chance.' He grinned. 'You two are fine young boys. I'm sure some folks would want to spend a lovely evening with you both.'

Smiles formed on the twins' faces. Never had villagers of Whitstead felt for the Readfusses. Never had they seen such joy in suffering. Never had they wanted something so much.

The two desired the peace of the poor folk.

'Thank you, sir,' Thaddeus said genuinely.

Terrence nodded. 'You've shown us kindness even though we are Readfusses.' He looked at the others gathered around. 'Would you like to join us for a bountiful feast to celebrate the New Year?'

The poor folk looked at each other in surprise. Delicious food and warm comfort sounded too good to be true.

'We mean it!' Thaddeus exclaimed. 'You've been very kind to us. Let us be kind to you.'

The elderly man grinned. 'We thank you for your invitation.' He looked around for approval. 'And we accept.'

● ◇ ● ◇ ● ◇ ● ◇ ● ◇ ● ◇ ● ◇ ●

Theodore Readfuss awoke the next morning with a foggy mind. He was laying across the floor of the Clockwork Study. Two empty wine bottles stood beside his head. With a groan, he shakily stood to his feet.

'Theodore!' Willow the maid called. She rapped on the door but let herself in before receiving permission. She saw Theodore sprawled across the wood floor but did not falter. She was used to the sight, unfortunately. 'It is Christmas Day,' she whispered. 'I've made a bountiful breakfast for you and the boys. Are ya hungry?'

Belching, Theodore leaned against a chair for support. 'I suppose, Willow,' he slurred. He staggered out of his study and to the kitchen.

Terrence and Thaddeus were seated at the table already enjoying their delicious meal. Theodore plopped into his seat and waited for Willow to pour him a glass of water.

Terrence swallowed his bread. 'Merry Christmas, Father,' he said slowly as if he was afraid to offend him.

Theodore managed a smile. 'Merry Christmas, my boys.' He ruffled his hair and wiped his dry eyes. 'How were the festivities last night?'

The twins' faces lit up as they explained their joyful adventure.

Theodore did his best to show enthusiasm, but he was still groggy and his mind was tangled. That would be fixed soon. 'I'm pleased to hear that,' he said as they finished. 'And were you able to find guests for our party?'

The two nodded. 'We made new friends,' Thaddeus explained. 'They let us warm ourselves by their fire last night.'

'They are a little different, just like us,' Terrence put in.

Theodore managed a smile. 'Different is perfect.' He sipped his warm coffee, thinking about the celebration and the New Year.

Thinking how he would be free at the start of 1845.

•◇•◇•◇•◇•◇•◇•◇•◇•

It was the eve of the New Year. For the first time in years, a celebration at Readfuss Grange was about to begin.

Terrence and Thaddeus were overjoyed as they dressed their best and combed their unruly hair.

Willow rushed about the kitchen, preparing delicious dishes for their guests.

Theodore stood in the study, adjusting gears on another clock. Once it was set, he placed it back upon the wall.

Everything was ready.

A loud knocking on the door echoed through Readfuss Grange. The twins flew down the stairs to answer it.

Standing behind was the elderly man from the poor houses and a few other kind faces. They wore the nicest clothing their humble earnings could buy.

'Welcome to Readfuss Grange!' the boys exclaimed in unison.

The guests exchanged greetings with the twins as they wandered into the house. Their eyes were wide with curiosity and bewilderment at the beautiful interior. For the first time, warmth and love battled the grim atmosphere.

Theodore stepped out of his study and into the foyer to greet the guests. A few stopped chattering and stared as if they waited for him to do something.

They waited for him to blink.

Even though he didn't, he left no time for them to worry about his quirk. 'Welcome, friends!' he exclaimed with open arms. 'My name is Theodore Readfuss, if you did not know. I tasked my boys with finding lovely guests to celebrate with us and I say, they chose well.' A smile painted Theodore's face, and he radiated friendliness.

The guests forgot all about how everyone in Whitstead disliked Theodore and thanked him for the invitation and his hospitality. Theodore nodded and led them through to where Willow had prepared a lovely meal. Meats, cheeses, breads, potatoes, vegetables, and more covered the long dinner table.

The guests drooled over the food before them. While the village was generous to the less fortunate on Christmas, the poor folk never expected to be fed by generosity twice in a month. Theodore led them in a blessing, then they began.

The guests did their best to eat slowly and politely, but they could not help themselves. Willow was an excellent cook and their portions were generous. They swallowed every last bite. Throughout the meal, Theodore was friendly with the guests and started pleasant conversations. Never once did anyone point out his oddities or treat him as an outcast.

For the first time in a while, the Readfusses were simply human.

The twins were overwhelmed with joy.

After everyone had their fill of dinner and dessert, Theodore stood and addressed his guests: 'My dear villagers of Whitstead. I thank you for joining us this evening to celebrate not only the lingering joy of Christmas but also the start of a New Year. I could not be more grateful that you gave our family a second chance despite the hurtful rumours spread. I thank you for that. Henceforth, I promise to keep an open home to kind folk like you.'

Acclaims filled the dining hall as Theodore finished.

'Now, I would like to show you one more thing before our celebration ends,' he added, stepping out from behind the table. 'If you are finished, come with me. As a new start, I would like to show you something. Something I would like to give you as we go into the New Year.'

All the guests rose and followed him out of the hall.

He led them to the Clockwork Study.

Theodore stood outside the door as the guests filed in. The twins were about to follow when their father stood in the way. 'Not yet, boys,' he whispered. 'Wait here until after I present them my collection. When the clocks chime midnight, then you may come in.'

The boys were about to protest, but Theodore shot them a look. His unblinking gaze was cold and serious. The twins nodded and backed away as their father shut the door behind him.

Terrence and Thaddeus sat on the floor. Patiently, they listened to the mumblings of their father speaking. The two wondered what he was talking about, but assumed he was describing each clock in detail. He often did that in a monotonous drone that would put anyone to sleep.

Time passed and it was a few moments before midnight.

'It's almost the New Year, Thaddeus,' Terrence whispered as he lay on the hardwood floor.

'Another year without Mother,' Thaddeus mumbled.

Terrence sighed. 'It is true, but at least Father is promising to be better.'

'But don't you find any of this strange?' Thaddeus cried. 'I know he's odd, but he's been even more so since Christmas Eve Day.'

Terrence shrugged. 'Christmas Eve has always been hard on him, but perhaps he's trying to get better. Let him prove himself. He may be giving another apology speech. Although I don't know why he needs to,' he added under his breath.

Thaddeus chewed on Terrence's quiet comment. 'You're right, though,' he whispered. 'The Readfuss family has never done anything wrong. Father may be odd, but he never hurt anyone.' His mind flashed back to his memory of Mother. The tears streaming down her unblinking eyes, the pocket watch in her grip. He shook off the thought. *Mother leaving was never Father's fault,* he told himself.

Even though he never knew the truth.

Chimes, cuckoos, and tings resounded from the clockwork study. It was midnight. The start to a New Year.

The Readfuss boys rose to their feet. They were about to approach the door when it slowly opened on its own.

Theodore slipped out into the hallway, barely closing the door behind him. His face radiated with joy and he let out a low chuckle. 'It's the New Year,' he whispered. His gaze met his sons' and they stared for a while.

Then, Theodore blinked.

Startled, the boys jumped back. Theodore laughed and said softly, 'My boys, it's all right.' He extended his arms. 'I am better now. Things are going to change.' Tears of joy streamed down his face. 'I promise to never withhold you from anything again.'

The twins were amazed. They didn't know what happened; they didn't care. They embraced their father who blinked repeatedly to clear the tears from his burning eyes.

Terrence clutched his father tightly. 'I wish Mother was here,' he choked.

Theodore rubbed his sons' heads. 'Me too, boys. Me too.'

Thaddeus quietly rested in his father's embrace. He turned his head to peer into the Clockwork Study.

To his shock, the wall that was covered in clocks was now barren. Out of all the guests that entered, only the elderly man remained.

He stood in the centre of the room. In his frail hands, he clutched a small clock with an *O* and *X* painted on its face. His expression was blank. 'Do not harden your heart; be joyful,' he whispered in a monotonous tone. 'We will be fine. You are free. All will be well.' The corner of the old man's mouth twitched upward.

But he never blinked.

The Will of the Goddess
by Dana Bell *(mythology)*

Editor's note: We have written a varied anthology concerning Whitstead, with many fantastical figures involved. This story is unusual even in this collection. It concerns a mythological character and is told from the point of view of a most extraordinary cat – and cats are notoriously full of themselves and their own concerns! Yet the themes of the story fit in with the others in this book, when read with a little imagination…

Snow landed on my grey fur and I ignored the drips of water seeping through onto my skin. The cold no longer troubled me, and I continued down the white covered road, my paws silent on the icy surface. Wood smoke tickled my nose and my yellow eyes darted to the house sitting slightly outside the main village.

I stopped, my tail slightly twitching, pondering if I should visit. Long ago I had resided with an old woman who practiced herbal medicine. She cared for many cats and I had joined their number, having been abandoned by my mother. I'm sure she gave me a name, but it was so long ago I no longer remember.

What I do remember is that she was accused of being a witch by the superstitious leaders and executed. They killed as many of the cats as they could find, myself included. My death I had long forgotten, but the warmth of Bast's greeting when I came to her I have not.

'Greetings warrior,' she had purred, her tawny fur and black spots making her the most beautiful cat I had ever seen.

'I am no warrior,' I'd answered, feeling ashamed, lowering my head so I no longer looked at her.

'You fought for the kittens and saved them along with their mother at the cost of your own life.' A kitten played with her tail and I wondered why she did not hiss at it.

I had blinked, having no memory of my actions, yet the goddess seemed to know what I had done and considered it a noble deed.

'Such bravery should be rewarded.' Her head had turned to a large male with fur similar to hers who sat beside her. 'What think you?' she'd asked him.

'A worthy addition,' he'd agreed.

'And so he shall be, if he so chooses.'

'If I choose what?' I'd interrupted.

'There are many battles to fight on Earth and I have chosen the best warriors to serve my purposes.' The goddess had risen and came to stand before me. 'You may stay or return to serve me.'

How could I have said no? I'd given my permission and she touched my nose. When I'd awoken, my body lay on the ground where I had fallen. The smell of blood and death hovered around me. Human laughter and voices receded as I slowly got to my feet, my body whole and healthy.

For a long while I wandered the countryside, often hunting for females as they nested and cared for their young. I brought them prey so they could eat and survive. Other times I would drain the rats or mice, saving a farmer from having their seeds eaten, which could mean the difference between surviving or dying from hunger. Death was a common companion to so many living in chilly hovels.

I shook my head away from the past and again pondered whether or not to visit the older woman living nearby. She had a small garden as most humans do, now barren and covered in thick snow. Smoke danced out the chimney and I smelled a rat nearby.

Hunger awoke and I stalked the creature, ending its life before it could slither inside the crack it had found between the bricks. The limp, drained body I carried into the nearby skeleton trees, leaving the carcass for scavengers. No doubt the birds would pick it clean or another predator looking for an easy smell. My unusual scent did not offend them.

Other cats however, no matter how hungry, would not touch my prey. No doubt out of respect or fear for the Chosen Ones. Or perhaps they simply did not remember Bast and her ways. I had met many who had never been taught about the goddess.

Tempting as it was to visit the old woman, I decided instead to venture into the village. Heavy white blanketed every lawn and hugged the house's roofs. Even the church and graveyard had not escaped the storm's wrath.

Heavy smoke hung in the air and I marvelled at the silence. True, when darkness had fallen, the welcoming black had awoken me. Felines are nocturnal by nature, Chosen Ones even more so. We hide when the sun sets and journey until it rises.

The oldest ones speak of Ra's journey across the sky and descent into the underworld until he fights his way free. They are from the ancient land of our birth.

A soft cry echoed through the night, needing more attention than ancient legends. I followed the sound. My nature has always been to aid any who have need, be they cat or human or on rare occasion, other creatures.

I found a child huddled under a tree, her tiny shawl hugging her shoulders. In her arms she rocked a cloth doll with a torn dress. Taking care not to frighten her I approached openly. Her brown eyes darted up and she stared at me.

'Kitty,' she cried, as tears trickled down her pale cheeks, one thin hand extended.

Slowly I inched toward her, sniffing her fingers before sitting down just out of reach. I'd seen village cats do that and mimicked their behaviour. No need for anyone to know I am different.

The child sniffed. 'Are you hungry?' She pulled a few bits of bread crust from her pocket.

Pity for her rose in me. She was starving and yet she'd offered me a bit of her food she obviously badly needed.

'Cats don't eat bread,' a boy said, the expression on his face cruel. 'You're stupid not to know that.' His clothes were tattered, too, and his shoes had holes.

'Shut up.' She pushed back into the tree as if to hide from her tormentor.

I hissed.

'I'll kick you,' the boy threatened.

Like I'd allow him to get close to me, not that he could do any damage since my body healed quickly. With another hiss I dashed at him, racking his leg. My claws didn't reach skin, but the fabric tore.

'You stupid cat!' He chased me, making several dives to catch me.

Even mortal cats are fast, and I soon escaped. Looking back, the boy had stopped, breathing hard. He tossed what I assumed was a rock. I heard the dull thud when it fell several body lengths from me. Furious, he stomped away, grabbing the girl and yanking her up. She protested as they headed back toward a building where I assumed they lived.

'Not what you seem to be.'

I blinked, not certain where the woman had come from. Her wild hair framed her dirty face, and her eyes reflected her madness. 'Birthed by a goddess,' she accused, her offensive body stench trying to envelop me.

Hissing, I leapt up, grabbing a wobbly branch, continuing my journey along the frozen bark. Not that I bothered to look back at her.

'You'll find no prey here!' she screamed.

I already had, but she had no way to know that.

I watched the village from my perch as it fell asleep, the flickering in the windows disappearing, silence broken by the dogs barking and howling at one another.

I had done service this night, killing the rat that might have harmed the old woman or perhaps stolen food from her. Or left a darker gift visited upon humans long ago, or so I'd heard.

The child I could do nothing for. I'd seen others like her. I feared she might not live out the winter and prayed to whatever god she believed in asking she be taken into loving and warm arms.

The mad woman still raved, wandering about the trees and finally down the road, stumbling through the drifts.

'You're a Chosen One?'

I glanced below, where a small black kitten shivered.

'My mother told me about the goddess and her warriors.'

'Why seek me out?' My tale wrapped over my toes.

'My mother died.' The kitten mewed sadly. 'I will die too.' The young female shivered again. 'Is it warm where the goddess is?'

'Very.' I scampered out of the tree, my paws easily landing on the snow-covered ground. 'It is not your destiny to die this night.' Already I could hear Bast whispering to me, telling me to save her young life. 'Come.'

Together we journeyed over the lightly crusted white.

'My paws are cold.' She stopped, shivering, cold and no doubt tired.

Gently taking her by the neck I carried her out the village. I think it was called Whitstead. I can't be sure. Through the night we travelled until I came upon a farm. A lantern hung in the barn's rafters and I went inside. The cows made it warm and slightly smelly. Several cats lifted their heads where they rested in the hay.

'You're a Chosen One.' A multi-coloured female rose and greeted me. 'How can we be of service?'

Putting the kitten down, I nudged the young one toward the other. 'Care for this one. Bast commands it.'

'So shall it be, Warrior. We have a mother who just birthed. She will welcome this young female.'

'My thanks.'

The cat carried the kitten away and the others closed their eyes.

With a final look around, I left. My tasks for the night had been completed. Soon Ra would descend into depths to fight and I would need a safe place to rest. Finding a hole between thick roots, I hid myself as the first rays of light touched the new day.

Closing my eyes in the protective dark hole, I fell asleep, content. Bast's will had been done as I had promised her when I'd become a Chosen One.

Author's note: The Chosen Ones appeared many years ago based on both cat and Egyptian mythology. My first story, Chosen One appeared in an anthology when I had promised the editor a cat vampire story in outer space. Many others have followed and been published through the years. They can be written in any time period, any planet, and each has its own unique shared tale.

The Christmas Griddle Cakes
by Ronnell Kay Gibson *(drama/recipe)*

The aroma of baking soda and fried dough waft in the air as I enter our cottage. I sigh and unravel my scarf. 'Douglas Green! Not again!'

My husband greets me at the door, a mischievous smirk plastered on his lips. 'Viola, dear heart, let me help you.' He takes the bag off my shoulder and slides my wool coat from my arms, hanging both up on a wooden peg in our entryway.

'Don't try to sweet talk me. This is the fourth night in a row.'

His kiss on my crinkled forehead tickles. I laugh, and the stress of a long day's work melts away.

He returns to the stove as I slip off my boots and place them near the hearth to dry. I sit down at our old, worn kitchen table. My gardener husband has it decorated artfully with a centrepiece of green pine and pinecones. Our glasses are filled with his homemade mulberry wine. It's still warm, so I let my hands soak in the warmth, then let the alcohol and fruit warm my insides.

Douglas sets out a bowl of marmalade and a large stack of griddle cakes. 'Indulge me once again?' His eyes glimmer with hope.

I smile. 'Of course. Anything you make for me is a treat.'

'You deserve all the best, dear heart.' He kisses my lips then sits down to our late-night supper.

He takes the top griddle cake for himself then spreads the butter and dollops marmalade all over. Then grins as he dollops a little bit more.

I narrow my eyes. 'Mr. Green, remember what the doctor said?' I shudder remembering how just a couple months ago I almost lost him to heart issues. Doctor told him to work less and eat less sweets. As a groundskeeper to the Fentiman family, he can't control the work part, but I've ensured the sweet part. At least I try. I can't say the same for Lottie Baxter, the Fentimans' cook. It's not her pretty face that keeps him stopping by her kitchen.

'I remember, Viola. I just choose to ignore.'

I stab a piece of the thin, pan-fried dough with my fork and place it on my plate.

He watches me as I take my first bite, anxiously awaiting my response. I chew slowly, carefully, knowing he needs my honest opinion. The texture on the outside is crisp, with the inside soft and sweet. But it's too dense. I wash it down with a sip of wine.

He exhales. 'Another failed attempt.'

The disappointment on his face hurts my heart. I reach out and clasp his fingers. 'But it's close. You're almost there.'

He pops a piece into his mouth, swooshing it around. 'You're right. Close, but not perfect.' He tries another bite. 'It's beyond me, and no mistake! I finally coaxed Mrs. Baxter into giving me her recipe. I added the ingredients in just the right amounts. But it's still not like hers. I only have one more day till Christmas to get it right.'

'Why does it have to be—' I mimic his husky voice. ' —just like Mrs. Baxter's?'

'She makes the best Christmas griddle cakes. And I want to make something special for my family.' He pulls my hand close and kisses my wrist.

I stare at the third chair at our table. With Charlie now married and working miles away, not even Mrs. Baxter's Christmas griddle cakes can fill the void left by his absence.

We eat the rest of our meal in silence.

When we're done, he picks up both plates. 'That's it. No more. Instead, tomorrow I'll make you a big feast.'

'Do you forget so easily? It's the big Christmas Eve extravaganza at the manor. I'll grab a quick bite with the other servants and won't be home till very late.'

'Then it will be a very late Christmas Eve feast.'

***

The next day, while my lady is resting, I head to the kitchen. Mrs. Baxter is in in a dither, barking orders at the footmen like they're her own personal army.

'Mrs. Baxter, is there something I can help with?'

Her eyes raise and head cocks as she notices me. 'Normally, I don't want anyone else touching my food, but since I'm already behind, I'll ask you to take the tarts out of the oven and put them on the cooling rack.'

When I reach for a spatula, she adds, 'Carefully.'

I don't blame her for being leery. Last time I offered to help, I accidently let the cream soup curdle. I grab a kitchen towel and carefully remove the tarts onto the rack. When I'm done, I rinse the hot pans in cool water and add them to the pile of dishes stacked in the sink.

When she slows down long enough to stir her gravy, I see my chance. 'Mrs. Baxter, can I ask you a quick question?

'You have as long as it takes me to congeal this sauce.'

'Mr. Green keeps attempting to replicate your amazing Christmas griddle cakes, but there's always something off. Do you use any special ingredients he's missing? Something I could buy for him for Christmas?'

'Nope, nothing special.'

I bite my lip.

She must sense my disappointment because she stops stirring and stares at me. Then she wipes her hand on her apron, reaches for her recipe box, and flips through the slips of paper. 'Here.' She hands me one that reads, 'Christmas Griddle Cakes.'

'I thought you already gave him the recipe?'

'Kind of. He kept comin' in here pesterin' me while I was working. I kept spoutin' out the list of the ingredients and measurements.' Her voice softens. 'But I forgot one key detail. It's not what's in the batter that is key, it's the order in which you put them all together.'

She touches my arm. 'Mr. Green is such a dear man, and I know this means a lot to him. Tell him to follow this recipe as listed, and the results will be just what he's hoping for.'

I give her a quick hug. 'Thank you.' I start to leave but stop. 'Mrs. Baxter, do you know why this means so much to him?'

Her face flushes and her eyes mist. 'He loves you so much. I'm sure he just wants to give you the perfect Christmas.'

And with that she turns back into commander, snapping new instructions.

•◊•◊•◊•◊•◊•◊•◊•◊•◊•

Lord and Lady Fentiman's party was a brilliant success, but by the time I make it home, it's after two a.m. Douglas is sleeping in his rocking chair, a blanket snuggled up to his chin. A simple plate of chicken and vegetables sit on the table. My head and heart swoon like our courting days.

I slip out of my snowy outerwear and tiptoe to our fireplace. I place the recipe with the red bow I had tied around it on the mantel for him to see in the morning. We aren't exchanging gifts, but this will be the perfect Christmas surprise.

Heart full of love, but physically exhausted, I collapse on our bed, still in my clothes.

I awake the next morning to the aroma of coffee and banging in the kitchen. And chatter? Who would be stopping by so early on Christmas morning?

Rubbing the sleep out of my eyes, I trudge into kitchen. Someone is sitting in our third chair.

'Charlie?'

He spins around. 'Surprise!' Then jumps up and twirls me around. 'Merry Christmas, Momma.'

My breath catches in my lungs. As he puts me down, I notice Charlie's bride, rocking in the chair, a large bulge around her belly.

Mrs. Sarah Green eases out of the rocker and gives me a hug. 'Surprise.'

I stutter, trying to make sentences. 'How? When?'

Charlie's grin lights up the room. 'The coach dropped us off early this morning. Our Christmas present to you.'

81

Douglas slinks up next to me.

I playfully hit his arm. 'Mr. Green, and you didn't tell me?'

'They made me promise not to.' He kisses my cheek and wipes a tear from my eye. 'Now, dear heart, you slept so late, breakfast has turned into luncheon. But everything's ready. Let's eat.'

We gather around the table decorated with a centrepiece of green pine, red ribbon, and fresh holly berries. On either side are taper candles, their flame flickering. My grandmother's red, linen placemats peek out underneath porcelain dishes.

And among the platters of plum pudding, roast hen, and corn dressing, sits a stack of griddle cakes.

I glance at our fireplace. The red bow is there, but the recipe is gone.

Douglas whispers in my ear. 'I hope you don't mind, but I opened my Christmas present early.'

We hold hands and said grace, thanking God for family and being together.

As we start feasting, Charlie adds a couple griddle cakes to his already full plate. 'Dad, these smell wonderful. Just like the ones Mrs. Baxter used to make.'

I turn to Sarah. 'They were his favourite growing up. Every Christmas the cook would make them for the servants and their families.' As the words leave my mouth, I realise why. Why getting the griddle cakes just right was so important to Mr. Green.

Douglas and I watch as Charlie butters his griddle cakes, dollops marmalade, dollops a little bit more, then takes a bite.

His eyes widened as he chews. 'These *are* just like Mrs. Baxter's! Dad how did you—' His voice trails as he stuffs two more bites in his mouth.

'It's my Christmas present to you.' He glances over at me. '*Our* Christmas present to you.'

● ◊ ● ◊ ● ◊ ● ◊ ● ◊ ● ◊ ● ◊ ●

Author's note: 'The Christmas Griddle Cakes' is based on a true story. My grandpa, Lloyd Loucks, was a conductor on the railroad in Wisconsin in the 1940s-50s. In those days, the dining cars were the equivalent of five-star restaurants. Grandpa Loucks tried repeatedly to coax a pancake recipe out of the Jamaican chef working on his route. Finally, after months of experiments, the chef told him the same thing Mrs. Baxter did, 'It's not just the ingredients, but how you put the ingredients together, that is the key to making the pancakes special.' When Grandpa tried it the next time, it turned out perfect. Our family has been enjoying them ever since.

Grandpa's Pancakes

Ingredients:
3 eggs
½ cup sugar
1 ½ cup flour
3 teaspoons baking powder
¼ teaspoon salt
¾ of a stick of butter
milk (not exact, but between a half and a cup).

Directions: Melt the butter. Cream the eggs and sugar. Add the flour, salt. Batter will be thick. Add a little bit of milk (try 1/8 of a cup at a time), then mix. Continue doing this until your batter is the consistency of pancake batter (you'll want it on the looser side, rather than too thick—the butter and baking powder will thicken it). Now add the melted butter. Mix well. Lastly, add the baking powder. Mix well again.

Spoon batter onto a medium heat griddle. You will know the pancakes are ready to flip when the sides are slightly firm and the centres are bubbling. If they are getting too dark before this happens, lower the temperature.

Makes about 4-6 servings.

Jacob Needsworth's Second Christmas
by Sarah Falanga *(fantasy)*

Jacob Needsworth was said to be the proudest, greediest man in the town of Whitstead. A man who even the stray dogs shied away from. But that was last year.

All the year of 1844, the townsfolk had known a generous, gracious man who knew all the wants of the poor and the joys of living. In that chilled month of December — the very month when he had changed a year ago — he joined in the festivities of the season as never before, and Whitstead knew a Christmas like no other.

24 December found the town in a bustle, with children playing in the streets, and the pleasant hurry of preparation for the next day. The blind pedlar, Dermot, sung a carol in the town square; the travellers went from door-to-door to sell holly; the shopkeepers were busy at their work; from hilltop to doorstep could be heard the sound of laughing; the smell of smoke was on the air and the warmth of joy was profound.

And old Jacob Needsworth sat in his office. A fire blazed pleasantly in the fireplace with a cat curled in front of it. The clerk, Bill Cuthbert, sat in the outer office, humming.

A knock came at the door.

'Only let 'em in if they're singing carols. It's too late in the day for businessmen,' Needsworth bellowed, chuckling to himself.

Bill opened the door, letting in a bitter wind. He stood in the doorway a minute. Finally, he turned and went to Needsworth's desk.

'What is it, my man?' Needsworth asked, putting down his *pen*.

'It's a boy, Mr. Needsworth,' he answered, 'He says his mother needs your help — that...'

'Yes, Mr. Cuthbert?'

'He says bad fairies took his mother.'

Needsworth's eyebrows rose.

'So, it wasn't a dream,' Needsworth muttered under his breath. He leaned forward and said, 'Show him in at once.'

The boy was brought in and made to sit down. He looked small in the big oak chair, his shoeless feet only just touching the floor. He stared at Mr. Needsworth with fear and doubt in his face.

'Well, young fellow,' Needsworth smiled. 'What's your name?'

'Tommy, sir.'

'How can I be of service to you, Tommy?'

'Please, sir,' the boy spoke breathlessly, 'Mother told me to come to you. The bad fairies took her... Will you help me, sir?'

'Where did you last see her, Tommy?' Needsworth asked, speaking softly.

Tommy bowed his head. 'Father died a year ago, Christmas Eve, sir. Mother went to the graveyard...' his voice faded.

Needsworth nodded slowly, muttering to himself, 'To the very day, just as I was told. And God give me the courage to stand it.'

Tommy looked at him, tears in his eyes.

'Please, sir,' he said. 'Will you help me?'

Needsworth didn't answer for a moment.

'Yes, Tommy, I will help you,' he said, standing. 'At once!'

He went to the cabinet in the corner of his office and brought out a small wooden box. He unlocked it and examined the contents, nodding slowly.

Then, he quickly went past Tommy, into the outer room. Bill stared at him from his desk.

Cautiously, Needsworth opened the door and peered outside.

The busy street looked much as it usually did. But Needsworth gazed long at the corner next to the grocer's shop, and then quickly shut the door again.

'Sir.' Bill half rose. 'What's the matter?'

Needsworth turned to him, smiling.

'It's Christmas Eve, Bill! What are you still doing here?' He took the man's hand, shaking it. 'A very Happy Christmas to you, Bill, and to all your family!'

Bill smiled faintly, returning the salutations slowly.

In less than five minutes, Bill was stepping out of the building, a jolly spring in his step, but one curious glance back at his employer before the door shut after him.

'And now we must be on our way, Tommy,' Needsworth said, quickly going back into his office. He went to the window, prying it open with some difficulty.

Tommy stared at him, the astonishment wiping away his tears and worries for a moment.

'Through the window, sir?' he asked, stepping forward.

'There is a certain amount of danger, Tommy,' Needsworth said. 'Come, we must be going.'

Quickly, Needsworth climbed through the window and then lifted the boy through. He shut the window again.

They were in a small, dirty alleyway between Needsworth's row of buildings and the next.

Needsworth turned and went quickly into the fields behind the buildings. Tommy followed as quickly as he could, but soon Needsworth picked him up and carried him.

They left the town behind them. The chill wind surrounded them until they seemed alone and no sound could be heard. Evening came on quickly and the air grew steadily colder.

'Where are we going, sir?' Tommy asked, looking around as they went on their way.

'To the woods.'

'Why, sir?'

'I shall need you to do something for me, Tommy,' Needsworth answered. 'But you must be very brave.'

'Will it bring mother back?' the boy asked.

'Yes, it shall.'

'Then I'll do it, sir.'

They were silent for a moment.

'Tell me, Tommy,' Needsworth said, as they continued on their way. 'What does your mother do for work?'

'She cleans, for Mrs. Hubbard, sir,' Tommy answered.

'Is she paid well?' Needsworth asked. Tommy didn't answer. Needsworth said, 'Do you have enough to eat?'

'No, sir,' he said.

'Then you shall, Tommy, after we find your mother. She shall come work for me,' Needsworth answered, smiling.

The smile soon faded.

The wood was within view, looking dark and ominous against the fading light of the sky.

Tommy stared up.

'Sir,' he whispered. 'I thought – I thought I saw something above us. A *huge* thing.'

'You'll see many strange things tonight, Tommy,' Needsworth answered. 'Don't let them worry you.'

'Mother's spoken of seeing things. She says she must just be overworked.'

'Quite likely, Tommy,'

They entered the wood. The trees towered over them and the wind quickly died down.

As soon as they were in the depth of the wood, and the town was out of sight in the dark, Needsworth let Tommy down again.

The boy looked around.

'I used to go here with father,' he said quietly, following Needsworth as he walked on, 'But I don't remember it looking like this. Have the trees grown so very much, sir?'

The man laughed quietly.

'These are not our woods, Tommy,' he said.

'Have we wandered into fairyland, sir?'

Again, Needsworth laughed.

'God bless me if I know,' he said. 'Shall I tell you a story while we go?'

'Yes, please,' Tommy answered. 'I don't much like these woods.'

'It is not an old story, for it happened a year ago to the day.' Needsworth glanced at Tommy.

The boy looked at him.

'Much happened on that day, Tommy.'

'Yes, sir—it was a bad day. That was when my father died.'

Needsworth nodded.

'It was a terrible day—a day made to change a man,' he said, 'The strangest day of my life—unless this adventure goes on as strangely as it has begun—but it made me a better man.'

'How can a day do that, sir?'

'Ah, that is a mystery except to the One that owns the days,' Needsworth said. 'But upon that day, I experienced many strange things—or rather that night. That very night, creatures visited me. Whether they were angels... fairies... ghosts—I don't know. They showed me my fate.

'I used to be a different man, Tommy. If you had come to me for help a year ago, even to the hour, I would have turned you away. I kept my money to myself and, worse, was no friend to charity or joy.'

Tommy stared up at him.

'When I saw my fate, I changed—gladly.'

'What was your fate, sir?' The boy asked.

Needsworth narrowed his eyes a little.

He turned and picked up the boy again, speaking in a softer tone.

'Today was not the first time I had seen you, my boy,' he said, 'I saw you that night, a year ago. You were sitting on your doorstep, weeping. I passed on into your little house, and saw your mother weeping over your father, who had just died.'

Tommy hid his face in Needsworth's shoulder, weeping.

In a moment, Needsworth went on, 'That was not all I saw. I was told that one day I would need to help you, for I held in my possessions—passed down from my father—something that would help your mother one day.

'But what I saw that changed me, was how much your father was loved, and how hard your life has been.

'I have been on the watch for you all year, but I was told we would not meet until this day. I am ashamed to say I *nearly* thought it was a dream.'

Tommy looked at him. 'But why, sir? Why was mother taken?'

'I cannot answer that,' Needsworth said. 'I knew that you would be in danger from the enemies of the creatures that visited and changed me, because they desire to crush even the simplest of man's joy. But I do not know who they are or even if they took your mother.'

Needsworth paused, leaning against a tree trunk as huge as a castle, which towered so high above them that the top could not be seen.

'Are you frightened, sir?' Tommy asked.

'I am frightened, Tommy,' he said. 'The creatures I met last year are not to be taken lightly, good though they are.'

They were silent.

It was now completely dark, but still the wood was visible around them.

A light shone, though from no direct source. Every branch could be seen easily, and beyond the trees, the stars shone brilliantly, moving as though in answer to a song.

The air grew colder, and a heavy frost fell on the ground until new trees formed, growing around the man and boy.

A new forest stood around them, as huge as the first, so that there was hardly any room between the first trees and the frost trees. The frost trees reflected the light of the dancing stars, lighting the way until it seemed to be daytime. In contrast, the first trees stood dark as the feathers of a raven.

Snow was falling fast, shining like the stars. It was now so bright that the dark bodies of the first forest was swallowed up in the frosty trees.

'Where are we going, sir?' Tommy asked at last, looking around in awe.

'I was told to go on, no matter what may try to stop us, until I find a child,' Needsworth said. 'When we find the child, you are to go on with him alone.'

'Must I, sir?'

'You said you would be willing to, if it would bring back your mother,' he said, looking down at Tommy.

The boy nodded slowly, saying, 'I'll try.'

'There shan't be anything too frightening in a small child,' Needsworth said.

The bodies of the trees had completely joined together, so that the path was narrow.

Bits of the frosty trees started to break off, falling softly to the ground.

'Look, sir,' Tommy said. 'They're windows!'

He had stopped in front of one the sections that had fallen off. It was hollow, and, looking in, a huge white house was visible. It was completely white, but still looked strangely familiar.

'Look, sir — the same huge monster I saw above us!'

Needsworth, eyes wide, jumped back as the creature passed just beside them.

'Come, Tommy,' he said. 'We must continue.'

'But I'm so tired, sir.'

'I shall carry you for a while,' he said, picking up the boy. 'We mustn't stop — not yet.'

'There are many strange things inside those trees, sir,' Tommy said, peering in at the windows as they passed. He added, 'I think it's Whitstead!'

They came to a sudden stop.

A strange woman stood in their path. She also was white, but her eyes glowed like crystals.

'Who is she?' Tommy breathed.

'I met one like her, last Christmas Eve,' Needsworth whispered back; 'She is a dryad.'

He stepped forward. The woman stared up at him.

'Excuse me, madam,' he said. 'I must go on.'

'Jacob Needsworth, I need your help,' she said in a distant voice. 'You must leave Tommy and go on with me for a little while. My people are in need.'

'I am exceedingly sorry to hear that, madam,' Needsworth said. 'But I cannot leave Tommy here, and I *must* go on. That is what I was told to do.'

'You were told to continue until you met a child,' she said. 'I have spoken to him and he says I may have your help for a moment. It will only take a matter of minutes.'

Needsworth shook his head.

'Now I must believe that you are not my friend, lady,' he said. 'For I think you would rather I go to the child *first* than make him wait. I was told to go on until I met the child, no matter what may stop me, and, indeed, that is what you are trying to do. So, I am forced to believe you an enemy. Unless you can prove otherwise, I ask that you step aside.'

The woman smiled.

'I am not your enemy, Jacob Needsworth,' she said. 'For I am only a mirror of another mortal being, but you are right. And so, I step aside.'

Suddenly, the dryad disappeared.

Needsworth walked on, doubling his pace.

They went on and on, but there was no end to the white forest in sight, and no sign of life.

'Climb onto my shoulders, Tommy,' Needsworth said, 'And see if you can see anything.'

The boy carefully climbed onto Needsworth's shoulders, with Needsworth holding onto his legs. He looked around.

'No, sir,' he said, 'I don't see anything at all. The forest just goes on and on.'

The soft sound, similar to singing, grew louder and louder. It was soon deafening.

Suddenly, the snow started to harden, becoming diamonds. It fell to the ground, where it shattered to pieces, flying into little bits that struck like glass.

Needsworth continued quickly.

A hollow in one of the frost trees appeared in front of them, and Needsworth ducked inside.

Tommy, ducking his head down next to his, carefully lifted his head.

'Must we go on, sir?' he asked. 'I don't like this place.'

'Indeed, we can't stay here,' Needsworth said. 'We *must* go on.'

'Can't I stay here, sir?'

Needsworth hesitated. He half moved to let Tommy down, and then stopped.

'I cannot leave you here, Tommy,' he said. 'We must go on together.'

'But we'll be crushed!'

Needsworth thought a moment and then quickly let Tommy down. He pulled off his overcoat and gave it to Tommy.

'Put it on to cover yourself,' he said, picking him again and putting him on his shoulders. He added, 'You'll provide some cover for me too.'

Moaning softly, Tommy pulled the coat over himself, and held it out in front, so that it covered Needsworth as well.

Needsworth leapt back onto the path, walking on as quickly as he could.

On and on they went, over the mounds of diamonds.

Presently, the force of the diamond-fall started break off the branches, bringing them crashing down to the ground.

Needsworth came to a sudden stop. Their way was blocked by branches.

Quickly, Needsworth let the boy down.

'Stay here, Tommy,' he said. 'While I make a way.'

Tommy, huddling in the coat, quickly moved into a hollow, where he was safely out of the way.

Quickly, Needsworth picked up a branch and started working at the mound of diamonds and branches that stood in his way.

He had been working at it for several minutes when he suddenly stopped, staring at Tommy.

He joined Tommy in the hollow, feeling the wall behind the boy. Tommy stared at him.

'What is it, sir?' he asked.

'I was told to *continue*, no matter what,' he said. 'Perhaps... *this* is where we're supposed to go.'

Tommy stared at the wall.

It was not solid frosty wood as the other walls were. It was a thick layer of ice, through which another path could be seen.

Needsworth looked back at the mound in the way of the path they'd been on, and then back at the wall of ice.

Quickly, he picked up the branch again, and started hammering it against the ice.

The ice soon shattered, falling away in huge pieces. Needsworth and Tommy stepped into the path beyond.

This path was inside the huge trees, but it shone as though the stars were out.

Needsworth walked forward, going toward a light that shined at the end of the pathway.

They reached it in about ten minutes, and found a huge feast laid out. It was a Christmas feast, with pies, meats, puddings, fruits of all the seasons, and green trees grew all around, though the snow lay thick on the ground.

'Have I made the wrong decision?' Needsworth muttered. 'Have I gone astray?'

'Needsworth, my fine fellow,' a huge, happy voice said. 'Do you see a joyous feast and assume you have chosen wrong?'

Needsworth's face lit up.

'Joyous One,' he said, stepping forward and turning around and round like a little boy. 'I am so pleased to find you again! You see I have lived as I promised you!' He stopped, rubbing his eyes, and said. 'But where are you, Joyous One?'

No one answered.

The great room around them was completely still.

'What shall we do, sir?' Tommy asked, stepping forward. He stopped suddenly, staring at the ground. He laughed, and, suddenly falling to the ground, shouted, 'The snow is warm! The snow is warm!'

Needsworth fell to the ground and they both frolicked in the snow like a couple boys, making snow angels, building a fort, and having a snowball fight.

At last, breathless, Needsworth stood up and looked at the table.

'Now I'm quite hungry! Shall we have a bite to eat, Tommy?'

'I've never seen so much food!' Tommy stood up. His face fell and he went on, 'But there's no plum pudding. Mother makes the best pudding—we were to have some tonight…'

Needsworth turned and saw a doorway he had not noticed before. Standing in the doorway was a small child.

He looked no more than a few days old, and yet he looked at Needsworth the wisest, kindest eyes he had ever, or would ever, see. He was clothed in a great gold fur robe that trailed behind him.

Quickly, Needsworth bowed.

'Child, sir,' he said. 'I have come, as I promised, and here is little Tommy.'

The child only nodded slightly.

Needsworth smiled slightly, muttered, 'You are silent as the other one was last Christmas Eve. Will you take Tommy to his mother?'

The child merely blinked.

'Will you take Tommy home?'

The child smiled.

Needsworth turned to Tommy, saying, 'Well, in any case, Tommy, go with the child now.'

Tommy looked at him, and back at the child.

'Goodbye, sir,' he said. 'Thank you so much. But will I ever see mother again?'

'Go with the child and find out,' Needsworth said.

Slowly, Tommy went to the child, who turned and went back outside the doorway. They were soon out of sight.

In a moment, a woman dressed in beautiful clothes entered. She was beautiful and happy, but there were tears in her eyes.

'At last,' she said. 'Who are you?'

'I am Jacob Needsworth,' he answered, bowing slightly.

'*You* are Mr. Needsworth?' she asked, staring. 'Oh, sir, it's such a great pleasure to meet you! I have wanted to meet you for ever so long, ever since my mother told me stories. I never dreamt I would be taken, and that I *would* need your help. Do you know who they are, sir?'

He shook his head.

'I feel they are good,' she said. 'Though they should have asked me if I *wanted* to go.'

'Would you have, unless you had seen what it would be like?'

The woman, smiling, shook her head.

'Indeed, no, sir.'

'Are you Tommy's mother?' he asked.

'Yes, sir,' she said, 'And did he bring you here?'

Needsworth nodded.

'He has gone with the child,' he said.

'Ah, good then,' she said, 'He's only gone to find some pretty clothes to wear for the feast. And do you have the final ingredients? I simply *can't* make plum pudding without it!'

Needsworth quickly pulled out the small wooden box and gave it to Tommy's mother.

She opened it and, sniffing the contents, nodded.

'It's my mother's recipe, and they're eager to taste it. My mother used to bring them plum pudding, but she's been gone many a year, and they only found me last year when…' her voice faded, 'When my husband died. They're ever so sorry he died, but they've missed my family's company since my mother died.'

Tommy's mother looked at him again and asked, 'They said they have enemies who were trying to take us. That was why they took me so suddenly. But who are the enemies, sir, and why did they want to take us?'

'I know less about their enemies than I do about the good ones,' Needsworth said, 'I used to walk in their invisible company until last year, because I did nothing to share or promote happiness.

93

'Last year, I was shown what companions I have, and that they will go to great lengths to take any joy from mankind that they can. I know, from Tommy, that you have experienced great sorrow this year…'

Tears in her eyes, she nodded.

'It's been horrible, Mr. Needsworth,' she said, wiping away the tears, 'But the last few days have been good. Tommy laughed for the first time yesterday, and we were to have a wonderful — but humble — feast.'

Needsworth nodded.

'The — well, as Tommy put it, the bad fairies — saw that, and they couldn't have it. But the good creatures will not leave their own to the mercy of the bad.'

Suddenly, with a huge rush, Tommy re-entered the room, running to his mother.

They embraced.

'It's so wonderful and good here,' Tommy said, 'I knew it would be all right! I knew you'd be here too!'

Tommy's mother, smiling, looked at her son long. He was now wearing a green velvet tunic.

'Don't we look splendid, Tommy,' she said, picking him up as she stood. 'Ready for the biggest, most wonderful feast we'll ever enjoy!'

Suddenly, there was a loud crashing sound from the other room.

Gasping, Tommy's mother turned to go back towards the kitchen.

'I must get back to my pudding, sir,' she said. 'Won't you stay?'

Needsworth smiled, saying, 'Thank you, madam, but I wasn't invited. There's a lovely party tonight, though, and the church services will be quite wonderful.'

'Indeed, sir,' she said. 'And Merry Christmas, sir; and thank you so, so much!'

A Clean Rise
by Joanna Bair *(fantasy)*

artha Baker stumbled into the doorway of the Whitstead Bakery, knocking into a wreath decorating the door. She hopped out of the way, startled by holly pricking the bottom of her chin. In her surprise she slipped on a small patch of black ice amongst slush and fell headfirst into the bakery. She froze on the floor gathering her bearings then pulled her woollen cloak out of the way and stood carefully.

'Morning, Miss Baker,' Jeremiah Ellicott, the current baker, came out from behind the counter, a smirk developing in the corner of his mouth. He offered a hand, but Martha had already stood. 'Are you all right?'

'I'm fine,' Martha said. She shouldn't be embarrassed by her fall, this sort of thing happened all the time to her. Falling. Everyone who knew her always took care to warn her of puddles or slippery spots. She brushed off her cloak. 'I didn't see the ice.'

'Or the holly?' Mr. Ellicott asked.

'I guess not,' Martha said.

'Did you ever consider getting spectacles?' Mr. Ellicott suggested. 'It could help.'

'They don't help. My eyesight is fine.' She shrugged.

He laughed. 'You're just always moving quickly then. I see.'

She touched her cheeks, suddenly warm despite the cold air blowing through the open door. She shut the door with gentle hands then turned to him. 'I can move slow, but that's a waste of time. I'd like a loaf of your sourdough please.'

'Anything else? I'm making Christmas pies and fruit cakes today if you come back later.'

'Not today. Mother specifically requested your sourdough.' She hoped to get out of here quick and return to the comforts of laundering alone with her sisters where she didn't need to make idle talk with a man who always left her feeling out of sorts. What was it about him?

'Did you forget to save some of the starter again?' he asked. His bluntness put her off. Why did the man always point out her faults? Was it because she had so many? She couldn't even bake bread. Not that he made her feel bad about them, he didn't. It's just that she wanted him to have a better opinion of her, yet every time she was around him she came across as such a blunderer.

Martha shrugged at his comment, not bothering to answer. He knew.

'It's fine. Keeps me in business, but I can run in the back and grab you a piece.'

'Don't bother. My mother will get some from Cousin Hazel. It has to be in the family.' Martha's guilt rose in her the longer she stayed talking to this man who knew most of her weaknesses.

Mr. Ellicott ran in the back anyhow and returned with a loaf of bread, too hot to touch. 'For yourself, to start your own, if you like. Keep it separate from your mother's.' He spoke with almost a question.

Martha raised her eyebrows as if unsure what he implied. Would she ever separate from her mother? Not if her mother's illness kept getting worse. She'd never have a clear conscience marrying and leaving her mother alone with her sisters. As clumsy as she was, her sisters were silly and couldn't be trusted to keep track of all the laundry that came in. She'd be stuck caring for Mother for years. She turned her gaze to the trays of biscuits in the glass. 'That's a lot of gingerbread.'

'I got a head start. I'm baking some for the Whitmore Christmas party. They've hired me to do the cake. I guess their cook had enough to do.'

'What an honour,' Martha exclaimed.

'I hope it will show more families in the village that I'm capable of more than just breads,' Mr. Ellicott said.

Martha nodded, understanding his desires. Her own hopes and dreams centred around people seeing her as more than just a clumsy girl who fell into holly branches and couldn't tell salt from sugar.

Martha couldn't imagine Jeremiah feeling inferior to anyone or anything. He seemed too knowledgeable. He'd picked up her own father's trade better than any of her siblings. Granted she only had sisters, which is why her father had chosen Jeremiah as his apprentice. No one had anticipated him passing the same year he took on Jeremiah. But the young man had learned quickly, and he had the love of baking Martha had never acquired.

'How is your mother today? Let me know if she needs anything,' Jeremiah said.

'She had a fit yesterday and it wiped her out in bed with a headache again. The healer brought some more belladonna, but if you ask me, she's just getting worse. Although she woke up tired this morning, she was up and about harping me about the sourdough,' Martha said.

Martha's mother had been having fits that came and went since her father had passed. They were often short, but then it meant Mother spent the rest of the day in bed unable to do anything. Some mornings she'd wake without a headache and help them with the washing. More and more frequently the fits had gotten severe.

Jeremiah nodded. 'How are you on firewood?'

'I think you chopped enough to get us through Epiphany. Thank you.' Martha turned slowly and walked with caution by the holly boughs hanging on the door, muttering, 'Who hung these?'

'I did. I found them in the woods when I was chopping firewood.'

Martha jerked her hand back, annoyed he'd heard her words, and knocked against the door barely missing the pointed plant — again. She sighed, ignoring any looks from Jeremiah, and slammed the door shut behind her, managing to exit without tripping or destroying anything.

The sun shone, though the day was bitter, and it brought a nice change from the endless dreary rain they'd had. The cold must have frozen the puddles causing black ice. She kept her eyes out along the dirt path as she headed toward the back garden path leading to her family's rooms above the bakery.

A street urchin sat on the path outside. Where had she come from?

'Matches?'

Martha glanced again at the two meagre matches in the child's shivering hands. She wanted to buy the matches and light them for the child to have some warmth. Should she bring her inside to their house? She didn't have any more coins left. Instead, not wanting to waste time, she broke off a chunk of bread and tossed it to the girl. 'No thanks, but here, have some breakfast.'

The girl eyed it as if she'd never seen bread in her life before.

'Eat,' Martha encouraged.

The girl then shoved it in her mouth as fast as anything, and Martha turned onto the path leading to the garden behind the bakery. Glancing behind her once more she noticed the child had disappeared. Odd. All the children in this village who were poor didn't usually resort to begging. They got sent to the charitable children's home, or they belonged to the gypsies. With her pale skin, blue eyes, and well-brushed hair this child appeared to be neither.

•◇•◇•◇•◇•◇•◇•◇•◇•◇•

Jeremiah shook his head as Martha left. Strange girl, so nervous, yet her striking eyes always drew him in. Although he knew she hated it, he found it highly amusing how she managed to break something or hurt herself whenever she stepped in the bakery. He assumed that's why she'd given up trying to learn her father's trade. The door swung open, disturbing his thoughts.

'Morning!' A cheery twelve-year-old Emily Winterhurst bounded into the bakery, eager to help. 'What are we working on today?'

His self-proclaimed assistant, who he'd never asked for but had turned into a blessing in disguise, grabbed an apron and followed him into the kitchen. The girl's dream was to be a baker.

'I have a request to bake a cake for the Whitmore Park Christmas party. I'm going to cover it with decorated gingerbread telling the Christmas story.'

'And put an almond in the middle?'

'Where did you get that idea?'

'It's tradition.'

'I'll have to check with the estate.'

'Don't check, just surprise them.'

'I can't do that.'

Emily's face sank. 'Well, can I help?'

'If you can bake a few more loaves of bread for me while I'm working on the cake, I'll show you.'

Emily went to work quick, and Jeremiah couldn't help wishing Martha had the same sort of interest and excitement to learn baking. Maybe her father just hadn't shown her? It would certainly benefit her to learn. She always said no when he offered his help to teach her. What was the point?

• ◇ • ◇ • ◇ • ◇ • ◇ • ◇ • ◇ • ◇ • ◇ •

Martha finished eating her bread and cheese then grabbed her satchel to go pick up the laundry from the Bradbury's house. Their last customer before Christmas. Her younger sister, Jemima, whined after her, 'Come right home because I don't want to scrub Mr. Land's suits all day by myself.'

Martha sighed. She had forgotten about the suits Mr. Land needed for the Christmas party. Ignoring her sister, she raced down the stairs thankful to get out of the worst part of laundering. Scrubbing. It chipped away at her skin and nails and this weather only made it worse. Let Millie and Jemima do the hard scrubbing while her mother boiled water. Mother had seemed well enough for it today.

Martha scanned the muddy street corner for the match girl. If she still had matches maybe she'd buy one, or on her way home she'd invite the poor girl in. She didn't have time now though. Not even a minute down the road she heard footsteps running after her. It was Jemima. 'Wait!'

'What did I forget?'

'It's mother! I think she's having one of her bad fits.'

'Why aren't you with her?' Irritated, Martha waved her arms to shoo Jemima back inside.

'Millie is with her. She laid her down on the kitchen floor where she was washing the breakfast dishes. Go get Reverend Hollybrook. Or Widow Larkin. Or both.' Jemima's voice gasped between breaths, but she didn't stop to wait and see what Martha did. She turned and ran back down the path and behind the house.

Martha bolted. The Bradbury's house was on the other side of town from the church. They'd understand if she didn't come straightaway for the washing. She could run to the church, or closer yet was the Widow Larkin's cellar on the edge of the woods. She had plenty of herbs that often calmed her mother and at this point they would do more good than the Reverend's empty prayers. It wasn't that she'd lost her faith in God, but after months of the reverend's visits nothing had changed. Yes, the healer it was. As scared as she was of the woman.

She recalled Jeremiah mentioning something to her a few days ago about another healer who had healed Mrs. Jones's gout, but no one seemed to know where she had disappeared to. She wouldn't know where to look. She'd have to go to the Widow Larkin.

The old hag, for that's how Martha and all the village children thought of her, lived in a hovel with an old cellar brim full of remedies and herbs. The lady's wrinkles and scratchy voice creeped her out, but she was her only option besides prayer – which she could do herself while running down the main road to the edge of the forest near where the less fortunate lived.

Martha ran in a very unladylike fashion lifting her freshly laundered skirts a tad too high. She'd be the one having to scrub out the mud if she soaked them through again. The light rain melted the patches that appeared to be ice, but she hopped over those careful not to cause another catastrophe. The baker had such an ability to send her nerves into a state of overreacting. No wonder her mother had been prone to daily fits since Father's passing last year.

'Lord, help me get the right help,' she prayed out loud. Jemima would not have run after her to fetch help if it had been a minor incident. The fits had been getting worse and worse. The belladonna Widow Larkin had given their mother should have helped by now. The healer had warned them that the herb could make things worse in the beginning, but the fits were supposed to lessen and eventually leave; as time went on and their mother's body would balance. Perhaps she should just race to fetch the vicar. She didn't know where she'd find this other healer Jeremiah had mentioned.

About halfway to Widow Larkin's 'dungeon,' as Martha often referred to the cellar, she missed toppling over a child sitting on the street corner as she turned down the trail to the healer's.

'For Pete's sake,' she muttered, regaining her balance and in the process recognised the little match seller from outside the bakery. 'It's you!'

'Matches?' The dirty face peered up at her with such bright blue eyes Martha paused.

'Not now, but if you follow me, I'll need some.' Martha kept running, and she heard a patter of feet sloshing through melted puddles after her. The child must have followed, but she couldn't turn around now. Every second was crucial. Her mother's fit would have stopped by now. She'd either be fine or be in bed the rest of the day, or week, or month. No one ever knew what to expect.

She reached Widow Larkin's cellar in record time. The old woman stood in her doorway, staring at melting icicles dripping off the roof. Martha shook her head. Had the lady nothing better to do? The widow snapped out of her trance as Martha ran closer.

'Your mother?' She moved fast for someone who had to be a hundred years old. The lady didn't even wait to see Martha's nod and grabbed a couple vials, a mortar, pestle, and a couple ceramic pots that she crammed into a black leather bag. The match seller had caught up with them, but watched in silence.

They moved much slower heading back to the bakery, so Martha stopped at the Bradbury's and collected a basket of laundry while the lady and match girl kept walking. She caught up with them then waited as the lady climbed the stairs above the bakery, with rather agile limbs for her age. Perhaps she was only ninety, not one hundred. The little girl was almost as tall as the lady.

Martha turned to the match seller. 'You should probably stay outside, I'm not sure what's going on.'

The child, expressionless, turned away.

'Wait. Go to the baker and tell Jeremiah that Martha sent you to help with the bread. Tell him her mother had another fit.'

The child's eyes widened.

Martha nodded, raced up the stairs, and entered the kitchen bracing herself for the scene played out in front of her.

Jemima knelt next to their very still mother laying on the floor. Her sister, Millie sat by their mother's head. The healer pulled a small milking stool over and arranged her wares on the table before them.

'Is she—?' Martha didn't finish her sentence, afraid to ask.

'Her heart beats,' Jemima's voice was barely above a whisper. She'd never seen such fear in her sister's face before. Without asking, she knew it had been a bad one. Martha watched the healer mix another one of her potions. She longed to say something and question the many herbs laid out. But what did she know? If only the village had a real doctor. Or they had time and money to get one from another town.

A knock sounded at the door before any of them could move. Jeremiah entered, stepped to her side, and asked quietly, 'Is there anything I can do?'

Martha shrugged. He stood so close she didn't want to turn for fear he'd be right in her face and she wouldn't know how to react. Why did that scare her, yet excite her so much at the same time?

'Should I get the reverend?' he asked.

'You could, if you like.' She mustered up the courage to look him in the eyes. Those dark, searching eyes. Searching for what? A way to help? He'd already helped the family so much. He patted her arm, his touch soft, and she turned back to her mother as she felt her cheeks warm. But then watched as he exited the upstairs living space.

The healer coaxed another spoon of her concoction into her mother's mouth, but it dribbled out.

'Place her in bed. This will keep her asleep so her nerves can relax.'

'Will she make it?' Jemima asked the question no one else dared to ask.

The healer checked their mother's pulse again. 'Her heart is beating very fast. Too fast. Only time will tell.'

The healer left them feeling hopeless as ever.

'What an awful Christmas.' Millie slumped into the chair, none of them bothering to move their mother. They sat in silence, time slipping away silently until they heard a creak at the door. The little match seller poked her head into the doorway.

'I thought maybe my gran could help.' The child's words gave them a measure of hope. An older lady pushed open the door behind her granddaughter. The new healer who'd been seen in town?

The lady's face held a warmth that even with her age made her appear years younger than Widow Larkin, and much kinder. Her smile was soft and sweet. Her shoulder-length hair glistened a brighter silver than the old hag's. She was well-kempt, but was she a *she*? She wore a robe like a priest, but the villagers had called her a lady. The match girl said this was her grandmother, yet left to her own devices, Martha would not have been able to determine if the figure in front of her was male or female.

'Are you another healer?' Millie asked.

Her face simply smiled. The lady walked, almost floated over to their mother, and placed her hand on their mother's head and declared, 'The same spirit that raised Jesus from the dead is alive in you and bringing to life your mortal body.'

Martha had never heard that verse before. Was it in the Bible? Was it the lady's own words?

Martha heard Millie gasp, and they stared as their mother's eyelids fluttered open. Mother sat up and looked at everyone in the room.

'Why am I on the floor?'

'You had another fit.' Jemima's words were soft.

Mother caught the eyes of each person in the room. 'But I don't have a headache this time. I always have a headache after a fit.'

'And you're always tired,' Millie muttered.

Mother rose carefully, the older lady giving her a hand.

'Your hand is so nice and warm. Who are you?' Their mother spoke as if in a daze.

The lady didn't respond, but turned to the little match seller. 'It's time for us to leave them.'

'Where? Stay here, spend the night, let me thank you,' Mother said.

'We have more fresh bread,' Jeremiah offered from the threshold. Martha started. When had he appeared? That Emily girl must be working downstairs. The girl loved baking.

'We're fine. We have more people to visit,' the lady said, her voice lilting like a young choir boy's.

The match girl followed obediently, and as fast they'd come, they left.

The sisters huddled around their mother. Jeremiah put out a hand to help Martha stand, then grasped her elbow and didn't let go. The sisters stared at their mother in amazement.

'Are you really fine?'

'She looks better than ever.'

'Her skin is glowing.'

'You should still rest.'

'Stop fussing, all of you. I feel healthier than I have in my entire life,' Mother said as she grabbed a towel, shooing them away. The sisters eyeballed one another and finally moved with caution back to the chores they'd begun.

'I've never seen anything like that in my entire life.' Jeremiah had let go of Martha's elbow to allow her to fill the washtub with what was left of the boiling water on the stove. 'Where did that girl come from?'

'She was sitting right outside the bakery when I left this morning. I've never seen her before.' Martha chose her words carefully, pondering the morning's events. She poured the water without spilling it into the washtub. She determined there would be no more accidents in front of Jeremiah today.

'It's strange how they didn't want to stay for breakfast. They hurried on as if they had somewhere to be,' Jeremiah said.

'She did say something to that effect. I'll keep my ears and eyes open today as I collect laundry.'

'I'm glad your mother is well.'

Martha nodded, holding his gaze.

'I'll be working late tonight, but stop by and let me know if you hear about who they are.'

As the day went on and Martha delivered the laundered clothes to the last families before Christmas Eve, she asked if anyone had seen a little match girl or an old healer. But the villagers only knew of Widow Larkin's attempt that morning.

'No one knows of them,' Martha told Jeremiah that evening when she brought him supper that her mother had made.

'It's a Christmas miracle.'

'You don't think...?' Martha paused. She waited while he ate the potatoes and turnips.

'Think what?'

'Never mind. Are you ready for the Christmas party?' Martha looked around the bakery for the cake.

'Wait.' Jeremiah took her hand in his and she glanced down at their fingers entwined with one another. 'Will you come to the Christmas party with me?'

Her heart raced and leaped, but she smiled up at him.

'I promise I won't come anywhere near your confections except to eat them,' Martha said.

He laughed. 'Do you really think something would happen to them?'

'I'd ruin them. Knock them over.'

'I'm not worried about that.' He shook his head. 'Is that why you won't learn to bake?'

'I never did anything right when my dad tried to teach me,' Martha said.

'I'd teach you how to bake your own gingerbread if you like?' Jeremiah suggested. She shrugged, then nodded. He smiled. 'The cake is in the back; would you like to see it?'

'Yes,' Martha moved carefully through the kitchen, being sure not to bump into anything. She stopped at the sight of the cake covered in gingerbread cookies telling a story. She walked around it slowly studying the cake, then studying Jeremiah just as closely. 'Shepherds, sheep, are those the angels?'

He nodded.

'Do you think that lady today —? I mean her granddaughter — Well, do you think we're like the shepherds?'

'Because God sent them angels?' Jeremiah asked, finishing her thought.

She nodded and he squeezed her hand.

'Perhaps,' he said. 'Perhaps.'

A Christmas Promise Kept
by Nathan Peterson (fantasy/adventure)

I was close to dozing off, eyes drooping shut. Then the band around my arm began to warm. My mind slipped away into a too-vivid dream.

A crackling fire lit up the parlour, playing off bright bits of paper and sweetmeats hanging from boughs of greenery. Off to one side stood Esther's sewing mannequin like a dilapidated sentry keeping watch on the stairs down to her shop.

Knees tucked up under her as always, Ada perched on the window seat. She pressed her nose against the cool glass. Across the heath, the pink sun hung just above the horizon. The snow sparkled like guttering coals.

On and on she stared, the window fogging under her breath. With uncharacteristic dark wavy hair and olive skin, she looked like my twin, Esther always said. But the look on her face filled me with a hollow ache.

'Ada,' came Esther's voice from across the room, one part cross, two parts playful, 'do you wish to scrub that window?'

'No, sorry, Mother,' Ada turned to face her. 'I just was looking for Father.'

Esther's face fell as she settled on the window seat. The ache in my chest redoubled. Esther said nothing for a long while, no doubt trying to reframe the same worn excuse that I was off on some 'last-minute errand.'

'Ada,' Esther began slowly, 'your father warned that he may not be home till late tonight. He's a busy man, you know.'

'But it's Christmas Eve.'

'I know, I know. I wish he was here too. But,' Esther rallied what little excitement she had, 'but we must be leaving for the party soon. Let's see if your new dress fits!'

Ada nodded. 'I can try it on myself, Mother.'

'Very good, love.'

Ada trotted across the parlour into her room. She glanced out the window once more, absently rubbing the silver bracelet upon her wrist. Many Christmases ago, I'd given it to her, telling her it would keep us close even when I was far away. Now, being nearly eight, she was of course 'too grown up to believe such silly things,' as she reminded me nearly every day.

'Father… please hurry,' she whispered.

That was enough. I sat up, eyes open, and the vision faded. The silver band beneath my sleeve cooled. 'I will, I *will* hurry, Ada,' I mumbled through cracked lips. 'I promise.'

This set off a series of wracking coughs that left me gasping. As I sucked in the icy air, plunging like blades into my chest, my shivers settled in once more.

It was dark all around me. Even the snow looked muted, dirty, cheerless. I could see only a handful of yards between the shaggy, black-needled firs.

My coughing soon drew the pair of stone golems back to me, tramping through the trees. Of middling size—their faces too crude and crumbling to be Lord Bentham's—they glowered down at me with yellow-orange eyes like sparks.

I did my best to stay still, regain my breathing, till finally the dumb brutes lumbered away. Taking note of the directions they both went, I sat up against the nearest tree. Cold and aching as I was, the chances of falling asleep again soon weren't good.

So I settled back into my work. The problem with not binding a prisoner's feet is that they tend to wriggle around. And in an inhospitable forest of trees with unnaturally sharp branches, it's doubly a problem. The third mistake my captors made was opting for leather chords instead of shackles.

I was halfway through my bonds, I guessed. My wrists were chafed and bleeding as I sawed the leather back and forth against a low-hanging branch. But it was a small price to pay to be rid of this place.

Besides, I had what I was after. With nothing but rock for brains, the idea of searching their prisoner would never dawn on the golems. But whoever had ordered them here wouldn't likely be so dense. One still could hope, though.

I paused in my sawing after a few minutes. The labour only exacerbated my coughs. And I didn't need the golems tramping back on me again in the middle of escaping.

As best I could with bound hands, I checked the left corner of my jacket. Yes, the lodestone was still there hidden within the lining.

Better be worth the trouble, I thought.

Ultimately, I knew it wasn't up to me to assess the lodestone's worth. I was just the local Guild's pathfinder. The 'gallivanter' as Marta so fondly, obnoxiously called me. The one who ended up climbing down old abandoned wells, hiking down old abandoned mineshafts, and whatever else old and abandoned that proved to be a terminus to another realm.

Pity that terminuses never are found in the local pub or a nice manor house.

I soon gave up on that cheery line of thought. One had to make a living, and contenting myself with being some trite tinker or simpleton tilling a field would never do. Better to be venturing to new realms, hunting for artifacts, which the Esteemed (Secret) Guild of Snatchers & Grabbers could sell for a tidy profit.

Getting tied up and left in a forest of perpetual night was just a hazard of the job. And not the worst of them either, unfortunately.

After another half hour's on-and-off sawing, I was able to snap my bonds. Rubbing the feeling back into my hands, I set off through the trees, swift and silent.

At every opportunity, the fir tree needles pricked me. Wherever they touched bare skin, they left a slight oozing puncture. The pain was minimal, but I still began to feel the leaden effects of their venom slowly worming into my limbs. There was little I could do but turn up my collar, stuff my hands into my pockets, and press on with thoughts of hearth and home to fight back the weariness overtaking me.

I came across a slight clearing where the snow was furrowed with clods of dirt and dead grass. And half-buried in a drift, a sliver of moonlight gleaming off the mahogany, was my cane. I reached down fondly, almost reverently, and reclaimed my prized possession.

As soon as my hand settled around its black leather grip, I felt a surge of strength and courage. Perhaps a quarter hour more, and I should be out of those ghastly woods with my prized lodestone in hand, or rather in pocket.

I'd gone scarcely a dozen yards when I began to see them. Slivers of sick green glowing among the shadow-loving trees. They seemed to multiply with each step, tracking my every movement. Images of any number of gruesome creatures from past exploits crowded my mind.

Whoever my antagonist was, he or she had exposed my arrogance, believing I was being held captive by nothing but a pair of thick-headed golems. *Well-played,* I conceded with a sigh.

I slid the flat grey blade free of my cane's sheath. 'Don't worry, Ada,' I murmured. 'I'll be home soon.'

And so the chase began.

I sprinted through the trees, hacking at impeding branches. Behind me, to my left and right, I heard paws or hooves chuff through the snow. I caught flickering glimpses of long, lithe bodies keeping pace with me with enviable grace.

They began closing the distance, hemming me in on three sides. It was only a matter of time till... yes, there they were. Three of the abominations directly ahead. Six-legged, their pelts full of glowing iridescent quills, their mouths full of teeth thin as Esther's sewing needles. Dusk-jackals. Lovely . . .

Less than six feet from them, I sheathed my blade, slipped my cane into its holder on my back, and jumped. A thin whip of cable hissed out from my wrist. It looped around a tree branch, and I went soaring right over the top of the dusk-jackals' snapping jaws.

Soon I was crouched upon a bough sixty feet off the ground. I allowed myself a grin at the jackals' bewilderment as they scrounged through the snow, trying to regain my scent. They would soon enough, I knew. But for all their speed and dexterity, dusk-jackals are lousy climbers.

I respooled my wrist cable and then sent it out once more. I settled into a steady rhythm, swinging through the treetops, pausing on branches before relaunching once more. The dusk-jackals' grating bays of frustration slowly faded into the distance.

Up ahead, I saw the edge of the cursed forest, a plain of white beyond. And dangling straight out of the thick snow-burdened clouds was a rope and a bucket. My escape.

Another minute, and I was back on the ground, trotting through the last line of trees, barely winded. 'All in a day's work,' I smirked to myself.

'Indeed.'

Too many things happened at once. The cold sneer from behind. The ground before me dropping away into a near-bottomless trench. And a chorus of snarls, laughter, and clunks of shifting stone.

I turned around slowly, hands raised. There must have been a half a dozen dusk-jackals, nearly as many hooded men with rifles levelled my way, and the two dumb golems. Even they looked smug. And right in the centre of them... was my father-in-law. Fletcher Kershaw.

My hands flopped down to my sides as my eyes split wide. Snickering at my absolute shock, Kershaw picked his way through the snow toward me. 'Fancy you here.' His emphasis made the last word come out with the grace of a phlegm-filled cough. 'I thought you'd be at Whitmore by now, drinking punch and serenading my Esther.'

Words refused to come. I could only gawk. I knew it was him. He'd all but confirmed that himself. And yet, he was so... changed.

Without his familiar stoop, Kershaw stood nearly half a foot taller. His shabby greatcoat was replaced by a much finer navy smoking jacket with gold buttons and a sweeping grey inverness cape. His ever-present top hat was missing, allowing his long white hair to hang loose in the chill wind. At his neck, he wore a jade pendant in the shape of an egg. It glowed and pulsed with miniature sparks of yellow lightning.

'Fine manners you have, Roebuck,' Kershaw mocked. 'No word of cheer, no embrace for your dear father-in-law.'

I could only shake my head and mutter, 'So you're the broker we've been running up against? I suppose you were behind Sullivan's capture at Belfast?'

Kershaw gestured as though tipping an invisible top hat. 'Your acumen, as usual, is bafflingly delayed. But still mildly entertaining.

'Unfortunately, I've no time to dawdle tonight. It is a special occasion as you should well know.' He smirked as he held out a thin gloved hand. 'If you'd be so kind as to hand over the lodestone . . .'

'Load-shtone?' I made a show of exaggerating each syllable. It was well past time for me to get over my shock. I had made a promise to Ada after all, and I was going to keep it. Even if I had to thwart her grandfather's schemes to do so.

'Very droll.' One of Kershaw's unruly brows arched as he snapped his fingers. Two of his cowled henchmen swathed in black overcoats lowered their rifles and started digging through my pockets. It took nearly a minute for them to find the lodestone hidden within the jacket lining. They tore it open and offered up the stone to Kershaw.

'Hold now!' I took the tone of a parent chastising a naughty infant. 'Your daughter made that jacket for me. There's no call to be so heavy-handed about this.'

Ignoring my complaint, Kershaw eyed the lodestone, a fist-sized lump of granite completely unobtrusive down to its mottled flecks of grey and white. 'This will fetch a fine price.' His voice hitched. 'A fine price indeed.'

'You must be careful,' I warned, bluffing for all I was worth. 'You can't sell a relic like this just to anyone! You know what it could do in the wrong hands.'

Kershaw ignored my theatrics, wrapping the stone in a silk kerchief before pocketing it. 'Oh, I don't doubt it.'

'You slimy, thieving cur.' I lunged toward him, but his thugs were too quick, clamping their gauntlets tight around my arms.

'Cur?' Amusement made Kershaw's voice sound even more sickly and hoarse. 'You of all people call me a cur?'

As he continued, growing louder, his eyes darkened to match the jade pendant at his neck. 'Where would you and your family be without my patronage? Esther and you would never have had the capital to open that shop of hers.

'Without me, you'd be living under some hedgerow! Of all people, a smooth-talking thief, a swarthy foreigner like you has less than no place insulting me!'

Heat boiled up in my chest. My mouth opened. But I held my tongue. Foreigner, outcast, ingratiating, slippery Spaniard—I should be unvexed by such taunts, jibes I've heard all my life. An angry outburst would get me nowhere, I knew all too well.

Kershaw hacked a wad of phlegm at my feet. 'Showing some sense at last, I see. Too late, I'm afraid.' His eyes began to return to their normal frosty blue. 'I had a mind to spare you, given the occasion and all. But now...' He trailed off, letting his threat linger.

He motioned to the hooded guards as he turned away. They wrenched my arms up high behind my back, and manacles clanked into place around my wrists.

'And you...' Kershaw stalked up to the stone golems, who loomed a good two feet taller than him. 'I ordered that you allow him to break his bonds, *not* get within inches of escape with my lodestone. I've no time nor patience for imbeciles.'

He clapped his palms together, index fingers extended, brought them up over his head as if hoisting a sword, and then swung them down through the air. Tendrils of gold and emerald helixed down his arms, blasting the golems to smoking hunks of rubble. A wave of heat gushed across the plain like ripples across a pond.

I stumbled, regained my footing in time to see Kershaw staring me down with a wicked smirk. He bent down, picked up a lump of the exploded golems, and stuffed it into his pocket.

'Farewell, Roebuck,' he scoffed over his shoulder. 'I'll give Esther your regards. Pity how many accidents happen upon the road this time of year. Too sharp a turn, a buggy tipping, and all inside dead upon impact. Shameful, really.'

He swept around the chasm in the snow in front of me and headed across the plain, flanked by all but one of the dusk-jackals and three henchmen. The latter clustered around me.

A combination of shock and flagging hope roiled within me as I trudged back the way we'd come. But I forced it down with a strong will.

I waited till we were well outside of earshot of Kershaw and his cronies. Then I dropped to the ground. Two of the guards tripped, collapsing right over the top of me. I wriggled my way free, managed to stand, and bowled the last man over.

I sprinted in the opposite direction, fast as my bound hands would allow. Something darted across right in front of me. The dusk-jackal's snarling hiss forced me to a standstill. It sunk low to the snow, poised to spring with quills flared.

'You idjit!' one of the guards barked as he jogged over to me. 'You thought you could outrun a dusk-jackal just like that? Forget it, mate, that bloke Kershaw's been onto you Guilders the whole bloody time. No way you're getting out of 'ere. But just so you don't get no more ideas...'

His fist slammed into my stomach. I doubled over, and he and the other guards rained down a flurry of blows. My vision flickered in and out.

When I regained full consciousness, my feet were bound in shackles as well, and I was being half-dragged, half-carried through the forest. It had grown even more bleak, shadows seeping into the snow itself. The fir needles jabbed at me with noticeable hostility. It only added to the leadenness already within.

The guard was right. There was no escape. I'd let down both Ada and Esther. That this had come at the hands of my own father-in-law paled in comparison to this gross failure.

We did not return to the previous spot where the golems had brought me. Instead, the dusk-jackal trotted along in front deeper into the woods till a cave appeared drilling deep into the side of a small rise. The men shoved me into the cavern's stygian dark, illuminated only by the faint glow of the jackal's quills.

At last, we stopped. The guards shoved me onto my knees before a stalagmite jutting up from the cave floor like a giant reverse icicle. They bound me to it, even hammering a spike down into the stone, severing all my hopes of escape.

Two guards headed for the mouth of the cave. The other remained within a couple feet of me, weapons close at hand, and the dusk-jackal settled onto its haunches, staring at me, salivating for a taste of flesh.

My spirits dropped lower and lower. Getting out of tight spots was a pathfinder's bread and butter. But this was different. My first capture had clearly been a ruse. Kershaw had baited me. How long he'd known I was a member of the Guild, I couldn't guess. Why he'd allowed me to escape I couldn't fathom either, other than a pure stroke of malice.

We had never been on the best of terms since I first began courting his daughter, but needless to say, this stretched far beyond my wildest suspicions of what he was capable of.

And yet the details began falling into place. I never could get a straight answer out of him when it came to his vocation. And just before the mess at Belfast, the Guild's worst setback to date, Kershaw had departed for a 'promising business venture.' The irony that I'd said nearly the same thing to my Esther before setting off with the rest of the Guild was abominable.

The dusk-jackal began to doze, snuffling quietly, and the glow from its quills faded to almost nothing. The band around my arm began to warm. My eyes closed.

I saw Ada tugging Esther down the path, pointing at the decorations in Whitmore Park. Fires blazed, dancers whirled and twirled, fiddles and guitars made the air pulse like a living thing.

Soon Ada charged off into the throng, linking arms with her friends, Diggory and Sylvia, and jigging in a tight circle. Esther hesitated upon the fringe. She glanced over her shoulder down the path to our home and pulled her shawl tight against the chill. At last, she settled down at a table next to the reverend's wife. They chatted politely, but Esther's eyes constantly strayed back to the dancers.

No more! my eyes snapped open. The band on my arm went straight from warm to frigid.

Knowing how dearly Esther loved these parties, the energy, the life, and laughter, I couldn't bear seeing her so miserable. And it was all my doing. I knew how much she worried when I left, when she saw the fresh bruises and wounds from my latest venture, things I'd casually dismiss whenever she broached the subject with me.

But chained to a stalagmite with a dusk-jackal at my feet and a guard ready to put a bullet in my chest, I saw the truth all too clearly: I revelled in this double life.

Whenever Esther became too pressing with her requests—demands, I called them—whenever Ada grew too needy or too persistent, I could leave. Not quite at the drop of a hat. But nearly. Roaming on my own wherever I pleased.

I couldn't help it, I'd told myself. Our information on new artifacts came like sparks, quick to come, quick to fade. If we didn't act within hours, there was no point at all.

But that didn't change how selfish I'd been. It wasn't right, wasn't fair to Ada and Esther.

'I'm sorry,' I whispered into the dark. If only they could hear.

'Leave off!' The guard's rifle butt slammed into my head.

•◇•◇•◇•◇•◇•◇•◇•◇•

I came to as a faint scuffing echoed down from the mouth of the cave. 'Hoi, who goes der?' one of the guards barked.

I straightened, rolling my stiff neck with a sigh. Probably Kershaw coming back, for interrogation, gloating, or both more than likely. Then came a gunshot.

Immediately, adrenaline surged through me. With nothing and nowhere for it to go, it just set my heart pounding in my ears. I strained to see what the commotion was. One distant thud echoed down to me, then another.

The dusk-jackal went from sprawled across the floor to charging in a moment, snarling at a small globe of light that swung closer. It made it halfway down the cavern's length when the light reached it, sent the creature slamming into one of the walls.

'Marta?' I croaked.

The guard closest to me had his rifle levelled. He squeezed off a shot. But the light dodged it and darted forward. A flash of brown, a hefty wooden smack, and he crumpled to the ground.

'Marta, is that you?' I blinked in the lantern's sudden glow.

'That's *Sister* Marta to ya, gallivanter!' came a thick Irish brogue. 'I see ya made a right bags o' this night's work.'

I slumped back down against the stalagmite. Relief seeped out of me in a heavy sigh.

'Don't suppose ya need a hand, boyo?' She was already at work, fiddling with the manacles behind my back. 'Or do ya prefer to keep acting the maggot?'

The chains dropped from my hands and feet. I shot up, wrapping Marta in a tight hug. 'Thank you, thank you, sister.'

Tensed, clearly not expecting my rare burst of affection, she just nodded. 'Ya all right there?' She stared at me more closely.

'Now I am.'

'An' the stone?'

'Gone.'

Marta's broad brow furrowed for a moment before her perpetual smile returned. 'Well, we'd best crack on, all the same. 'Tis Christmas Eve after all, places to be and all that.'

I took a deep breath. 'Aye, that we do.'

•◇•◇•◇•◇•◇•◇•◇•◇•

After passing through the terminus, back into our own realm, we worked our way to the edge of the woods on the outskirts of Whitstead. 'There's tell that there may yet be a score to be had tonight, gallivanter. A big 'un,' Marta said with a merry gleam in her gaze. 'Keep an eye out.'

I nodded without a word, too weary to speak.

With that, Marta set off on her way back to the convent in the next town over. As I crossed the heath, exhaustion hung on me heavier with each step.

But I set my gaze upon our parlour room window, third from the left in the small row of shop fronts and second-story apartments. The window was dark as I expected. All the same, I felt disappointed.

What did you expect, fool? Esther and Ada sitting around moping on Christmas Eve of all nights? came my sluggish thoughts. *You chose this life. And you can make a new choice too. Whenever you muster the courage.*

I had no energy, no will to respond to that.

All I could do was keep tramping on through the snow, eyes still fixed on the parlour window. With a bright sliver of moon, the way across the heath was easy to follow. Soon I reached the narrow back stairwell and slipped into the dark rooms. I'd just begun stoking a fire when I heard voices coming from down in the shop.

Moments later, the door opened.

'Father!' Ada screeched. She bolted across the parlour and launched herself into my arms.

'What's all this then?' I laughed as her contagious energy filled me with a second wind. 'Hello, my dear, how are you? How was the party?'

'Lovely! Father, you should have seen, Edith and Ellis were gobbling down nearly everything in sight. And Mr. Draco brought his huge dog. I mean, it was quite simply enormous and then—'

'Slow down, child,' I teased. 'You make me breathless just listening. There will be time soon for a full report, I expect nothing less. Can you manage that? But first I must say hello to your mother, if I may?'

'I suppose,' Ada said, still beaming ear to ear.

'Hello, Esther.' I opened my arms wide.

For a moment, she hesitated, removing her bonnet, glancing over her shoulder, before stepping in for the embrace. 'Happy Christmas, Mortimer,' she whispered.

I closed my eyes as I held her close. There was a faint hint of cinnamon on her skin. I breathed it in as I savoured her soft hair against my cheek. There was so much to say.

'Esther, I must tell you—'

Esther held up a hand, 'Mortimer, we have a guest...' She withdrew a few steps, and I saw a stooped silhouette make his way into the parlour. For the second time tonight, my jaw hung slack. But this time, his expression was equally full of shock and disgust.

I recovered first. 'Evening, Mr. Kershaw, fancy meeting you here!'

'Indeed,' he murmured. He stared hard at me, eyes boring deep, trying to discern how his scheme had gone awry.

Esther seemed to sense the tension though she could never have known its source. 'Ada, dear, fetch Grandfather's coat. He must be boiling.'

Ada skipped forward and took Kershaw's ratty overcoat and top hat. He took a moment to smooth down his wispy white hair.

His shock enlivened and terrified me all at once. I knew we were safe here. The statutes are strict. All conflicts and rivalries must be limited to the nether realms. Earth itself is neutral ground. Anyone violating these edicts risks grave peril. So we discovered at Belfast.

I forced a broad smile as I offered my hand. 'Happy Christmas, Mr. Kershaw.'

'Yes, yes, indeed.' He shook my hand with a venomous glare.

'Oh, Father, look, look at that!' Ada grabbed my other hand and pulled me away to the back window. 'Look, Father, see the light just like in your stories. The highwaymen must be celebrating Christmas with a party of their own!'

There, out on the heath, was a single lantern. It flickered faster and faster, weaving through the air like a manic firefly. It had to be Hobbs, signalling the other Guilders. Once more, Marta's parting words passed through my mind. Without thinking, I glanced over to my coat and boots, weariness swallowed up in pumping adrenaline. To be flashing so fast, it had to be quite the prize awaiting us.

'Father, where are you going?' Esther's strained voice broke through my trance.

Kershaw was gaping at the light upon the heath just as I was. He soon roused himself, snatching up his hat and coat. 'My apologies, Esther. I'm afraid that I have forgotten something rather important.'

'But you just arrived.'

Kershaw was already halfway out the door. 'It cannot be helped! Good night all.' He paused long enough to exchange a hard look with me. *This isn't over*, his eyes said loud and clear.

And then he was gone. I felt my hand reaching for my own jacket when Ada asked quietly, 'Father, are you alright? What happened to your hand?'

I looked down to see her fingering the raw skin beneath my wrists where my shackles had been. Memories of tonight's harrowing escape flooded fresh through my mind. I had been a fool one too many times to make the same mistake again. Not tonight of all nights.

'It's fine, Ada.' I reached down and scooped her up into my arms. Walking over to where Esther stood watching the last few minutes' commotion, I drew her in close for another embrace. 'I'm fine. It's Christmas Eve. And there's nowhere I'd rather be!'

To Make a Merry Christmas
by Erika Mathews *(children/drama)*

hristmas in Whitstead has to be the most glorious time of year, if I do say so myself.' Eleven-year-old Evelyn Weston clasped her hands together dramatically for a moment before spinning back to the old wood stove to peek at the rising loaves under their warm cover.

'It *is* cosy; thank the Lord for that.' Her mother smiled as her needle whisked over a cuff hem and disappeared underneath again.

'I cannot wait for Christmas Day! Won't it be gloriousness and delight, all pine and mistletoe and candles everywhere — and snow and moonlight and gifts together before the roaring fire!'

'—and puddings, and meat, and cake with raisins!' put in nine-year-old Ellis, poking his head up from the reader he laboured over, prone before the wide hearth.

'I want to go sing for the neighbours, like we did last year,' little Edith added as she turned her own small lump of bread dough round and round on the table.

'And I want to give us a roaring fire worthy of a Christmas Day.' Eldon, the oldest, kicked off his boots at the door and dumped a load of logs into the wood box.

Their mother dropped her sewing in her lap to smile upon each of her four children. 'My dears! I hope Christmas shall be all you wish! Nothing brings me greater happiness than having us all together, especially while celebrating the birth of our Saviour.'

Evelyn glanced keenly at her mother. The purse-strings were drawn tighter than ever this year, she knew — but surely there would be enough for a festive Christmas. So many times during the summer months her heart had turned eagerly to the anticipation of the first snow, sledding, decorating their small cottage, planning the modest feast that they might be able to afford, preparing surprises for each member of the family, crunching in the snow to the Christmas Eve service at St. Nicholas — and oh! perhaps finally having the crowning delight of carrying a glorious Christmas pudding to grace the Christmas dinner table!

The bread baking, she tackled the rest of her daily tasks with zeal, her mind busily and happily occupied in planning pleasures. Eldon could cut boughs of greenery just as easily as not from the forest when he chopped wood. Grandpapa's candle supply would do nicely for the decorating. Paper couldn't be spared; it must be saved to light the fire. Perhaps they would be able to get fruit to hang on the greenery and then enjoy for a special Christmas breakfast.

Once the cottage lay in its usual neat order, Evelyn skipped downstairs to the cellar and then upstairs to the loft to search for extra supplies, odds and ends, and bits of things that could be turned into Christmas cheer.

'What are you doing, Evelyn?' Ellis leapt to his feet and clattered up the stairs behind her.

'I'm finding things for Christmas.'

Edith's humming rendition of *O Come, O Come, Emmanuel* ended in an abrupt squeal. 'Can I find some too?'

'Of course! Get anything you can. Any little scraps, anything! We'll make a merry Christmas!'

'Is it tomorrow?' Edith asked, jumping up and down.

'No, it's more than a week away still.' Evelyn knelt by the trunk in the loft and rummaged through the treasures collected therein.

A happy hour later, a pile of short yarn ends, twisted nails, three shredded rags that couldn't be patched again, wick ends too tiny for Grandpapa to use in a candle, a pheasant feather, and various other items lay collected in a bucket on the floor, and a second happy hour followed as all three younger children engrossed themselves in cobbling together a variety of decorative items.

'Mumsi, can we have some of your yarn for the tree? We'll be sure to wind it up nicely and put it back in your basket after Christmas.'

'Yes, you may, Evelyn.' Her mother glanced up from another long seam.

'I'll go collect some sticks to make things with.' Ellis raced to the door, shoving feet into boots almost midstride. 'Eldon can always burn them afterwards.'

'Excellent plan! You just wait and see! The Christmas of 1844 will be the most beautiful Christmas the Weston family has ever known!' Evelyn spun, her dress puffing out around her. Surely it would be! It had to be!

●◇●◇●◇●◇●◇●◇●◇●◇●

'Dear Father up above in Heaven, please send us a Christmas pudding for Christmas dinner.' The slender form knelt by the old brass-knobbed bedstead, her brown head bowed low over her tightly-clasped hands. 'Thank You for answering my prayer. Thank You for Grandpapa, and Mumsi, and Eldon and Ellis and Edith, and please bless us all and help us all to love You with all our hearts. And thank You for sending Jesus to us. Amen.'

The prayer finished, Evelyn snuggled into bed next to her little sister, her old stuffed dog tucked neatly under her arm. Christmas Eve—tomorrow night—floated into her visions under her tightly-closed eyelids. For the whole week, she'd done her best to set the stage for a merry Christmas: helping Eldon cut and bring in greenery from the forest, trimming it with Grandpapa's newly-made beeswax candles and bits of odds and ends around the house that anyone else would term as 'trash' with no hesitation, trying to piece together something—anything—for a surprise gift, and tiring her poor little brain in a vain attempt to find something for a special Christmas dinner.

Only potatoes and carrots filled the cellar, and only flour for plain bread or porridge rested in the old grey cupboard. How could one possibly create a special meal from the same ingredients she cooked with every day?

But God could send the Christmas pudding. Of that she was certain. All her life, it seemed, her chief dream had been to crown the Christmas dinner with a pudding, and every year she'd waited in vain. But surely this would be the year ... despite the leaky roof and leaky stove that had eaten into every bit of Mumsi's meagre savings only a few weeks ago. Celebrating the birthday of the Saviour of the world in a grand and homey way was worth all the trouble.

The next thing she knew, early sunlight streamed into her attic window and it was Christmas Eve morning. The fire must be built, porridge must be stirred up, and Edith, trailing downstairs with one sock on while humming *Joy to the World*, must have her dress buttoned.

Yet heaviness weighed on her heart as she cleared away the breakfast dishes. Mumsi hadn't been able to finish her last dressmaking project, so no money would be coming before Christmas. The Christmas pudding seemed further off than ever. At this rate, she'd be faced with serving stew and plain bread for Christmas dinner.

Not a very festive dish with which to celebrate the Saviour of the world.

The bits of thread and rusty nails decorating the boughs looked shabby and sad, and even the prospect of twinkling candles didn't raise her spirits. As hard as she'd worked, as much as she'd planned, and as faithfully as she'd prayed, it didn't seem that there would be much of a Christmas at all.

'May I go for a walk outside when Eldon does?' she asked Mumsi, putting the broom neatly in its corner.

'You may.' Her mother smiled.

'May I come? Please?' Ellis jumped up, his prized accordion—a blessing from Grandpapa—in hand.

'Me too?' Edith stopped humming long enough to ask.

Permission granted, the four headed outdoors. Eldon disappeared in search of more firewood, and the three younger children wandered away from the road—even from the tantalizing aromas drifting from the bakery next door—towards the seclusion of the trees behind their small cottage.

Ellis softly played on the accordion as they walked, and Edith joined his tune here and there. Evelyn, in silence, listened to the pensive notes and words:

Come, Thou long-expected Jesus, born to set Thy people free;
From our fears and sins release us. Let us find our rest in Thee.

Christmas isn't about making everything perfect, Evelyn reminded herself. It is about what matters. Forever, not just for today. How could she and her family find their true rest in Jesus in this season of difficulty?

Suddenly inspired, she made a decision. She'd take this question upon herself as a personal challenge.

Back at the house, she pulled back the curtains, letting in the sunlight that reflected dazzlingly off the snow. She set the tea kettle on, and she kneaded the bread, shaping it into festive and exciting angels, mangers, and crosses rather than just plain rolls.

'Can I help?' Edith crowded against her elbow.

Evelyn wanted to say she could finish faster herself, but instead she agreed. 'Of course you can. Here's dough. Shape it into whatever you want.'

A merry hour followed. Project after project leaped to Evelyn's ready brain and was carried out as best as possible under the circumstances by her eager fingers, aided by her brothers and sister. After a cold lunch, the family settled into the main room, delighted with the rare opportunity of a chance to sit together in the middle of the day without pressing work clamouring. Cheerful chatter followed, and gradually the conversation became more serious as Evelyn attempted to express a few of her conflicted feelings and efforts.

'It's not whether we end up with enough for a merry Christmas or not. We are together, and Christmas really isn't about decorations, or delicious things to eat, or presents, or anything at all that we have.' Mumsi's soft voice reminded Evelyn.

'I know — but I do want to celebrate Jesus properly. I want to make it special for us to remember Him.'

'But, Evelyn, don't you see? He doesn't need any of these things, so why should we?'

'I suppose,' she said reluctantly. Then suddenly a light burst across her face, illuminating it with a divine glow. 'Oh! I see it now! Of course! Why, it's just that *He* is the gift. He is the feast. He is the decorations. He's everything Himself — the Bible says all this — so that means if we have Him, we have everything with which to make a merry Christmas.'

'Let's name everything He is.' Eldon turned from tossing another log on a roaring fire. 'I'll start. He is joy — the joy of the season and joy in us, no matter what.'

'He is our peace,' Evelyn added, quoting a favourite Scripture.

'He is our Christmas present,' Ellis put in.

'He is the bread of life that satisfies us forever,' Mumsi contributed.

'He is the Shepherd who takes care of his smallest and weakest sheep.' Grandpapa's eyes twinkled.

'He is the Baby in the manger!' Edith exclaimed. Then she burst into song. 'Joy to the world, the Lord is come!'

'He is our provider,' Eldon said, his voice low.

Round and round the circle they went, naming more and more elements of who their Saviour and Lord had made Himself to be to them. As the declarations flowed, Evelyn found her attention drifting away from the things they didn't have to gratitude for the things they did. A cheerful, healthy family, all together on Christmas, knowing and welcoming Jesus Christ the Saviour of the world—what more could she ask for?

Yet again, the prayer tugged at her heart. 'O Father above, please grant us a Christmas pudding.'

In light of the many blessings recounted, it seemed such a trivial thing to request. Yet had not her Father repeatedly assured her that He loved to give good gifts to them that asked Him? 'A Christmas pudding for Christmas dinner,' she repeated. 'Thank You that You have already arranged it.'

'Now let's count all the nice things about this Christmas,' Evelyn suggested as the fire burned lower and conversation dwindled. 'I'll start. A nice, warm, cosy fire.'

'Snow all week!' Ellis rushed to look out the window.

'The party at Whitmore Park!' Edith squealed.

'Being all together,' their mother spoke.

One by one, each shared little blessings, and Evelyn found her spirits soaring.

Sunlight's shadows lengthened, and it was time to get ready for the grand party at Whitmore Park, the chief estate of the village of Whitstead. Even if she barely knew Lord Fentiman and his family, the prospect of a grand time and a hot supper shone enticingly in the light of their own meagre fare.

'Perhaps God will give me a Christmas pudding there,' she sighed to herself. That would be delicious, though it wouldn't be the same. But no, Jesus was enough. If God gave her anything more, it would simply be extra.

The flurry of preparations, the brisk walk to Whitmore Park, the lights and colour and dazzling array of decorations, chatter, and aromas fell like heavenly bliss on Evelyn's senses. She so thoroughly enjoyed the chats with her good friend Emily Winterhurst—even though she missed Aurinda Button—as well as with various and sundry other Whitstead folks both well-known and little-known. How delicious was the little supper, and how her spirits soared once she left the mansion to tramp to St. Nicholas for the Christmas Eve service!

Inside, the still reverence awed her heart. Notes of carols wafted from somewhere up front, and candles—most of them made by Grandpapa—lit the congregation. She slipped into her place, holding Edith's hand tightly.

O come, O come, Emmanuel… Rejoice, rejoice, Emmanuel shall come to thee, O Israel.

She let the words wash over her. 'Thank You, God, that You *are* with us, and You are enough.' Despite her faded dress, scuffed shoes, and threadbare coat, despite the utter ordinariness of home, despite her own failure to create something special for her family, she had Jesus. And somehow, that knowledge filled her with utter joy and peace. She hugged the familiar words of the service to her heart.

'For unto you is born this day in the city of David a Saviour, which is Christ the Lord...'

Unto *her*. Just as surely as unto the shepherds, unto Israel, He was born unto Evelyn Weston and her family.

Snowflakes landed gently around her as she crunched back over the roads to the little cottage. The splendour of talking with and being in the presence of God filled her heart on this most holy night, and a determination seized her.

Back in the warm kitchen, she scooped the fancy-shaped bread she'd made into a basket and plunged back into the night. Two doors down, the Griffith family cottage stood, even smaller and more dilapidated than their own. Surely, they too would have little hope of a happy Christmas, but perhaps she, in her own small way, could help.

Leaving the basket on the doorstep, she knocked loudly, then retreated out of sight. Hiding behind a birch trunk, she watched the littlest Griffith boy pull the basket inside, and she heard the echoes of the shouts of his many brothers and sisters as they discovered the contents.

With a smile dancing on her face and a lump resting in her throat, Evelyn skipped back to her own front door. As she paused just before reaching the doorstep, she turned her face to the night sky. Stars shone out from between wispy and fleeting clouds. The full moon hung halfway up, shedding its brightness over the entire street. The snowfall had stopped. A single shooting star streaked across the dark expanse, clearly visible even in the moonlight.

All was right with the world. God had provided again. Even if there was nothing special to look forward to in the morning.

•◇•◇•◇•◇•◇•◇•◇•◇•

Christmas Day dawned as usual, bringing the normal daily work of staying alive and keeping warm, fed, and clean. The children played before the fireplace; Eldon tackled little repairs around the house he'd put off while he was out doing odd jobs around town; Mumsi sewed; Grandpapa studied Scripture and polished candlesticks. Evelyn put the house in order, started bread and stew for lunch, and kept Edith occupied.

Heaviness threatened her heart at the meagre fare, but she resolutely put it aside. 'Jesus will give us Christmas pudding,' she thought. 'He laid it on my heart to ask. He will not fail me. He said, "Whatever you ask in my name, that I will do. If you shall ask anything in my name, I will do it."'

But hadn't He also said, 'If two or three of you agree on anything in my name, I will do it'? She hadn't thought to share her request with the rest of the family. After all, it was only a silly little desire of hers—it wasn't earth-shattering. But He'd said....

'Ellis,' she whispered. 'Come here. I have something to tell you. And Edith, you come too.'

Together, the three of them scampered upstairs to Eldon, who was nailing a board onto the window frame. Evelyn gathered them around her. 'I have something important to say. I've—I've been asking God to send us a pudding for Christmas dinner. I know it sounds silly, but I think He wants me to ask. He says, 'Ask, and you shall receive.' So, if you would, I'd like to request that *you* also ask Him with me. Together.'

'I will! God will send pudding!' Edith exclaimed at once.

'And I will,' Ellis readily agreed.

Evelyn looked up into Eldon's eyes. Her older brother was always so cautious.

'Are you sure God wants you to ask? It seems… maybe… presumptuous.'

'He says, 'Ask whatever.' Ask in faith. It will be done. I think He means what He says.'

'But…' Eldon began.

'In faith,' Evelyn interrupted firmly. 'No doubting. If you don't want to, that's fine, but don't doubt us.'

'No. I will ask.' Eldon's eyes still held hesitancy, but he folded his hands together. 'Dear Father, we ask for a Christmas pudding, and we believe You will send one.'

'For Christmas dinner,' Ellis added. 'Make sure to send it on time, so it won't be spoiled.'

'That's today,' Edith put in. 'Send the pudding, God, please.'

'Thank You that You hear and answer our prayer,' Evelyn concluded. 'And thank You for sending Jesus to earth. We want to celebrate and worship Him. And we want to live in Him every day. Amen.'

'Amen,' her siblings echoed and then trooped downstairs once more. Dinnertime awaited.

'We must set the table,' Edith piped up. 'I will get the pudding spoons.'

'But…' Eldon began.

'No, she's right. God will send it, so we must be ready.' Evelyn handed Edith the six precious spoons that didn't see daily use in a stew or porridge bowl, and Edith skipped happily to the table.

Evelyn quietly set the bread and stew on the table, poured water, and slipped into her chair. Her family gathered around her. 'Grandpapa,' she said, a bit shyly. 'I've been praying for a pudding. Couldn't you pray for one too?'

'Why certainly,' he replied. 'But why a pudding?'

'Just because… I've always wanted one to celebrate Jesus' birth, and we've never had one, and God seemed to want me to ask.' A nagging thought lingered in the back of her mind, wondering how God could possibly get them a pudding now, but she pushed it away. Of course, God could.

'Our Father in heaven, we thank You for sending Jesus, our Emmanuel, to be with us forever. We thank You for Your provision today and every day. We thank You for our daily bread. We thank You that we are all well and together. We thank You for our kind neighbours and friends, and we pray Your blessing upon them. Bless our home, our table, and this food. If it is Your will, we ask for the Christmas pudding that Evelyn desires — but most of all, we ask for Your glorification and for Your kingdom to come on this earth, today and forever. Amen.'

'Amen,' the family echoed.

Evelyn took a deep breath. Now was the moment she'd hoped to crown the table with cutting a pudding… but it would have to be stew. 'In everything give thanks,' her heart reminded her. 'Thank you, God, for stew.' She heroically lifted the ladle.

Somewhere outside, a dog barked.

Ellis's head jerked up, then he ran to the front door. 'I'm going to look for the dog,' he exclaimed. 'Just a minute.' He flung the door open, then let out a shriek. 'Something is on the doorstep. Come see!'

In a twinkling, Evelyn dropped the ladle and flew to the door. A bowl sat on the step — a small bowl, but a beautiful one to her eyes.

With trembling fingers, she carried it to the table and opened it, never doubting a moment, yet with a heart that throbbed in anticipation and awe.

Under the towel lay a gorgeous, magnificent-looking Christmas pudding.

'Thank You, Father. Thank You, Father. Thank You, Father.' Evelyn's eyes nearly brimmed over in gratitude and joy. Jesus was enough — but look at how He delighted to bless His children! See how He answered the smallest and most trivial of prayers! Evelyn lifted the dish, placing it in the centre of the table, and though it was small, it seemed better than the most magnificent feast to her eyes.

For it was the answer to a child's prayer to her loving Father.

With shaking fingers, Evelyn cut the pudding, each movement a small miracle in her estimation. As delightful as the pudding was, it paled in comparison to her Father's wondrous love and care — for *her*. He had personally answered her prayer. He had given her *exactly* what she'd asked for. Not a roast, not a feast, not a houseful of gifts and decorations… but He'd given her Himself.

And the Christmas pudding would forever be a symbol in her mind of just how much that Christmas gift meant to her.

She handed the first plateful to her mother, her heart full. 'Merry Christmas, Mumsi. A merry, merry Christmas indeed.'

An Unexpected Christmas
by Lauren H. Salisbury *(science fiction)*

Syuch and Harsci trudged through the thick frozen water particles piled between tall, skeletal plants, their eyes on the weak lights blinking in the distance. Their ship lay hidden behind them, the branches of a rather prickly plant covering a small section where the cloaking device was glitching.

'Can you see any of the lifeforms yet?' Syuch asked.

Harsci scanned the area. 'Not yet, but as long as we change shape before any of them see us, we should be perfectly fine.'

Syuch grunted. Harsci had never been stranded anywhere before, but she had. She rubbed the scar on her side, a constant reminder of the perils of close-quarters data collection. At least this planet had a breathable atmosphere—and no draconis.

She followed Harsci around a particularly tall plant with a rough outer layer and bumped into him when he came to an abrupt stop.

'What is it?' she hissed.

'Lifeforms. Scanning now.'

He showed her the reading, and she scrunched her face at the awkward-looking shape she would have to imitate. 'How do they cope with such spindly appendages?'

Already transformed, Harsci inspected his body, bending and twisting to test its limits. 'I think they are fascinating.'

'You would.' She morphed her features into an approximation of his, then checked it against the palm pad's female parameters.

A noise beyond the collection of plants brought her head around, and she peered at a group of short lifeforms walking along a track with a taller one at the rear. They wore layers of material over their bodies—yet another sign of their species' inferiority—and they created much noise as they moved.

Syuch tilted her head and adjusted her appearance to include long fur on her crown. Then she held out her hand to Harsci. 'Pass me the replicator. We will need to copy their body coverings.'

They followed the line of lifeforms towards a cluster of buildings perched between the tall plants, a rise in the land, and a flat, open area. Smoke drifted from the top of some of the dwellings and voices floated across the freezing tufts of green edging them.

'May I collect the linguistic data?' Harsci asked, to which Syuch merely shrugged. The less interaction she had with any indigenous lifeforms the better. She left him running the speech patterns they could hear through their translator and peered through narrowed eyes at the first line of structures in the settlement.

'Got it,' Harsci said. He held up the palm pad. 'We should have enough here to be able to make ourselves understood. Let us go.'

He started for the buildings, but Syuch grabbed his arm and pulled him back. 'What are you doing?'

'Making contact? You agreed we would attempt to blend in while we are stranded here.'

'Yes, but we should examine the surroundings first — see what we are dealing with. You have no idea whether they are dangerous or how many of them we might have to face if they attack.'

His lips compressed into a thin line. 'For a data collector, you have a distinct lack of curiosity. How have you managed to keep the position for so long?'

'By being cautious. The last curious partner I had is now an incinerated husk on Dracon.'

She cast him a warning look and made her way around the habitation, dragging the ridiculous layers of fabric encircling her lower appendages through the frozen water particles.

They passed a large building with a square section at one end that rose into the sky and emerged into a field covered in carved stones. What was this place? Syuch had never seen anything like it. She walked over to one of the stones and wiped a thin layer of plant matter from the surface.

Something had been etched into it. ARTHUR COBBETT. 1735-1754

'It must be a name,' Harsci said from beside her. 'There are remains approximately one-point-five spans beneath us that resemble the lifeforms here.' He consulted his palm pad. 'People, they call themselves. Maybe they store their dead underground.'

'Maybe,' she said, moving on. More carvings appeared in the rocks littering the ground, each one in the same formula.

Harsci stopped beside a large stone shaped as a people with wings attached to its back. He gazed up into its face, his brows pulling together. 'There must be more than one lifeform on this planet. I did not see any of these winged creatures in the settlement. Did you?'

Syuch stepped closer to the back of it, inspecting the detailing on the feathers. 'No. Our initial scans showed only earth-bound sentient creatures, but the advance teams sometimes miss things.'

He turned around. 'I have seen enough. We should find a domicile before night falls.'

'Night falls?'

He waved his palm pad over his shoulder as he walked away. 'It is one of their expressions.'

She hurried to catch up to him. 'Are you sure we could not stay in the ship?'

'I told you, the atmospheric controls were damaged on impact. And you agreed we would take the opportunity to explore.'

'Hah. You left me little alternative when you set out for the nearest energy readings.'

He did not meet her eye, which she took to mean he conceded her point.

They walked back the way they had come, around a line of structures that decreased in size and solidity of construction as they progressed. At first stone, then brick, and finally pieces of plant with a composite filling in the gaps, the majority contained heat signatures of at least two, sometimes as many as seven or eight lifeforms.

Eventually, when Syuch's body coverings were wet and heavy, they came across a small structure set slightly apart from the others with no inhabitants inside.

'Do you think it is vacant?' she said.

Harsci stowed his palm pad. 'There is only one way to find out.'

He crept to the window and looked inside, then pushed on the door and disappeared into the dark depths. A moment later, he reappeared and waved her over. 'It appears derelict but should suit our needs.'

Syuch slipped inside and looked around. A reasonably sized room with a section of stone wall at one side, a blackened stone slab at the base, and a small table and two chairs in front of that. At the other side, a low construction with some fabric coverings resembled a sleeping mat, and a shelf held a collection of items, all of which besides the cups baffled Syuch's mind.

The furniture was entirely made of brown plant material, and she ran a hand over the surface of the table, surprised at the smoothness beneath the thick layer of dust. Half a cycle with a cleansing wand, and the room would prove adequate indeed.

By the time they finished stowing their supplies, her eyelids drooped. She collapsed on her sleeping mat and fell asleep within moments.

•◇•◇•◇•◇•◇•◇•◇•◇•

She woke early the next morning and eased into one of the chairs, holding her breath in case it broke under her weight. When it held, she settled back against the spindles and board behind her.

'Comfortable?' Harsci asked.

She sniffed. 'I suppose so.'

Grabbing her palm pad, she skimmed through the data she had transferred from the ship. Deep grooves soon etched her forehead, and she started again from the beginning, scrutinising each performance readout in turn. She must be missing something, for she could find no reason for the collapse in their orbit that had forced them to land.

Harsci tugged the device from her hands. 'We should observe the settlement.'

Reluctantly, she agreed, and they left the domicile, walking along the packed gravel at the front of the building towards the larger structures.

They were nearing a bend when two short peoples ran out in front of them and jerked to a stop.

'Who are you?' one said.

'I am Syu—'

'Arthur Cobbett,' Harsci said. 'And this is... Elizabeth.'

'Is she yer wife?'

'No.' Syuch had no idea what that was, but the people's tone did not make it sound agreeable.

The second people scrunched her face. 'Sister then. My brother's annoying too.'

The male glared at her. 'Take that back.'

'Can't make me.'

She ran off, the male chasing her, and Syuch stared after them. What a strange first contact.

At the earliest opportunity, she returned to the domicile and spent the rest of the morning scouring the ship's data. Whatever Harsci said, she had no intention of venturing out again until she had discovered how to get them back into space.

Sometime later, the door opened, and he walked in. He whistled as he carried a box of provisions to the table and unpacked them.

'Did you find something to help us fix the ship?' she asked.

He winced, pausing for a second before returning to his task. 'No. But I bought ingredients for something called a Christmas pudding. I thought we could try making one.' His eyes twinkled when he looked at her, and she stowed her palm pad in her pocket with a sigh.

'I suppose so. What do we do?'

His lips pursed. 'I am not exactly sure, but the people I spoke to in the shop gave me some written directions.'

He fished in his pocket and produced a piece of paper with squiggles all over it. Smoothing it out on the table, he scanned it and tapped his palm pad's display a few times. Then he grinned and showed it to her.

'What do you think?'

She read the instructions. 'Seems simple enough, and non-toxic, but what does this mean?'

She pointed at a line towards the bottom, and he scrunched his face as he read it. 'Tokens. She said something about that... Ah, I know. We add a piece of metal to the mix.'

Syuch stared at him. 'Why?'

'I do not know.' He shrugged. 'For us to find when we eat it?'

That made little sense, seeing as they would be the ones to put it there, but they could add metal if it would make him happy. She walked over to the replicator standing on the stone plinth at the side of the room.

'What type and size?'

'She did not say, but it seemed to have significance, so a metal precious to them.'

Syuch programmed the replicator to generate a piece of gold the size of her thumb, then looked at the bowl Harsci held and cut the size by half. That should do.

Three quarters of a cycle later, they were both covered in a fine white powder, and Syuch's nose tickled. The mixture was wet and slimy, but it did not taste bad when she touched a drop to her tongue. Still, it did not seem right.

She consulted the instructions again, picking up the original sheet of paper and turning it around and then over. Typical Harsci—another line had been written on the back that he had not scanned. She did so and read the translation. The pudding must be boiled for eight hours and set aside.

Boiled? What in the universe did that mean? She stared at the gloop, and an idea occurred.

'I am not sure this is the correct consistency. Do you think we need to heat it? Chemical reactions often need heat, and this has many compounds in it.'

Harsci dropped the spoon he had been licking and wiped a smear of the mixture from his face. 'Maybe. But will that change the taste? I like it the way it is.'

'Let us see.'

Syuch heated the bowl with her cauteriser set to the lowest setting, watching the mixture turn brown around the edges. It gave off a pleasant, spicy smell, so she kept going until the entire top matched the colour of the dry fruit they had added.

Harsci leaned over it and breathed in, then let out a groan. 'That smells delicious. Want to try a piece?'

'No.' She whipped it away from him and placed it on a shelf above the replicator. 'The sheet said to eat it at Christmas, and that is not for another five rotations.'

'The word is *days*,' Harsci grumbled, glancing at her from the corner of his eye.

'What?'

He sighed and turned away from the pudding bowl. 'It is not rotations. They call them days.'

'You know what I meant. Now clear up this mess while I replicate some real food.'

She bent over the replicator, scrolling through the list of options, while he banged around behind her. Her mouth watered as she breathed in the tantalising aroma of the pudding, but she swallowed and clenched her jaw. There was no way this side of the Pyricon nebula she would admit she wanted to try it too.

●◇●◇●◇●◇●◇●◇●◇●◇●◇●

The next morning, Harsci's sleeping mat was empty when she awoke. Where had he gone now? She stood and stretched, morphing into the people form in case anyone was spying on them. It paid to be cautious, as she kept trying to tell Harsci.

She replicated some fressil gar and sipped the warm beverage while she searched for her palm pad. The diagnostic she had set to run on the ship's systems the previous evening would be ready to review by now. Where was it? She was certain she had left it on the chair by the table.

The door swung open, causing her heart to miss a beat and her hand to reach for her blaster, but it was only Harsci. She relaxed and lowered her arm. 'Where have you been?'

'Exploring.' A broad smile spread across his face, and the corners of his eyes wrinkled. 'And I have found an instructional document.'

He held up a sheaf of papers bound together inside the skin of a deceased animal. Did peoples record their writings on the flesh of their vanquished enemies? A shudder ran through her. She had assumed only the inhabitants of the Dendar system did that.

Harsci continued as if nothing were amiss with what he held in his hand. He placed it on the table and opened it to the first page, scanning it with his palm pad.

'Where did you get it from?'

He turned to the next page. 'Someone called a pedlar. He speaks a slightly different language to the others we have encountered. Did you know peoples have more than one?'

She shook her head.

'Anyway, I learned a few new words, and while we were talking, I noticed this in his portable domicile.'

'His what?'

'He lives in a domicile on wheels and sells things from it to other peoples. I gave him three of their little metal disks for this, and he seemed quite happy. He told me it was published last year, so it must be full of current information.'

She edged closer, curious despite herself, then frowned. She should know better — curiosity got data collectors killed. Draining her fressil gar, she returned to her search. 'Do you know where my palm pad is? I was sure I left it right here.'

'Um, no. But look at this.' He held up the translation of a section involving something called a ghost. 'It seems this planet has non-corporeal lifeforms as well as peoples. I wonder if we will meet one.'

He walked towards the door.

'Where are you going now?'

'To try out some of what I have learned.' He looked back at her, his brow furrowing. 'You should come with me.'

She shook her head. 'I would rather be eaten alive by a graxyl.'

'Come on. You have not left this room since yesterday morning. Are you not at least a little curious?'

She started to deny him again, but he strode across to her. 'Please. I assure you there is no danger, but there is much for us to discover. These peoples are extraordinary creatures.'

'Very well.' She sighed and snatched up the bonnet he had replicated for her. 'Half a cycle, and then you leave me in peace.'

'Absolutely,' he said, his mouth stretching into a wide smile.

They walked down the main street in the village, greeting the peoples they met the way Harsci said was their norm. The first were a young couple, who responded to Harsci's 'Bah humbug' with strange looks and a shuffled half-step away from him.

He added a bright smile for a plump female. 'Bah humbug.'

'Foreigners,' she said, giving him a sharp look as she stomped past them.

'I do not think that word means what you think it means,' Syuch whispered to Harsci after they were out of hearing.

He frowned. 'But it was in the instructional material. Maybe I am just saying it wrong.'

He tried again as they approached a male with iron grey hair, blue eyes, and a tall hat. 'Bah humbug to you.'

'Hah, very amusing.' The people lifted his hat a fraction and dropped it back onto his head. 'New to town, eh?'

'Yes,' Harsci said.

'Just passing through,' Syuch added.

'Well, if you're available on the twenty-fourth, you should join us at Whitmore Park. We're having a Christmas gathering, and the whole village is invited.'

'I am not sure we will be here—'

'We would enjoy that very much,' Harsci said over the top of Syuch's answer. He grabbed her arm as he nodded to the people, then walked on, pulling her with him before she could protest.

It seemed they were going to a gathering, whatever one of those was. Well, Harsci could discover the details on his own. He was the one who had got them into this mess. Him and his bah humbug.

•◇•◇•◇•◇•◇•◇•◇•

Three evenings later, they arrived at a vast domicile spread out beside a frozen pool of water. Inside, branches from various plants had been laid along shelves above roaring fires and tied to the handrail of a staircase that wound up to a second level. What strange creatures peoples were. If they wanted to see the leaves, why not simply go outside?

The first room was filled with peoples standing about and talking while they sipped from glasses and cups. Their conversation hit Syuch like a swarm of kaffle flies, incessant and grating on her ears.

She sidled along the wall towards an open doorway, hoping to avoid the crowds, but there were yet more peoples in the next room. At least the scent of their various perfumes was not as overwhelming in there. She spotted a table covered with food and headed in that direction.

When she was halfway across the room, the flash of a silver mane disappearing behind some thick fabric hanging over the window caught her attention. She sucked in a breath. Was that a...?

She darted a glance around her, but none of the peoples appeared aware of the draconis hiding in their midst. She would need to deal with it herself. It shifted position, and she narrowed her eyes, keeping it in her sight while she rounded the table.

As she drew closer, her steps faltered. This was no advance scout. Its scaled body was too diminutive for one of their warrior caste, and the colouring was all wrong—deep purple rather than mottled grey.

Her hand went to the scar on her side even as she breathed out the tension in her shoulders. But if it was not a draconis, what was it? And what was it doing here? The same as she and Harsci?

She ambled across, feigning interest in an image of a group of peoples dangling on the wall.

'Are you here to observe people behaviour too?' she asked the winged creature.

It looked up at her and, in a velvety smooth voice, said, 'They're much more interesting than I remember.'

He had been here before—and chosen to return? How... perplexing. She gazed out over the collected peoples, tilting her head as she tried to see them in a different light. Maybe they were not dangerous creatures after all.

She nodded to the draconis-like being and moved on. Where was Harsci?

A female appeared in front of her, slim and smiling. Hair as black as deep space curled around her face, some of the prickly green plant's leaves and berries peeking out from where they were pinned to the side of her head.

'I am Elizabeth,' Syuch blurted, Harsci's reminder surging to mind.

'Georgiana. Nice to meet you.'

Syuch was about to edge around her when she said, 'I hope you don't mind me saying, but your dress is simply stunning. Wherever did you find it?'

Syuch looked down, then glanced about for Harsci, twisting her fingers together. 'I, um, made it.'

Was that an adequate response? The last thing she wanted was to draw attention to herself and end up being driven out of the settlement at the end of the peoples' weapons. She had only copied the design Harsci had scanned during his trip to the trading places earlier that afternoon.

'Oh, how clever. I'm useless when it comes to the feminine arts, especially sewing, so I'm in awe of anyone who can produce such a masterpiece.' The people drained whatever was in her cup, giggled, and covered her mouth with her hand. 'I'm so sorry. I think I've had too much of the punch. Will you excuse me?'

Syuch stared after her as she walked away. What was sewing? And why would she laugh if someone hit her? Blast Harsci's stupid translation. She should have done it herself.

Still, Georgiana had paid her a compliment, and her cheeks warmed at the realisation. Were they always so encouraging of each other? If so, she might be able to handle having to stay a while longer.

She shook the thought from her head and continued the search for her wayward pilot.

A group of peoples had gathered around a large wooden contraption in one room, and she paused to see what they were doing. A male sat behind it and moved his arms, producing rhythmic sounds that were surprisingly pleasant. The rest of the peoples began to sing, their voices, while not all harmonic, collectively cheerful and enthusiastic.

Syuch found herself swaying to the tune and tapping her foot on the floor in time. She did not know the meaning of the words, but the music washed over her as she stood transfixed.

After a few renditions, she backed away lest she be called to join the ever-expanding group. Her feet took her back to the room with the food, her mouth watering at the collection on offer. Maybe she could try one or two dishes before they left.

She was approaching the table when the cloth draped over it twitched at one end. A moment later, a small arm appeared from under it and reached up to snatch one of the pieces of food on a plate near the edge. Syuch looked around, but no one else seemed to have noticed the incident.

Cautiously, she bent down and lifted the cloth. A small people—boy, Harsci had said—sat beneath the table with a selection of food in front of him. His cheeks bulged, and crumbs and a blob of something gooey and red decorated his front. He started when she cleared her throat, his eyes going wide.

'I din't mean no 'arm, miss, honest. I jus' wanted a few more o' the tarts.'

He held out a crumbly concave filled with the red goo, then shoved it in his mouth as if afraid she would take it from him if he showed it to her for too long.

'You like these?'

'Oh, yes,' he said around a mouthful. 'It's one o' the best bits o' Christmas.'

'Hmm. What else do you like?'

His face scrunched, then lit. 'Snow. We get to make snowmen and have snowball fights, and if you go out when it's snowing, you can try to catch them on your tongue.'

He liked the frozen water particles? How strange. She was about to ask what a snowmen was when his eyes rounded at something behind her. Footsteps approached.

She dropped the cloth and stood, spinning to find Harsci grinning at her like a fool. Huffing, she straightened her dress, avoiding his eyes.

'Making friends?' he said.

She glanced down at the cloth, then lifted her chin. 'I suppose peoples are interesting enough up close.'

His smile widened. 'Admit it. You're enjoying yourself.'

Her lips twitched, but she pressed them together. 'Fine. There are several aspects of their culture I would not mind experiencing again. This has been... agreeable.'

'I told you so.' He reached around her for one of the tarts and popped it into his mouth. 'Ready to go?'

She eyed him, wariness stirring. What was he up to now? 'Go where?'

'Home,' he said. 'Or at least, back to our original flight plan.'

Her heart lifted. 'You discovered how to fix the ship?'

He rubbed the back of his neck and glanced aside. 'Something like that. Do not be angry with me, but I wanted to visit the surface, so... I faked the malfunction.'

'You did what?' Her voice rang through the room, loud and sharp. She advanced on him, her finger poking into his chest. 'Anything could have happened, and you stranded us here on purpose.'

He looked around them, a nervous smile on his treacherous face. 'I read the initial reports about this planet,' he whispered. 'The lifeforms here pose no threat to us, and I thought you could do with a reminder that not all missions are filled with perils. You did just admit it has been pleasant.'

Her mouth opened, but no words came out. She closed it and narrowed her eyes. 'Fine. But that is the last time you ever lie to me or sabotage our ship.'

He held up a hand in a two-fingered salute. 'I promise.'

'Good.' She hmphed. 'Let us go then.'

He turned to leave, and she snatched one of the tarts from the plate behind her, then followed him out into the entrance hall.

They said a brief farewell to their host—apparently a requirement of leave-taking Harsci had uncovered—and trudged back to the domicile to gather their equipment.

Syuch could not wait to revert to her true form and divest herself of the uncomfortable layers of clothing female people were required to wear. She was also looking forward to a long soak in a cleansing unit.

It was only as they left the small structure that she noticed the bowl tucked under Harsci's arm.

'What are you doing with that?' she asked, pointing to it.

He glanced down at the Christmas pudding. 'I thought we could —'

'No. There is no way you are bringing anything from this planet onto our ship. The universe only knows what contagions it could contain.'

He took a half step away from her. 'But I wanted to try it.'

'Then you should have waited to confess your sabotage until tomorrow. It serves you right after putting me through all of this.' She held out a hand. 'Pass it over.'

His brows lowered, and his lips pinched, but he did as ordered. Glancing around, Syuch dumped the bowl on the nearest doorstep. That would do.

The corners of her lips twitched, and she straightened them before turning back to Harsci. He deserved the punishment, but she had kept the recipe, so they might be able to replicate something similar once they returned to orbit.

Their ship was undisturbed where they had left it, the prickly plant still hiding the visible section. Syuch glanced at the smooth metal hull. Was the glitch in the cloaking device another of Harsci's fabrications?

Regardless, they would be leaving soon, returning to the familiar, sterile, wonderful routine of space. A deep breath eased the tension in her muscles as she boarded the ship and morphed back into her true form for the final time.

She double-checked every calculation and control sequence Harsci entered before launch, making only one adjustment. Then they strapped in and powered up the engines.

The flight through the atmosphere was uneventful and silent, but Harsci peered at her from the corner of his eye once or twice. When they reached orbit, he swung his chair around to face her and said, 'The ship overcompensated for our heat signature during our departure.'

'Really?' She busied herself transferring the data from her palm pad to the ship's system.

'Yes. I noticed because I made that mistake on the way down and made sure to adjust the calculations this time. But it happened again anyway.'

'Mmm. Maybe we should run a diagnostic.'

He gasped, and she looked over at him.

'It was you,' he said. 'You did it. Admit it.'

She waved him off, but her body flickered orange, and she shifted in her seat. 'Fine. I did. Happy now?'

A mischievous blue twinkled in his face. 'Only if you tell me why.'

'One of the small peoples mentioned that they like the frozen water particles, and it made no difference to our safety parameters.'

'I knew it.' He turned back to his control panel, the blue replaced by a happy yellow swirling over his head. 'Do not worry. I will say nothing else. Today.'

Syuch glanced down at the yellow dancing under the surface of her own skin, then up at the sun appearing beyond the planet in their forward viewer. 'Merry Christmas, Harsci.'

He turned, his mouth opening, but she cut him off. 'Yes. I read the rest of the instructional document. Now, if you can take us to the Esarelian system without incident, I will program the replicator to make another Christmas pudding for us to try.'

He spun back around. 'Yes, sir.'

'And Harsci? Next time you want to go planet side, just ask.'

Puck Takes a Chance
by Ari Lewis *(fantasy)*

ying on his back near the fire in his guest room, Robin Goodfellow sulked. When his king had originally said that Robin would be going to a mortal home during a party, he had been rather pleased. Granted, the idea of being at the mortal's discretion as to when he could leave did not sit well, but it was his monarch's decree so he would obey. However, he had expected more fun during his stay. It was bad enough that he had been temporarily exiled by Oberon for 'taking his duties as jester too far,' as if any jest could be taken too far; but to be forced into a mortal home and have nothing work out his way was just too much for his faerie pride.

He threw the apple progressively higher as he thought of each failed escapade.

First, since preparations for a large party were underway, he had kept the cream from churning, hoping to watch the mortals run about worried. However, one of the staff had been sent with directions for greater delicacies that could only be made with unchurned cream. With his first attempt foiled, he had tried to make a fool of Lord Arthur Fentiman, the head of the household, by making an illusion of where the lord's chair was so that he fell backwards just as he was trying to make a decisive point. Robin had been sure that the fall would have made him lose all credibility in the argument he was waging, but Lord Fentiman's mother, the dowager countess Eleanor, had just turned it around and brought the family closer together. Finally, he had led the youngest Fentiman, George, out at night with promises of secret flowers and insects that he could add to his collection. Then he purposefully lost the boy and waited out of sight for the child to continue to lose himself in the darkness and despair. Unfortunately, someone found George and used the opportunity to reveal a new patch of sky to fascinate the budding naturalist.

However, creeping in between the fits of outrage and self-pity, Robin felt something else, something completely new. He caught the apple and twisted it in his hands as he followed this new feeling. With each failure, the mortals had been made happy, and in their happiness, they included him even more closely in their celebrations. A part of himself that he had hitherto tried to suppress and ignore called out for more: more time with the mortals and more participation in their doings. Perhaps they were more than just playthings. With a vigorous shake of his head, he shoved away these absurd notions. What sort of faerie wanted the company of mere mortals?

Suddenly, the perfect idea burst upon him—swap the family newborn for a faerie changeling. It was one of the oldest and greatest jests that could be played on a mortal. He could envision it now: Queen Titania's joy at a new addition to her nursery and the complete distress and disorder of the mortals as they had to deal with a troublesome faerie for the rest of their lives. A smile of mischievous delight spread across his face. He sat up and tossed the apple into the fire and watched as it popped and crackled into ash.

He waited until the Christmas Eve party was in full swing, but after the very youngest members had been put to bed. When everyone had gathered around the piano to sing carols, he slipped away quietly. Going up the stairs to the family bedrooms, he looked back down the hallway to make sure no one had noticed him. No one was there and he heard no sounds except for the echoes of carols from the company below. He opened the doors to one of the rooms and crept inside. Without bothering to light any of the lamps, he made his way towards the cradle that sat to one side of the large bed.

'What are you doing, Robin?'

The young faerie froze where he stood in the semi-darkness. Slowly, he turned his head to look back over his shoulder. Silhouetted in the doorway stood a female figure. Though only of average height, she seemed taller because of her rigid posture and aura of authority. He felt a familiar urge steal over him and just caught himself from falling to one knee in genuflection. With a toss of his head, he stood erect and turned fully around to face the lady.

'Just checking on the baby, Lady Eleanor,' he said, a disarming grin sliding into place. 'I thought I heard him crying and so came to make sure all was well with him.'

The dowager countess did not move from her place in the doorway. Silence fell and deepened, weighing upon the young faerie in an unfamiliar and most unpleasant way. He was not accustomed to being so blatantly ineffective against a mortal. Normally, she should have believed his effortless lie and gone away with thoughts of what a conscientious guest he must be for taking such notice and care on behalf of his hosts. Instead, she stood in his way, preventing him from either escaping into the hallway or resuming what he had come to do. His smile began to crack.

Shaking her head, Lady Eleanor Fentiman started walking into the room, her cane ringing on the panelled floor. Robin took an instinctive step back. She stopped with only the cradle of her great-grandson between herself and the young faerie. Leaning down, she tucked a blanket in more tightly around the little form. As she did so, Robin surreptitiously raised one hand and started to move his fingers.

'No, no, my sweet Puck—none of that now.'

Robin felt his arm and fingers freeze in place, the wisps of magic dissipating into the darkness. Eyes wide, he stared at the still, silhouetted figure in front of him. Lady Eleanor straightened and, withdrawing matches from an unseen pocket, lit the oil lamp that sat on the nearby mantle before throwing the match into the fireplace. Robin took a few respectful steps back, conveniently putting more space between himself and the dowager countess. The light from the lamp danced across her green eyes reminding Robin of the way cats' eyes reflect light at night.

'How...' he began.

'My dear boy, have you really given no thought as to why your esteemed lord would send you to this house of all places?' She tutted several times. 'Sometimes I do despair of young people, mortal and fair folk alike. None of you seems to be able to think properly. Besides, you think too much of yourself if you believe that you are the most remarkable thing in Whitstead. I know for certain of at least a dragon and a young woman from another time. There is also an elderly woman and a young relation that I am sure are special, though I have yet to discern how.'

As she spoke, she reached into the cradle and removed a swathed form to cradle it in her arms. Then she pulled back the blanket enough to reveal the face. To Robin's amazement, the face was made of porcelain.

'But that was a child! I know it was,' Robin protested.

'What you saw was a small glamour, nothing more. As I said before, if you had been thinking and paying more attention, you might have noticed. To be honest, I was hoping it would not have come to this.'

Trying to recover his lost poise and make his escape, the young faerie retreated to feigned innocence.

'What do you mean?'

The dowager countess fixed her eyes on him. He could feel her gaze penetrating into him, seeing into what would have been his soul if he had one. The intensity of it made him look away.

'Must we play these games?' she asked, all matronly tones now vanished.

The light from the lamp dimmed so that the shadows that had been held at bay now grew and deepened across the room. Something oppressive entered the air and held there, like a storm on the brink of breaking. Only the old lady's eyes seemed to shine brightly in the darkened room. A sinister smile crept across Robin's handsome face.

'But I am good at games,' he said, eyes returning to meet hers, 'and mortals are so much fun to play with.'

Lady Eleanor laid the doll back in the cradle, never letting her gaze leave that of the young faerie before her. Her hands free once more, she smiled back at Robin. He felt that smile laughing at him.

'Oh, Robin, you are not nearly as good at games as you think you are, but I daresay you are more insistent than most at playing them.'

Robin's smile shifted into a scowl.

'I am the BEST at games — you can ask my lord and he would say the same.'

Lady Eleanor shook her white head, her smile warming slightly.

'I don't believe he would.'

'What do you know of my lord?' Robin burst out. The shadows deepened behind him and rose like a wave threatening to crash and consume the old woman before him. 'What does any mortal know of him beyond their superstitions and stories? Your poets and playwrights create fanciful pictures of my lord and his domain but what does of any of you really know of us?'

'I met the lord Oberon many years ago, when I was but a child of twelve, and played a game with him.' she answered mildly.

Her simplicity and directness took Robin aback. The shadows receded to their normal bounds.

'Yes,' she continued, 'One of your fair folk had whisked away my eldest sister Diana as a dance partner, and being a nosy child, I had followed her one night when she was being escorted to one of your balls.'

Lady Eleanor smiled and shook her head at the remembrance.

'Everyone was so surprised to see a child in the middle of all their revelries. I surprised them further by breaking into the dancing and trying to forcibly drag my sister away. Of course, I did not get far. For my insolence I was brought before the lord Oberon, in whose honour the festivities were being held. He promised me my sister's freedom if I could give him something of equal value and beauty, something befitting a Diana.

'I agreed to his terms and asked for one of their empty bowls. Running to a nearby stream, I filled it with water and brought it back to the lord Oberon. I told him that he now held the whole heavens in his hand. He stared at the reflected sky and laughed. I cannot recall when I have been more frightened in my life than when I heard that laugh. When he looked at me, it felt as if something of great weight were trying to settle itself on my shoulders. Fortunately, childish defiance came to my aid and kept me from looking away. He set the bowl aside and beckoned me forward. With slow steps, I came. He smiled, and it was as if the sun itself had arisen during the night.

'Cleverly done, young one,' he said. 'You have earned your sister and my respect. Now go.' And so we left.'

During the whole of this story, Robin had stared open-mouthed in utter amazement. Even when Lady Eleanor finished, he continued to stare, unable to put his astonishment into words.

'Now, Puck,' she began again, 'you have a choice to make. I have done all I can to make you see the error of your ways as your lord had requested.'

'What do you mean?' Robin interrupted. 'What have you done at all?'

She shook her head ruefully. 'I told you before that you simply did not think properly. Did you really believe that all your lovely plans fell through by chance? No, no, sweet Puck; that was my doing.'

Robin finally fell to a sitting position on the bed.

Lady Eleanor continued, 'When the cream wouldn't churn, I suggested to Mrs. Ellsworth that she request the cook to prepare a special recipe that I had recently rediscovered that required the same amount of cream that had been unsuccessfully churned. When you played that trick on my son, I saw an opening in conversation to turn it around for the benefit of all. When you tried to worry poor George by getting him lost, I found him and spent a lovely hour with him explaining about the stars.'

She strode up to Robin so that they were face to face with only her stick between them.

'Now you have a choice to make. First, you may return to your lord with word that I have released you having done all I could. Second, you may remain with us in Whitstead until Epiphany. What say you?'

The young faerie looked down at the old woman, her thin hands laid one over the other on top of her stick. Her green eyes looked back into his expectantly. Closing his eyes, he thought back over his experience at Whitmore Park: of his attempts to spoil the food only to create opportunities for better cuisine; of how he had tried to make a fool of Lord Fentiman and only brought the family closer together; of how he had tried to get young George Fentiman lost and had only brought him new wonders. Through each of these diverted mishaps, he felt in his heart the unfamiliar and newly desired warmth of belonging. Perhaps there was something more to mortals than mere entertainment; perhaps they could fill what nothing in all Faerieland could, the desire for community.

Opening his eyes, Robin answered, 'I will gladly accept your invitation to stay, Lady Eleanor.'

A beaming smile burst across the old lady's face and into her eyes, and for a moment, Robin thought he saw her grow younger. Then it was gone, but the joy was still there. He felt it spread towards him, and for the first time in his long recollection, he let the feelings of a mortal touch his own. He smiled back. Lady Eleanor wrapped her arm in his.

'Shall we return to the festivities?' she asked.

Robin pulled the dowager countess's arm in closer and led the way back to the rest of the assembled company. They were all still around the piano, but the singing had transitioned to those songs popular amongst the company. He noticed a bowl of apples that sat on a table near where a group of young people were dancing to the music. The image of them sprawled on the ground due to apples underfoot flashed through Robin's mind. Looking down at the old woman on his arm, he let the thought pass. Instead, he picked up an apple that fallen of its own accord and replaced it in the bowl. Smiling to himself, he drew near to the piano and joined in with the singers.

Tangled Worlds
by Mary Schlegel (*fantasy*)

Alexandra wanted to cry at the emptiness yawning inside of her.

'Ladies and gentlemen,' Lord Fentiman called from the foot of the grand staircase to the crowd of guests, 'I present my daughter, Miss Caroline Fentiman, and her esteemed guest, Miss Alexandra Randolph.'

Thirty or forty faces young and old turned up towards them amid a sea of glimmers from candles, jewellery, and crystal glasses, and a scattering of applause drifted through the gathering as Alexandra followed her hostess' lead and began a slow, graceful descent down the stairs.

Caroline caught her hand and gave it a squeeze. 'They're all looking at *you*, darling!' she whispered, softly enough that the silken rustle of their dresses covered the sound. 'You look divine, and *all* the young gentlemen are taking notice!'

So they were.

'They needn't,' she whispered back.

'Oh, darling!' Caroline said with another squeeze of Alexandra's hand. 'I thought if anything would bring you back to Earth this party would, but you still seem as though you're... adrift. It's as though your mind is somewhere else entirely.'

Because it was.

'I did not realise you had noticed,' Alexandra said.

Caroline laughed good-humouredly. 'Noticed? How could I not? Ever since our visit to Cumbria you've done nothing but devour books of fairy tales and sing strange songs I've never heard before. Whatever has come over you?'

They reached the bottom of the stairs, and Alexandra realised that there was at least one reason to be thankful for all the attention from the other guests: she did not have to come up with an answer to give to Caroline right away.

But that was the only reason she could think of to be thankful for it.

She put on a smile, exchanged light embraces or hand clasps with the women, offered her hand to be kissed by the men, and exchanged insipid pleasantries. She tried to pay attention to the meaningless small talk surrounding her, but found too much of her attention occupied by once again fighting tears at the immense emptiness that threatened to consume her.

How had this once been her entire world? How had this farcical society, these vapid conversations, these masks of people, once been all she knew — and how had she been *happy* in it?

'Alexandra, dear, come with me,' Caroline said, leading her out of the crown at the foot of the stairs and towards one of the many refreshment tables situated around the hall.

Alexandra drew a breath, relieved at being out of the centre of so many people's attention.

'A glass of punch is just what you need to lift your spirits,' Caroline said, gesturing to the servant at the table to pour two glasses. 'They *can* be rather a lot, can't they?' She slid her eyes sideways, indicating the crowd they had just left.

The servant ladled punch into two glasses. Caroline took both from him, handed one to Alexandra, and led her by the arm again to the other side of the room.

'Carefully look over there,' she said, too quietly for anyone to overhear, and smiling to look as though they were casually discussing the weather or commenting on the party decorations. 'In the far corner, near the library.'

Alexandra discreetly looked where Caroline indicated and spotted a tall young man with a handsomely-cut face and chestnut-brown hair. He stood with two other men but was looking towards Alexandra and Caroline.

'That is young Lord Melville,' Caroline said. 'He just inherited his father's estate and fortune last year. He is *immensely* wealthy, and he has been staring at you for no less than five minutes!'

Oh, good heavens…

'I will wager,' Caroline continued in a conspiratorial tone, 'that if he asks you to dance, and you work your magic on him, you will have gotten a proposal out of him by Epiphany.'

'Caroline —'

'And he is wealthy enough, you may want to consider accepting this one.'

A bolt of grief, like lightning, shot through the empty void in Alexandra's heart. Last Christmas — indeed, until the aforementioned trip to Cumbria a few weeks ago — she would have jumped at the opportunity to 'work her magic' and see how quickly she could make a conquest of Lord Melville's heart, only to reject his proposal and leave him heartbroken, merely for the sport of it.

Alexandra couldn't even remember for certain now — how many bleeding hearts had she collected like trophies since being introduced to society three years ago? Now that she knew for herself the pain she had so heedlessly dealt, now that she saw how utterly stupid and cruel she had been, and since she could not undo what had been done, she wished she could simply vanish from society and never have to attend one of these silly functions ever again.

She took a sip of the punch. Its sweetness surprised her, and she realised that she had been expecting instead the heady flavour of mead. How long would things like that keep happening?

'I don't want a proposal from Lord Melville,' she said.

Caroline's eyes lit up like a bonfire. 'Oh? Then there is someone else? Alexandra, shame on you for not telling me sooner! Who is it? I must know!'

Oh dear. 'No, I—'

'Of *course*!' Caroline went on, grinning and giggling like a little girl. 'How absurd I didn't guess it sooner! So *that* is why you've been so out of sorts lately! Well then it must be someone we met on our holiday in Cumbria! Who is it? You *will* tell me!'

At once a sense of panic and a well of grief and longing opened in Alexandra's heart, and tears sprang into her eyes. What could she say? Caroline was so far from the truth of the matter and yet so very close that there seemed no way to answer. The truth would sound so much more false than any lie Alexandra could possibly concoct anyway, that neither would be believed... even if Alexandra had thought for a moment that her experience in Cumbria was something she could tell to Caroline.

'I... I don't... no, Caroline,' she said, 'there is no one.'

'I don't believe you. There must be someone, for you to be behaving this way.'

'No,' Alexandra repeated. Her heart ached to say it—ached at the fact that it was true. 'There is no one in Cumbria, no one...' She paused to draw a steadying breath. 'No one in the world. I give you my word.'

'Well, then what in the world is the matter with you?' Caroline burst out. 'You've never been like this before, Alexandra, and it's beginning to be very tiresome.'

Alexandra felt the situation slipping from her control. There were still tears in her eyes, but a newly familiar fire kindled in her chest at the same time, in resistance to Caroline's petty fixation—in resistance to all this soulless pomposity.

'I can't explain it, Caroline,' she said. 'Not in a way you would understand. I am not the person I was when we went to Cumbria.'

'That is apparent,' Caroline said. 'Very well.' She tossed her head and sniffed. 'I see you are quite determined to be gloomy and obstinate, but I shall not allow you to spoil my evening. If you wish to stay here in the corner and sulk, it is nothing to me. Good evening.'

And with that, Caroline sailed away on a swirl of her skirts, vanishing into the crowd of glittering guests.

Alexandra let out a sigh that felt oddly like relief and took another drink of punch. That had been unexpected, but perhaps it was for the best.

She shook her head at herself. She still didn't know what to call it—not that it mattered, since she had vowed never to tell anyone about it.

Anyway, all of the friends she had now were made prior to the trip to Cumbria with Caroline, when Alexandra had been a very different person—vain, proud, cruel, and empty headed. She had returned to her world, yes… but she could never go back to who she had been before. She would never be the person who had found comradeship in the company of people like Caroline.

Perhaps, then, it was time to be free of the friends she had had before. Alexandra let her eyes rove over the party—the smiling faces, the din of laughter and conversation—and wondered if there was anyone in the world she could be friends with now, if there was anyone who could ever even begin to understand.

'I beg your pardon?'

Alexandra turned to see a beautiful girl with dark hair, blue eyes, and a generous sprinkling of freckles across her nose and cheeks, smiling at her.

'Forgive me if I'm too forward,' the girl said, coming closer. 'We've not been properly introduced, but Lord Fentiman *did* announce you when you came in, and that's rather the same thing, isn't it?'

Alexandra couldn't help a smile. 'I think that's quite sufficient.'

A smile burst across the girl's face, and she laughed. 'I've always thought that waiting for an introduction was the silliest thing,' she said. 'I'm Felicity Kerrington. I saw you standing here all on your own and decided to see whether it was because you prefer to be alone, or if you would like some company.'

Alexandra toyed with a few possible answers before deciding that honesty was the best policy. 'I don't know what sort of company I would be,' she said. 'I find I'm not much in the mood for dancing or the other usual festivities.'

'Oh, splendid!' Felicity exclaimed. 'Would you like to steal away to some secluded corner and talk?' Before Alexandra could answer, Felicity moved even closer to whisper: 'If we felt especially dull, we could even smuggle ourselves into the library and read books to each other and not speak of the party at all!'

Again, Alexandra smiled, and this time a warm glow filled her chest to accompany it. Perhaps no one would ever understand what had happened to her… but perhaps here was someone who wouldn't demand to be told anyway, someone with whom she could at least share a pleasant evening.

'I would like that very much, Felicity.'

•◇•◇•◇•◇•◇•◇•◇•◇•

They had been cloistered in the library for hours when Felicity's head jerked up to the sound of the clock chiming the half hour. When it had finished, she turned to Alexandra with a conspiratorial smile on her face.

'It's ten thirty,' she said. 'There is going to be a midnight service at St. Nicholas Church in the village. Shall we send for a carriage and venture out for a daring midnight adventure?'

Alexandra hesitated. 'Oh, I… I don't know…'

'Well, I won't insist,' Felicity said, already rising from the corner settee they had stuffed themselves into, 'but I think I shall.'

She said nothing more but stood staring at Alexandra as if expecting an answer, either way.

Alexandra was about to decline the suggestion, but there was something so winsome in Felicity's face, and she *had* saved Alexandra from an awkward evening at the party. 'Why not?' she said, rising to follow Felicity's lead.

When they had sent for the carriage, retrieved their wraps, and made their way as unobtrusively as possible back through the crowd of party guests, they stepped outside to find it snowing—a snow that could not have begun more than an hour before, judging by the thickness on the ground.

'How *perfectly* lovely!' Felicity laughed. She rushed down the stairs and into the carriage, beaming.

But Alexandra stayed where she stood at the top of the stairs, eyes closed, breathless at the nearly imperceptibly soft brush of the snowflakes against her face. The breeze that set the snow dancing carried with it, somehow, the echo of wind through leafless forests ancient beyond memory, the sigh of the snow on the hills of the wild country…

'Are you coming?'

Alexandra opened her eyes at Felicity's call and tried to remember where she was, where they were going. Had—had that truly happened? Had Alexandra's imagination merely taken flight with her wishful thinking, or… was there truly something on the wind?

She hurried down the steps and into the carriage without a word, her thoughts consumed with this sudden confusion.

The entire drive into the village, she tried to hear the wind over the sound of the carriage, but to no avail. When they arrived at the church and disembarked, she tried to listen again in the open air, but there were too many parishioners crowding past them, too much chatter to hear anything, too many distractions to feel anything… if there was or had ever been anything to feel. By now Alexandra had all but convinced herself that it was nothing but her imagination.

She tried to pay attention during the service but found herself distracted by a continuous onslaught of seemingly insignificant details that somehow had the power to fling her back, if only for an instant at a time, into another existence.

The church glittered with scores, perhaps even hundreds of candles, and their glow on the church walls recalled the dancing light of bonfires on standing stones. The reverend's voice speaking the service could have been the voice of a bard reciting stories older than anyone remembered. The sacred anticipation on the faces of the people all around her could have been…

Wait.

No, that was real—the solemn expectance Alexandra saw in everyone's eyes as they listened to the reverend speak was truly there, not just reminiscent of it. She had seen it before—knew it well, knew the internal hush that accompanied it, knew the awe it spoke of.

What was it doing here? What was the reverend saying?

Alexandra turned her attention to the reverend, a small, ruddy figure in the flickering candlelight, and focused on his words for the first time.

'Emmanuel—God with us,' he was saying.

God with us...

The reverend continued: 'The book of John tells us that "The Word became flesh and dwelt among us..."'

Alexandra's eyes widened as it suddenly occurred to her that she was not the only one to have entered another world. The Son of God had done that when He was born as a man. And, just as Alexandra had come back to her own world, He had returned to Heaven.

Had He felt this way too? This feeling of being so out-of-place? Of no longer truly being of one place or the other, but somehow forever tangled in between?

She scarcely noticed the rest of the reverend's message, but when every voice suddenly joined in singing God Rest Ye Merry Gentlemen, Alexandra's throat caught and tears turned the points of candlelight into wide, quivering pools of gold in her vision. This—the joining together of everyone to share in song—this was real too. Another piece of the Otherworld that translated to this world, and in doing so carried her back.

Alexandra forced a swallow past the knot in her throat and took several breaths to relax her voice enough to join the singing. How she had missed this, the sharing in song of an ancient story everyone knew but still held in awe!

As her voice melted into the others, Alexandra closed her eyes and let everything else vanish. When the song ended, she hesitated a moment before opening her eyes again, relishing the feeling that she could have opened her eyes to find herself in either world and that the Other was just as likely as this one.

When she did open her eyes, she stood staring into the rafters of the church, feeling more alive than she had felt in weeks—'since the trip to Cumbria,' as Caroline had repeatedly phrased it. She did not fully understand what had happened, or how, or why, but for those few moments she had ceased to feel the emptiness, the ache, the longing of being severed from the world she had come to love as her own. For those moments, the empty lifelessness she had come to identify with this world had flushed with colour and meaning, and the shallow had suddenly run deep, from a surface world of insipid modern society into something ancient and profound.

She pulled her gaze down and looked around to see Felicity standing a few feet away, only glancing at her intermittently. The parishioners were quickly funnelling out the door to return to their homes, and the nave was emptying.

'I'm sorry,' Alexandra said, moving towards Felicity, 'I didn't mean to keep you waiting.'

'No need to apologize,' Felicity said with a smile. 'I could see that you were very moved and didn't want to interrupt.'

Alexandra suddenly felt rather shy at having been so transparent. It was an unfamiliar feeling. 'Thank you.'

Felicity reached for her hand and gave it a squeeze. 'Shall we return to the party — truants that we are?'

Alexandra smiled, and followed Felicity outside.

As they walked to the carriage, Alexandra noticed a lingering scent of smoke wafting among the snowflakes. There was a wildness to it — a wildness that once again served, for a fleeting moment, as a flash of connection, drawing her back to where she had come from, to where her heart remained.

They climbed into the carriage, and the footman closed the door. Alexandra felt a little pang of regret as he did, as it shut out the breeze and the snow and the smoke.

'I am so glad you came with me to the service,' Felicity said as they settled into their seats and the carriage began to move. 'You're an absolute *dear* for spending the evening with me the way you have. I'm afraid I would have had a terribly dull time without you.'

Alexandra smiled. 'And I am quite certain I would not have enjoyed myself at all, had you not sought me out. So I thank you.'

Felicity giggled and leaned in close to whisper: 'What a matched pair of rebellious girls we are! Hiding away for the entire party, and then sneaking off in the dead of night!'

Alexandra could laugh at that too. 'Indeed, we are.'

Felicity straightened, folded her hands in her lap, and looked Alexandra in the eye. 'I like you, Alexandra Randolph. I don't know what it is, but there is something very special about you that I quite enjoy. There is something... magical about you. As if...' She searched for words. '...as if you come from one of the fairy tales you so love to read. And I quite like the idea of having a friend who's come out of a fairy-tale.'

Alexandra had no words to put to the feeling that rose in her chest at that. She cast about for something to say, some reply that she could give, but at that moment a gust of wind rushed over the carriage, audible even through the closed door and the covered windows.

And in the wind... Alexandra could not describe it as anything other than a call. A song, a voice... and it came from the Otherworld. There was no question about it; somehow, she was absolutely certain. It had come on the wind, but the source was out there—out on the heath or the hills above the village, somewhere very close by. She could feel it, and it was strong.

Without pausing to think about what she was doing, she threw up the cover over the nearest window and banged her fist on the side of the carriage.

The driver pulled the horses to a stop, and the footman jumped from his perch and came to the side of the carriage to look in the window Alexandra had opened.

'Is anything the matter, miss?' he asked.

'I want to get out,' Alexandra said. 'I want to walk back to the manor from here.'

The footman's eyebrows went up and he blinked in surprise. 'Miss Randolph—Whitmore Park is nearly two miles away, and it is snowing!'

'I know,' Alexandra replied, already gathering her skirts to climb down. 'I'll be all right.'

'Alexandra!' Felicity said. 'You'll catch your death of cold!'

Alexandra pushed open the carriage door and held out her hand for the footman's assistance, which he provided rather confusedly. She stepped down into the shallow snow, thankful she had changed from her dancing shoes into warm boots before leaving the manor to come to the village and turned to look back at Felicity.

'I won't,' she said. She looked up at the sky, where the clouds were segmenting and scattering, revealing a velvety-dark-blue sky and a brilliant white moon. She pointed up at it, smiling. 'See there? The snow is stopping, and it's clearing off.'

Felicity hesitated, thinking, then took a decisive breath. 'Well, then I suppose I will come with you!'

Alexandra smiled. 'Thank you, Felicity. You are a dear. But I would like to be alone for a while. Go back to the manor where it's warm.' She backed away from the carriage, so that it could continue without her.

'We can—drive along beside you, if you like,' the footman offered, clearly perplexed by the situation he had been placed in.

'Thank you. No.' Alexandra gestured up the hill, where the lights of Whitmore Park were just visible in the snowy night. 'I can see the lights of the house. I won't get lost.'

The footman looked up the hill as if to confirm that it was true, then looked back at her. 'Very well then, Miss Randolph… if you are quite determined.'

'I am.'

She waited while he closed the carriage door and returned, looking reluctant, to his place on the carriage.

Inside the carriage, Felicity leaned forward to peer out the still-open window, her eyes slightly narrowed.

'You *are* from a fairy tale, aren't you?' she asked. 'I knew it.' She sighed. 'Well, in that case, you'll likely vanish or return to your true form at dawn. But if you do return…' She stuck her open hand out the window. '…will you write to me?'

Alexandra clasped her hand, smiling. 'Of course I will, Felicity. Thank you for everything.'

The driver called to the horses, and the carriage rolled away. Felicity stayed at the open window, watching, and just before the carriage rounded a bend in the road and took her out of sight, Alexandra waved goodbye.

As if it knew that she was now alone, the wind whistled by her again, laden with the scents of snow and fir and earth... and the wild. The Other.

Out on the heath—something was there. Something that bore the scent, the sound, the soul of the Otherworld.

Alexandra glanced up the hill again at the lights of the manor. She would return to it—she had told the truth about that—but she hadn't said she would go by the road. She could cut across the heath, perhaps not as easily, but more directly, and satisfy her curiosity on the way.

She left the road and struck out, her coat wrapped tightly around herself but hardly feeling the cold at all. The ground was frozen, sparing her a slog through mud, but making every clump of earth as hazardous as a stone for tripping or turning an ankle. She didn't know where she was going, exactly, or even how far of a walk it would be—or really, if there was even anything out there to reach—but she trekked on, guided only by the pull in her spirit.

Breadcrumbs of sensation led the way—the rhythm of dancing, an echo of music through the winter-dead heather, a remnant of bonfire smoke.

She continued as the ground rose towards a patch of forest. The trees were young, but the song whistling through their bare branches was ancient and familiar. And the music grew louder, clearer, with every step. Perhaps it was there, concealed by the trees, that Alexandra would find what she—

'Oof!'

She came to rest with her hands and arms in the heather and her legs and posterior ignominiously draped over a knee-high rock.

She extricated herself and got to her feet, scolding herself for not watching where she was going. The full moon's light on the snow made the stone very plain to see, had she been looking. She turned to continue towards the trees but stopped short only a few steps further on.

Another stone stood in front of her, this one nearly to her waist. With her gloved hand she brushed the snow from the top of it, revealing a pocked, weather-eaten surface. The wind stirred again, and this time the music was so clear it seemed as though she must be hearing it with her ears rather than just in her spirit.

She turned, looking all around her, and now that she was looking for them, she could see them all—a dozen or more, some obscured by heather and gorse, some fallen down to lay horizontally, but most of them still upright.

A stone circle.

With haste made difficult by the sudden shaking of her hands, Alexandra pulled off her right glove. Then she reached slowly, almost fearfully, to touch the nearest of the stones.

The remnants of music and bonfires and stories came again, but no stronger than they had been when she had entered the ring of stones. This circle was not a gate—if it had been at one time, it had weakened beyond usefulness.

She felt a pang of disappointment, which was silly of her, really. Even if it had been a gate, she could never again cross into the Otherworld. But somehow it seemed that just knowing she was outside a gate, knowing she was so near, would have been a comfort.

And yet... hadn't there been many things throughout the evening that had comforted her with the nearness they seemed to imply? The scent of smoke on the breeze, the candlelight in the church, the voices joined in song, the reverend's message...

God with us.

Again, Alexandra turned to look around the stone circle, her eyes now wide with new and sudden understanding.

The Son of God had come to Earth and had gone again—but did He not also remain in the hearts of His followers? Alexandra had returned here to her own world, but did the Otherworld not still dwell in her heart?

It all made sense now: the worlds themselves were tangled.

The stone circle did not open into the Otherworld... but it touched it. Like snowflakes brushing skin, the singing, the candlelight, the smoke, everything that had called to her so deeply since leaving the manor, were all tiny kisses of world against world.

Heaven, Earth, the Otherworld—they were inextricably entwined. Parallel, invisible to each other, but tightly tangled and touching in many places. Alexandra could never go back to the Otherworld, but she could touch it and be near to it, in places like this.

A strange and sudden sense of satisfaction filled her at the thought, and the pull she had felt so strongly before seemed to fade—as though this place had shown her what it wanted her to see, and then released her. She laid her bare hand once more on the nearest stone of the circle, smiling fondly at it. Then she pulled her glove back on, drew and released a deep breath that swirled, shimmering silver, beneath the full moon, and turned her face to the lights of Whitmore Park, gleaming on the hill above her.

•◇•◇•◇•◇•◇•◇•◇•◇•

The fire in the library fireplace was dying, but Alexandra could still feel its warmth as she sat curled on the settee, her boots drying on the hearth before her, and her hands wrapped around a cup of hot mulled wine.

The party had long since ended, and the family and guests had all departed or gone to bed. The house was quiet—so quiet that Alexandra could hear the singing of the wind in the forest through the library window.

She thought back over the evening, from the moment Lord Fentiman had introduced her, until now. She could never return to the Otherworld… but the night's events had made it clear that she did not entirely belong in this one anymore.

Where did that leave her? She was forever tangled somewhere in between, no longer fully in either one. She was like the stone circle out on the heath; not completely in either world… but… touching both?

Alexandra suddenly sat up straighter, staring into the fire as though she had spied the answer in the shrinking flames and glowing coals.

She lived tangled between two worlds now, just as the stone circle was between two worlds. Just as the smoke on the breeze and the song in the church and the wind on the heath were between the worlds. And, she realised, there must be countless other places where the worlds touched, scattered everywhere.

She smiled as clarity finally came to her. She knew, now, what she would do with herself. Tomorrow morning, she would bid farewell to her hosts, and to her new friend, Felicity. And then, fulfilling Felicity's prophecy, she would disappear. From now on she would travel the world seeking the smoke and the heath and the song and the fire—any and every place where two disparate worlds came together.

Those places were home now, and they were where she belonged—between the tangled worlds.

The Snowmen and the Treasure Hunt
by Abigail Falanga (*fantasy/adventure*)

Windows got ever so grimy in the winter. This room wasn't bad, though—hadn't had fires in a week, maybe, so there was little soot. It was a big house, Mr. Pembroke's, and with nobody but him and the sickly niece, many of the rooms were disused—though that meant more cleaning, with more family expected.

But clean it, tip-to-top!

Be a good maid, Miss Rossiter always said, and you'll always have work. That's how to keep food in your mouth. How to stay respectable.

Nell couldn't resist looking over her shoulder at where a new book lay on a table. It looked far more interesting than most of those Mr. Pembroke got.

The chair teetered.

'Vinegar-water over the floor…' she whispered to her reflection. 'Careful, now, else no reading.'

She reached into the highest corner, gave it a final polish, then climbed down.

Nell dashed across into the kitchen, threw the newspaper into the fire, slopped the bucket into the corner, then darted back.

Then, wiping her hands on the cleanest corner of her apron, she took the book and curled up in a dark corner of the floor, where light from the hall just touched the pages.

•◇•◇•◇•◇•◇•◇•◇•

'Careful, Charlie!'

The noise jolted Nell from a dream.

The curtains were drawn. Lamps shone on the table and mantle. A fire crackled, sending warmth and comfort into every inch of the room, which seemed even fuller of people than the Charitable School:

Five children of various ages, fine clothes bright and colourful, played with toys beyond interesting. A nursemaid, about sixteen (only a few years older than Nell, though far prettier, perter, plumper) reprimanded a boy of about ten years, with a metal toy horse that had nearly crushed a small girl's set of wooden animals.

She seized the boy's jacket by the shoulder and gave him a shake. 'Can't you listen and behave?'

'Sorry, Gladys.' The boy looked a little ashamed of himself.

'I *don't* know what to do with you all!' Gladys clutched her hair. 'Your grandfather said he left a book in here as a gift, but I can't find it no matter how I look.'

Nell's finger ached as she squeezed the book around it.

'Couldn't you tell a story, Gladys?' The small girl sniffled, hugging her wooden animals. 'A Christmas story?'

The other children stilled.

'I don't know any! We could sing carols or —'

'You know lots of Christmas stories, Gladys. Tell us one!' Charlie insisted, impudent as a demon. 'One about *here*, this house. That one your dad used to tell you that was so scary you couldn't sleep a wink afterwards!'

'*That* was nothing but a syllabub truth.' But Gladys' eyes grew a little wider.

'Tell us!' chimed all the children, dragging at her hands until they clustered near the bright fire.

'Very well!' the nursemaid gasped a little laugh. 'But shut the door first; there's a draught.'

Charlie broke away, slammed the door, and was back before the others settled.

Botheration! With the door open, Nell at least had a *chance* of escape! Now what was she to do?

'A *very* long time ago!' Gladys was saying. 'Back when the roads were all mud, and there were highway robbers! My story has to do with the most famous one around these parts: the daring Tobey Fitzgerald himself.'

'Oooh!' breathed the children.

Fitzgerald?

Nell nearly dropped the book and forgot escape.

'Bold as brass, Tobey was,' Gladys continued. 'Used to hold up every likely-looking coach on the High Road. Never let the magistrates or the farmers with their big blunderbusses scare him. One evening near Christmastide, with the snow thick on the ground and darkness falling —'

'Just like tonight!' interrupted the little girl.

'Much foggier. Proper, thick fog up from the river. The torches barely lit it and lanterns were nothing! Nobody was out in it but the snowmen — and Tobey Fitzgerald. *He* was mounted on his big grey horse, wearing a big grey cloak, and looked as much like the fog as something that wasn't fog *could*. That night, he was going to —' there was a thrill in her voice, ' — *this* house!'

The children all gasped and leaned in closer.

'That's right,' Gladys nodded. 'Your grandfather's great-great-grandfather had taken a treasure out of the hills, maybe even from...'

Nell couldn't make out what she said, but an instant later —

'From the *fairies*?' scoffed one of the older girls. 'There's no such thing!'

'Oh, yes, there is, Miss Janet, and don't you forget it.' The nurse gasped, cheeks going pale. 'They're rare in the cities. But around here, forget them if you dare! Now, whether it was the fairies' treasure or not, he had no more right to it than anyone else. So, Tobey Fitzgerald thought to take it for himself.

'He crept along the High Street, past all the snowmen down, which looked like real men in the fog. It startled him, so out came his pistols! But just in time, he saw their branch-arms wave in the wind (or so he thought) and realised what they were. "Thank ye kindly, wind," said he. "I near shot and gave myself away, if 't'weren't for your blowing." And—what do you think? The snowmen bowed in return! For they were fairies too, and were saying (without words, you understand) "Thank you, for not shooting us."'

'Snowmen don't bow,' laughed one of the boys. 'Their tops would fall off!'

'Go on, Gladys,' Charlie urged.

'Well,' she obliged. 'Up Tobey crept, right to the gates and over he went, and tiptoed through the fog up to the house.

'*But* something *else* was in the fog! Something that watched as he went, and slunk behind him, its long claws making skritch-scratches in the snow. *Skrritch-crunch…* Tobey Fitzgerald thought it was nothing but the ice. Up he went, right to the front door, thinking everyone would be inside making merry for Christmas. And he was right. All he had to do was force the lock with his big old knife—*crack!*—then slip in. And there it was! The treasure.'

'Right there in the open?' Janet asked sceptically.

'Of course not, silly! Locked up in an old sea chest. But cunning Tobey had it open in the bat of a cat's eyes. And there inside—what do you think?'

'Doubloons!' Charlie shouted.

'No,' laughed the maid. 'But gold in plenty, glistering and shining jewels— everything! Tobey Fitzgerald wrapped it up in sealskin and put it into the pockets of his greatcoat and made his escape.'

Escape…

The word reminded Nell how late it was. Oh, she would get it from Miss Rossiter if she caught her coming back.

She laid the book on the floor and rose softly, creeping along the shadows by the wall toward the door, listening as the nurse went on:

'Out Tobey went, back into the fog. But *something* watched him come out, smelled the treasure on him, and followed him, licking its teeth. Still, Tobey Fitzgerald didn't know it was there. He went down the drive softly as he could in the snow without a fear of *it*.'

'What was it?' breathed the little girl, eyes reflecting the firelight clear over to where Nell was against the opposite wall.

'I'll tell you now.' Gladys glanced down at her, and at Janet, and at the closed door.

Nell hadn't made it that far yet, thank goodness.

'It was a monster—the guardian of the treasure! It had followed old Sir Reginald Pembroke and was waiting its moment. Just as Tobey Fitzgerald reached the gate—it lunged at him and caught at the heel of his boot! He let out a yell and kicked, knocking the monster backward. Then he jumped over the fence and galloped off! But...' She leaned forward. 'The monster shot over the gate and was after him in a flash.

'Through the streets he galloped, never mind the noise; for he knew every step of the way. The *thing* streaked after him, screeching, screaming, hunting. But Tobey Fitzgerald was too fast for it and reached the heath. He had his own secret paths, and the monster *nearly* missed him.'

Nell reached the door and turned the handle but hesitated, caught in the story.

'Well!' Gladys continued. 'Tobey Fitzgerald thought he'd lost the monster, for he heard nothing of it through the fog. So, on he rode to his secret hiding place, and there put the treasure and locked it up.'

Nell eased the door open.

'He started back, thinking himself safe... When out leapt the monster! And that,' Gladys finished, voice shuddering, 'was the *end* of Tobey Fitzgerald.'

The children *oohed*.

'He was killed?' Charlie said.

Gladys nodded. 'They found him, frozen to the ground in the heath, weeks later.'

'What about the treasure?' Janet demanded.

'Lost forever!'

'What about the monster?'

'They say it roamed back and forth on the heath, seeking and shrieking. Until...'

'Until what, Gladys?'

'Well,' she shrugged. '*Some* say that it returned to linger near Sir Reginald Pembroke, as the one who'd last had the treasure. Or perhaps it still roams out on the heath, hunting after its lost treasure.'

The heath was just beyond the garden wall at the Charitable School. Nell had heard strange sounds from out that way, which Miss Rossiter said were wild birds. But what if...?

Charlie's eyes were full on her.

She froze.

He opened his mouth slowly.

Her mind went blank.

'But Gladys...' Charlie said. '*You* think it came back here?'

'Who knows? Perhaps it's just a story.'

Nell slipped out.

The house was lighter than she had ever seen it; candles stood on every table and sputtered in sconces. The door into the drawing room stood open and from within, querulous voices were raised.

'…might have made more of an effort to pay a visit, Jane…'

'…such danger to my health and the children…'

'But you have the Pet to look after you, dear.' That was Mr. Pembroke, none too pleased.

'…Impossible to get Henry to leave the 'Change, Father, with his business the way it is.'

'Couldn't someone ring for tea? This pot isn't *quite* hot…'

Mr. Pembroke must have his son and daughter up from London for the season, and their children.

Nell ran for the kitchen while she had a chance.

Mrs. Ellis was busy and red-faced, preparing dinner with the help of a cook Nell didn't recognise. Neither paid her any heed as she dashed out the scullery door into darkness and snow.

Cold struck her harder than usual. The path was icy, and she skittered along, feeling every slick and crackle through her shoes.

'Silly chit,' she mimicked Miss Rossiter's voice. 'Don't grow accustomed to warm fires, when you've a little blanket and no supper to look forward to.'

She ran through the large garden, around the house and to the drive. It was lit with torches down to the open gate.

Something loomed out of the darkness right in front of her.

Nell thought of the monster and nearly screamed.

But it was only Charlie, who grinned and cocked his head at her. 'Sorry I scared you,' he said. 'I thought you were a ghost, back there inside.'

'I wasn't supposed to be there,' she confessed in a sputter. 'Don't tell, sir—please don't.'

'Sir?' he repeated and laughed outright. 'Why do you call me 'sir?' Are you a servant or something?'

'Yes, of course, Master Charlie. That's why I was there inside. I was cleaning out that room and fell asleep.'

'You don't look like a maid.'

Nell glanced down at the thick brown stuff dress and the thin grey shawl she had over it. 'Miss Rossiter makes sure that we are all clean and presentable.'

'Who is Miss Rossiter?'

'She runs the Charitable School. And I'm late getting back, sir, if you will excuse me.'

'I'll come with you!' Charlie announced, swinging toward the gate.

Nell nearly had to run to keep up with the boy. 'If you're coming, shouldn't you have your coat on, Master Charlie?'

'You have less on than I do,' he pointed out. 'What's your name?'

'Nell Fitzgerald, sir.'

'Fitzgerald? Like the highwayman Gladys was telling us about?'

'Yes.' Nell flushed. 'He was my great-great-great-grandfather.'

Charlie stopped right in front of her, mouth open. 'That's splendid! I would much rather have a highwayman ancestor than one who stole from the fairies.'

'Not much good when he's been dead for hundreds of years and left nothing to show for it,' she retorted.

'Nothing?' He sounded disappointed and sighed before he turned to tramp on ahead of her. 'Guess that's why you have to be a maid.'

It rankled something deep in Nell, until at last she pulled at the frayed cord that hung about her neck. 'There was *this*. An heirloom, mama called it—she said it was a key, though I've never seen another key like it. She said Tobey Fitzgerald left nothing to his son but ten pounds and this key, and the ten pounds was quickly spent.'

'It's rusty and grimy.' Charlie poked it. 'D'you s'pose it's the key to that secret hiding place, where he put the fairy treasure?'

'Mayhap…' The idea sparked and fluttered a moment before Nell rammed it down. 'Don't matter, anyhow. None knows where that treasure was hid, so what good'd a key to open it be?'

'Won't know 'til we look.'

'Can't. Have to be at the School when I'm not out on a job.'

'Still…' Charlie shrugged. 'Bet I could get that key clean. Could you let me try? Please, Nell?'

She hesitated, stopped in front of the tall gate at the end of the village. 'Daresay I'll be back at Mr. Pembroke's house soon enough. Goodnight.'

'This it? Looks grim.' He looked up at the house and made a not-very-gentlemanlike grimace immediately followed by a gentlemanly question: 'May I call?'

'No,' said Nell, and went inside.

•◇•◇•◇•◇•◇•◇•◇•

Gladys' story kept swimming in her head. The monster, the fairy treasure, the snowmen bowing, the fog, the highwayman…

It was nothing special to have a highwayman ancestor, Mama had said…

Very late, Nell rose and passed by the window. Outside, starlight sparkled on the three lumpy snowmen they had made yesterday.

Were they…?

She pressed her nose against the icy glass.

155

The snowmen were sliding closer to each other, then back, bowing and sweeping their branch-arms through the snow.

She watched until her eyes strained from watching.

•◇•◇•◇•◇•◇•◇•◇•◇•

Next morning, she couldn't be sure it hadn't been a dream.

Nevertheless, after lessons, as Nell was passing down the path on her way to the church where she was to clean the choirboys' room, she stopped by one of the snowmen and dropped the tiniest of curtseys. 'Good morning, Mr. Snowman. Are you a fairy creature, too?'

If Miss Rossiter heard her, she'd give extra lessons to drive the nonsense out!

The choirboys' room was filthy as ever. She never could tell how boys always managed to make such a mess what with rubbish and floors to scrub...

The third trip to slosh a muddy bucket out the door and fetch a clean one from the pump, she passed the crypt for William and Felicity Fitzgerald. That was Tobey's father and mother — wealthy and respectable, at least enough to afford a place in the church and a carved relief to mark it.

Nell stopped to look at it, examining the names and dates and the carved flowers. Above the names, though not too large, was a symbol she didn't recognise; something like a crown set in a circle of twined antlers.

Perhaps the vicar Mr. Hollybrook would know what it was. She could hear him talking somewhere near.

No! Here came the vicar, but with him came the querulous lady of last night, wrapped up in furs and supported between a gentleman and a lady.

Nell hurried on. Questions could wait.

•◇•◇•◇•◇•◇•◇•◇•◇•

The very next day, Miss Rossiter received a request for extra help at the Pembroke house.

'Nancy is engaged, and Ida has a fever...' she muttered, tutting over the message, then lifted her cold eyes to Nell, who pretended to have been doing her sums rather than listening. 'Nell, come forward.'

So, off Nell went at an eager run, pausing only to curtsey to the snowman, who now sported a tattered scarf thrown away by a choir boy.

It was a fine day, and all five of the children were out in the yard of the Pembroke house amidst a full snowball war. Charlie gave a whoop when he saw her and abandoned his side to catch up with her by the scullery door.

'Can't stop, Charlie,' she panted. 'But I'll let you clean the key if you want.'

Charlie whooped again and took it.

Cleaning hearths, polishing the railings, sweeping out the side corridors, scrubbing the pots—Nell kept busy the whole morning and into the afternoon. Then, Mr. Ellis gave her the broom and the bucket and sent her to clean the front step. Again.

'But it was cleaned this morning, Mr. Ellis,' she objected, confused.

The broom-handle met the side of her head. 'Don't talk back, chit. Steps're muddy with all this tramping about, and Mr. Rattinger expected any minute.'

So, out she went, rubbing at her stinging head with her shoulder.

Muddy the steps were. The children were nowhere in sight, but they had done their play well. She scrubbed and swept, as the clouds thickened and sent a few snowflakes down.

Nell was nearly finished when the gates creaked open and a carriage lumbered down the drive. She squeaked and gathered the tools before Mr. Ellis discovered her still at it. Down she jumped and concealed herself and everything behind the nearest boxwood.

The carriage, loaded with luggage up top and a large, enclosed cage at the back, pulled to a stop just as the door was opened by Mr. Ellis, looking far more correct and butler-like than usual.

The man she'd seen earlier at the church came out a moment later, with a smile that wasn't quite happy, and called, 'Here at last, Henry? Good to see you could make the journey after all.'

'...these incessant letters!' a voice grumbled from within the carriage, as the coachman opened the door and adjusted the steps. A tall man stepped out. 'There lacks three days till Christmas—why I must be bothered to leave business and come early baffles me.'

'Jane could not rest without you—or her pet.' The other man eyed the cage, which shook and rattled as the footman struggled to unhook it. 'A party at Whitmore Park may bring her here, but home with Father would not be complete without the pet.'

'And well I know it.' The newcomer glowered at the carriage, and then shouted, 'Have a care, man!'

Too late. The cage jostled and broke free, sending the coachman tumbling back in the snow.

It broke open and out streaked a *thing*. Huge, long, dark, slavering.

At first Nell thought it was a large dog or wolf. But it was big as a tiger and crouched low to the ground, with a tail large as its body and claws instead of paws. Its round head was full of teeth, flashing and dripping in the steam from its mouth as it snapped and then screeched.

The noise sent terror shooting through her.

It snarled and snapped at the three men and, before the two gentlemen could seize it, streaked across the snowy yard, up a tree, and disappeared over the wall.

The new gentleman swore, sounding annoyed. 'Now we'll have to catch the thing! Stop wallowing in the snow, man, and gather whoever's at hand to search.'

They went inside, leaving Mr. Ellis to finish with the luggage, as the coachman, holding his bleeding hand, ran around the house.

'D'you s'pose *that* was the monster that guarded the fairy treasure?'

Nell stifled a scream and spun around, to find Charlie behind her, eyes and mouth round.

'What was it?' she asked. 'Why would it be *the* monster?'

'It's Aunt Jane's pet. She took it to London with her because she was fond of it, and it stays in the kennels at their house. But it's been in the family for years and years.'

'It's *horrible!*'

Charlie nodded, consideringly. 'Ordinarily, it's quiet as quiet can be—hasn't killed anyone since Grandfather was a boy.'

'Why would you keep something like that?'

'It's just always been there. I don't know that we could get rid of it even if we tried! That's why I think it might be *the* monster from Gladys' story; 'cuz she *was* scared to tell about it—like she was telling the truth.'

Nell admitted this, but— 'I must get inside, before Mrs. Ellis thinks to look for me.'

'I cleaned your key!' Charlie shoved something still warm and grimy into her hand. 'And I found a new cord for it.'

'Thanks, Master Charlie!' She looked at it before slipping it round her neck. It shone, clean and coppery, and she could make out the design. 'This mark... It's a symbol, ain't it? I've seen it before, in the church.'

'*I've* never seen it before.' He peered at it close. 'What's it mean?'

'Dunno! Maybe something...' She stopped herself before she said 'important,' and ran off.

It didn't do to hope like that.

•◇•◇•◇•◇•◇•◇•◇•◇•◇•

Nell made it back to the Charitable School just as the sun was setting. Somehow, she thought of fairies the whole trip, imagining them in every sunbeam and swirl of mist.

Soft sobs coming from just inside the garden bumped her back to earth.

It was Lucy, new to the Charitable School, curled up under a bush and in danger of getting covered in snow if she moved much.

Nell crouched beside her. 'What's wrong, Lucy?'

The mite shook her head, but then reluctantly showed her wrist. It was red from twisting. 'Some boys were mean.' She nodded beyond the gate. Village boys, then. 'Uncle Mattie said cool it in the snow.'

'Well, you'll freeze to death out here,' Nell said crisply.

She jumped up and ran to the snowman, whispering, 'She's more need of it than you' as she unbound the scarf from round his neck. Shaking it out, she wrapped it round the little girl, then scooped her up to carry inside.

'But Miss Rossiter —'

'Tell her a kind gentleman gave it you. It's true enough!' She smiled to the snowman.

•◇•◇•◇•◇•◇•◇•◇•◇•◇•

On Christmas Eve, Nell went to help Mr. Needsworth's housekeeper decorating his house.

It was a pleasanter job than most, since Mr. Needsworth was kind and made little mess, living all by himself. Besides, he left out books and didn't mind that she looked at them now and again.

Nell glanced at a dull-looking tome open on his reading table, between pinning bits of holly over the picture frames, and saw little more than long dry words. She turned a page — and gasped at what she saw.

Among illustrations of various symbols was the crown in the antler circle she'd seen twice before.

Nell stared at it, then ran over the mark with the tip of her finger.

'What captures your interest so thoroughly, Nell?' Mr. Needsworth came in softly and stood beside her. 'Interested in old symbols of a sudden?'

'This one!' She nodded up at him. 'What's it mean, sir? I've seen it in the church and — and somewhere else.'

'Oh! That one.' He smiled rather sadly. 'It's very old. Long ago, it marked sanctuaries during dangerous times, and then clean areas during the Plague. In fact,' he added with a twinkle in his eye, 'it indicated safe places to observe the Christmas Feast, back when old Cromwell outlawed it in 1652.'

'But why?'

'D'ye see?' Mr. Needsworth pointed. 'It's holly in a wreath of mistletoe. There used to be a great deal of holly on the heath in the old days and not much mistletoe, though I'm afraid the other way round now. One place, called Holly Hollow, was where the Christmas services were held in secret.'

He then went on to talk a great deal about how Christmas used to be celebrated — or not — as he helped her pin up the decorations.

•◇•◇•◇•◇•◇•◇•◇•◇•◇•

Christmas Day, fresh snow covered the ground.

After church and a splendid dinner, Miss Rossiter allowed the children out into the yard of the Charitable House to build an army of snowmen.

Nell was out near the lane when over the wall popped Charlie's face, grinning and grubby.

'Nell!' said he. '*There* you are. Guess what? I've found that symbol again!'

'You have?' Her ears instantly perked up.

Charlie nodded. 'Two *days* ago. But I couldn't come tell you, because you're always out, or having lessons, and at night I can't even get close because the pet is prowling around the fence.'

'It was?' The perk of interest turned to a prickle of fear. 'Why?'

'Probably because you have the key, and it's looking for the treasure. Want to go find it?'

Nell very much did but doubted she would be given leave. Yet the snowy garden was unusually frolicsome and Miss Rossiter unusually absent. She made up her mind in an instant. 'All right. But how? The gate's locked.'

'Climb over,' Charlie prompted, and helped her with the rather slick and slippery process.

Then they were off through the snow drifts up the High Road through the westering sunlight. The church loomed ahead, but Charlie turned off before, cutting between the houses and shops.

'It's up this way in the heath.' Charlie puffed, pushing his way through the snow. 'It was much easier to find yesterday, but even then, I only knew this was a path by the guidepost here.'

Outside the village boundaries, Nell recognised it at last—even despite the cloaking white. 'Oh!' said she. 'You mean the old bridle path to Whitmore Park?'

The heath was always hard to traverse; but at least the cold hardened the ground. They made quick enough progress, though there were strange sounds that startled Charlie.

'Just a fox hunting,' or 'That's a rabbit in the brush over there,' Nell would say, nearly too cold to be amused by the city-boy.

'I saw the symbol round this bend,' Charlie said. 'Found it while I was helping the men look for Aunt Jane's pet.'

'Are they still hunting it?'

He shrugged. 'They put out food. It'll come back sooner or later.'

'But what if—'

'There!' Charlie pointed a shivering finger at a thin stone, nearly three feet tall and covered in moss and lichen, grown over with ivy. He brushed away the clinging snow and, sure enough, there was the same symbol carved deeply into the stone.

Nell stared at it, the chill chattering in her knees. It *would* be quite nice to have boots. 'Can we go back now? If I'm gone too long—'

Something caught her eye and all other thoughts dropped from her: Red. Bright red from holly berries!

She plunged off the path toward it.

Sure enough, there was a holly bush, bright and merry as befit the day! And another further down the little hill, beside another stone.

Down she slid, Charlie close behind and asking questions faster than he ran.

Then—she stopped. Holly crowded around and over the bottom of a valley, formed against and partly sheltered by a huge rock. A scraggly old tree scratched into the sky overhead, hung generously with—

'Mistletoe!' Nell said. 'This is it—this is Holly Hollow.'

'What's--?'

A shuddering shriek cut short Charlie's question and the monster bounded down the side of the hollow straight at them. Shuddering muscles, chattering teeth, red eyes filled with murder and hate.

Nell screamed and clutched at Charlie, who was also screaming.

Down it came at them—faster, faster! Only a claw-swipe away!

Nell couldn't think of anything but a prayer and tried to close her eyes but couldn't. It almost had them! They were dead—

Three snowmen suddenly formed out of the snow and brush just ahead, facing the monster. They threw it backwards, then slid forward and stabbed the creature again and again with their branch-arms.

The snowmen turned to face the children.

'Thank you!' Nell whispered.

They bowed courteously, and then all three snowmen settled back into the snowdrift.

For a moment, the children stood there, gaping.

'Why did it attack?' asked Charlie.

'Because it was guarding the treasure,' Nell gasped. 'Which means it must be here somewhere.'

'There!' Charlie shouted, almost in her ear, and ran to the rock.

The symbol was in the rock face, low to the ground, above a round door with a keyhole in it.

It took some trying, what with cold hands and rusty lock, but at last Nell and Charlie got the key to turn and the door to open.

Nell crouched to peer inside and pull out a box.

'T. Fitzgerald,' Charlie read the tarnished brass lettering on the lid.

He pulled out a pocketknife and they forced the lid off. Within was a leather bag; they separated the folds and there within lay—

A small mound of rough yellow and red rocks.

'It's the fairy treasure!' Charlie yelped.

'Nothing but rocks.' Disappointment clutched. 'Just like fairies. Worthless, rough, stupid, cheap...'

'It's gold,' Charlie laughed. 'Saw some in the British Museum! And these glass things? That's amber! It's not worthless — this is worth a lot. You'll be rich now, Nell!'

'But —' She shook her head. 'But it's not *mine*.'

'Of course, it is! You found it, and it's *your* key, and that's your name on the box, isn't it?'

'But I'm not worth wasting such treasure on. I'm just a silly, rough orphan.'

Charlie waved a lumpy gold piece in her face. 'And this is just a rock? Both of you are worth a lot more than anyone thinks!'

Amid the Winter's Snow
by Steve Rzasa *(fantasy)*

The night air sang with joy.

Faint music drifted down the lane as Alicia Adair trudged away from the dark cottage. The flickering orange flames in the hearth had died out hours ago. If she was to freeze, which she'd convinced herself was her destiny, then she would do it out of doors where God could see her plainly among the cold indifference of her creation,

That music—carols. A year ago, she would have clung to Harold's arm, laughing at his silly riddles. The scent of wood shavings would have enveloped her as his lips brushed her cheek in a kiss that jolted warmth through the bitter night.

She pulled her cloak tighter around her shoulder. There would be no more of those moments. Not since Evan was taken. Her tears stung. She wondered if they clung as ice to her face as the water did to the rocks in the river ahead,

Alice lost track of the people she passed—the band of carollers working from door to door, the gaily laughing couples, the flocks of boys and girls wheeling after each other like flocks of gulls vying for a lone morsel.

'Happy Christmas!'

'And a very Merry Christmas to you!'

She deflected every greeting with a shift of her hood. There was naught merry about it. In the midst of gaiety, she was forsaken.

The stone bridge beckoned. She imagined the bone-crushing cold of the water below, the icy liquid filling her lungs. It had to be frigid. She fled from warmth. Anything that would scour the memory of Evan's blazing skin, boiling her touch as the fever took him.

Alice's shoulder collided with another. The tall figure doffed his hat, allowing thick white snowflakes to alight on a mop of curly black hair. The lamplight caught his young, craggy features and glinted off eyes as blue as stained glass at St. Nicholas.

'I beg your pardon,' she murmured.

'And I yours.' His voice was quiet, yet deep and steady, like the rumble in the wake of a passing thunderstorm. 'A Merry Christmas Eve to you, Mrs. Adair.'

Alice glared at him, her features frozen by the umpteenth greeting. 'You know my name, and so one would imagine are privy to my life's current state. Yet still you have the gall to offer glad tidings? I do not trifle with mockers, sir.'

She brushed by him. Of all the impudence. Why then did she expect him to follow, and offer apology or explanation? When Alice glanced back, he had already proceeded down the lane, black cloak a shadow between pools of golden light,

She shook her head. He was new to town—Reginald, she recalled as his Christian name. He might very well be the only one who didn't know the details of her recent past, ironically. But surely, he could see she wore a widow's garb and carried herself without the air of frivolity.

The church bells chimed. The seven o'clock Christmas eve service was beginning soon. In the distance, she could hear the tinkling of sleighbells as a carriage rolled into town, no doubt leaving fresh tracks on the newly fallen snow. Peals of laughter travelled with it.

Laughter like Harold's. But there had been precious little of that a month ago. No sooner had they buried Evan than he'd given himself to a mistress—the very drink that turned him from gay companion to sullen, angry lout, right up to the moment he collapsed face down in the woods beyond their cottage. He had drunk too much and wandered too far.

Her heart seized within. Why should she suffer so?

She lost her footing on a slice of ice at the base of a lamp and fumbled for support. Fingers found the snow-covered rail of the bridge.

There she stood, gasping for breath, holding back tears, as the river's dark depths streamed below. The water gurgled under thick, cracked sheets of ice. Smaller chunks broke free, crashing against larger sentinels as the current ground them downstream.

Giggles cut across nature's cacophony. A child nearby?

No. Months ago, when the grass was green, and the sky was blue, Evan had splashed in a shallow pool by the riverbank. Harold sang a hearty tune as he whittled a stick.

Alice had laughed and clapped along, until Evan slapped chubby hands in joyous mimicry...

Enough.

They were gone. No more than tombstones, now, on the fringe of the cemetery, Harold's savings afforded them that decency. She prayed their faith afforded them further consolation and an everlasting home for their souls.

Alice gripped the rail until she was certain the white of her knuckles could be seen from the sky. What of her, then? What would she be left with, when the money ran dry, and she forced herself into ever-increasing loneliness? Her aunt in Hastings had offered her lodging. Perhaps she could bring herself to leave Whitstead.

The Lord is with you, always, my child. He will never forsake you.

The words blanketed her. She looked over her shoulder. Surely, they had been in her head. They had come to her at dark moments like these, of which she had experienced many of late. She knew Scripture promised such, yet they seemed faint succour to the dark thoughts roiling in her mind.

Perhaps she should leave, without Harold and Evan.

Alice's stomach churned at the admission. Whom was she fooling? How could she be so selfish? There was nothing for her in Whitstead.

'I just want to hold them again,' she whispered at the night sky.

There was a way, of course.

She balanced a shoe on the lower rail of the bridge. If she were quick enough, she could be up and over the top before anyone noticed, plunging headfirst into the frozen depths —

'Oy, mum!'

The boy was ranging, clad in weather beaten coat and trousers against the chill. His cheeks were rosy, and a plume of frost feathered before him with each exhalation. 'Here you go!'

He shoved a small parcel at her.

Alice frowned at white silk, bound into a misshapen lump with brown string. 'I wasn't expecting a delivery.'

"Course that's what the gentleman said, didn't he? Paid me a whole shilling to bring it to you!'

'Gentleman?' Alice glanced the way she'd came. That Reginald, no doubt. Of all the nerve, offering a token to a woman so obviously in mourning. She saw no sign of him among the adults visiting in warmly lit doorways, or children sprinting down the alleys as they flung snow at each other.

'Well then, here!' The boy thrust the package into her hands, and as soon as her fingers closed around it, he tipped his cap. 'Happy Christmas, mum!'

Snow smacked into the side of his head. He yowled and spun at his opponents, a pack of four boys all around his size. 'Come on, you slug!' one hollered.

The boy scooped twin handfuls of snow and charged after them, laughing and letting a fusillade fly. They raced off across the bridge.

Alice couldn't bear to watch them go. That should have been Evan, years along.

Her fingers caressed the silken bundle. There was embroidery on the back. She flipped it over and found a red 'L' in extravagant script.

The jingle of sleighbells grew louder.

Alice was tempted to toss the bundle far from her, but curiosity — the same curiosity that brought the Adairs to that shallow pool to examine its contents at summer's end — forced her to unwrap the silk.

Cool metal fell into her open palm.

It was unlike any pendant she had ever seen. Whoever had forged its shape had created a diamond, as long as her longest finger, the side points rounded. The top points had been sheared off, intentionally it seemed, and a hole punched through one end. Worn leather cord looped through.

But it was the metal itself which held Alice's gaze. There was the strangest shimmer to its surface, like silver mingled the opalescence of a mussel shell. Along the bottom right quarter, where a portion had broken away long before, mesmerizing patterns protruded. When she tilted the pendant, their golden hue gleamed.

There was no inscription, save for a faded marking that might be a foreign letter. She had seen the reverend's Greek and Hebrew translations of Scripture. Perhaps it reminded her of one of those —

A sharp crack echoed, like a gun's report. Laughter turned to screams. A man cried out in pain. Horses whinnied, the sound verging on panic.

Beyond the houses and shops on the side of the road, she glimpsed the terror in flashes — she had not heard a sleigh but a wagon, laden with two mothers and seven children. It careened downhill, behind Whitstead's homes, the tongue badly splintered. Their horses must have broken free. A man was limping through the snow far behind, shouting. Had he been thrown free?

None of that mattered. In seconds, the wagon would overturn in the river. Even as she stared, horror-struck, it was less than twenty feet from the embankment.

And there was nothing she could do.

Just as there was nothing she could do to cure her son of his fatal ailment.

Just as there was nothing she could do to pull her husband back from drinking himself to death.

The fingers of her left hand closed around the pendant, metal cutting into the skin, as the silken handkerchief fluttered to the ground. Alice reached her right hand, desperation overwhelming her senses. *Save them!*

Cold sliced through her, as if a sudden wind had rushed over the bridge — yet the tree limbs remained perfectly still. The pain cut deep into her chest, freezing her very core.

The wagon left the ground.

And continued through the air.

It barrelled along, as fast and out of control as before, but it soared ten feet or more over the water. Dirt clods and snow clumps spattered the ice and splashed in the water.

Alice stared at the miracle before her, outstretched hand framing the wagon. If only it would land without damage…

The wagon lurched to a halt, mid-air, and gently sank in a shallow arc to the opposite bank.

Townspeople ran from all corners, attending to the crying children and shaking women. The man who had been thrown free reached the bridge, where another fellow caught up with him. 'Did you see, Henry? Did you see what happened?'

'By God, James.' Henry helped James limp at high speed across the bridge. 'He said he would never let one of us be snatched from his hand!'

They paid her no mind. No one did. Alice withdrew her hand, unable to make it stop trembling.

'Do not be afraid.' Reginald was there. Given the sudden conflux of townspeople passing her on the bridge, and gathering around the wagon, she was not surprised he had managed to double back. 'Here.'

He took her hand, enclosed it in his gloved ones. Warmth suffused her icy fingers. 'Better?' he asked.

Alice gazed up at him. 'What… What has happened?'

'You happened, Alice Adair. It was a reflex, as involuntary as pulling one's hand out of a fire.' He raised his hands—and hers—to his lips and blew additional warmth. 'It was your first step into a world few see and in which fewer still exercise the gift.'

Alice yanked her hand free. The warmth had travelled all the way to her face. She avoided Reginald's piercing gaze and stared down instead at the pendant in her other palm. The cold in her chest faded, the icy prickles receding to the fingertips that still clutched the strange metal. 'What is this?'

'The keeper of the gift. A bulwark against darkness.' Reginald leaned on the bridge rail. 'Which you've no doubt discovered.'

'It did this.' Her muscles tensed. 'Some manner of witchcraft.'

Reginald chuckled. 'Hardly. You speak of parlour tricks while I talk of divine power, granted in limited fashion to mere mortals.'

'Power for what?'

He gestured at the wagon and the crowds of people coming together. 'The power to do far more than arrest a wayward wagon. The power to put to a stop the machinations of those who possess the same strength yet would use it to bend the world to evil. We are the garrison against the men who would leave their surroundings in ashes.'

'The men.' Alice held out the pendant. 'Perhaps you lack sharp senses, Mr. …'

'Lark. Mr. Reginald Lark.' He covered the pendant with his hand, turned hers over, and kissed her knuckles. 'Delighted.'

When he released her hand, the pendant was still in her possession. 'My senses have not taken leave, Mrs. Adair,' he said. 'We have rather strict rules about this sort of thing. It was no mistake, my finding you in Whitstead. The medallions go to where they are intended. Where they are destined.'

'I do not understand. What use would you have for a widow?'

'I have use for an agent. I have use for a woman who can go unnoticed among crowds, but who can exercise the medallion's powers with skill, even unconsciously.' Reginald smiled. 'Which you have so aptly demonstrated.'

The promises were grand, but Alice shut her eyes against them. It was not the power. It was the hope of *purpose*.

'This is an awful manner in which to spring this upon you,' Reginald said. 'Perhaps a warm cider and a warmer fire? I understand there is a festive gathering at Whitmore Park, amongst a great crowd — the perfect place for subtle conversation, without the raised eyebrows a handsome single gentleman escorting a beautiful young widow would elicit?'

Alice could not help a small smile at his impertinence. Her mind reeled from the implications of what happened — of what she'd done.

Reginald extended an arm. 'Shall we?'

Alice brushed back her hood. Blazing red hair caught the lamplight. She scooped it out of the way and looped the pendant around her neck, before replacing the hood. Then she rested her arm upon his. 'Very well.'

They left the bridge in companionable silence, Reginald humming a tune. A bit classier than Harold would have chosen, but a pleasant sound, nonetheless.

'Tell me, Mr. Lark,' Alice said. 'This medallion — will it do more than lift a runaway wagon?'

'Quite a bit more, but the bulk of that work will be done in secret.'

'I see. Will it fly, then?'

'No, my dear Mrs. Adair.' Reginald locked his gaze with hers. 'When we are finished, you will.'

On Whom His Favour Rests
by Pam Halter (fantasy/spiritual warfare)

10 December 1844

ophiel crossed the dark living room of the small cottage they'd been using as their base in Whitstead. A single log glowed bright orange as the flame died. 'Any word on why the Most High is keeping me here?'

'Nay.'

'Does it involve the woman? Alice Adair?' Zophiel persisted. 'Her son, my charge, died a month ago. And her husband is gravely ill now.'

Aar'in shook his head. 'Unknown, as well.'

The two angelic beings stood silently for several minutes. The town clock struck midnight. Zophiel spoke first. 'Let's go then.'

They assumed their night forms and slipped out of the cottage. Light from the waxing moon gave the landscape a metallic glow. Nightly rounds in the village were not untypical, however, as each night passed, more and more angels were going on rounds. None of them questioned it. Orders from above were followed absolutely. But they *were* curious.

Of course, they could also feel the demonic presence growing, as well.

As they passed the cemetery, a huge rust coloured wolf darted between the stones, sniffing the ground. His nightly hunt. Nothing out of the ordinary there.

Aar'in motioned for them to cut through to High Road. They drifted between houses, crossed the road, and made their way into the forest.

Do you hear that? Zophiel telepathed.

Aar'in nodded. They continued toward the sound. It was quiet singing. As they rounded a giant oak, they saw an old woman, raggedy and unkept, a faded red shawl around her shoulders, sitting next to a pine. It was the woman, Maisie Bloom, who often looked in on Dermot, the scarred, mostly blind young pedlar man who stayed near the Romani Camp. He sold or bartered his items and toys with the town people, and he was often asked to sing, as his baritone voice was as lovely as his face was ugly. Maisie looked up as they approached and smiled at them, never stopping her song.

'Veni cito, Domine meus,' she sang.

Patiently wait on the King, daughter, Aar'in spoke to her spirit. *His timing is perfect.*

She sees us? Zophiel asked.

She senses us. Those with a deep reverent love for the Most High are more spirit sensitive.

They turned and walked away, her song following them until they left the woods. The rest of their rounds were uneventful. Nothing out of place. They saluted their fellow angels at each house they passed. Until they reached St. Nicholas Church. Aar'in stopped and held up a hand.

Zophiel felt it, as well.

There. Aar'in pointed to the southwest corner of the building.

Where he pointed, Zophiel saw it. A thin wavering shadow, unfamiliar to Whitstead. *A new demon? Why?*

If there's a new one here, there are new ones in other places. I'll have to telepath the others.

Back in the cottage, Zophiel made sure the window coverings were secure and the door locked. 'Has everyone checked in?'

Aar'in nodded. 'Eight more sightings of new demons.'

'Same as the one we saw? Just standing?'

'Same,' he responded. 'No movement anywhere, but I have a feeling.'

Zophiel cocked his head. 'What kind of feeling?'

'Anticipation. And not in a good way.'

•◊•◊•◊•◊•◊•◊•◊•◊•◊•

12 December 1844

Twilight settled over the town like a blanket. Zophiel stood before the fireplace, offering praise to the Most High and waiting on Aar'in to return from checking on Alice Adair and taking herbs to Miss Rossiter at the orphanage. Several of the children had a cough, and the Most High directed him to bring them yarrow for tea. It made Zophiel smile as he thought of the great love the Most High had for young children.

The door opened and an old woman wrapped in a dark grey wool cloak stepped in. She looked frustrated. 'That woman who runs the orphanage needs a new heart!' she cried as she took off her cloak.

As the cloak slid to the floor, Aar'in stood, momentarily in his glorious form. 'Most High, have mercy on the children!'

The brilliant light faded and Zophiel grinned. 'Why would you think this time would be different?'

Aar'in's human embodiment, Aminta, had been trying to help the children at the orphanage since he and Zophiel had first arrived in Whitstead. Certainly, their main assignment was Alice Adair and her son. Alice's husband's angel was Jasper, who was sitting at his side right now until the Most High called him home.

But Miss Rossiter wouldn't budge. Aminta went there, day after day, bringing broth and bread or herbs for healing teas. If the formidable woman accepted Aminta's offerings, Aminta was sure the children didn't receive them.

Zophiel shook his head. 'We can't let her take our focus off our assignment.'

'That is true.' Aar'in swung his arms back and forth then clapped his hands once. 'Let's give praise to the Holy One while we wait to go on rounds.'

•◇•◇•◇•◇•◇•◇•◇•◇•

Aside from more demons showing up, rounds that night went well until they approached Alice Adair's cottage. They could hear her weeping, a sound that cut through the night and seemed to echo off the walls of the other cottages.

Aar'in rushed in. Jasper knelt next to Alice's husband, Harold, his hand on the man's forehead.

'O Most High, receive Harold to Yourself and give him eternal rest.'

Alice, who was sprawled over her husband's body, wailed her grief. Aar'in placed a hand on her shoulder and the other one on her arm. 'Peace,' he whispered. 'Peace. The Most High will take care of you.'

Zophiel stood with his head bent, honouring the prayers of his fellow angels.

Jasper looked up. 'It seems the Most High has assigned grief to this young woman once again. You need to stay close, Aar'in.'

Aar'in looked around the cottage. Alice had little. The small amount in the bank would enable her to lay her husband to rest beside their son. But not much more than that. Aar'in would, of course, stay close to his charge, but he also knew the Most High had more for he and Zophiel to do. Still, he didn't need to understand God's full plans to carry them out.

'Aminta and her 'granddaughter' will bring her physical comforts tomorrow,' he said. Then he and Zophiel left, puzzling over God's ways, but knowing He always had a plan for good.

•◇•◇•◇•◇•◇•◇•◇•◇•

15 December 1844

Ella Zoe, Aminta's great-granddaughter, walked past the orphanage on her way to town. A few children were playing stick ball in the front yard. They waved as she went by.

'Come and play,' one of the boys called.

'I can't today,' she answered. 'But I'll try to come tomorrow.'

Ella Zoe had a mission this morning. She left Aminta ministering to Alice Adair and made her way to the small bakery shop. Not for bread, although she'd buy some, but to meet and encourage the new gentleman in town, Reginald Lark. Why the Most High wanted Zophiel to encourage the man who would encourage Aar'in's charge, he didn't know. But he obeyed.

Ella peeked in the front window. Mr. Lark, as she must remember to call him, was standing in line behind the Reverend Hollybrook's housekeeper. She pushed the door open and stepped in quickly. The air had the chill of snow in it, and she had learned humans detested it when a door was left open to let that chill in. Angels, of course, didn't feel the cool or heat of weather—only demonic cool or heat.

The reverend's housekeeper left, nodding and smiling at Mr. Lark, who tipped his hat, as he stepped up to the counter. After receiving his wrapped loaf of nut bread, he turned and saw Ella Zoe.

He tipped his hat again. 'Good morn, young Ella Zoe.'

Ella curtsied. 'Good morn, Mr. Lark. I see you purchased the last loaf of nut bread. It's very good. You'll be sure to enjoy it.'

Reginald chuckled and leaned down to place the loaf in Ella's hands. 'I can't have you leave without it, then. I can come back this afternoon.'

The baker's wife, who had seen, gave Reginald a dimpled smile. Ella Zoe had noticed all the village women smiled at him. No idea why.

She took the loaf in her small hands. 'Thank you, sir.' Then she whispered, *'The Most High says to keep your course. You are not wrong about the woman.'*

The baker's wife could not hear the angelic whisper, but Reginald did. His eyes widened a moment, then he tipped his hat at Ella again and left the bakery.

Ella Zoe followed him out, satisfied that her message had been received.

She gave the nut bread to the children who were still playing outside the orphanage. They eagerly tore into it as she watched their angels block the scene from Miss Rossiter.

•◇•◇•◇•◇•◇•◇•◇•◇•

20 December 1844

Aar'in kept close to Alice Adair as she sat in her dark cottage, the candle long burned out. He kept giving her the nudge to eat some of the soup and bread Aminta had brought. She always accepted it thankfully, but after a few sips, she left it to grow cold. Her heart was always moved to take the leftovers to the orphanage, but she really needed to keep it for herself.

As Alice dozed, Aar'in patrolled the outside of her cottage, invisible. The demons who wanted her life were also invisible, but he could feel them. Just as they could feel his presence. So far, none had made a move, but he would not let his guard down. As he had told Zophiel, he felt anticipation. And not in a good way.

•◇•◇•◇•◇•◇•◇•◇•◇•

22 December 1844

Ella Zoe thanked the servant who handed her an envelope. They'd never gotten mail before. Why now? She closed the door and opened it. An invitation to a Christmas

Eve party? All the years they 'lived' here, and she was just getting a party invite? Well, she had more important things to do, so it didn't really matter.

'You should go,' Aar'in said.

Zophiel nodded. 'Aye, if the Most High desires it.'

'Of course.'

Rounds that night were tense. More and more demons were arriving, which put all the angels on alert, paying more attention to them than their human charges. Aar'in didn't like it. He stood across the street from Alice Adair's small cottage. A wavering demonic line hovered at each corner now.

Prince Michael, he prayed. *What are we preparing for?*

•◇•◇•◇•◇•◇•◇•◇•◇•◇•

23 December 1844

Aar'in patrolled around the outside of Alice Adair's house before taking his place inside, next to her. He had gotten the word not to leave her or the cottage to join the nightly patrols around the village. Zophiel kept him appraised of the situation; demons were gathering at the river where the road crossed it by way of a stone bridge.

It seemed the demons thought themselves stealthy, but the Most High knew. He knew everything, even before it happened. So clearly, something was going to happen at the bridge, and soon.

Aar'in would like to engage the demons at Alice's house, but he had not been given the go-ahead, so he kept silent vigil. He wasn't going to be going back to Aminta's cottage in the morning, as usual. He could rely on Zophiel, as Ella Zoe, to cover for him.

In the bed, Alice Adair slept uneasily, as if she knew the coming danger.

•◇•◇•◇•◇•◇•◇•◇•◇•◇•

24 December 1844
Christmas Eve morning

Dermot bobbed his head at Ella Zoe. 'I thank ye, miss. Ye'll be makin' the wee ones at the orphanage merry this Christmas.'

Ella lifted the bag of toys, remembering to make it look like it was heavy. 'I hope so,' she said. 'Happy Christmas, Dermot!'

When she was out of sight of the pedlar, she walked quicker. She'd hide the toys until it was dark and everyone was sleeping. Then she'd distribute them to the foot of each bed in the orphanage. She smiled as she thought of each child. Most of them were sweet, some were hard. All were sad. Not for the first time did Ella ask the Most High to change Miss Rossiter's heart.

After stashing the toy bag in the cottage. Ella dropped off a loaf of brown bread and a jar of beef broth at Alice Adair's house 'from Aminta' and continued on into town to look at party dresses.

•◇•◇•◇•◇•◇•◇•◇•◇•◇•◇•

24 December 1844
Christmas Eve, near time for the seven-p.m. service

Alice Adair stood, gripping the icy cold railing of the stone bridge. Curse that Reginald Lark! His completely inappropriate Christmas greeting had interrupted her purpose. Aar'in stood close, waiting to see if the Most High willed him to intervene with her obvious plans.

He touched her shoulder. *The Lord is with you, always, my child. He will never forsake you.*

She looked up, as if she had heard him. Then she whispered, 'I just want to hold them again.'

Aar'in forced himself to be still as she placed a foot on the lower rail of the bridge. But before she went any farther, a boy ran up with a small package. Aar'in smiled in relief as the Most High revealed to him what was to happen.

The bells in St. Nicholas rang the beginning of the service.

Zophiel came up. *The demons in the forest are on the move. Their attention lies on a wagon coming toward town.*

Aar'in nodded. He turned back to Alice, who was gazing in wonder at the metal pendant. *Get ready* he told Zophiel.

There was a loud crack. The demon battalion had broken the tongue of the wagon and tossed the man driving out. Shrieking in delight, they gave the wagon a great heave and it picked up speed, heading straight to the river.

Brilliant angelic light knifed through the trees as a legion of warrior archangels burst into their glorious forms. The demons roared their rage. Aar'in stood still, itching to join the fray of angelic blades against demon, but the Most High's instructions were clear. His place was with Alice.

Zophiel had jumped into the battle, his sword and shield blazing with the glory of the Lord.

The wagon sped toward the river. It would reach the bank in seconds! Aar'in nudged Alice. *Save them!*

The women and children in the wagon screamed. The noise of the spiritual battle almost covered the sound. Aar'in was the only angel not fighting. Not that war. His battle was to help hold Alice's arm up as she used her power for the first time.

The wagon flew up over the water, crossed the river, then floated a moment before settling on the ground. The moment its wheels touched land the demonic army vanished with an explosion that shook the spiritual realm.

One of the archangel captains, Rafael, approached Aar'in. Zophiel stood beside him.

Well done, Aar'in, he said. *The Most High is pleased.*

All to His glory! Aar'in responded.

One by one, the angel army left, passing through the houses, cottages, and the church. The congregation started singing O Come All Ye Faithful. The man who had been thrown from the wagon helped his family out.

The townspeople who were still on their way to the church ran up. Everyone exclaimed in awe at the miraculous rescue.

Another man ran up to the wagon. 'Did you see, Henry? Did you see what happened?'

'By God, James.' Henry helped one of his sons across the bridge. 'He said he would never let one of us be snatched from his hand!'

The mother wept and hugged the little ones close. Then she looked up. 'Where is William? Henry, where is William?'

Zophiel waved from the back of the wagon. Aar'in gave Henry a nudge to look there. He glanced at Alice, who was talking with Reginald Lark. Good. Just as the Most High planned.

Henry gave a cry of relief. 'He's here, Anna! I found him!' The crying four-year-old boy in his arms clung to his neck. 'It is well, William. It is well!'

The family rejoiced, thanking God and holding each other close. Alice Adair walked off, arm in arm with Reginald Lark.

Aar'in and Zophiel followed behind. *So, it was the boy?* Zophiel asked.

Aye, the boy.

I wonder what part he will play in history, Zophiel remarked.

Aar'in grinned. *I have a feeling William Crook Graham* will make a mighty difference in the lives of many.*

Zophiel flexed his arms. *Well, now that's done, I have a party to attend.*

Aar'in laughed. While Ella Zoe was getting ready for the party, Aminta would slip into the back of the church. Aar'in never got tired of hearing the Word for tonight. From the first time, when he had sung it with the heavenly host, to all the years of Christmas celebrations since, it never lost its power to stir the hearts of people.

Glory to God in the Highest, and on Earth peace toward men on whom his favour rests!

*Author's note: William Crook Graham, grandfather of Billy Graham, was born September 1840.

Christmas Ember
by Ellie West (*fantasy*)

et out, ye vermin!'

Ten-year-old Clara Moore flinched at the angry note in old Mr. Winthorp's voice. How often had she heard the same words aimed her way when she tried to visit the horses in his livery stable? Papa had taught her to show respect to all people—rich, poor, or somewhere between. Mr. Winthorp hadn't learned the same lesson, and the man had never heard of Christmas charity.

Curious about the identity of the so-called vermin, Clara crept toward the front of Winthorp's Livery. The snow crunched beneath her worn shoes, and her threadbare cloak was barely adequate for the late December chill. Papa would be angry if he found out she'd gone to town to look at the fine clothing of the ladies, but she longed for the day when she could afford to hire the town seamstress to make her a new wardrobe instead of having to rely on the castoffs of her betters. He thought she should be content with the meagre living he managed to eke out through odd jobs.

Reaching the corner of the stone stable, she peered around the corner. Mr. Winthorp had gone back inside. There was no sign of a child, leaving Clara to wonder if the offending creature had been a stray dog or perhaps a cat that had already run off.

A soft whimper came from behind a barrel near where she stood. Maybe the offender hadn't run off after all.

Clara eased over to the barrel and peeked behind it. A pair of bright golden eyes stared up at her from a brilliant green, scaled face. The dragon wasn't any bigger than a cat and looked miserable as it shivered.

'Oh, you poor thing!' Clara knelt to get closer, taking care not to scare it. 'You must be freezing.'

A sudden sneeze shook its scaly body, and steam rose from its nostrils. The dragon sniffed and crept closer to her.

She reached out a hand and gently stroked the smooth scales of its head, noting how cold the poor creature felt. The dragon made a sound almost like a cat's purr.

'Papa won't like it, but I can't leave you out here to freeze. You're coming home with me.'

She scooped the dragon into her arms. It wrapped its legs and tail around her and rested its head on her shoulder, pressing its chilly body against her as though trying to absorb heat. She pulled her cloak around them both and hurried back the way she'd come.

Passing between a pair of shops, she turned onto the lane and headed across the bridge. The river looked calmer than usual, good for fishing. If she was lucky, Papa would bring home a fish for dinner. She glanced at the dragon she carried. Maybe even two.

The one-room stone cottage at the end of the lane wasn't as nice as many of the houses she'd passed to get there, but she loved it. Papa kept it in good repair, and Clara couldn't imagine a cosier place to spend a cold winter day.

Well, it would be cosy as soon as she got the fire going. The last one out of the house always banked the fire to conserve firewood while no one was home. It made for a chilly homecoming, but a nice fire would warm up the cottage.

Clara struggled to open the door while keeping a firm hold on the dragon. It seemed perfectly happy to snuggle against her no matter how much jostling it got as she unlatched the plank door and pushed it open.

The dark interior of the cabin was barely warmer than outside. The curtain made of an old hessian sack let little daylight in through the single window.

'Here we are!' Clara shut the door and opened her cloak to give her passenger a better look at its new home. 'I know it's cold right now, but it'll warm up as soon as I stoke the fire.'

After a lot of coaxing, the dragon finally let go of her and allowed her to set it on the fieldstone hearth. It huddled close to the ash-covered coals as Clara stirred them up and added a few small sticks. The tiny fire put out enough warmth for the moment. She'd add a larger piece of wood closer to time for Papa to come home.

The dragon purred as it leaned toward the flames, warming itself in the golden glow. Clara pulled out one of the two chairs at the rickety table and sat down.

'You need a name if you're going to live here.'

She pulled her cloak around her and resisted the temptation to stoke the fire higher now instead of waiting. They didn't have much firewood at the moment. Once she was sure her new friend was settled, she could go look for more in the woods beside the cottage.

The dragon looked at her and tilted its head. Did it want a name? Did it already have one?

An even more important question came to mind, and Clara tilted her own head. 'Are you a girl or a boy?'

The dragon stared at her for a moment, then turned back to the fire with a contented hum. She waited for any sign of whether it was male or female, but it offered no clues. How did one tell on a dragon, anyway?

Her new friend stood and stretched. Then it circled for a moment before curling up in a ball and burying its nose in its tail. Soft, snoring whuffles joined the quiet crackle of the fire, and Clara smiled.

'Sleep well, my friend,' she whispered as she stood. 'I'll be back soon.'

She paused at the door and glanced back at the dragon. It still slept soundly, so she went outside.

A light breeze brought the sounds of children playing to her ears. Although tempted to go join them, she turned toward the woods. It was her job to collect fallen sticks and small branches for firewood. Papa sometimes brought home larger pieces of wood if someone he worked for was feeling generous, but mostly they relied on what she could find.

By the time her arms were full, twilight was falling. Papa would be home soon, and she needed to be there when he arrived. Otherwise, he might toss the dragon out into the snowy night without hearing why it was in the cottage in the first place.

Clara fumbled with the door latch, but she managed to keep her grip on the sticks. The moment she stepped inside, she spotted her father standing by the table, wrapping his finger with a strip of cloth. The dragon crouched by the fire. Its glare burned hotter than the flames.

'What happened?' Clara asked as she closed the door and crossed the cottage to dump the sticks in the basket by the fireplace.

'I came home expecting to find my daughter, but I found a small dragon napping on the hearth instead.' Papa tied off his bandage and focused on Clara. 'Why is she in our cottage?'

'It's so cold outside, and Mr. Winthorp kicked it out of the livery and...' She stared at him as she realised what he'd said. 'She? The dragon's a girl?'

'That's right.'

The dragon grumbled and turned her back on them.

Clara looked at her father again. 'How did you figure it out?'

'I wasn't going to let a male dragon stay here, no matter how cold it is outside. They get too territorial.' Papa glanced toward the dragon now ignoring them. 'So, I checked, discovered she's female, and got bitten for the effort.'

'Does that mean she can stay?' Clara clasped her hands and hoped he would say yes.

'She may stay with us until the cold weather breaks. But'—he held up a finger, stealing some of her excitement—'you have to provide her food.'

'Food?' She hadn't thought about what the dragon would eat. The fish in the middle of the table caught her eye. Would that be enough for all three of them to eat tonight?

'That's for our supper,' Papa said. 'You'll have to find something else for her.'

'What do dragons eat?' If she'd eat holly, Clara knew where to find plenty of it.

'They like rabbits, fish, things like that.'

'Oh.' Clara looked at the fish again and sighed. Maybe the dragon would be happy for tonight if she shared a bit of her dinner.

The dragon's head popped up, and she stared toward the back corner, behind the straw tick mattress. She slowly rose and crept over, intent on whatever she was doing.

Clara glanced at her father and opened her mouth to speak, but he held a finger to his lips and indicated she should watch their new friend.

The dragon froze, almost vibrating as she stared at the corner. Then she launched herself behind the straw tick. Lots of rustling interspersed with squeaking ensued. Quiet fell over the cottage once more, and the dragon trotted out with a rat dangling from her jaws.

Papa chuckled and turned toward Clara. 'I guess you don't have to find supper for her tonight after all.'

The dragon settled on the hearth again and began to eat. Clara thought for a moment, a plan forming in her mind.

'Papa, if she'll eat the rats that come in, maybe we should keep her even after the weather warms up.'

'We'll talk about it later.' Papa moved to the shelf with the pans and cooking utensils. 'For now, we need to cook our own meal before it gets any later. I'll prepare the fish, but you can put the pan on the fire. I don't think your friend has forgiven me yet.'

Clara caught the way the dragon watched every move he made and pulled the remainder of the rat closer any time he turned toward the fireplace. 'I think you're right. Maybe she'll forgive you by morning.'

'One can always hope.' Papa cut the head off the fish and tossed it in the scrap bucket.

•◇•◇•◇•◇•◇•◇•◇•◇•

Clara stroked the dragon's head. 'You be good today. It'll get a little cool before I get back to stoke the fire, but you'll be all right.'

'We need to go, Clara,' Papa called from the door.

She gave the dragon one last pet and received a purring hum.

Papa guided her out of the cottage and closed the door. 'I hope it's not a mistake to leave her alone in there all day.'

'It'll be fine,' Clara said as they walked up the lane. 'She was fine all night while we slept. Besides, maybe I can come check on her around lunch time.'

'No, you'll be busy all day helping Mrs. Parkhurst and her maids prepare the house for Christmas.' Papa laid a hand on her shoulder. 'I expect you to stay at the Parkhursts until I pick you up this evening.'

'Yes, Papa.' She didn't like the idea of not seeing her new pet all day, but he was right. The Parkhursts had hired her to work the entire day. Taking off in the middle of it to run home, even if only for a brief peek to make sure the dragon was okay, wouldn't be right.

Clara hoped to one day marry and have a family of her own, but until then, she would continue to do whatever work brought wages in, whether it was assisting a family with decorating for a holiday or sweeping the floor in one of the shops.

Several other people who lived in the small houses along the lane joined them as they headed toward town. Workdays started early and ended late, but each person walking along the lane was grateful for their employment.

Papa left Clara at the last house before St. Nicholas Church and continued down the road toward Cobbles to do some work for Mr. Huffam. She went to the back of the Parkhurst house and knocked on the kitchen door.

Mrs. Banks, the housekeeper, opened the door and ushered Clara inside. 'Ooh, it's nippy out there this morning!'

'Yes, ma'am.' The warmth of the house surrounded her like a luxurious blanket. 'But it's nice in here.'

'It certainly is.' She showed Clara where to hang her cloak. 'We have a lot to do today, so let's get to work.'

For the rest of the day, Clara swept floors, cleaned fireplaces, scrubbed pots, and performed numerous other tasks to ready the house for the holiday celebrations the next day. She'd hoped she would get to help decorate with greenery, but Mrs. Banks and the footman took care of that.

As Clara put on her cloak at the end of the day, Mrs. Parkhurst swept into the kitchen.

'Ah, Clara, I'm glad I caught you.'

She bowed her head and hoped she wasn't in trouble. She'd worked her hardest all day long, and she thought she'd done a good job.

'I know Mrs. Banks has already paid you for your work today,' Mrs. Parkhurst said, 'but I want to give you a bonus.'

Clara lifted her head but didn't meet her employer's gaze. 'Thank you, ma'am, but you don't have to do that.'

'Nonsense!' Mrs. Parkhurst waved a hand as though chasing away an annoying fly. 'You've worked harder today than I expected, so you've earned it.'

Mrs. Banks appeared behind the lady of the house with a covered dish in her hands and a smile on her face.

Mrs. Parkhurst took the dish and handed it to Clara. 'This is for you and your father. I hope you enjoy it.'

The rich scent of beef stew seeped from under the lid on the heavy dish, and Clara smiled. 'Oh, I'm sure we will. Thank you so much, Mrs. Parkhurst.'

'You're welcome, Clara. Have a happy Christmas.' She left the kitchen in a swirl of skirts.

Mrs. Banks ushered Clara to the door. 'You can bring that dish back the next time you come out this way.'

'I will, Mrs. Banks. Thank you.'

As Clara headed around the house to the road, she spotted her father coming toward her. He met her in the road and took the covered dish from her. She breathed a sigh of relief to be rid of the weight.

'What's this?' Papa asked.

'Stew. Mrs. Parkhurst said it's a bonus for my hard work.'

'That was kind of her.' They started down the road toward home. 'I assume she paid you too?'

Clara nodded and handed over the few pence she'd earned. He slipped the coins into his coat pocket, and she hoped it would be enough to help buy a nice Christmas dinner. Maybe even a goose.

Her dreams crashed as the cold wind cut straight through her cloak. No, spending the money on a fancy dinner wasn't in their future. There were too many practical things they needed.

The walk home was a quiet one. It had been a long day, but it wasn't over yet. They still had to attend the Christmas Eve service at the church.

Clara followed Papa into the warm cottage and stopped. Why was it warm? It should have been as chilly as ever, especially with the wind sweeping down the chimney.

'Close the door.' Papa didn't sound happy as he set their supper on the table.

She shut the door and joined him.

'We need to talk about your pet and why you came home after I told you not to.'

'But I didn't!' She glanced toward the fireplace and found the dragon curled up with a pile of everything metal they had in the cottage—silverware, pans, cups. Behind her, a nice fire blazed where there should have only been banked coals. 'Who stoked the fire?'

'That's what I would like to know.' Papa crossed his arms, a stern expression on his face. 'I told you to stay at the Parkhursts until I came for you.'

'I did!' She remembered meeting him in the road. 'Well, they told me to go home before you got there, but I stayed there until I met you outside.'

'The fire didn't build itself, and I certainly didn't come home to do it.'

Clara sighed, sure her father wouldn't believe her no matter how much she protested, but she couldn't let herself be wrongfully accused without attempting to defend herself. 'I don't know who built it. Maybe the dragon did it.'

'Animals don't build fires.' Papa went to the hearth and reached for a spoon, but the dragon pulled it toward her and hissed. He blew out an exasperated breath and straightened. 'Clara, see if you can get enough away from your friend so that we can eat supper.'

She went over to the hearth and knelt near the dragon. 'I know you like all this stuff, but we need to use some of it. Could I please have those things?'

The dragon studied her, huffed out a breath, and pushed the spoon toward her. Then she laid her head on her front feet and watched intently as Clara collected another spoon and two cups.

'Thank you.' She stroked a hand along the dragon, earning a soft purr.

She carried everything to the table and set it down. Papa scooped stew into wooden bowls, and Clara filled the cups with water from the pitcher on the shelf. Once they were seated at the table, Papa said a quick prayer over their meal. Clara whispered her own prayer that he would realise she'd told him the truth.

The first taste of the rich, meat and vegetable-filled stew made the exhaustion from working all day worth it. She'd never had a more delicious meal in her life.

A sigh from the direction of the hearth interrupted Clara's enjoyment. She glanced over and found the dragon watching them with a longing expression. She peeked into the dish in the centre of the table and found more stew. Her father wouldn't like it, but maybe he'd grant permission since tomorrow was Christmas.

'Papa, since we have stew left, could I give a little—'

'No. We're saving it for tomorrow.'

'But she needs—'

'I said no.' He set his spoon down and met her gaze. 'We know she can hunt. There are plenty of rats and rabbits if she gets hungry enough.'

'There aren't any rabbits in here.'

'Then she can go outside.' Papa held up a hand to stop her protest. 'She's an animal, Clara. Dragons aren't meant to spend all of their time indoors, just like you.'

'But she can come back inside to sleep, right?'

'If she wants to.' Papa resumed eating, and Clara did the same.

•◇•◇•◇•◇•◇•◇•◇•◇•

'Clara, it's time to go.' Papa's voice interrupted her dream of warm summer days.

She shifted under the blanket and rubbed her eyes. 'What?'

'We need to leave for church.'

'Oh!' She hurried off the straw tick and straightened her dress. The rest had been nice, but she hadn't meant to sleep so long.

Papa set her cloak around her shoulders, and she tied it at her throat as he opened the door. She glanced toward the banked fire in time to see the dragon dart toward the door.

'Papa!'

He didn't move as the dragon slipped out into the darkness. 'She probably wants to hunt. If she's here when we get home, we'll let her back in.'

Clara nodded, fighting tears as she blew out the candle burning in the middle of the table. Either the dragon would come back and have a warm home for the winter, or she'd disappear into the night and Clara would have to forget about her.

She didn't want to lose the only pet she'd ever had.

Papa ushered her out of the cottage and closed the door. They joined the other families from the lane as they all headed across the bridge. The group was mostly quiet while they walked, although a few of the children chattered excitedly about being up so late.

Many of the townsfolk were arriving at the stone church when Clara and her father reached it. They filed inside with the others and found seats toward the back of the sanctuary. Candles flickered around the room, casting golden light that almost appeared alive as it wavered across the walls and the congregants.

Clara did her best to hold still while they sang hymns and listened to Reverend Hollybrook's sermon, but it was difficult. Her mind kept wandering to the dragon, alone in the cold night. The gust of wind rattling the church windows midway through the sermon didn't ease her worries.

When Reverend Hollybrook finally dismissed them, Clara walked beside Papa toward the door, wishing he would move faster. He kept the same measured pace as they stepped outside, and her heart leapt. Snow fell, muting sounds and covering the world in a white blanket. Others leaving the church exclaimed over the beauty of a Christmas snowfall, but Clara's worry increased with every snowflake drifting down.

The dragon would be so cold by the time they got home. Would she even be able to make it to the cottage door? She'd barely been moving when Clara first found her, and it was colder and snowier now.

Clara couldn't bear the thought of the dragon suffering. Tears stung her eyes long before the cottage came into sight, but she held her tongue. Papa had made it clear he wasn't happy about having a dragon living with him, especially one who still held a grudge against him for checking to see if she was male or female. He'd probably be happy if she never came back.

A small, dark shape huddled against the door had Clara running the last few feet home. The dragon looked so miserable as she shivered and tried to pull her tail out of the falling snow.

'You poor thing!' Clara scooped her up and tucked her into her cloak as Papa arrived. 'Hurry, Papa! We need to stoke the fire and warm her up.'

'Have patience, Clara,' Papa said, opening the door. 'She'll be all right.'

He closed the door behind them and went to the fireplace. The dragon launched herself out of Clara's arms and rushed to her usual place on the hearth. She looked toward where a fire should be and drooped, her disappointment at the lack of flames apparent.

Papa collected a few sticks from the basket and stirred the ashes in the fireplace. Instead of glowing coals, Clara saw only darkness.

'Papa?'

He laid the sticks down and sighed. 'The storm put out the coals.'

'Do we have any matches?' They'd been using the coals in the fireplace for so long she couldn't remember the last time they'd started a fire from scratch.

'No.' He stood and shook his head. 'I'll have to see if I can borrow a coal from one of the neighbours.'

As he headed for the door, a sound from the hearth caught her attention. She looked over to find the dragon dragging sticks into the fireplace.

'Papa, look!'

He turned around and stared. 'What is she doing?'

'Maybe she's hoping a fire will magically start.'

Clara watched the dragon now sitting before the piled sticks and taking deep breaths. She sounded almost like the blacksmith's bellows as she breathed in and out.

A slender stream of flame shot out of the dragon's mouth, igniting the sticks. Clara jumped and glanced at her father. The dragon could start fires?

'Well, I'll be...' Papa scratched his head as the dragon curled up beside her fire and purred happily. He looked at Clara in the firelight. 'Do you suppose she built her own fire this afternoon?'

'She must have done.' She wanted to remind him that she'd suggested it, and he'd told her animals didn't build fires, but she resisted.

He walked over and put his arm around her shoulders. 'I'm sorry, Clara, for not believing you when you denied coming home to build that fire.'

'It's all right.' She leaned against him and smiled. At least he believed her now.

'You know, if your friend there is going to live here, she needs a name.'

Clara gasped and looked up to find him smiling. 'I can keep her?'

'She hunts rats and can start fires. I'd be daft to refuse such a useful creature.'

Clara went to the hearth and knelt by the dragon. 'What shall we call you?'

The dragon stared up at her with eyes glowing like embers in the firelight.

'That's it! We'll call you Ember.'

The dragon closed her eyes with a happy hum. Clara stroked the smooth green scales, her heart full. Not only did she get to keep the dragon, she never had to worry about going cold in the winter again.

Petals, Thorns, and Moth Feathers
by Valerie Shaw (*fantasy*)

The snow was thick on the ground, but Triss was warm and snug in his home burrow beneath Buttonstead, surrounded by his family and friends. He was sitting at the dinner table, a wooden plate piled high in front of him. Kade was on one side, Fren on the other. Kade bounced a pickled frog egg off his plate, to connect with Squim's ruddy cheek across the table. Squim's thick brows drew together, then the red-haired gnome burst into hysterical laughter.

It was a pretty normal night for Triss. He was a fifty-two-year-old gnome, still bare chinned, with twinkly brown eyes and dark eyebrows. Sandy blond hair spilled over his brow, curling at the ends.

Across the room, Elder Ram stood up, and even the pickled egg, now rolling off the table, couldn't distract Triss. When an Elder spoke, you listened. Especially if the Elder was your grandfather.

Ram raised his bonemug.

'Tomorrow,' he said, 'Tomorrow is Christmas Eve.' To anyone not of Buttonstead, Ram's accent could have been difficult to understand. A sort of cockney slosh mixed with remnants of their faraway home, the gnomes spoke a mumbling kind of language that only a drunken leprechaun might decipher. To Triss, of course, it all made perfect sense. He'd grown up here.

Ram's face reflected his reverence. 'Tomorrow, we will do what we 'ave always done. We will Remind the Buttonstead o' their blessings, an' gift their wee ones with strong memory.'

The gnomes rubbed their hands together, the sound like waves sighing at the sand.

'The Buttons 'ave produced another dear lass,' said Ram. 'Born jus' three days ago, an' early, at that. They 'ave named 'er Ottilie.'

A buzz of approval went through the crowd. The Buttonstead gnomes admired a good name.

'We take care o' the Buttons,' declared Ram. 'We dunna let 'em forget, as we promised, so many years ago. And Christmas Eve night, 'tis our night to Remind. This year...' The revered gnome trailed off.

Triss went still as his grandfather's gaze centred on him. The older gnome, his hair still reddish at the roots, looked with fierce pride at his grandson. Triss felt his face go hot and awkwardly stiff as Ram's eyes filled with fond tears. 'This year, the honour o' Remindin' the newborn Buttons will go to me grandson, Triss Buttonstead.'

Triss swallowed and stood. The eyes of the room rested on him; encouraging, strengthening, measuring.

'Thank you,' he said. Thirty-six pointed red and blue caps nodded up and down, up and down, acknowledging his gratitude.

Triss sat down, cheeks blazing as red as his hat, and the meal continued.

But now, nothing was the same.

Triss was to Remind the Buttons, and gift their newborn. Ottilie. She would be his charge, then, for the rest of her childhood.

Triss's heart blossomed with emotions. He had a charge! His hand strayed to his chin, finding it yet smooth. Soon, though, he would grow a beard, take a wife, begin his own home burrow. His cheeks flushed with the excitement of it all.

Then, just as quickly as joy had come, ice cold fear flooded his gut.

What if he *failed*?

The Buttonstead gnomes had been Reminding the Buttons since grey-bearded Nowell of Eire, had been saved from a determined fox by Adair Buttons, of Britain, nearly three hundred years ago. In gratitude, Nowell had promised to always watch over the Buttons, and the entire Nowell clan had moved to England's strange lands to do just that.

Every December, the carefully preserved raspberry sprigs would be unwrapped. Dried in the warmth of the summer sun, these were sprigs nearly the length of a gnome, thick with sharp thorns. A Reminder sprig would have its delicate white flower still attached, with great care taken to preserve the shape of the petals. The glass vials of rose oil would be brought out, and each fragile, dried petal rubbed gently, daily, until they plumped and softened again. The work was done in the Gathering cosy, the main hall beneath Whitstead's livery stable.

This was important work. Guards would patrol the tunnels, even more so than usual, for the fragrant smell of the flowers would bring rats, and moles, and sometimes even chitter beetles. The scent would waft up, mingling with the warm, sour smell of the horses, and the sweet, dry scent of hay. Triss directly associated the roses with Christmas, as all gnomes did. Smelling them in the summer, fresh and alive, was like a heady reminder of their work, of the joy of the gift.

Triss took a breath. He'd helped the crew cut sprigs this summer, helped hauled them back on his own padded carry. Little had he known, then, how important one of those would be to him.

•◇•◇•◇•◇•◇•◇•◇•◇•◇•

A scant hour's jog away, another family was discussing Christmas Eve.

186

'I want to go to the party!' Aurinda Buttons stomped her foot.

Her father was unimpressed by the display. 'Calm yourself down, girl. You know very well why we must remain at home on that night, of all nights.'

'The curse,' the children all said, together, with some eye rolling.

'It's not a curse,' said their mother, Eleanora, while at the same time, their father exclaimed, 'Exactly!'

He looked incredulously at his wife.

'It *is* a curse! Imagine if anyone else in this town knew about it! We'd be the laughing stocks of the village. We'd be right up there with that Maisie woman.' Sigel Buttons shook his elegant head, his jaw setting. 'Ever since Adair was befuddled by the fairy, our family has borne this curse, and fought back against it!'

'But it's just a bit of rass-berry,' said Clara, who, until recently, was the littlest of the Buttonses.

'Every Christmas Eve, they come for our children,' said father, his voice thrumming with the might of a true defender. 'And every year, we thwart them. That 'bit of raspberry' is a talisman of evil, and this year, you know very well who they will be after.' He punched his fist into his hand. 'They shall not have our little Ottilie!'

Eleanora clutched the bundle sleeping in her arms a little tighter. 'You're scaring the children,' she said. She'd married into the Buttons household and had laughed at the whole idea of the fairies until the raspberry twigs began to appear. She'd pricked herself on the first one, nestled down near baby Arthur's feet, and bled all over his nice white blanket. The stains were still there, faded brown now, on the very blanket snugging Ottilie's sleeping form.

'Let them be scared!' roared Grandfather Buttons, coming into the room. He was holding his old sword, which was never a good sign.

Arthur, the oldest of the children, perked up. Grandfather Douglas usually spent his time napping by the fire. It wasn't properly Christmas until the sword came out. Arthur decided to reveal his plan for this year.

'I've got a right sharp trap this time,' he said, confidently. He'd caught five mice with it thus far, and one rat. No little fairy was going to mark his newest sister. He knew the stakes—Uncle Gregory said that if the fairies marked her, they'd be able to find her, wherever she went, and steal her away. Only sheer vigilance had protected the Buttons children for centuries, else their children were gone into the night. Only a generation ago, Grandfather Buttons had awoken to his son's empty bed on Christmas morning. The toddler was found, eventually, wandering in his nightie down in the stables, his lips the ruby red of the fairies' bait. The Buttons, admittedly, concentrated more on the empty bed part, and less so on the 'found safely' bit. The fairies, had they succeeded in luring the boy away, would have won for the first time in two hundred years.

Grandfather Douglas was never going to lose another child again.

'A trap, hmm?'

Arthur nodded, and ran off to fetch it. When he returned, Uncle Gregory was there, too. The men were bending over a map of the house, drawing up their plans.

'Don't feed the dogs tomorrow,' said Grandfather. 'It'll make them sharper.'

'I know, father,' said Sigel, somewhat wearily. He'd been fighting this battle his entire life.

Aurinda was watching all of this sulkily, with her arms crossed over her chest. Twelve years old, she was finally old enough to go with her parents to the fancy party in Whitmore Park—*if* her parents would actually go. They never did. Every year, they would attend the Christmas Eve service in the big church, which, admittedly, Aurinda loved, then hurry home and prepare for the vigil. The children would be escorted to bed, and have to remain there for the entire night, under lock and key. You couldn't even get up to go tinkle, it was that serious. It wasn't easy falling asleep under the blazing gaze of Grandfather Douglas, or, maybe even more intense, her own father. They always had the dogs in, too, their collars jingling, their nails clicking on the wooden floors.

Aurinda thought the whole thing was ridiculous. She hadn't even gotten a raspberry twig last year, and Arthur had stopped getting them too. Only Clara had found one, sitting on her dresser. Fat lot of harm *that* would do. Clara had boasted about it, coming out with her lips all cherry red, and her breath smelling of sweet.

So the fairies only liked Clara, now. Aurinda thought she wouldn't mind if they actually took her. Aurinda didn't really need two sisters. As if reading her mind, Clara glared at her from across the room, then skipped off, bored with the whole subject.

Aurinda sighed. Even her mother was lost to this cause, bending over the map with the men. Resigned to her party-less fate, Aurinda shuffled out of the room, and headed to her sewing.

•◇•◇•◇•◇•◇•◇•◇•◇•◇•◇•

Triss barely slept that night, even though he knew he wouldn't sleep at all the next. He crawled out of bed early, and the day proceeded to snail by anxiously. A counter-sounding description, he thought, but accurate. He'd never lived such a slow fast day, or the other way round.

Finally, the time came.

Triss reported to the Gathering cosy, dressed in his Christmas clothes. Once his task was complete, he would join the others in the celebration. His shoes were the plain brown leather of work, his pants and shirt similarly devoid of the usual embroidery and colours the gnomes preferred. Christmas, after all, was a day of humility, of remembering, of celebrating the wonder of the gift.

He stood very still as his friends wound his torso with padding and placed the sprig on his back. Pliant now, and fragrant with rose oil, the raspberry sprig was ready to travel. The padding was a necessity. Without it, the huge thorns on the stalk could pierce his back, and he could bleed to death swiftly. Sharp as a cat's claw, and twice as thick, the thorns were suitably formidable. He hoped Ottilie, and her parents, would take great meaning from them.

Elder Chorlee gave him his mouse-leather pouch, filled with sleeping dust, and his wooden pot of sweets. Triss' vest had pockets for these, sized to ensure nothing would jiggle. Then cousin Sharn carefully handed him the silvery moth, bound gently in a thin line of spider's web. Triss took the creature and tucked it into the special pocket made just for this. The moth would remain there, perfectly safe in his padded sleeve, until the right moment arrived.

His mother kissed him on his cheeks, tears sliding down her face from her love and worry. She beamed at him proudly, clasping her hands together, and he had to rein in his own tears. His father limped over, and did the same as mother, and then the rest of the family followed suit. The other Reminder-Bearers were treated to the same send off from their families, then, to the sound of many hands rubbing in a sigh of warmth, the gnomes headed out on the most important journey of the entire year.

There were only three bearers this year. Only two Buttons children were still young, Aurinda and Arthur having passed the Year of Grown. Lollith carried one for little Clara, the white flower bobbing in the tunnel as the girl gnome ran ahead of Triss. Next to him, cheerful Mukin was bearing a sprig for a newly made widow. While she was not a Buttons, the Buttonstead had heard of her plight, and cried for her. It was their hope that a Reminder would do the widow's heart good, bringing light to her darkness.

Mukin peeled off down another tunnel, waving as he went.

It was only Triss and Lolli, now. They ran together. Lolli was Clara's bearer, so she had done this for five years now. Triss was glad to be with her.

It didn't take long for trouble to arise. It always did, on this run.

Triss was prepared, and so was Lolli. When the rat charged at them, both gnomes drew their pin needle swords, and drove it away. Squealing and hissing, it ran down another tunnel, bleeding. If they were lucky, its companions would smell the wounds and attack their fellow, leaving Triss and Lolli unnoticed. The gnomes ran as quietly as they could.

They came to the Buttonstead hole. This would take them into the cellar of the Buttons' house.

The year before, Lolli, doing this alone, had run into not one, but *four* cats in the large basement. Knowing that there was no serious rodent problem — the Buttonstead gnomes took care of that for their beloved family — the presence of the cats was puzzling. So was the fact that when the gnomes visited several days later, the Buttons were back to only having one of the deadly creatures. Ram thought the whole situation was perhaps due to the habits of the older girl, Aurinda. She was fond of leaving scraps of food here and there, and it made the scant few mice bold. Extra cats must have been needed, he supposed.

'Remember,' said Lolli. 'We must no' be seen, nor heard. We canna break our promise.'

Triss nodded. 'I know,' he said. A good deed done in plain sight was a boasting deed, and worth little.

She gave him an encouraging smile. 'You'll do good, Triss. Jus' be careful.'

They moved the stone blocking the hole as silently as they could.

There *were* cats, Triss saw. Three of them. The gnomes crept, on padded feet, away from the hole, only daring to breathe when they had successfully made it to the next hole. This one led up, into the house, by way of a ladder system.

It was warm in the house, and Triss found himself sweating, five minutes into the climb. You had to be a fit gnome, to do this job. He found himself counting the rungs — a hundred and two, a hundred and three, a hundred and four....

They stopped to breathe at the mark of the first floor and slid open the peephole there.

Triss looked into the plush living room, taking in the evergreen boughs, the red ribbons, the candles in the windows. The smell of good things baking tickled his nose and made his stomach growl. He'd been too nervous, earlier, to eat. He was still too nervous, but, goodness, would he like a bite of it all!

A dark shape suddenly blocked his view, and something rammed against the wall, hard. The impact of it threw him back, and Lolli grabbed his shirt, saving him from falling.

'Dog!' Lolli whispered, fiercely. The beast's nose sucked at the hole, taking in their scent, and then it started to bellow. The sound was so close, and so loud, that again Triss's hands threatened to lose their grip on the ladder.

The creature started scratching at the wall, and the gnomes began to climb again, frantically. The claws on the beast were huge, and Triss imagined it smashing through the thin boards, the giant mouth devouring him in one gnashing snap. His hands and feet propelled him upward.

They reached the second floor, then kept moving. The children were on the third, with the nursery in the little chamber next to Eleanora Buttons' bedroom.

Triss's shoulders were beginning to ache, and the palms of his hands were being rubbed sore by the roughness of the ladder. He ignored it, kept going. He was a strong gnome. He would not let Ottilie down.

They stopped again only for a moment, taking a long draught of water from their pouches, and calming their lungs. Then it was back at it, until they reached the third floor, and carefully opened the tiny door into the hall.

It was time to separate. They would meet again, in the tunnel, once they had both accomplished their Reminder. Triss kissed Lolli's cheek, and she his, then they each turned away, and silently went to find their charges.

Triss entered the nursery by way of the door, carefully sliding beneath. Petrick had filed a spot there, years ago, ensuring that any gnome could fit under. Triss silently hid beneath the shelves, there, by the door, and looked out into the small room.

Eleanora slept next to the cradle, on a slender couch. Her long, blonde hair spilled over the pillow, catching the light of the dim lamps.

There was the father, in his chair by the cradle. The Buttons men were fierce protectors, watching over their children every Christmas eve.

Sigel Buttons was wide awake. So was the dog by his feet.

This was expected. Such a good father would never fall asleep on this most important duty. Triss's heart filled with love for the man. He vowed to himself that he would share the same devotion if he was fortunate enough to have a babe of his own.

Triss carefully took out the mouseleather bag tucked in his shirt. He poured the powder into his hands, and blew, being very, very careful not to inhale. His breath, dancing with the powder, spiralled out into the still room.

The dog fell asleep first.

Sigel looked down, saw the dog snoring.

'Wake up, you foolish beast!' he whispered, not wanting to wake his daughter. 'The hour comes!' The dog didn't budge, even when nudged with a foot.

Triss glanced at the huge clock on the wall. Midnight was only minutes away. He took out another handful and unfolded the moth from the silken bag. Whispering to the creature, he put the powder on the moth's back, and released the insect.

Dutiful as any gnome, the moth flew up, as smoothly as a moth could, heading for the father's face. Once close, it shivered, the precious powder spilling from its feathered fur. Sigel inhaled, smelling roses. Then, gently, immediately, he fell asleep, his fine head slumping onto his chest. The moth flitted away, heading to dance for the lamps.

Triss grinned. It had worked! He hurried towards the cradle. The powder would do no harm. Sigel would wake in the morning, with nothing but a deep, restful sleep to remember. Until he saw the gift, of course.

Triss climbed the cradle, the wicker worn thin by generations of gnomes climbing these very weaves. He reached the soft blankets, and gently walked out onto them.

Ottilie murmured in her sleep, and Triss looked at her.

His charge. His heart swelled in his chest, overcome by tender emotion. She was beautiful, tiny, innocent. Of course she was loved. Of course.

Her eyes fluttered open, and she looked at him with blue saucers, ringed with thick lashes.

'Hello, Ottilie,' he whispered. This, this first meeting, was the only time he would ever speak to her.

Ottilie watched him, too young to even smile. He saw it in her eyes, though, and he smiled back, full of affection.

Triss unstrapped the sprig, and gently laid it on her blanket, by her feet. She was too young to grab it and would be safe from the thorns. Next year would be different, and every year after. He would have to tie it up with spider silk, or leave it somewhere else in her room where she would find it. But this year, this special year, he laid it upon her sweet, blanketed feet.

'Here 'tis my Reminder for you, my sweet Ottilie Buttons,' he said, speaking as slowly and clearly as he could. He touched the leaf of the plant. 'With leaves o' care, for the women who bear,' Triss said, softly. His hand moved to the flower. 'A flower o' white, innocent an' pure, for our Lord who came to us helpless, an' bound to the care o' our hands. For 'is mother, so young, but yet she bore the pain, an' agreed to trust.'

His hand went to the thorn, and tears came to his eyes. 'Keep away o' these thorns, my darling.' Triss said. 'They are sharp, an' deadly, and will draw blood and give pain, as our Lord felt.' He touched the tip of the thorn, the bead of red forming there at even so light a pressure. 'Our Lord gave 'is life for you, my precious Ottilie, an' He did it because He loves you.' Triss looked at the sweet baby. 'He loves you, an' looks after you, as I will always do, until you, or I, am no more. Beyond that, you need not fret. We 'ave nothing to fear.' Triss smiled at her. 'May you 'ave a blessed Christmas, my Ottilie. Welcome to the world. Please accept my gift and be Reminded.'

With that, Triss bowed to the little girl. Then he went forward and drew his pot of raspberry jam. He took out the wooden spoon and placed a dollop on her pink lip. 'A bit o' summer for you,' he said. The baby licked it, and then her eyes widened with joy.

Triss laughed, forgetting for a moment where he was.

'Sleep well, sweet Ottilie,' he said, then he closed the pot, tucked away the spoon, and ran lightly over her blankets, climbing back down.

He was practically dizzy with joy. He'd done it! He'd brought her gift!

Wasn't Ottilie beautiful? Darling? He surely had the loveliest baby of them all. No other Buttons was as adorable as his Ottilie.

Triss ran, light as a feather, the sweat on his back cooling. He took a turn, ran into a tunnel of her dresser, then—

SNAP.

The world went black.

Triss had run into Arthur's trap.

•◊•◊•◊•◊•◊•◊•◊•◊•

192

Aurinda woke. She kept her eyes shut, and tried to go back to sleep, but it wasn't working.

She should never have had that last mug of hot cider, but Arthur had given her that look, as if he was her father, and so she had to down it.

She opened one eye and snuck a look at the man in the chair next to her. It was her Uncle Gregory, and he was asleep. Ha, she thought.

Aurinda wasn't about to use her pot when her Uncle was right there. Quietly, she snuck out of her room, leaving her door ajar.

She crept down to the kitchen and used the privy behind the wall. Hazel had left several platters of cakes on the table, in anticipation of Christmas day, and Aurinda put a few in her pocket. Chewing on a hunk of gingerbread, she headed back upstairs, as silent as a little ghost in her white nightgown.

Outside of Ottilie's room, she paused. The house was quiet, but not a spooky kind of quiet. No, it was a homey sort of silence, a comfortable, sleeping feeling. Still. Daddy and Grandpa's stories about the fairies were hard to forget. Just in case, Aurinda peeked into the nursery.

Her parents were sound asleep. So was Rufus, the wolfhound.

She stood on tiptoe, not daring to get too close, lest the baby start crying and blow her in. Ottilie was sleeping too, her tiny face so cute in the light of the lamp.

Aurinda smiled, then turned to go.

Her eye noticed one of Arthur's traps under the dresser. He'd shown it to her, before. It was a harsh little thing, a wooden box with a door that slammed down on springs and filled the box with spikes. He'd whittled the spikes himself and shown her the effect it had on mice. Arthur *knew* how much she liked mice.

This trap was closed.

Frowning, Aurinda risked a glance at her father, but he was still sleeping. She crouched and lifted the horrible box.

There was a weight to it that suggested something was inside.

That jackal! Another one of her mice, gone to Arthur's cruel games!

She hastily carried the box out of the room, and light-footed herself to the closet at the end of the hall.

Several months ago, she'd claimed this closet as her own, and hidden some essentials here. Now, she struck a match, and lit her candle, then made space and carefully pried the trap open.

She knew what she was going to find and steeled herself for it—while not losing hope that maybe, just maybe, this time, the mouse would have avoided the certain death.

To her great surprise, out onto her hand tumbled not a grey little mouse, but a shivering little man.

Aurinda stared. If she hadn't been herself, bricky and bold, she might have screamed. Instead, she held the fellow carefully, amazed at his tiny stature.

'Are you all right?' she asked, using her finger to lift the wee man's arms, head, leg, checking for blood. He was clinging to a funny red cap, which he put on his head immediately. She saw no sign of injury, though he seemed dazed. 'How are you not impaled?'

He was limp in her hand, then he shook his head, and looked at her, abject terror on his face. He said a flurry of words too quick for her to catch, then made to leap off her hand.

'Oh, whoa—no, no!' she whispered, catching him. She was careful not to crush him. 'I'll let you go once I know you'll not bleed to death.' He stopped, held in her grasp, and looked at her again. She could feel his heart hammering against her fingers.

'Please,' he said, in the strangest accent, 'I am well. Let me go.' His little red hat was pointy on top, and slightly bent. Even though he'd spoken very slowly, she could barely understand him.

Aurinda looked at the little man. This was obviously a fairy. Every instinct in her body said keep him, keep him, keep him. No one would believe her unless she had him. He was evidence, right there, that the fairies were real. They also had no wings, she realised, and looked hardly menacing at all. His little face was handsome, and pleasant, and his eyes had a kindness in them.

She could prove them all wrong if she kept him. Aurinda looked at his face again, seeing the desperation there.

Aurinda made up her mind. Holding the fairy with her right hand, she took a biscuit from her pocket with her left, and snapped it in half, then in half again. She offered it to him.

He took it, hesitantly, watching her with his brown eyes.

She set him down carefully. 'Go safely,' she said, reaching up to turn the knob. The door creaked open an inch, plenty large for him to run through. 'Merry Christmas, little fairy.'

He stood a moment, then a smile widened on his face and he raised the piece of cookie. 'Merry Christmas to you, Aurinda Buttons,' she thought he said, as he reached to tuck the sweet into his plain brown vest. She caught a glimpse of a little leather bag.

•◊•◊•◊•◊•◊•◊•◊•◊•◊•◊•

Aurinda woke the next morning. Puzzled, she sat up, chilly and confused. Why was she not in her bed? The scent of roses was in the air; Arthur's trap was open and empty. The memories of the night before washed back, like a story told before bedtime.

It was Christmas morning! Aurinda ran down the hall, eager to see the raspberry sprig that she knew would be on Ottilie's blanket. Now she had a new story to tell, one about happy little fairies that left gifts, and ate cookies. No one would believe her, but somehow, it didn't matter. She knew the truth, and it was good.

•◇•◇•◇•◇•◇•◇•◇•◇•◇•◇•

Not far away, Triss was sitting with his family, retelling the excitement of the night. The ceremony in the stable was over, the night had turned to day. He had been worried about his talking to Aurinda, but it turned out that nearly all of the older gnomes had a story similar — that was the excitement of working with children. They were clever, curious little people, rather like gnomes in that regard. They'd all enjoyed his story of tangling with the deadly trap. It had been touch and go, pinning himself to the side of it like that. Grandfather Ram had winked and praised his instincts. The night had been a success!

Across the room, Lolli raised her mug of tea to him, and he returned the greeting. Maybe, he thought, she would like to go see the horses, together, later. He was already planning to cut a strand of tail from the grey, and weave Lolli a new rope to climb with.

Triss's eyes sparkled. The years stretched ahead, filled with purpose and excitement, God willing.

It was a merry Christmas, indeed!

The Rossiter Letters
by Sarah Levesque *(fantasy)*

To Miss Rossiter, Charitable School, High Road, Whitstead
HMS *Dovecot*, Bristol
25 November 1844

My dear Fanny,

As my ship is in for repairs these next few weeks, I shall *repair* myself to you for the holidays. Please advise me of the number of children under your care, that I may be prepared.

Your faithful brother,

Mattie
(Matthew Rossiter, Midshipman)

•◊•◊•◊•◊•◊•◊•◊•◊•

To Matthew Rossiter, Midshipman, HMS *Dovecot*, Bristol
Charitable School
Whitstead
Friday 29 November 1844

Brother Matthew,

I am grieved that after all these years you still have not been promoted even to third lieutenant. Yet you are family, so I shall prepare a room for you, as our father did not outlive your mother by even a month. I have twelve souls in my care, and I am surprised every day that my hair is not yet fully grey because of them. You need not prepare anything for the brats; they are well enough off as they are.

As per usual you neglected to write your arrival date. Do let me know.

Your sister,

Frances Rossiter

•◊•◊•◊•◊•◊•◊•◊•◊•

To Mr. John Bradshaw, 227 South Road, Bristol
Charitable School, Whitstead
2 December 1844

Bradshaw, my friend, I told you aboard the *Dovecot* about my sister Fanny. I have safely arrived at her Charitable School, seemingly ahead of my letter which told her what day I was to arrive. She seems to view me as just another charitable case, but she is fifteen years my elder and ever aloof in her manner. I feel sorry for the children under her care, but perhaps I might be able to give them a small portion of the joy of the season.

I wish you a very happy Christmas.

Your friend,

M. Rossiter

●◇●◇●◇●◇●◇●◇●◇●◇●

To Mr. Matthew Rossiter, Charitable School, High Street, Whitstead
Bristol
6 December 1844

Rossiter,

You told me your sister ran a Charitable School, but does she in truth lack the imagination to name it anything besides 'Charitable School'? It seems so cold and formal and serious. Do keep me informed. It is quite dull here with only my aging parents and their aging friends. All they talk of is the weather (which varies but slightly, as you know), their aches and pains (likewise) and their food. What I wouldn't do to have some children underfoot to liven things up. But alas, I have yet to find a woman to suit me, and I have no siblings to give me nephews and nieces.

Thank you for your season's greetings. I hope your time in Whitstead will be amusing, if only for my own sake! And that your holidays are joyful.

Yours,

J. Bradshaw

●◇●◇●◇●◇●◇●◇●◇●◇●

To Mr. John Bradshaw, 227 South Road, Bristol
Charitable School, Whitstead
9 December 1844

Bradshaw,

I'm so glad you expressed your interest because there are such goings-on here in Whitstead that I must share them with someone. Let me begin by telling you something about the orphans in my sister's care. They really are an adorable and mischievous lot, and I've quite fallen in love with the group. There's Robby at 5 years, who has the voice of a cherub, and his sister Margie at three years who never says a word. If I didn't know better, I would say they could turn invisible. I've been here less than a week and there has been more than one occasion where I've seen them go into a room and were gone when I entered behind them. Perhaps my eyes are playing tricks on me, or there are secret passages. I think the latter more likely, for I've never known my eyes to be wrong in the middle of the morning, but many an old house has a secret passage or two.

As for the other children, there's Freddie, a lame lad, poor chap, and Eliza and Nell and John and Lottie and Charles and Claire and Jim and Martha, of varying ages and sizes. Though my sister is quite strict and they are rather afraid of her—a sentiment I cannot blame them for, having shared it during my own childhood—they are not a meek bunch, on the whole, and quite merry when Fanny's back is turned. I am convincing them to call me Uncle Mattie. It is delightful.

My sister has many of the orphans working for the townsfolk, and she intends to apprentice one of the boys to a chimney sweep. I have tried to persuade her otherwise, for crawling up chimneys is no life for any chap, spry though he may be. My pleas have fallen on deaf ears. Fanny does not even plan a festive meal or presents for these poor parentless children, so it is all up to me. I suspect all of my pocket money shall be spent in this endeavour, and Fanny will certainly tell me I'm a reckless fool, but I care not. I am excited to see what I can get away with, much like the children. More soon,

Your friend,

M. Rossiter

●◇●◇●◇●◇●◇●◇●◇●◇●

To Mr. Matthew Rossiter, Charitable School, High Street, Whitstead
Bristol
12 December 1844

Rossiter,

Do tell me more about these children. The only things of interest in this house are the cat, Milton's *Paradise Lost* (rather lost on me, I'm afraid), and your letters. There was a dance the other night that I was invited to by a cousin, but I turned my ankle, so even that was out of the question. God knows how I, who can walk a heaving deck in a heavy storm without a stumble, could turn my ankle on dry land. But then again, there are no small holes in the deck of the *Dovecot*.

I await your next letter impatiently.

Your friend,

J. Bradshaw

●◇●◇●◇●◇●◇●◇●◇●◇●

To Mr. John Bradshaw, 227 South Road, Bristol
Charitable School, Whitstead
16 December 1844

My dear Bradshaw,

The disappearing children really did disappear for a time! I checked every hidey hole I could think of, every nook and every corner, and they still could not be found. When they didn't turn up for supper I got really concerned. I sat up all night in the kitchen, hoping they would return. It was a bitter cold night, and I was quite worried, though I could quite understand why they left—though Robby is quite young, it was he my sister intended to apprentice to the chimney sweep. And there's a rumour around that a boy in the next village died in a chimney, sent up by a sweep. But after a dreadful two nights, and putting up with my sister shaking her head at me dolefully for my seeming folly in staying alert for them, I was lucky enough to come upon them suddenly the other evening. They were having a jolly visit with the tinker who has come to town, and were quite glad to see me, and I them, as you can imagine. I tried to convince them to come back with me, but Robby was quite insistent that they were safe and warm. For such a young lad he has an old head on his shoulders. I of course promised that Fanny would know none of it, and I certainly didn't tell her, but she found out somehow – the children were at the home of the Winterhavens, not far away. I'd met Mr. and Mrs Winterhaven at church, and they seem like a nice old couple. Well, somehow the Ws convinced my sister to let the children stay with them—wonder of wonders! For apprenticing the boy to the chimney sweep (I always forget his name)

199

would bring her in a small fund, which would be used, I suppose, in clothing and feeding the mites. But, as I said, the Ws prevailed and the children are safe from Fanny and chimneys, for the present.

The candle burns low, I must conclude. How is your ankle?

Your friend,

M. Rossiter

•◊•◊•◊•◊•◊•◊•◊•◊•◊•

To Mr. Matthew Rossiter, Charitable School, High Road, Whitstead
Bristol
20 December 1844

Rossiter,

The ankle is much better, thank you. We have had snow, but like all city snows it is lovely for little more than an hour, then gets grey and trampled, worn and tired. Yet in those lovely hours I was much amused by imagining all sorts of accidents, happy and tragic, that may have resulted from it. You would have enjoyed the pastime, I suspect, if you were not busy with the children, who are far more entertaining. Do tell me more about them.

A happy Christmas to you and your children, and to your sister since politeness demands it.

Your friend,

J. Bradshaw

•◊•◊•◊•◊•◊•◊•◊•◊•◊•

To Mr. John Bradshaw, 227 South Road, Bristol
Charitable School, Whitstead
23 December 1844

My dear Bradshaw,

I have come to the conclusion that I am visiting Fairy Land! A few days ago, we had a lovely snowstorm and consequently the children wanted to build a snowman. Of course I helped, for it has been years since I had the chance to enjoy this most festive of pastimes, and I yet well remember how much larger a snowman could grow with the help of someone larger than my child-self. But Bradshaw, I swear they moved. You know that I am not prone to hallucinations, and I have had no drink, for Fanny does not keep any. So I conclude I am in Fairy Land, for that explains the disappearing children, the frolicking snowmen and the dragon. For yes, I've seen a dragon! A small one, to be sure, like they have in the Pacific Isles but—well, more dragon-like, somehow. More dangerous, and cunning, by the look in its eye. I looked at it for a long minute, and he looked back at me, when I was off to the butcher for a turkey. How it will get cooked I have yet to discover. Wish me luck on that account! I have succeeded in procuring an armload of boughs, berries, and candles to decorate with. These I shall keep hidden in my room until my sister has gone to bed on Christmas Eve. Won't the children be surprised! Speaking of children, we've gotten a new one—a young girl named Lucy. I shall have to find a way to get her a present, for we can't leave her out just because she arrived close to Christmas.

How's the ankle?

Your friend,

M. Rossiter

•◇•◇•◇•◇•◇•◇•◇•◇•

To Mr. Matthew Rossiter, Charitable School, High Road, Whitstead
Bristol
26 December 1844

Rossiter,

Thank you for your letters. They have kept me entertained much more than Father's gout and Mother's swollen feet. Still, it is not their fault. Would that I were in Fairy Land with you! We have had more snow, and it, too, has turned grey. Christmas was rather peaceful, but rather dull. I gave Father a new pipe and Mother a pair of knitting needles, for the shop girl told me those would be best. In return I received two pairs of wool socks and that dratted copy of Milton. But tell me, however did you get your turkey cooked? Or was it your goose that was cooked instead? And did you manage presents for all those children?

Oh, and my ankle is just fine now. Not even a twinge left.

Your impatient friend,

J. Bradshaw

•◇•◇•◇•◇•◇•◇•◇•◇•◇•

To Mr. John Bradshaw, 227 South Road, Bristol
Charitable School, Whitstead
30 December 1844

Bradshaw,

I have had the most glorious Christmas! It began with the Christmas Service at Midnight, with the children singing. Our own Robby sang the sweetest carol. And there was a pageant, with Margie as Mary. It was touching. I snuck them both their presents after the service. Back to the house afterwards with the rest of the lot, and once everyone was asleep (and I was yawning prodigiously), I quietly snuck downstairs and spread about my candles and boughs and berries in a most festive way. I plunked the turkey (which I had picked up earlier and left in a shed) onto the stove—Fanny was obliged to cook it, for I am quite clueless about those matters and she will not see food wasted. I managed to put a small brown-paper parcel and some sweets at each child's place at table—even Lucy's, though that was a trick as she had arrived but a few days prior, you remember, and I was nigh out of money—and took myself back upstairs. And oh! The shouts of glee in the morning! No fairy elves could have made the children happier, I do believe. It was most gratifying, and I lay there in my bed quite satisfied until the children knocked thunderously on my door and demanded entry. I bid them enter, of course, and they all piled atop of me in order to convince me to come downstairs and see the presents, a rather backwards way of doing it, now I think of it. But they were delighted at the sweets and toys, and all the while Fanny had a face of stone as she prepared the turkey. The glare she gave me made it clear she, at least, knew from whence the goodies came. It was the most fun I've had in years, which, as you know, is saying something.

To make everything that much sweeter, Robby and Margie will be kept by the Winterhavens, and Lucy seems to have found a good home as well. A bittersweet parting will have to be held soon, for I received a letter just this morning that the *Dovecot* will be ready to sail again in a fortnight. But as fond as I am of these children, I will be glad to be at sea again. I shall have to remember to pick up presents at all the ports for the children against the day we return to Britain.

I wish you and your family a happy new year!

Your friend,

M. Rossiter

Three Ghosts: A Whitstead Christmas Carol
by Laura Nelson Selinsky (drama)

Author's note: On the day our editor/inspirer-in-chief Abigail Falanga announced the collection, I immediately replied that I'd love to write the obligatory homage to Charles Dickens' A Christmas Carol, a novella I have often taught. I began writing before Whitstead was named, mapped, or peopled. Why would I write for a place that didn't yet exist? Because certain truths inhabit all towns in all times; that's why we still read Dickens. A Whitstead Christmas Carol was created with the help of the 1843 public domain edition of the Dickens classic, as reproduced by the marvellous folk of Project Gutenberg.

Merry Christmas and God bless Us, Every One.

Laura Nelson Selinsky

Stave I: The Captain's Ghost, The Past

The Captain was dead to begin with.

Agnes shuddered awake from *that dream* when the mail coach crunched and juttered across frozen wheel ruts. Her heart hammered like a steam-driver. A cloud of mist surrounded her as the cold translated her panting breaths. The other passengers edged away. Agnes felt shame redden her cheeks, but she drew herself to proud uprightness — back straight, chin high.

In *that dream*, the Captain was always dragging her from her grandmother's house. His hand clutched so tightly that her arm bore fingerprint bruises for a fortnight. The captain, her father, kept shouting that if he must suffer the misfortune of a daughter, instead of a son, he could at least train her to follow his trade… even if he had to beat the lessons into her. Hot spittle had sprayed her cheeks as he raged.

No one need ever face his wrath again, she reminded herself.

Now, the Captain lay silent in the urn tucked under her arm. And she certainly couldn't condemn the — uhm — sternness that had rendered her capable of captaining his ship, Aurora Risen, from Surat to London. She turned to the window, hoping to distract herself from the distressing dream. But she longed for the hot crowded glory of India and grimaced at the muddy high street that led to her grandmama's village. For the first time in a decade, she was back on English soil. Why must she arrive in the dreariest of months?

'Whitstead,' brayed the coachman. His lad flung wide the door and set the step.

Agnes jumped from the stage. *No ladies' step for me.* She tossed coins to the coachman's boy for delivery of her gear and took her first stride toward… *Home?* Perhaps Whit Willow farm was still home despite her years at sea.

Perhaps the lad could deliver the urn, too. She turned back to the coach, thinking to pass it to him. But abandoning the Captain, even his dust, seemed cruelly disloyal. Agnes clutched the cold metal urn closer.

A bellow blasted. Agnes jumped, slapping a gloved hand to her ear. Her watch cap tumbled off her head and into muddy slush. She shook off the muck and shoved the abused cap into her greatcoat pocket. *Hardly matters whether the uproar is a pet dragon or the steam-driver at the mill, my cap is destroyed.* The loss of her perfectly good sailor's cap seemed an ill-omened symbol of her return to Whitstead. The landlubber populace would expect her to don bonnets and prance down the street like a lady. *Not likely.*

A flurry of carol-singing school children jostled the dispersing passengers, as they did each time a carriage arrived. Mittened hands extended for pennies. Agnes tightened her fingers on the urn, even as the music intruded on her preoccupation. For a moment, she remembered being ten and singing for treats. Scowling, Agnes waved off the children.

One ragged youth brandished his empty cap in front of her. *'Penny for the song, Mistress?'* Her glare sent him running, tugging his small pale sister behind him.

Ignoring passers-by and decorated shop windows, Agnes strode down the high street, bound for Whit Willow Farm. The crowds gradually thinned. The church and churchyard loomed from the dusk. She couldn't avoid wondering which stone was Grandmama's. When she'd disembarked from the ship, a messenger had stuffed a black-trimmed envelope into her hand. At once, she'd known that the one person who made England worthwhile was gone. Tears, repressed for a decade, shimmered in her eyes. *Coming here is turning me maudlin. After all the time Father spent toughening me, he would be livid.* She looked down, trying not see the graves or hear the wind whistling around the cypresses.

Best get moving. Agnes hurried from the high street onto a narrow lane. No fine horses hoofprints or carriage tracks here. Her sturdy boots left a trail of prints among the ruts left by cartwheels. She lengthened her stride. It would be a long walk, and the sun already languished on the horizon.

Night tightened wintry claws around Agnes as she climbed brick steps to the front door of Whit Willow House. The doorhandle refused her tug. *Locked? But I sent word.* Agnes wrapped her fingers around the bronze angel's folded hands and raised the knocker. Angel's wings spread and arced around her hands, sheltering them from the icy wind. She snatched her hands back, and the knocker fell with a single decisive thwack. Agnes looked fixedly at this phenomenon and it was a knocker again. Inanimate. Unmoving.

More landlubber superstitious nonsense. The dark. The cold. Lack of supper. Making me see things.

An unpleasing braying grabbed her attention. Someone inside the house was howling *The Holly and the Ivy*. Loudly. Footsteps approached the door. The ritual turning of keys and lifting of latches began inside it.

Agnes rolled her eyes at the singing. *I'll take an honest sea shanty any day. Give me Christmas on the Captain's ship. Extra tot of rum for the sailors and back to work.* The singer came to a decisive cadence. *Seems to be done. Thank...* A memory of childhood lessons stopped the oath.

Then the unseen singer screeched into another verse.

Vaguely queasy at the idea of touching the knocker, Agnes slammed her fist against the oak. The singing ceased. A pale-faced and apologetic maid let Agnes in and guided her to her room, promising tea and hot bricks.

'Oh, Miss Agnes. I didn't expect you 'til the morrow. Sure, I didn't.' She helped Agnes off with her greatcoat. A flicker of puzzlement clouded her face as she registered that it was a man's coat she held.

'The Captain's,' snapped Agnes by way of explanation. 'I've come to see him buried and sell Whit Willow Farm.' She saw the maid flinch at that. 'Now I need supper, tea, and silence until morning.'

'I've made up your old room. I'll send up your dinner right quick. Shall I, ma'am? If you need anything meantime just call for Molly. That's me.'

Agnes replied with a sharp nod and collapsed on her bed. She was asleep before the door clicked shut.

•◇•◇•◇•◇•◇•◇•◇•◇•◇•

Stave II: Grandmother's Ghost, The Present

A raucous rendition of *Hark the Herald Angels Sing* careened up the stairs and shattered Agnes' nap.

'Of all the bloody ways to wake a woman,' muttered Agnes, squinting into the dark. She flailed for the bell cord that would call the servant and still the noise. As she fumbled for the cord, her hand struck something hard, and sent it tumbling. Glass crashed against hardwood.

Agnes opened wide eyes and peered over the edge of the bed. She lit the candle at her bedside. On the floor lay the palm-sized portrait of her grandmother that had travelled with her from London to Zanzibar. Mild grey eyes, tempered with regret, gazed up at her, as they had a decade earlier when her father hauled her away to learn the family trade. How often Agnes had wept over the precious gift Grandmama had given her on her last night in Whit Willow Farm. The sweet portrait that had hidden beneath her bunk, a sweet-faced contradiction to the Captain's harsh lessons.

'Grandmama,' Agnes whispered, her voice softening from hard seafarer to young lady. Agnes shook off a momentary wish to join in the singing that still scraped along the hallway. She had loved Grandmama and their Christmases in Whitstead. But she was no longer that child who decorated the parish church hall with holly from Whit Willow's overgrown woodlot.

She slid from the tall fourposter, careful not to land on broken glass, and realised she had fallen asleep in her boots. After lifting her grandmother's image to the bed, she began picking the pieces of glass from the floor. Some fragments had bounced onto carpet, and Agnes was picking them from the pile when her door swung open.

Agnes glanced up and saw Molly approaching with a heavy tray. She lugged it to the table by the fire. As she came around the bed, she saw Agnes on her knees picking at the carpet. 'Oh, Miss, that's no good. Let me clear up that mess for you.'

Molly dropped to the floor beside Agnes, who grunted and went on cleaning. 'I prefer to run my home as I run my ship. Anyone who causes disorder must take responsibility for clearing it up.' She dropped a handful of glass shards into the wash basin Milly held out.

'Your grandmother was much the same. I hear her voice in yours. And you have her eyes.' Realizing that she had overstepped, Molly added, 'Begging your pardon, Miss.'

Molly rose, set the basin in the hallway, and returned with an oil lamp. She turned up the wick. The last few shards of glass caught the lamplight. She and Agnes plucked them free.

'Enjoy your supper, Miss. And ring if you need any wee thing.'

Agnes looked up and caught Molly's eye for a moment before the maid looked away. Molly was young, seventeen or eighteen, yet her shoulders hunched and dark rings circled her eyes. Strength and sadness contended in her posture and expression.

'Wait. Did you work for my grandmother long?' She lifted the little portrait and cradled it in her palm.

'Nearly five years. Since I come from Ireland. A green girl, I was, but she plucked me off a street corner and brought me here to train as her housekeeper. Oh, she was a grand mistress, was Mrs. Collins. A good kind lady.' Molly set the lamp beside the dinner tray. She pulled back the chair.

'And you miss her?' Agnes sat, startling when Molly pushed in the chair to seat her.

'I do. Every day. Gone two months, and I miss her every day.' She paused a moment, composed herself. 'Here I am thinking of myself when it is your granny who was lost. Forgive me, Miss.' She uncovered a dinner plate, piled high, and poured a cup of tea. Agnes saw her bite her lip, a sure sign of worry. 'I guess I'll be off home to Ireland once you close up Whit Willow and go back to yer ship.'

'Back to my ship. Hmmm.' Agnes nodded and lifted her teacup. 'You'll be returning to family then?'

'No, only me lives in England. When we lost the farm, we scattered. To America. Even Australia. But if I return,' she hesitated, then raised her chin. 'Someone will take me on. Neighbours perhaps, for my parents' sake...' Her words drifted into a sigh.

Agnes had sailed with enough Irishmen to know what that sigh meant. Men could go to sea, but harsh as the sailor's world was, the landsmen's world was far crueller to a pretty, unschooled girl. No welcome for Molly in Ireland, no future if she stayed here.

Grandmama's portrait studied her from beside her fork. Agnes was troubled by the sense that Grandmama would do *something*. But Molly's future was not Agnes' affair. She had a farm to dispose of, a ship to sail. She raised her teacup to her lips with her right hand. With her left, she pointed to the door until Molly curtsied her way out, a stiff smile on her pale face.

Agnes pushed the portrait aside and lifted the fork to a very fine lamb pie, but she couldn't ignore a certain inner turmoil. *Grandmama was loved even after the Captain hauled me away.* Would the sailors miss Agnes, as Molly missed Grandmama? They surely hadn't missed the Captain and his cat-o-nine-tails. When he died in India, Agnes had heard them murmuring relief and joy. He was not missed as Grandmama was. After he died, Agnes had the Captain cremated, as Indians did their own dead, so she could carry his ashes back to England. Then she donned his greatcoat and ruled the return voyage with the steely discipline he had taught her.

Did anyone miss her now?

No.

Too deep a thought, too frightening. She turned the portrait face down and gasped in shock. A note in Grandmama's tidy copperplate was written across the back of the image. It had been concealed by the now-broken frame.

> My Dearest Agnes,
>
> Remember that in my heart, I am always beside you, even on your papa's ship. Think of me as your guardian angel, invisible hand beside yours on the tiller, guiding you to safe and Godly shores.
>
> Your loving,
> Grandmama

...safe and Godly shores. Grandmama wished them for me, and she would wish the same for Molly. With that disquieting thought, Agnes folded her napkin and readied herself for bed.

Exhaustion should have granted her a night of dreamless rest. Instead, her repose was shattered by nightmares. At first it was that dream. Over and over her father dragged her from her home, taught her to call him Captain, crushed every gentle impulse she might express.

But then came nightmares of Molly: *Weeping as boys who shared her black hair boarded separate ships. Fleeing a family 'friend' who promised refuge but demanded her virtue. Trading her last coins for passage to England. Selling flowers in London's November rain. 'Please, miss, think how pretty these would look on your table.' 'Please, sir.' Both her coat and her beautiful ebony braids were gone.*

Each brief nightmare ended before Agnes' grandmother appeared and whisked Molly to safety. If Grandmama had not appeared on that November night, then what? Molly would have died in the street.

The clock struck ten and midnight and three before Agnes slept soundly.

•◇•◇•◇•◇•◇•◇•◇•◇•

Stave III- The Future

Whitstead's country air always roused Agnes early, and the next morning was no exception. Before the sun was fully up, she dragged her tired body out of bed. She felt more than a twinge of guilt to see that her supper dishes had been cleared away. Molly had stoked the morning fire, too. *I could at least have set my tray in the hall, so Molly didn't have to tiptoe about while I slept.*

Water steamed in the wash basin, and tea steamed on the table. Agnes welcomed both. She enjoyed the eggs, bacon, toast, and jam that Molly had provided. There was little enough of such luxury onboard ship, and Agnes felt a pang at the idea of returning to the seafaring life. Today, she must scatter the Captain's ashes. Cold weather for walking, so she pulled on the scandalous breeches she'd worn at sea and concealed them beneath petticoats and skirts.

Her breakfast done, she tugged the pullcord. A distant bell chimed and brought Molly hurrying to Agnes' room.

'Thank you for your hard work while I slumbered,' Agnes said, stiffly. 'Pray do not set luncheon for me. I am off to the village for the morning, and I am not sure when I shall return.'

Donning the Captain's greatcoat, Agnes nodded goodbye and left her cosy chamber. She had promised the Captain that she would scatter his ashes in the churchyard as soon as she returned to Whitstead. This she must do quietly and early, so as to avoid offending those unfamiliar with the practice of cremation or fearful that it was dangerously pagan.

With the urn under her arm, she strode out the front door and into the lane. The steps and path had already been swept clear of snow. *How early did Molly rise to make my way so easy? The farm taught Molly to set to work at dawn... just as my father's ship taught me.*

The morning walk to Whitstead seemed far shorter than it had the previous night. As the Captain taught, she kept her head up, back straight, and eyes ahead, focused on her task. But snow gowned the tree limbs and icicles decked them like jewels, drawing Agnes' eyes again and again. *So beautiful. 'Christmas perfect,' as Grandmama always said,* she thought.

Unwillingly, Agnes remembered her last walk to the village with Grandmama, a trip to buy Boxing Day gifts for the staff at Whit Willow Farm. They'd selected a length of fine wool fabric for Mrs. Willet, the housekeeper, a knitted waistcoat for Mr. Clark, who managed the property, and a new cap and sweets for Dawson, then their boy-of-all-work. The next day, her father arrived. He had dragged her off to sea before the holidays arrived, so she had not helped Grandmama hand out those gifts.

Gifts were not a consideration at sea. Such foolishness was not to be thought of.

With her grandmother's ideas and her father's engaging her thoughts, the churchyard appeared in Agnes' path unexpectedly. She took a deep breath and reviewed what she must do: enter quietly, find her family plot, and scrape back the snow. Then she would sprinkle the Captain's ashes over the plot and brush a veil of snow over them to prevent idle questions. Finally, she must slip away unnoticed. *I shall do my duty as the Captain taught me.*

The churchyard gate swung open with a screech of rusty hinges. A snow-heavy cloud skidded past the winter sun, chilling the air. With a shiver (half cold, half fear), Agnes stepped onto hallowed ground. Then the distinctive ring of a hammer on stone startled her. The clangour rose from the furthest corner of the graveyard, where five generations of her family slept.

Amidst that cluster of gravestones and memorials loomed a black-clad apparition. Agnes hesitated, the superstitious tales of a hundred sailors thronging her imagination. Then she remembered her father whipping a lad who hesitated to carry out an order. He ordered her to this churchyard with his ashes. She jolted into action.

'Ho, who goes there?' Agnes called. 'What are you doing in the Collins plot?'

The shadowy figure spun around, cloak belling around a huge man, heavily muscled. He raised a great hammer. Agnes flinched back, ready to flee.

'I be the stonemason, Miss,' came his gruff voice. 'I be adding dates on this stone. *Angela Mary Collins, 7 October 1844.* A good kind lady, that Mrs. Collins; I knowed her all my life. And this note come from a shipping company in London, says carve *Captain Robert Collins, 11 August 1844.*' He waved a crumpled workorder. 'Heard he was a hard man what went to sea years back.'

'My father and grandmother,' Agnes said, approaching slowly. She couldn't feel easy about stepping on graves, so she wove between them. Deep snow filtered into her boots.

'I'm that sorry, Miss Agnes. Meant no disrespect. I'll just be going. Let you pray in peace.'

She shrugged off his apology. 'How do you know to call me 'Agnes'?'

'Family plot. Frugal to carve a bunch o' names at once, add dates later. Yer name's right here, innit? No date a course.' He pointed at the stone, his gesture swinging the great black cape into dark wings.

He loomed like the angel of death from her Bible, and Agnes trembled, almost dropped the urn. The dark angel indicated an obelisk of grey marble at the heart of her family plot. At the top were the names of her great grandparents. Further down was the grandfather who died before she was born. Next a roll of aunts and uncles lost to smallpox. Her mother's name and her death date—the year Agnes turned two and her father went to sea. Then her grandmother *Angela Mary Collins, b. 5 May 1780- d. 7 October 1844* and *Captain Robert Collins, b. January 1799- d. 11 August 1844*. Their dates, newly carved, shone white, against the sooty grey monument. Last…

Agnes Elizabeth Collins, b. 29 July 1821- d.

Her name. Her grave. Missing only that final date.

The shock of her grave choked her, made her want to run straight to the docks. To take ship and forget love and life and loss. To run as her father had when her mother died.

She was all that was left of their family. And she had a job to do.

Pouring the ashes took only a moment. She used the lid of the urn to brush a layer of snow across the mingled dust and marble chips. *Someday, just as quickly, I'll be dismissed and forgotten*, she thought, as she crouched to examine her work.

A handcrafted holly wreath was propped at the foot of the obelisk. Who had taken such trouble for the nearly extinct Collins family? She leaned closer to examine it. A red paper heart was tied amongst the boughs. Awkwardly lettered on the heart was 'Mrs. C.' and on the reverse 'Molly.'

Molly had left this tribute to her grandmother.

Molly, whom Agnes might easily leave homeless and destitute, had spent her free half day making this wreath and carrying it to town. *Have I ever done anything so thoughtful?* As the question formed, Agnes heard her Grandmother's promise to be beside her, and she knew what she must do.

She had Boxing Day gifts to purchase.

•◇•◇•◇•◇•◇•◇•◇•◇•

The End of It

By the time Agnes was ready to return to Whit Willow Farm, she had collected more gifts than she could carry. She gave half a crown to a ragged youth and his wide-eyed sister, entreating them to 'act as my porters. Please.' They stumbled down the lane behind her, sucking peppermint drops and valiantly lugging parcels that outweighed them. When she heard that they had neither family nor employer waiting in town, she welcomed them to her household.

'After all,' she said. 'I am an orphan, too. And we must stick together.'

Agnes gave the same explanation to Molly, who just shook her head and put on the kettle.

Soon Molly herded Jem, the new boy-of-all-work, and Sukie, the new kitchen girl, off to baths and clean clothes. At the doorway to the back stairs, she paused and turned. 'You do have exactly your grandmother's eyes... and her heart.' She disappeared up the stairs, but Agnes sat at the kitchen table and wept.

Agnes never had any further nightmares, especially not *that dream*. Reluctant to expel Molly, or Jem or Sukie or Dawson from the farm, she reopened it to the paddock and plough. But for the woodlot, where a neighbour uncovered standing stones, the long fallow fields flourished. The people flourished, too. And the house was always rich with laughter and good food.

Each Sunday, Agnes cut flowers or holly to place on the graves in the churchyard, for she said, 'These quiet folk taught me a great lesson once.' She never told the secret she had learned, but she showed it daily in every word and action. She became as good a friend, as good a mistress, and as good a woman as Whitstead ever knew. And she kept Christmas well.

About the Authors

Abigail Falanga

Believing firmly in magic and merriment, valour and peace, Abigail Falanga is a wildly ambitious author of fantasy and science fiction. It was probably insane to try pulling together an anthology at the very last minute, but bringing the jollity of Christmas to twenty-five authors and artists was well worth it. She lives in New Mexico with family, books, too many hobbies, and a distracting lab puppy named Zoe. Besides a plethora of flash fiction published with Havok Publishing, she has released her first book *A Time of Mourning and Dancing*, the beginning of a series of dark fantasy fairy-tale retellings.

Sarah Falanga

Sarah Falanga lives under the open skies of New Mexico, where she's growing her business of cosiness and enjoying simple pleasures. She started writing science-fiction stories when she became too old to 'make-believe' them. Her fiction is inspired by George MacDonald, C.S. Lewis, E. Nesbit, Ellis Peters, Doctor Who, Pixar movies, and Marvel movies. Besides writing, she loves to sketch, sew, bake, walk, and listen to music.

Joanna Bair

Joanna Bair has a BA in English and Theatre, having written and produced a handful of plays in the US and Malta. She's had short stories published in anthologies by Zimbell House Publishing, *Splickety, Spark*, and *Keys for Kids*. Her novella *Nightmare in Nice* is available on Amazon. A Connecticut native who has lived in England and Malta, Joanna now teaches in South Florida.

Dana Bell

Owned by two cats, Adara and Taj, Dana Bell writes stories starring her fur babies. She loves to tell tales set in places she has lived or visited, has a fascination for lighthouses, Yellowstone National Park, super volcanoes, and doll houses (which have taken over her basement). Her published books include *Winter Awakening* and *God's Gift*. Her short fiction can be found in various anthologies and she writes under Belle Blukat. She lives in Colorado and works a day job so her cats have a warm house, food, and lots of toys.

Melinda K. Busch

Melinda K. Busch has written four Arch Books and *The Maiden and the Toad* (a verse retelling of the Princess and the Frog). She is currently co-writing a series of World War II novels with her wonderful husband, Andy. A book lover from her earliest days, Melinda's childhood imagination teemed with hobbits and dragons, talking beasts, and all manner of faerie. As a mother, a grandmother, and a writer, she hopes to inspire hearts and minds through her stories. She lives in Southern California with her husband and their three crazy mutts, and when she isn't writing, she keeps busy chasing the world's cutest grandbabies around the house.

Hillari DeSchane

Hillari DeSchane's 'Fatally Fun' family friendly cosy mysteries combine her four favourite things: The Regency Era of Jane Austen, mysteries, humour, and pets. *A Christmas Tail*, Hillari's debut novel, received a certificate of merit from the Cat Writers Association. When not traveling internationally to research her novels, Hillari enjoys training therapy dogs, volunteering with youth at her church, and serving on the board of her regional opera company. She lives in California with her 'Fur-rensics Team," Jocko the black Labrador and Ambrose the Siamese cat. Find Hillari's books including her latest pet cosy *Throw A Dog a Dead Man's Bone*, on Amazon in both digital and paperback formats. Follow her at hillarideschane.com or on Facebook and Instagram.

Sara Francis

Sara Francis is an author, media designer, and speaker. She has written/published the YA Dystopian/SciFi trilogy "The Terra Testimonies", the children's series "Adventures of Wobot", and the poetry collection "Stardust". When she is not writing, she is designing for clients and assisting indie authors with social media marketing. Outside the professional realm, she loves a good mystery and playing games with friends. With everything she does, Sara Francis hopes to light a torch in the darkness with the desire that others will do the same and make the world bright again.

Ronnell Gibson

Ronnell surrounds herself with words and teenagers. She specializes in young adult contemporary with a sprinkling of the mysterious. She also writes youth and adult devotions and is one of the editors for HAVOK Publishing. Self-proclaimed coffee snob and Marvel movie addict, Ronnell has also titled herself a macaron padawan and a cupcake Jedi. High on her bucket list is to someday attend San Diego Comic Con. Ronnell lives in central Wisconsin, with her husband, two teenagers, and two Pomeranian puppies. Find out more about Ronnell at http://ronnellkaygibson.com/.

Pam Halter

Pam Halter is a children's picture book, middle grade, and YA fantasy author. She is also a freelance editor of picture books and the children's book editor for Fruitbearer Publishing. When she's not writing, Pam enjoys quilting, cooking, reading, playing the piano, and Bible study. Pam lives in South Jersey with her husband, special needs adult daughter, and three cats. You can learn more about her at www.pamhalter.com.

David W. Landrum

David W. Landrum teaches Literature at Grand Valley State University in Michigan. His fiction and poetry have appeared widely in journals in the US, UK, Canada, and Australia.

Sarah Levesque

Sarah Levesque loves stories, whether she is reading them, writing them or editing them. She is a high school teacher and the Editor in Chief of LogoSophia Magazine, as well as a freelance editor in her spare time. She loves the snows of her native New England and may be found curled up with her dogs near the Christmas tree with a Jane Austen book or her *Lord of the Rings* fanfiction.

Ari Lewis

Ari Lewis has always loved stories, especially fantasy and mysteries. Her love of stories drove her to study literature at the University of St. Katherine and then to pass on what she learned and loved to students as a high school English teacher. Her favourite authors include C.S. Lewis, G.K. Chesterton, Terry Pratchett, and Agatha Christie. Currently, she is living happily ever after with her husband in southern California.

E. S. Marsh

A library employee by day and a writer by night, E. S. Marsh aspires to write stories that invite readers to ponder the divine, hug a box of tissue, or sleep with the light on. More of Marsh's stories can be read in *Warriors Against the Storm, Monsters: The Crossover Alliance Anthology,* and *The Whispered Tales of Graves Grove* (as Caitlyn Konze).

Erika Mathews

Erika Mathews writes Christian living books, both fiction and non-fiction, that demonstrate the power of God in the life of a believer, transforming daily life into His resting life. Her kingdom adventure novel series *Truth from Taerna* features spiritually challenging and refreshing adventure and unique Christian twists on cliched plots. Outside of writing, she spends time with her husband Josh, mothers her little ones, reads, edits, enjoys the great Minnesota outdoors, plays piano and violin, makes heroic ventures into minimalism, clean eating, and gardening, and uses the Oxford comma. You can connect with Erika at restinglife.com.

John K. Patterson

John K. Patterson is a lifelong lover of fantasy and science fiction. Fuelled mainly by coffee, Patterson is the author of the Arrivers series, and loves to challenge the word 'impossible' wherever it shows up. All the better that his stories can do so with aliens, dragons, dinosaurs, wizards, the undead, and on occasion all of the above. He lives at the roots of Pikes Peak in Colorado Springs, CO.

Nathan Peterson

Nathan is an aspiring novelist and artist. Growing up with a passion for all things Star Wars and Lord of the Rings, it's no surprise he loves weaving sci-fi, fantasy, and real life into his stories. When he's not drawing or writing, you can find him working out, eating 'rabbit food,' or watching movies. You can learn more about his new comic book series at https://vidarandhans.wordpress.com.

Steve Rzasa

Steve Rzasa doesn't slay monsters, but he defeats word count goals and vanquishes overdue books. He's the author of many novels of science-fiction and fantasy, gobs of short stories, and when he's not writing, he's running a library in Wyoming. Find his stories at www.steverzasa.com.

Lauren H. Salisbury

Lauren H. Salisbury is a lover of all things science fiction/fantasy, creative, and edible, but not always in that order. An English teacher for sixteen years, she now tutors part-time while trying to figure out how to use an MA in Education as an author. She lives in Yorkshire with her husband and a room full of books but likes to winter abroad, following the sunshine. Her favourite stories include faith, hope, and courage.

Mary Schlegel

Mary Schlegel believes in writing the stories that capture her heart and inspire her imagination, whatever the genre. She lives in southwestern Missouri with her husband and fellow author, Aaron, and their infant daughter. If she's not writing she's probably in the garden or brewing another cup of tea.

Marla Schultz

Marla Schultz is a freelance writer, the wife of Rick, and the mother of six amazing children. She graduated with a B.A. in Communication Arts and an emphasis in Literature, but her mother's love of books and her missionary experiences in other countries inspired her to learn more about different countries, cultures, and time periods through fiction, and to share that love of discovery with her children. In addition to writing, Marla currently homeschools her two youngest children, teaches online and, occasionally, creates art. Her first grandbaby is due in the summer of 2021.

Laura Nelson Selinksy

Laura Nelson Selinsky teaches British Literature, so she jumped at the chance to play with *A Christmas Carol* in Dickens' era Whitstead. She's published fiction and nonfiction in a variety of genres and is especially proud of her Christmas novella *Season of Hope* from Anaiah Press. If Laura can't travel the world with Barry, her beloved husband, and their family, then her favourite ways to have fun are teaching Chaucer, gardening, and leading second grade Sunday School.

Valerie Shaw

Valerie Shaw is a compulsive writer living in Upstate, NY, with her beloved husband and two tweenage kids. Valerie has written for the Upstate Gardener's Journal and blogged in women's ministry, but her real passion lies in writing fictional novels long past her bedtime. Valerie is a homeschool mom, an avid reader, and a staunch believer in both true love and second breakfast. You can find her on Twitter @EmersonGrey3 or on Facebook as VE Shaw.

Sarah Earlene Shere

Sarah Earlene Shere is an author, actress and cosplayer in her native home of Southern California. Sarah fell in love with storytelling at the age of eleven. As she's grown closer to God and fallen in love with Jesus, her stories have become biblical and allegorical, reflecting her favourite authors, John Bunyan and Hans Christian Andersen. Besides Amazon, Sarah's stories and writings can be found under Hosanna Heralds on Facebook and WordPress. Since 2018, Sarah has been acting with the Long Beach based Masquer Theatre Company. In 2017, she started volunteering with a local cosplay non-profit, Kids Can Cosplay.

E. J. Sobetski

Growing up, E. J. was usually outnumbered. Youngest of seven and the only boy, while an uncle of seventeen, Christmas can be very fun. (Or as he likes to call it, organised chaos.) E. J. loves fantasy with writers such as J. R. R. Tolkien, C. S. Lewis and Wayne Thomas Batson as inspiration. He has three books written with several more on the way. Find E. J. on Facebook and Amazon.

Ellie West

Ellie West is a sucker for happy endings. Tea and chocolate fuel her imagination. Her two dogs are her constant companions and have helped brainstorm more than one story, which could explain a lot. Ellie also writes contemporary fiction under the name E. A. West. Visit her website at ellie.eawestauthor.com.

Acknowledgements

The editors and compilers would like to extend deepest gratitude to…

Sara Francis, for designing a beautiful cover from our ideas and dreams of how we wanted it to look.

Hannah Falanga, for painting a delightful image and allowing us to use it as the cover. And for helping with other graphics.

Melinda K. Busch, for assisting in formatting and preparing this book for publication.

Marla Schultz, Mary Schlegel, Ellie West, John K. Patterson, Melinda K. Busch, and Wendy Falanga, for help in proofreading and editing.

Lauren Salisbury, for being our long-suffering Genuine Brit.

To the authors, for producing such amazing stories, and to all the Whits for their community and imagination.

To our family, for their support and food. (Not you, Zoe! Down! Crazy puppy…)

And to our Lord Jesus Christ, for inspirations, guidance, love, and most of all for being that little Babe whose coming to a lowly manger we celebrate with this book.

Printed in the USA
CPSIA information can be obtained
at www.ICGtesting.com
LVHW051228101223
766132LV00011B/1005